GW01339356

The Wisdom of Crocodiles

"The only writer, English or American, with the guts to take on the modern world in all its terrifying complexity."
The Week

"This is fiction on a grand and ambitious scale... inspires sensations of terror, nausea, bemusement and exhilaration."
Daily Telegraph

"His insights into some of the female characters are among the novel's most valuable details. And the chapter about the childhood of Fraud Secretariat deputy director Michael McCarthy, spent watching his father jump out of aircraft (Hoffman's father was a sports parachutist), is a masterpiece."
The Independent

"...the most horrible book I ever read and the only one I ever physically destroyed so that nobody else would have the displeasure of reading it."
Amazon review

The Golden Age of Censorship

"Hoffman's witty style and command of satire, coupled with the unique setting, makes this a hugely original and enjoyable novel."
Time Out

"Moves with the pace of the best thrillers."
Independent on Sunday

The Left Hand of God Trilogy

"Writers like Hoffman are too rare. This wonderful book gripped me from the first chapter and then dropped me days later, dazed and grinning to myself."
Conn Iggulden

"Brooding and magnificent... Hoffman has created a terrifying world and filled it with strange and complex characters."
Eoin Colfer

"Brilliant. Mervyn Peake takes on Dickens in a head to head clash with a manga comic that takes no prisoners. Strange, funny, violent and intriguing."
Charlie Higson

"A dark novel, haunting and exciting. If you do not enjoy this book something has died in your soul."
Harry Sidebottom

"A cult classic..."
Daily Express

"Tremendous momentum."
Daily Telegraph

SCORN

PAUL HOFFMAN
SCORN

RED OPERA

First published in 2017 by Red Opera

Copyright © Paul Hoffman 2017

The moral right of Paul Hoffman to be identified as the author of this work has been asserted in accordance with the Copyright, Designs and Patents Act 1988.

All rights reserved. No part of this publication may be reproduced or transmitted in any form or by any means, electronic or mechanical including photocopying, recording or any information storage or retrieval system, without prior permission in writing from the publishers.

This novel is entirely a work of fiction. The names, characters and incidents portrayed in it are the work of the author's imagination. Any resemblance to actual persons, living or dead, events or localities is entirely coincidental.

ISBN 978-1-911195-35-1

Available in paperback
ISBN 978-1-911195-43-6

Also available as an ebook
ISBN 978-1-911195-34-4

Typeset by Jill Sawyer Phypers
Cover design by Mecob Designs
Drawings by Nick Szczepanik
from designs by Paul Hoffman.

Printed and bound in Great Britain by Clays Ltd, St Ives plc

For Pauline Brook and Gordon Brook, whose kindness to me as a child cannot be reckoned.

'External validity in sampling refers to the approximate truth of conclusions that involve generalizations. Put in more pedestrian terms, external validity in sampling is the degree to which the conclusions in your study would hold for other persons in other places and at other times.'

The Web Center for
Social Research Methods

'The best way to drive out the devil is to jeer and flout him, for he cannot bear scorn.'

Martin Luther

PROLOGUE

Listen!

Why should I? (Yes, I can read your rebellious thoughts.)

I'll make you a promise: this story will end with a twist so astonishing you'll regard any other twist that ever existed as nothing more than the most mutton-fisted kind of anticlimax. The true identity of Keyser Söze? Piffle. The knifing in the shower at the Bates Motel? Utterly planking. *He was dead all along!* A sauceless non-event. Here, you'll experience a revelation to make your liver freeze, your eyes bulge in their sockets, and your hair stand out like quills upon a fretful porcupine.

So why not take this book over to the cash register, or add it to your basket on the world wide web, and coin me to be your designated guide across the river of forgetfulness to the place and time when eight-year-old Aaron Gall, in a matter of a few minutes, is to take the first step towards his transformation from one kind of creature into another.

'One time, I heard a father in a meeting with married couples say, "I sometimes have to smack my children a bit, but never in the face, so as to not humiliate them," Pope Francis said. "How beautiful," he added. "He knows the sense of dignity! He has to punish them but does it justly and moves on."'

Pope Francis, 2015

'Get 'em young — they're yours for ever.'

Jesse Pinkman, *Breaking Bad*

CHAPTER 1

THE WORST OF TIMES

... One times seven is seven ...
 ... Two times seven is fourteen ...
 ... Three times seven is twenty-one ...
 ... Four times seven is twenty-eight ...
The teacher sitting on the desk was in her late twenties. In many ways, the clothes she was wearing – the brown, ribbed top, the short skirt, the tan tights – would have seemed entirely modern to us. Only the unpleasing textures of the cloth and the cut of the clothes would have marked this out as a scene from decades in the past. Sitting to one side was a priest, Father Thomas Lloyd, whose clothes would have been pretty much the same in the late eighteenth century, enjoying the sight of thirty contented children and waiting to begin instructing them for their Confirmation.

'... Svens svens are forty-nine ...' they chanted, suddenly and inexplicably changing the rhythmic pattern: 'Eight svens are fifty-six.'

There was something pleasantly boring about the mood in the room, something secure in the repetitious nature of the schoolroom tasks: the children enjoying the irresponsibility of rote (the obligation to be the engine of endless creativity was a decade away), the paintings on the wall of Mum and Dad (single parenthood on any sort of scale was also waiting in the wings), and the fish tank full of froglets, likewise consigned to history and a greater awareness of the rights of amphibians.

Then, very quietly, an internal door opened and a woman entered. Only some of her face was visible, and nothing of her shape, beyond the fact that she was thin rather than fat. She had no hips, no breasts, no hair; neither did she have feet. She was encased from head to foot in black, the only exception being the white wimple that enclosed her head and neck and ears, leaving just an ellipse of flesh from the middle of her forehead to the edge of her chin. The edge of her weighty black habit touched the ground.

Her eyes were cast down and she moved without sound, only the click of the opening and closing door signalling her presence. The teacher stopped talking and moved to one side as the shrouded woman took her place. She had clearly been expecting her. The nun put a pile of blue exercise books down on the table. There was an extraordinary calm in her expression, though not that exactly: at any rate, fear and doubt were strangers to this woman. The children stood, silent in a way they had not been silent all that day. There was expectancy here, but it was of an odd kind. All of them, even the inattentive ones who had been occasionally whispering, or daydreaming throughout the lesson, spoke as if with one voice.

'Good morning, Mother Mary Frances.'

She waited, not reacting, her eyes moving once from side to side, seriously considering something. Then she nodded her head, barely moving it, as if to emphasise the scale of her power. They sat.

The nun opened the exercise book up at the middle

The Worst Of Times

and showed the class a picture of a harlequin and, beside it, a carefully written account of its history. This was predictable enough in its childish way, clearly copied, very neatly, out of a book. But her most admiring remarks were for the drawing. She praised not only the care with which it had been coloured in but the sense of movement which the child had given the figure. It was impressive, and certainly the product of a childish hand, for it was not especially precocious technically but it was full of vigour. But the girl whose book it was seemed neither pleased nor indifferent – she exhibited instead an uneasy vigilance.

The nun turned to the other books in the pile. None of them was praised in such terms; a few were given commendations here and there. Most were handed over silently. Although she could be pleased, it was clearly difficult to do so. About fifteen books in, she stopped and looked carefully at the stack of books, then turned to face the class. They sensed something; the watchful silence deepened. All the while, the young teacher had been looking into the distance, as if at something far beyond the high Victorian rafters of the room. At no time during the handing-out had her expression altered. When the nun spoke again, her voice was quiet, but her face was stern.

'Every year I look at the work you have done – a practice I have observed throughout the fifteen years since I became headmistress here – but never have I seen, and never do I expect to see, an exercise book like this.'

She turned and picked up the topmost book.

She flicked through the pages irritably. In the absolute silence, the noise of the paper, harsh and angry, filled the room with menace. She looked up, her lips tight together, staring around the room. Then she held up the book and panned the centre pages around the class for all the children to see. There was a terrible waiting as they looked. The girl whose book she had praised did not lift her eyes at all, and some of the others, whose books had been returned quickly, looked away. She brought the pages, like a searchlight, to bear on the desk of a small boy, sitting halfway to the back of the class.

The colour drained from the child's face, his eyes opened wider and then everything seemed to stop: his breathing, the movement of his eyes, his hands.

'Aaron Gall,' said the nun. 'Come here. Come here, to the front of the class.'

The boy stood up. He was short compared to the other children, and a little fat. His black hair was dishevelled and his navy-blue sweater had a small hole on one seam. He walked to an adjacent desk and the seated child hurried to let him pass by pushing his chair into his desk. In his desperation to give him space, he seemed to squeeze his stomach so that he was only three or four inches wide. The frightened boy slipped past and walked up the aisle to the nun, who held his book open, as a beacon to the advancing child. He came to a stop in front of her, dazed by terror, face completely white.

The blow, when it came, seemed to arrive from a great distance. She raised one arm almost outstretched behind her head then turned her body into the movement. It was not a slap. Her open hand took him just above the ear. He staggered back from the force. The teacher stared into the distance, but the priest flinched as if the shock wave of the blow had passed straight through him. He raised his left hand slightly as if to protest, but then something held him back, in the way of a polite visitor suddenly finding

The Worst Of Times

himself in the middle of a dreadful family row.

'Stand still!' she screamed. 'Stand there!'

She raised her arm again as she waited for the boy to move back into position. Slowly, he did so. Again, she swung her arm with all her strength; again, the boy staggered back.

'Don't you move!'

The scream made the girl sitting at the desk closest to the boy wince with the fury of it. The teacher blinked, and her hand shook slightly, but still she kept her eyes in the distance. The priest moved in his seat a little, back and forward. Then he made his decision; he signalled to Mother Mary Frances and pointed to the door, as if he'd remembered some urgent appointment. She did not acknowledge him. Silently, he left and quickly made his way out into the playground. 'Old bitch,' he said to himself, as he headed back towards the church, a hundred yards away.

Inside the classroom there were no tears from the boy, but a terrible whimpering sound emerged from somewhere at the back of his throat. The nun waited, and he moved back towards her. She made a feint with her upraised hand, once, twice – each time matched by the boy moving his head away from the direction of the blow and holding up his hand to protect his head. She waited, still staring at him.

Slowly, he let his hand drop.

'Don't you move,' she repeated, barely audibly.

When the blow came, his head seemed to bounce, but he had set his legs wider apart in order to remain still, and he stayed where he was. She hit him again. The noise in his throat was now continuous, exhausted and high-pitched, like the grizzle of a two-year-old. She pointed to the book and, page by page, shared the source of her anger with the thirty children. With each new blasphemy – an inept drawing, a clumsy crossing-out, an unmade punctuation mark – she hit the boy. A blow, then an error pointed out, then another blow. And throughout, the terrible noise from his throat and the deadly white face. The boy stared ahead, in a private world in which there was only pain, humiliation and fear. And the woman in front of him defined its beginning and end, its limits in every direction. She could do whatever she wanted – there was no one to stop her, after all. A horrible quiet had fallen over the class, of a kind none of them would ever experience again. They were in the presence of a violence and hysteria of unique quality. And she'd not finished.

'Come here!' She turned and walked around the table. She picked up a piece of white chalk from the blackboard and held it out to Aaron Gall. He looked at her, stupefied.

'Come here,' she repeated quietly. The boy approached and took the chalk, his hand shaking so badly he could barely hold it.

'Write a nine on the board. Go on.' The boy hesitated, then awkwardly began to scrawl on the blackboard. As he tried to draw the loop of the nine, the skin on the nun's cheeks darkened. The flush deepened and spread across her face, as great a contrast with the white of her headpiece as the boy's black hair to his pale face. Her rage seemed almost ready to spread into her clothes, to infect the floor, the wall, the board itself. She looked at the clumsy number nine and turned to the class.

'Do you see that?' she asked, incredulous, unbelieving. Two white spots formed in the middle of her dark-red cheeks. She grabbed the boy by his chalky hand and with great deliberation forced him to redraw the nine. Then she took the chalk and corrected it by adding a slight tail to the loop.

'A nine has a tail! It has a tail! Do you understand?' She drew a tail-less nine.

'Put in the tail, Aaron Gall.'

An enormous, wet sob broke from the child as he took the chalk and drew the tail. The nun turned again to the class, appealing to them: 'Look at the tail on the nine! Look what Aaron Gall has done!' She hit him across the face and, for the first time, he began to cry. The tears fell in large drops on to the floor, without touching his cheeks, and his nose started to run. She stared at him as he sobbed, and for a moment there seemed to be a terrible struggle within her, as if her rage threatened to break the very flesh and bones of her body.

Then she raised her hand again.

Feeling sorry for little Aaron Gall? I wouldn't waste them, those tears, if I were you. What's a few blows to the head, given the horrors of the years in which Aaron grew up? While he was waiting to be branded on his little soul in a small school in Abingdon, Chairman Mao's Great Leap Forward was creating the conditions for thirty million people to starve to death. While a few dozens of children were living in dread of Mother Mary Frances, some parents in Xingyang were eating theirs.

Aaron failed completely to see that there are always people worse off than you. It was a decade in which the most famous murder of the century saw a tourist filming Jacqueline Kennedy scrambling over the boot of a car, trying to collect pieces of her husband's skull and bits of his brain. And, shortly afterwards, new technology also preserved forever Ian and Myra recording on tape for their mutual pleasure the dying cries of children even younger than Aaron.

Aaron took his first fearful steps into the hands of Mother Mary Frances while three million or so Biafrans were dying in a now forgotten civil war in West Africa. In 1977 he had his first serious attack of depression (not, of course, recognised as such) during the month the Khmer were forced to end the process of killing off one citizen in every three. In the spring of 1994, as Aaron was hospitalised for the first time with severe psoriasis, probably rooted in what his psychiatrist at the time called 'negative life events', somewhere around three quarters of a million Tutsis were massacred in less than a hundred days.

He received the decree absolute ending his first marriage in July 1995, a month in which eight thousand men and boys were bound and shot by Bosnian Serbs on the football pitches and the agricultural co-operatives of Srebrenica.

September 2001 saw him in New York to receive the little-known Noether Prize for Physics for his paper 'Fractional Edge States of Heisenberg Spin Chains'. The ceremony was cancelled.

The deep cut on your finger is bound to be more pressing to you than a bomb shattering a busload of Muslims in some backwater shithole in Baluchistan. At any rate, for all the hideous crimes of man on man that had been the soundtrack to his life, Aaron Gall was bound to concentrate on the cut to his finger – which in this case was a cut into his soul, and one that had now decided to stop being a cross to bear and start being a crucifixion.

CHAPTER 2

THE BEST OF TIMES

The spirit of the times moves through everyone. Don't believe me? Ask yourself why aliens only kidnap the goofy and the no-account. Abducting a head of state, an A-list star or an oligarch is a pointless risk if the secret of what's going on, the human zeitgeist, is contained just as comprehensively in worm pickers, restaurant greeters, lap dancers and nail technicians. When he was a boy, Aaron made a great many jokes about homosexuals – benders, queers, shirt-lifters. One hundred and thirty-two derogatory remarks in 1974 alone, to be precise. But then, of course, homosexuality was still a criminal offence in Scotland and Ireland. Now such terms would never pass his lips, and the clang of the prison door for being gay seems to belong to the age of burning witches or the rack.

When he was six, little Aaron berated his mother for going out to work and not being at home to make his tea when he got back from school. By the end of the 1980s he was working part-time himself and looking after a baby and a toddler twice a week so that his wife would not miss out on her career. The word 'nigger' last crossed his lips when he was attacked by a black skinhead on Between Towns Road in Cowley (in those early, more tolerant days, being black was no barrier to being a crop-haired thug).

How puzzling it must seem to the aliens, anal probes

in hand, that things could change so fast, that a black man already six years old by the time the miscegenation laws forbidding marriage between black and white were overturned in 1967 would become the forty-fourth President of the United States at the age of 47 years and 169 days. What is to be made of the fact that, in a Europe where women have only had the vote in living memory (in Switzerland, it was 1973), they now outnumber men in medical school by three to two. What would our rectally curious extraterrestrial think of all this? What conclusions would it come to? What would be the useful generalisations it could offer about the fluid nature of the human personality to the alien high commander who had paid its bill? What apodeixis could he present, what comprobations, what inferential conclusions about the crooked timber of the nature of mankind could it set down to justify the trouble and the expense? He'd be zapped with a ray-gun for making it all up and swindling Lord Vader of his money, I suspect.

But talking of trouble and expense moves us to the great twenty-first-century experiment at CERN in Switzerland. What nobility was here (since we are looking on the bright side now), the greatest experiment in the history of mankind, the most expensive, the largest number of nations gathered together in a single enterprise, and for the purest of motives: for the joy of understanding, for pure nosiness and nothing more, simply to know the origin of things.

On the other hand, the frankness of a true friend obliges me to discuss an innovation from the previous century that tells another truth about human scientific endeavour: the double-blind trial. This is a way of assessing the effectiveness of a drug, for example, in which neither the patients, the experimenter nor any other assessor of the results knows which participants are subject to which procedure, thus helping to ensure that no bias or expectation will influence results.

In other words, one of the great inventions in the history of human understanding is a system, let's be clear, not to prevent the greatest minds from lying about their discoveries to others, but to prevent them lying about their discoveries to themselves.

This is rather harsh, I know, but the relationship between cruelty and kindness is clear to anyone who believes in the power of the truth to set you free. Whatever the validity of the view that human beings are fundamentally dishonest, there is no question in my mind that the Large Hadron Collider enables mankind to say on Judgement Day (along with, let's be fair, the eradication of polio and the moon landing): this is what we have done, this is what we are worth. It does not alter my admiration for you (when you're on your very best behaviour) that when the collider was switched on for the very first time there was an enormous explosion which forced it to shut down immediately. So extensive were the repairs required that it did not start up again for more than a year. These things happen. Indeed, they almost happened again just before the LHC was restarted, when a passing pigeon dropped a piece of baguette into the works and caused another massive fuck-up in the cooling systems.

Some would say that once is a misfortune but twice looks like carelessness. I am that true friend, my frankness merely proof of my generosity of feeling, but there are times when making a defence of your character and your potential is pretty trying. What else can you expect of a creature, admittedly blessed with a certain intelligence, if not in a widespread sort of a way, but who's mostly made of a bit of mud and a bit of snake and a bit of dog? What you get is exactly the kind of thing that happened at CERN: a typically flashy and pretentious experiment nearly blown to kingdom come by a flying rat and a slice of bread.

But that's the thing about human beings. It's not laughter or the ability to stand upright that distinguishes man from the animals, it's the capacity for incompetence. When any other creature makes a mistake, it gets eaten. I admit mankind is a bit of a bungler but, in his own way, a fairly successful bungler … despite everything. Although, to be fair, it also depends on your definition of success.

While Aaron was only a cog in the great experiment at CERN, he was an important one. He was not a great physicist, nor was he a great engineer, but he was perhaps the best scientist there at being both. It was his concern over the question of the overheating of the dewars containing the helium required to keep parts of the collider cold that brought him at the last minute to cross a gantry on his way to the control centre about thirty yards from the tunnel.

A small resistance had built up in a collider circuit, threatening to generate a vast amount of heat. Safeguards cut in, but in doing so an electric arc was triggered, punching a hole in the dewars. The gas expanded like a bomb and wrenched thirty of the one-ton magnets from the brackets holding them fast against the fundamental forces of the universe.

Startled by the sound, Aaron turned in alarm towards the explosion and in that moment experienced something that had never happened to anyone before.

The Best Of Times

There are theories from reputable scientists that predict the remote possibility of the collider producing black holes, but of a microscopic kind that would disintegrate immediately they were formed. Reassuringly, the theory holds that if such tiny holes in space were to be generated, they would also be very weak. Nothing to worry about, then.

Unfortunately for Aaron Gall, this vanishingly small eventuality took place as he turned his head, just as the collider generated exactly the microscopic black hole that had been predicted. And, unlikely as this event was, what was even more unlikely was that the black hole opened up in the centre of Aaron's brain.

It was as if time had been speeded up and slowed down and, also, as if he'd been, in the same moment, sent into the distant future and the remote past. Stars coalesced from gas and burst into life as the same star billions of years later collapsed in on itself and exploded like a million suns. He was inside the universe looking out a second after it began, and still inside the universe looking out as the galaxies crumbled and then were torn apart. He was there at 10^{20} years, one hundred quintillion years from now, as the atoms decayed into subatomic particles and were swallowed up by supermassive black holes. At 10^{40} years, he was watching as ordinary matter vanished and there was nothing left but holes in space; and at 10^{100} years, he gawped as even the black holes dispersed and there was nothing left at all.

And then he woke up two seconds later to find himself lying on a corridor floor and staring up at the ceiling.

'To solve a crossword clue the solver must understand not the clues themselves but the mind of the person who set them. Once you have grasped how that mind works, then clues that appear utterly inscrutable and impossible lead to solutions that come as naturally as leaves to a tree.'

Borg Larnson, *The Cruciverbalist and the Ant*

CHAPTER 3

TRANSMOGRIFICATION

Three days later, Aaron recovered consciousness in hospital, having already undergone as many tests, often vastly expensive, as it was possible to perform on a human being. This was partly to do with the considerable regard with which Aaron was held at the Large Hadron Collider, but the extreme devotion to his health was mostly to do with the organisation's terror at what a fatality might mean for its reputation and, more specifically, its funding. Despite a clean bill, Aaron was ordered to take two months' leave with a large grant loosely worded enough in its terms of reference to allow him to do absolutely nothing. By the end of the week, Aaron was sitting on his sofa in his Finchley Road flat, overcome with a depression so intense that all he'd done for the past two hours was stare at the wall.

Neuroscientists these days are pretty sniffy about the idea that the human brain is really three brains wrapped in one: the brain of a reptile, wrapped up in the brain of a mammal, wrapped up in the brain of the kind of higher mammal that can understand this sentence. That, in short, when you lie down to sleep at night you're lying down next to a horse and a crocodile. But this is just the fussiness of the academic. A simplification of this kind makes the point well enough. In short, to all intents and purposes, the unimaginably tiny black hole had opened up in Aaron's brain at the boundary where the snake begins to blur into the dog.

Ever stretched? Even the laziest of you, the most inattentive to the needs of the body, will have at some point dropped your shoulders after a hard day and groaned with pleasure at the slow easing of the strained muscles and tendons. But if you want to know even something of what happened to Aaron Gall the evening after a black hole formed and then collapsed in his corpus amygdaloideum as a result of the unfortunate and highly unlikely events at the Large Hadron Collider, you should consider the cat or the dog. You will have seen them stretch, reaching as if their bodies could lengthen until their paws elongated around the circumference of the world and they might come around to scratch themselves on the bottom. See the pleasure this gives to Puss or Patch, the joy and delight in the telescopic turgescence of their joints, the delicious elongation of the spine, the gorgeous, yawny discharge of the day's long wear and tear.

For now, Aaron was smog-bound in the misery that had afflicted him on and off for most of his adult life. But then something odd happened. He began to sense something in his back, a tickling, titillating prickle along the spine – a growing relish in his chest for a consummation of something his body now wanted as much as it wanted breath, like the waiting butterfly yearning no longer to be a caterpillar. His body began to shake as every cell grew avid to become itself.

No doubt you will have seen a man change into a wolf in films – but film directors, just like journalists or economists, always get everything wrong. The pain of utter change? Wrong. The horror of transformation? Wrong. The breaking of bones required to double their length? Wrong again. The cry of agonising pain? Wrong. All totally and utterly wrong.

Transmogrification

Call up now the stretching of the muscles of the neck. Remember the total easement of the dog or cat. Now multiply that pleasure by a thousand times and then a thousand more, and still it is not enough to replicate the bliss and rapture, the gloating luxuriance, as every single sinew, muscle, bone and gristle in hand and eye and ear, in bowel and toe and cock, expands utterly into its truest and most delectable form. Open-mouthed you would have been, eyeball-bulged to witness the doubling in height and width, the elongating of fingernail to claw, of nose to snout, of eyes moving backwards to the side of his head, all changing into something rich and strange and otherly in every way.

Aaron stood and yawned. But don't think of your own measly yawn, or even the totally-given-over-to-the-experience yawning of the cat or the dog. Think of an orgasm of a yawn, but ten thousand times the power of what before has passed for bodily delight. Then the creature, Aaron, sneezed. It felt like the power of an exploding sun bursting in his head and his heart.

Then he fainted and fell to the floor with an enormous crash. Fortunately, the builders were Swiss and, as a result, the floor held.

When Aaron woke up about thirty minutes later, he remembered absolutely nothing. There was, however, one thing more alarming than the matter of a little fainting fit: all his clothes had, in a most peculiar manner, been ripped to shreds.

CHAPTER 4

THE GLOOMY MASK OF TRAGEDY

'Depressed?'

'Miserable,' said Aaron, after a pause.

'I'm only a simple GP,' said Keffner. 'What's the difference?'

'Misery is even worse.'

'Escitalopram not working anymore?'

'Presumably not. Perhaps it's working but I'm getting worse.'

'We could try something else,' said Keffner, scrolling down the monitor at his new patient's records. 'You've tried quite a few.' He seemed surprised as he kept on scrolling. 'I mean, the deeper depression is very likely to be a temporary reaction to being knocked unconscious. Nothing at all showed up?'

'Nothing.'

'And you fainted just the once?'

'Yes.'

Keffner pored over his screen.

'Ah … you had another scan after that.' Another pause as he read the results. 'Nothing there.' If Keffner did not mention the business of the ripped clothes, this was simply because Aaron had not told anyone.

Keffner breathed out noisily. 'Still, it's a long time to be

The Gloomy Mask Of Tragedy

out. I think there's a fair chance it's just a delayed reaction – which will probably mean it'll pass in time. The depression, I mean.' Again, he was studying the computer rather than looking at Aaron. This, unfairly, gave the impression of a teenager talking to his mother while looking at a television programme he found infinitely more interesting.

'Had Reboxetine?' asked Keffner brightly. 'I've had patients who've done well on Reboxetine.'

'I have, yes. I seem to remember it made me feel as if a midget – sorry, little person – was frying eggs on top of my brain.'

Keffner sighed as he found it. 'Oh, yes. It's down here as Beroxetine.'

'Aren't there any new ones?'

Keffner sucked his teeth guiltily, as if there were some collective professional responsibility involved in not finding a cure for suffering. 'Not really. Since Prozac – what, twenty-five years ago? – we've refined a few things. What you're on now, Escitalopram, is glorified Prozac, basically.'

'Pity.'

'What about psychotherapy?' Keffner was looking at the monitor again. Aaron's muffled capacity for wondering considered whether all GPs now looked at their computer screens rather than at the faces of their patients.

'I've done about ten years of therapy. I know why I'm like this. I spent my childhood occasionally being beaten, sometimes badly, though not often, and slept in a dormitory with eighty other people for seven years, being fed horrible food, harassed, lectured, threatened, hit, menaced into believing things so obviously stupid it makes me ...' He stopped. 'I was a child living out the sick dreams of old men – I was too young, it went on for too long and they suffocated any capacity I had for feeling joy. Oh, and I was bored – hideously, horribly, soul-numbingly bored. Why I'm this way is obvious. That's why I was hoping for a new drug. My hopes are limited, Doctor – a sticking plaster will do.'

The doctor looked disappointed.

'I don't think there is anything, to be honest. Or one thing, perhaps.' Aaron looked at him, hope springing eternal even in the hearts of exhausted realists.

'A couple of my patients have been singing the praises of a therapist who's just moved in down the road.'

Disappointment. 'I told you, I've been to lots of shrinks.'

'I heard you' – a little annoyed at Aaron's tone – 'but these patients had also been to a lot of shrinks – and they swear by Lou Bettancourt. If the cost isn't a problem?'

'No.'

'Then what harm can it do?'

Even in hell, according to Lucretius, the tormented look for small distractions to pass the miserable time between the daily ritual of being swallowed whole or disembowelled on the rack. Aaron's diversion from pain involved the often surprisingly helpful habit of doing the crossword. The problem for him was less solving the clues, more finding a setter whose habits of mind he had not learned through sometimes hours of daily practice. There was now only one compiler who regularly stretched his capacity, having emerged from nowhere about two years before. He called himself Proteus and, frustratingly, created no more than two puzzles a week, one in the *Spectator*, the other in the *Financial Times*.

Aaron now had to hoard them so that they could be used to distract him in the period when things were bad

The Gloomy Mask Of Tragedy

but before the point when his depression became unbearable. When that happened, no diversion ever made could help. Restless and fearing the descent into hell, he turned to one of Proteus's puzzles and went to the first clue. This was always a kind of warm-up, not so much difficult as witty, capable sometimes of making him gasp with admiration at its cleverness and, usually, rudeness.

Today the first clue was: **WRINKLED OLD RETAINER**, 7 letters.

For three minutes, he stalked the clue like a safecracker turning the dial and listening to the clicks of notch and dog. Soon, as was intended, he was in. A grunt of delight even in the poison fog:

SCROTUM.

Ten minutes later, he was still smiling, an event that had become so absent from his life that he felt a rush of gratitude, followed by curiosity. The notion of finding out who the compiler was had struck him before but, a private person himself, he felt he should respect the implication behind the alias. It also seemed like the sort of thing a fan would do. But now curiosity got the better of reticence, and after ten minutes searching on the web he found the identity of Proteus and something about his background. He was surprised – the compiler had an odd profession for someone who created crosswords of such sly intelligence.

CHAPTER 5

EREWHON

'No British films, I see,' said David Lister, gazing over at the multiplex while chewing on his Hawaiian Burger (it was Flavours of the South Pacific month at Burger King).

'Something to be grateful for,' replied his partner, who was polishing off Jaffa Cakes from a box.

'Yes, something to be grateful for.'

Both of them chewed on as they scanned the car park, as indifferent as cows munching idly in green meadows.

'When was the last brilliant British film, d'ya think?'

A pause as George Scrope considered.

'*The Long Good Friday*,' he said at last.

'That was forty years ago,' said Lister, not so much dismissive as appalled that it might be true.

'Fine. Name one.'

'Well, you never can, can you, name one?'

He thought as hard as he was prepared to – which was not very hard.

'*Trainspotting*!'

'Yeah, *Trainspotting* was pretty good.'

'There are good British films since then. I just can't think of them. *The Queen*!'

They both laughed. A pause.

'I once spent half an hour with Zig Bramley in the mess at Bastion while he tried to persuade me that *Hawk the Slayer* was the greatest film ever made. He was surprisingly convincing – I just can't remember anything he said.'

'He tried the same with me in Musa Qala, only that time it was him claiming that the best ever James Bond was' – Lister screwed up his eyes, trying to remember – 'you know, the one in ... He was Australian ... *On His Majesty's Secret Service.*'

'I think you'll find a lot of people think *On His Majesty's Secret Service* is one of the best Bonds.'

'Dunno. Never seen it. George Lazenby! Zig said that only Lazenby truly captured the authentic moral woodenness of Bond in the books.'

A pause. More slow munching.

'European films are grim.'

'And as for American films – usually, they're not even grim.'

'So, we're agreed,' said Scrope, finishing the last of his fries. 'There hasn't been a decent film made anywhere in the world since *The Long Good Friday.*'

'*The Act of Killing* was a great film.'

'It's a documentary. I thought we were talking about fiction.'

'I'd say it blurs the line.'

Lister was still finishing his Hawaiian Burger.

'*Twenty-four-hour Party People.* Very underrated.'

'It's true. You couldn't make a film like that anywhere else but here.'

'Definitely not.' An appreciative pause. '"On a *good* day, Shaun Ryder's lyrics for the Happy Mondays are on a par with those of W. B. Yeats on an *average* day."'

'My favourite bit was when the band find out that Tony Wilson has spent £10,000 of their money on a conference table.'

Laughter followed by a pleasant silence.

'*White Mischief*,' said Scrope mischievously. 'Also underrated.'

'You're right,' replied Lister. 'I can't think of another film that gets it right about how horribly mad the upper classes really are.'

'You should know.'

'That's right. I should.' He smiled. 'Of course, there are honourable exceptions.'

'Right Honourable exceptions? You would say that, though. Are you really an exception?'

'You know, I've often wondered.'

They grazed the landscape for a bit.

'I'm writing a screenplay,' said Scrope.

'No.'

'I am.'

'No, you're not.'

'Yes, I am.'

'What's it about, then?' It was an accusation, not a question.

'It's *Moby-Dick*' – he paused for effect – 'in space.'

Lister thought about this for a moment.

'How does the whale breathe in the vacuum of outer space?'

Scrope looked at him, eyes narrowing. 'The space whale has evolved to carry its own highly concentrated form of oxygen, which it replenishes every few years by dipping into the atmosphere of suitable planets. This explains why space whales are so large and why they are hunted down mercilessly by gas pirates from the planet Nit-picker.'

'You know,' said Lister, 'you've eaten almost that entire box of Jaffa Cakes. Not worried about diabetes at all?'

'I happen to like biscuits, so why don't you fuck off and die?'

'Did you know,' said Lister, 'the law courts have ruled that a Jaffa Cake is a cake and not a biscuit?'

There was a silence. 'Why would the courts have a view on something like that?'

'VAT. The Inland Revenue wanted to define Jaffa Cakes as Jaffa biscuits because the tax system defines a cake as a staple food and so not subject to tax, whereas a biscuit is a luxury food so they get twenty per cent for the Treasury.'

'But it's a Jaffa *Cake*, not a Jaffa *biscuit*.'

'What's in a name? You just called it a biscuit.'

'A slip of the tongue.'

'Twenty per cent of the price of a billion chocolatey, orangey things – that's a lot of money resting on a word.'

'It's obvious it's a cake,' said Scrope.

'Since you're such an authority, what's the difference between a cake and a biscuit?'

'Actually, I don't give a toss,' said Scrope. 'But if you want so badly to tell me—'

'I do badly want to tell you.'

'OK.'

'The Queen's Counsel arguing the case earned his keep – he definitively, in my view, pointed out that biscuits get soggy when they go stale – but, as for cake, a cake hardens. Jaffa Cakes go hard when they get stale. Pretty good, don't you think?'

'You should get his name, that QC. Could be useful for when you're in the dock at the Old Bailey on a charge of corruption in a public office. It's only a matter of time.'

Their discussion was cut short by the gravel-throated roar of a motorbike clearly going much faster than the speed limit. They watched the road with the same slightly elevated interest that the grazing cow might have shown, as a Harley-Davidson doing about sixty came into view and dopplered past them, making a tremendous racket.

Pretending not to be surprised by anything was a face-saving matter to both of them and had been since they first met. Boeing-loud, the Harley made its illegal way into the distance.

'Now that's not something you see every day.'

'You saw it, too, then? I was wondering if I was hallucinating.'

What had amazed them both was that the man on the Harley-Davidson was carrying a tuba strapped to his back.

'We're going to have to do something.'

'Why?'

'Because I'd say it was a hazard to the public.'

'But it's not *our* hazard.'

'What if he kills someone? I think there's a fair chance.'

Lister sighed and turned on the engine.

'Jesus Christ! You're such a fucking sissy.'

Five minutes later, they were getting out of their car just down from the Polish war memorial, walking towards the Harley and the oddly decked biker sitting astride it. They were both hoping that the rider was going to ask, 'Is there something wrong?', but he just stared at them with a sort of shifty defiance.

'Where's the fire, Tubby?'

The defiance turned to affront.

'Why are you saying I'm fat? I'm not fat.'

'He wasn't talking to you, dickhead,' said Scrope. 'He was talking to the tuba.'

Erewhon

Almost immediately, a marked police car pulled up and two uniformed cops emerged. Putting his cap on with the care of a particularly fussy milliner, the senior policeman smiled. His tone was deferential.

'Are you Detective Inspector Scrope?'

'I attended a Catholic primary school from Grade 4, and then a private Catholic all-girls secondary school. I really enjoyed my time at the Catholic primary school, to be honest … I think what I liked about those years was the feeling of inclusion. Doing all of my sacraments, participating in Mass … I was part of something. I liked that.'

Lily, 28 herself.com

'We now have a very specific target: to get people to understand that neglect is often as bad as abuse. As the Jungian analyst Grotstein said: "When innocence has been deprived of its entitlement, it becomes a diabolical spirit."'

Leonard Shengold, *Soul Murder: The Effects of Child Abuse and Deprivation*, 1989

CHAPTER 6

THE PROBLEM OF SUFFERING

'Why don't you just kill yourself?' asked Lou Bettancourt.

A silence.

'Isn't that a strange sort of question for a therapist to ask a patient?'

'I suppose it depends on the kind of therapist.'

'So what kind are you?' asked Aaron.

'Well, for the sake of simplicity, let's say there's a school of psychology that says men and women are driven by the will to power, another that it's the will to pleasure – sexual pleasure, mostly – and then there's the school I belong with …' – she corrected herself – '… belong to … which believes that what drives mankind is the search for meaning.' Lou beamed. 'I'm a logotherapist.'

'Never heard of them,' he said, trying but failing to place her accent. German, certainly, but somewhere else as well.

A smile.

'We're a dying breed. The founder of the movement had the view that, without finding a way to deal with suffering and turn it into something useful, men and women were bound to become depressed or neurotic.'

'When someone gives you lemons, you must make lemonade,' said Aaron. The mockery was polite, but still mockery – yet Bettancourt laughed.

'Exactly so. I know many people regard it as a line of the goody-goody, but I find it witty. And you know,' she said, still smiling, 'it's extraordinary how many such clever people come into this room requiring to learn precisely that this is what you must do in life.'

Aaron realised he was being politely mocked himself.

'So, you can see,' continued Bettancourt, 'a therapy that regards turning patients away from any idea of inner peace and harmony into people who use suffering as an energy to power their way into the world is not so good of an idea to many.'

Aaron smiled.

'Whatever doesn't kill you makes you stronger sort of thing?'

'It's a tricky one, that,' said Bettancourt. 'Viktor Frankl … He was the founder, if you like, of logotherapy … He liked the phrase. But me, I'm not so sure. Viktor didn't have to hear it coming back to him on the television every night.'

'You're right now that you mention it – you do hear it all over the place.'

'For me, the trouble with the notion of the killing kind of suffering making you stronger is that, if you can survive, it may only turn you into the walking wounded.' She looked at Aaron. 'Like you. Break a child's leg bad enough and they limp their way in life, and then the limp makes him move awkwardly and his back hurts, and then the back puts out his neck and the muscles clinch up, and the pain in his head feels bad enough to make him blind. Ring a bell with you?'

A pause.

'Yes.'

'Did it in any way?'

The Problem Of Suffering

'What?'

'Your suffering in this school of yours, did it make you strong at all?'

A silence.

'In a way, I suppose it did. When I left, I didn't feel afraid about things in the way other people seemed to be. No failure would ever be bad enough to be worse than the first time I went through those gates. It meant I took risks within my work and sometimes I screwed up. But it never bothered me, screwing up, because no one could hit me or bully me or lecture me about what a terrible creature I was. I could always just walk away. And I did.'

'That doesn't sound too bad.'

'It wasn't. I thought I was OK. But I wasn't OK. I was a very angry man. I drove away my wife and I frightened my children.'

'Do you still lose your temper?'

Aaron looked at her.

'No, not really. I don't even have that any more. I just feel …' He stopped. 'I don't know what I feel … A sort of dirty fog, one it hurts to breathe'

'And suicide?'

'For some reason, I just couldn't do that.'

A silence, a long one.

'But I wouldn't mind being dead. That would be all right.'

By the time he left, Aaron had decided to return.

There's no such thing as a stream of consciousness. There are no watery whirlpools, gyres or eddies in the human mind. Let me be clear with you: this is not an opinion. This is a fact. It may be the case that nobody knows anything. But I'm not nobody.

SCORN

The best model of consciousness is not a stream but the Gravelly Hill motorway interchange just outside Birmingham, more usually known as Spaghetti Junction. With its unbalanced and unappealing loops and whirls, it unites all four quarters of the kingdom in a harmonious but revealingly ugly whole. The human brain grows, it doesn't flow; it drives endlessly along continuously budding paths and tracks and lanes and highways, carrying its traffic along its lush and blooming tiny thoroughfares that cross under and over and around and around in millions of directions, in awe-inspiring but not, in my view, elegant synchronicity.

A particular example? I like a concrete for instance myself. Try this.

During the conversation with Lou Bettancourt, given his very existence was at stake, Aaron had been entirely present. But he was not just in a room discussing with grim intensity the roots of the death of happiness, although he was certainly doing that. A part of the interchanging pathways inside his brain was controlling his breathing, ensuring that the levels of electrolytes in his bodily fluids remained in harmonious balance so that he did not drop dead, and so on and so forth. His brain was also in the room, considering the rather fetching arse of Lou Bettancourt – having dropped a pencil as she went to shake Aaron's hand, she'd had to scrabble under the table in a skirt just a little too tight and just a little too short. As she reached for the pencil, the skirt tightened and rode higher until it revealed just the tantalisingly darker edge of black almost at the top of her long and enticingly plump thighs.

Lou was no glamourpuss, but she was as sexy as hell precisely because of that. Fleshy by twenty pounds or

The Problem Of Suffering

more by the measure of *Vogue* or *Grazia*, she gave to every man she met the sense that she might spill out a little from her elegant but faintly over-worn blouse or dress, an effect partly created by the fact that, for several months, one of the straps of her bra had been held together by a safety pin. She was matter of fact about how desirable she was. If a man seemed not to find her alluring, she was not affronted, she was merely surprised that anyone could deny themselves the pleasure of desiring her.

Climbing out from under the table, somewhat flushed, she had quickly adjusted her skirt – a little awkwardly; so appealing, this minor inelegance – and then sat down with it slightly too high upon her thighs. At the moment when she proposed the unusual idea that suffering was a fundamental necessity in the human heart, she had crossed her legs and (gasp!) briefly revealed a glimpse of cotton white shrouded in a shadowy nylon gauze.

It is expected that your garden-variety basic male would be incapable of failing to be aroused by such a voyeuristic opportunity, even if he were in the throes of a heart attack or a stroke. But it's worse than that. Weep, ladies, weep for the truth your endless generosity causes you to overlook: not even the most enthusiastically reconstructed male rightly ashamed of his objectifying gaze would have been able to resist gawping and slavering at the sight of the intersection of her legs and thighs. The hope of decency in man is a gold ring in a pig's snout – and not your wild pig either, all virile potency and sinewed heftiness, but your big, fat, pink and snorey porker destined for the Sunday roast or the BLT.

Be assured, oh gentle sex, I feel your pain. But what can you expect from a creature made of mud? Inside the skull of every man at the sight of Lou's entirely private place, the grey-matter axons and dendrites would have been on the move to fix in flesh and blood forever that sleazy memory, to be visited and revisited, even up to the point of death. What can you do to modify the hairy beast? Indoctrinate the better sort of man about his disgusting soul so that he'll confine himself to just a guilty and reluctant glance? Lacking the right kind of box, you could always to get him to confess under the covers of the bed at night.

But the worrying thing about Aaron, the real sign of the desperate condition he was in was that nothing grew in response. The will to power, the will to significance, the will to sex – at least one of these was already dead.

'A light scratch, Mr Gall.'

'*Ow!*' said Aaron. What the dentist meant by a light scratch was that it would in fact be a sharp pain. Weird, isn't it, people's faith in the power of language? The fact that it didn't work on this particular occasion doesn't take away from just how amazing it is how many of you seem to get it to work on other people, in defiance of any kind of common sense. Stupid and, yet, brilliant. I take my hat off to your ways with language, intrigued yet somewhat disgusted.

'We'll just let that settle in,' he said. A silence. 'Pity, really. Your teeth are really very strong, apart from all those childhood fillings. See, they're so large and deep you can't just replace them. Most of them have got to be crowned. Lot of work, I'm afraid.'

He sighed. 'And expensive.'

'Moreover no Christian shall presume to seize, imprison, wound, torture, mutilate, kill or inflict violence on [the Jews] ...

And most falsely do these Christians claim that the Jews have secretly and furtively carried away children and killed them, and that the Jews offer sacrifices from the heart and the blood of these children ... We decree that Jews seized under such a silly pretext be freed from imprisonment, and that they shall not be arrested henceforth on such a miserable imposture, unless – which we do not believe – they be caught in the commission of the crime.'

Pope Gregory X, in a papal encyclical
'The Protection of the Jews', 1272

'Furthermore, all of their synagogues, besides the one allowed, are to be demolished.

Moreover, concerning the matter that Jews should be recognisable everywhere: [to this end] men must wear a hat, women, indeed, some other evident sign, yellow in colour, that that must not be concealed or covered by any means, and must be tightly affixed [sewn].'

Pope Paul IV, at St Mark's Basilica,
Rome, in the first year of our Papacy,
1555

'So long as Jews remain Jews, a Jewish problem exists and will continue to exist [...] It is a fact that Jews are waging war against the Catholic church, that they are steeped in free-thinking, and constitute the vanguard of atheism, the Bolshevik movement, and revolutionary activity. It is a fact that Jews have a corruptive influence on morals and that their publishing houses are spreading pornography. It is true that Jews are perpetrating fraud, practising usury, and dealing in prostitution.'

'... one may not hate anyone. Not even Jews [...] it is forbidden to demolish a Jewish store, damage their merchandise, break windows, or throw things at their homes [...] it is forbidden to assault, beat up, maim, or slander Jews. One should honour and love Jews as human beings and neighbours.'

Ronald Modras, Two letters by Cardinal August Hlond, quoted in *The Catholic Church and Antisemitism: Poland, 1933–1939*, 1994

CHAPTER 7

TREACHEROUS JEWS

'And how are your feelings today?' said Lou Bettancourt.

'A bit wan. All right. I've just been to the dentist. The other kind of pain.'

He was looking what Lou's mother would have called *wackelig* – shaky; her father, *la tremblote*. He had a slight, indeed almost feminine build, but a strong face. Five minutes after climbing the six flights of stairs up to her consulting rooms he was still out of breath. This was not a well man.

'Nothing hit you in this accident which you had? I meant to ask more last time, but we became distracted.'

'No – might have been an electromagnetic pulse of some kind. They gave me a good going-over. Terrified I'll sue.'

'And will you?'

'Me? God, no. It's a European institution – the health benefits are majestic. They made me take a couple of months.'

'Still, you don't look well.'

'I'm fine.'

Bad temper, thought Lou. *Interesting.*

'All right. But if you want me to halt at any time …'

Aaron just looked at her.

She cleared her throat and got down to business.

'When we finished our last session, you were telling me

how you made your way through your life at this boarding school. How many months in a year?'

'Ten – give or take. The RAF would only pay for two flights a year for me and my brother to fly to Africa, where my father was stationed.'

'Something of a prison sentence, then?'

A bleak smile.

'We used to call it the camp. It was a joke – a friend of mine used to draw cartoons with barbed wire and guards dressed in a sort of Nazi helmet and cassock.'

'One of God's concentration camps.'

Aaron looked at her.

'Your founder again? Let's be clear about it. For us, it was just a joke. You were powerless against the black bastards, so all you had was jokes, the sicker the better. But nobody thought we were in a concentration camp.' He laughed. 'It was bad, but it wasn't that bad.'

'Viktor Frankl wouldn't have been agreeing with you.'

'Right. Yes. Well, Mr Frankl is wrong. They couldn't kill us. I think that *is* a difference worth mentioning.'

'What about soul murder?'

Aaron was taken aback by the phrase.

'You know the term?'

'No.'

'It refers to the destruction of the love of life in a child.'

A pause.

'That seems a pretty extreme way of putting things.'

'You could say,' went on Lou, 'that I have two kinds of patients. One kind are born with thin skins – they feel everything more deeply than others. Like the pea and the princess. So what you have to do is, always very slowly, help them to build a thicker skin. But you're the other type.'

'Type?'

'We're all types, Aaron. It's just not *all* we are. You're ... *kind*. You see, I'm trying hard to be the sensitive therapist. Your type is the opposite in a way. Not that they're insensitive – too thick-skinned – but they can't bring themselves to accept just how terrible the disaster is that's been overcoming them.'

'You tell your patients to take their misery more seriously?'

'Yes.' Lou smiled, liking the phrase. 'Exactly that. You need to take your misery more seriously. Viktor Frankl would have – and he knew suffering like his waistcoat pocket.'

'Because?'

'He spent the best part of a year in Auschwitz. His wife and everyone in his family – except his sister, I think – died in the Holocaust. He wouldn't have had the slightest problem in calling you a brother in misery.'

Another pause.

'I can't accept that.'

'You should, probably. We all think, in the best spirit of humility, that we never could imagine what it would be like to be in a place so terrible. Viktor's idea was that suffering was like a gas that expands to fill the available space in the human soul, so that there was a connection between all human beings when it came to feeling pain. To be honest, I'm not sure about the comparison. I think my idea of the thin-skinned soul and the devaluing soul – devaluing their own suffering, I mean – that's more helpful.'

Lou smiled. 'See, I agree with you. Some people need to see their suffering in a better proportion. It's just that you're not one of them.'

'So, I should be more miserable?' This time Aaron's

irritation emerged openly. Lou smiled and crossed her legs.

'Of course. This is exactly what I mean.' She was quiet for a moment. 'I'm sorry,' she resumed. She did not seem sorry and was smiling broadly. 'My supervisor always was telling me off that sarcasm was not just the worst form of wit but a blasphemy in the treatment of patients.'

'Perhaps you've taken up the wrong calling.'

Lou laughed like a bell.

'Nobody's perfect,' she said. 'I think a picture-perfect therapist would be a bit of a wazzock.'

'A wazzock?'

'Did I not pronounce it correctly? My husband has tried to teach me how to be rude in English. Perhaps wazzock is a bit strong, but a goody-goody of an analyst is not much use to anyone, even if they existed – which they don't, in fact.'

Anyway, that morning Lou's Geordie husband of nearly twenty years had watched her putting on the new bra which she'd finally got around to buying after the second strap on the old one had snapped (it was, of course, not her only bra – she had three – but it was *extremely* comfortable). Unfamiliar with the clasp, she'd had to make several breast-squeezing attempts to get it on.

'When I die, pet,' he said, with all the generosity of a Toon alderman magnanimously ceding his most prized painting to the city, 'I'm gunna leave those breasts to the Laing Art Gallery.'

Her hair always seemed to be three weeks past the time it should have been cut; her make-up always looked as if it should have been repaired several hours before; and her clothes were often six months to a year past the point when they should have been consigned to the charity shop.

'I still think it's too much,' said Aaron. 'I've read and I've watched. Those places really were hell.'

'Yes, of course. But there are seven levels of hell – each one more terrible than the last. But what you're not taking into account is that the Nazis didn't try to tell us they were doing these things to us as an act of love. They didn't try to get us Jews to agree to murdering our bodies. But your priests were guards when they were supposed to be shepherds. Worse than the Nazis in some ways, they tried to get you to agree to let them murder your souls.'

She watched him for a moment and liked the fact that he was clearly working hard through something he did not want to accept.

'I grant you, Aaron, that advising people about making use of their suffering can be a bit ... What's the word?'

'Wazzocky?'

She laughed.

'Very wazzocky, yes. But Viktor Frankl suffered about as much as a person can suffer and still live – so you've got to listen to what he has to say.'

'But it could still be wrong,' said Aaron.

'But it could still be wrong.'

'So what is it, then, the point of suffering?'

'I'm not sure he would have said it had a point exactly, but it *could* have a purpose if you could make one.'

'Such as?'

'That's up to each man or woman. He was no fingerwagger. It has to be something meaningful, for sure, but meaningful to *you*. The human person who has a *why* to live for can bear almost anything.'

'But I don't have a *why*.'

'Find one.'

SCORN

'And if I can't?'

She did not reply at first.

'Look hard. It's there somewhere. Give your soul the question and wait patiently for its answer.'

'I thought my soul was murdered.'

'You know very well what I mean, Aaron. Being a smart-pants won't save you.'

'It's smart alec or smarty-pants.' A pause. 'Sorry. I'm too fond of having the last word. That's what my mother used to say.'

'I like mothers,' said Lou, as the clock approached five minutes to the hour and signalled that it was time for Aaron to leave. 'Where would therapy be without them?'

Aaron stood up and she shook his hand. 'I know you are in great pain at this point in your life, but it's exactly in such a time of crisis that life offers you a way forward … A purpose becomes clear.' She smiled. 'The darkest hour is just before dawn. As you can see, I'm having a cliché for every occasion.'

CHAPTER 8

A TOUCH OF CLASS

As Detective Inspector George Scrope and Detective Sergeant David Lister drove down Western Avenue to Paddington Central, they spoke hardly at all. After a silence of almost ten minutes, Lister said quietly but triumphantly, 'Anal speculum.'

Scrope sighed and looked mildly put out. His mobile rang. 'Scrope,' he answered, then listened for about thirty seconds. 'See you then, sir.'

'What's up?' said Lister.

'Odd. Calvin wants us in his office as soon as we get back to Paddington.'

'What for?'

'That's what's odd. He said it was urgent, that Bayley had been on the phone. Then he said, "Someone's eaten a priest."'

'What the fuck does that mean?'

'You've never heard it before?'

'No.'

The problem was that neither of them would be able to ask anyone at the station what it meant because they were sure that everyone at the station was waiting for them to do exactly that – admit there was something they didn't know.

They were loathed, the pair of them, for two main reasons. First, they both went to Eton. Strictly speaking,

Scrope had gone to Ampleside, but you may understand, as it was the Catholic equivalent, that this was not a distinction of much significance to their less privileged colleagues.

But, worse than this, they'd been fast-tracked into senior positions in the force above the heads of real coppers through a scheme to bring in new blood from the armed forces. The police – quite rightly – regarded this, in reality, as a dastardly scheme by the much-hated Home Office to bring to heel the famously stroppy British police force by undermining their highly valued working-class tradition of promoting only from the ranks.

There was nothing about the pair, in short, that wasn't a blatant offence to pretty much every serving officer in the Met. Lister and Scrope returned the general loathing of their fellow officers with a disrespect they never bothered to disguise.

Why had they joined? It was simple enough. While they both craved the intensity of danger and action, the wars in Iraq and Afghanistan were hazardous in a way that had proved increasingly unattractive: the risk of getting killed or having arms, legs or genitals blown off in order to bring the benefits of western democracy to peoples among whom many were either indifferent to its virtues or violently hostile to them had started to seem not just dangerous but odd.

Police work in London, on the other hand, offered the possibility of being relatively exciting without the risk of ending up in a ditch in Gereshk with both legs and an arm torn off, wounds already festering from the rancid dog shit the Taliban liked to mix with the nuts and bolts and washers and nails in their improvised explosive devices.

A Touch Of Class

The only problem with police work, as far as Lister and Scrope were concerned, was that it was done by the police. 'An interesting job done by horrible people' was Lister's favourite line – he liked it so much that he'd even stirred himself to find out who'd written it, in case there was anything more they had to say – but after a fruitless five minutes on Google he'd got bored.

'Someone's eaten a priest,' he said again, impressed by the ominous obscurity of the phrase.

'It means,' said Scrope, 'someone has developed a conscience about something – hence, they've eaten a priest.'

'Could be. Sounds right. So it must be someone with dangerous information who's decided to cough.'

'Corruption – someone's dobbing people.'

'*Police* people?'

'Could be.' A pause. 'Well, don't look at me. I haven't had long enough to get my feet under the table to be tempted into anything.'

'Everyone knows you like a bung.'

'I take great exception to that. And besides, nothing was ever proved.' Scrope laughed. 'Anyway, why would they ask *us* to investigate? They hate us.'

'That's why. They want us to sconce any Stasi on the take exactly because nobody likes us – we're not beholden.'

'But then no one would talk to us either. Because everyone hates us.'

'I suppose we could just try waiting until we see Bayley.'

'We could do that, I suppose. Don't ask any questions. In fact, don't say anything. Let him do the talking.'

There was silence for a while.

'Do you think they literally hate us?' asked Scrope.

'I would if I were them. We've had every privilege life

has to offer – education, money, opportunities. If I wasn't me, I'd hate me.'

'So would I. Hate you, I mean.'

'Do you know Scrope and Lister?'

'I've come across them a couple of times – a right pair of supercilious cunts.'

'Smart, though.'

'Look, sir, I know you think I'm just a flatfoot with his arse still on a canteen bench, whining about the old days, but I don't have anything as such against graduates. I just think they need at least five years doing the job on the streets before they get to tell the rest of us what to do.'

'OK, fine, Geoff. I know the canteen hates them, but the canteen is at the root of why the force has lost the confidence of the public, and the government, and everyone else. Things are going to change. The canteen has been drinking in the last-chance saloon for twenty years.' He paused. 'I know that doesn't sound right, but you know what I mean.'

The canteen he was referring to was a hostile and reactionary state of mind shared by white working-class males in the police force below the rank of sergeant – or so was claimed by the increasingly large number of people in society generally unsympathetic to the white, the working class and the male. All in all, it was a bad time for this last bastion of the working-class professional. Once, becoming an inspector had demanded twenty years of walking the beat and learning the hard way about the real world. Now what it required was a degree in politics and good marks in the racial-awareness test at Hendon Police College.

Chief Superintendent Bayley flicked on the intercom. 'Julie. Send them in.'

A Touch Of Class

There was nothing but watchfulness about the introductions. Scrope and Lister were told to sit down. The DCI waited for them to ask what this was all about, but they simply looked expectantly obedient. He had to give in, but he wasn't going to make it easy.

'I understand, Scrope, you're into crosswords.'

'Yes, sir.'

'You make them up – for the newspapers?'

'Yes, sir.' Cautious hammers working in his brain.

'All right. The thing is, there's been a murder and someone – we presume the murderer – left what looked to us like a crossword clue written on the wall where we found the victim. The clue was written in his blood.'

At least now it was clear why the head of the murder squad was here.

Bayley gestured to Superintendent Dawe to go ahead.

'The clue was,' said Dawe, *'Initially, the Supreme Court lacks a twisted method of execution for squealers.'*

It was impossible to say which one of them got there first; perhaps what delayed Scrope's response was that the answer was something of a shock.

'The pig Scrope!' said Lister, before he could stop himself. 'The initials of the Supreme Court are SC and "a twisted method of execution" means "rope".' He looked, with some pleasure, around the room. 'A squealer can also be a pig.'

The resulting silence was one that someone educated privately might describe as gravid. Both the senior policemen now took great pleasure in taking the pair by surprise.

'As it happened, we managed to work that one out for ourselves, Sergeant,' said Dawe. This claim depended on a loose definition of 'ourselves'. In fact, the solution had come from a secretary in the scenes of crime office.

'So, what I'm here to ask you is: why do you think a particularly violent killer who seems to have devoured the internal organs of his victim appears to be writing your name in large letters above the corpse?'

They'd shocked Scrope once, but a lifetime of emotional repression honed by public school and the army put him back in control almost immediately.

'Who was the victim?'

'A Father Seamus Malone.'

'Don't know him – as far as I know. I'd need to look at the file.' Scrope shrugged.

'Maybe the answer isn't just Scrope,' said Lister. 'So, OK. "Initially the Supreme Court" means the initials of the Supreme Court, hence SC. A twisted method of execution is a rope. So we have "Scrope" – but what about "lack"? It has to mean something.'

'Such as?' said Dawe.

'"Lack" means "wants". The killer wants DI Scrope on the case.'

'Why?'

'He fancies himself – the perpetrator thinks he's clever.'

'How would he know about DI Scrope?'

'The crossword fans know about him,' said Lister. 'He's a bit of a poster boy after that article on him in *Police* got picked up by the *Telegraph*. I'm not saying he's Justin Bieber – but those who are interested would pick up on it.'

'*Can* I see the file, sir?'

Scrope looked at Lister in a way that suggested that he might now want to shut the fuck up.

'You can,' said Dawe, 'but let's be clear that the Murder Squad isn't in the habit of letting perpetrators choose the officer who investigates their crimes. Just in case you were wondering.'

Dawe took out his card and handed it to Scrope. 'Let me know if there's anything in the file that strikes you.' He stood up and looked at the Chief Superintendent. 'Time I wasn't here.' He gave a nod to Scrope and Lister that was as minimal as it could be while still possibly being taken as a gesture of acknowledgement, and was gone.

'OK,' said the CI. 'I won't keep you, but let me know first if you think of any connection between you and the victim.'

'So, we're just going to ignore the clue?' said Lister.

The CI looked down at a memo on his desk. 'No, *I'm* going to ignore it. You're going to get on with whatever it is you're supposed to be doing.'

'Weird or what?' said Lister as they made their way to the canteen.

'The clue was easy,' said Scrope. 'It wasn't meant for me to solve. I'd say our murderer has a low opinion of the analytic skills of the Met. Next time, it'll be harder. We should say something.'

'Will they listen?'

'No.'

'Then why waste your time?'

'The moral principle?' said Scrope.

'Listen, chum, they're not going to bring you in on this. You heard him. If you tell them there's going to be another murder, this time with a clue they'll be too thick to understand. Then they'll dig in their heels, and it'll take another killing before they give in. Am I wrong?'

'But if I don't say anything, there'll also be another killing.'

'True. But you won't have proved them wrong if you keep your mouth shut. If you speak up now, it means they'll have made a bad mistake. If they ignore you – which they will – there's going to be another victim whatever you do. Keeping your mouth shut now means you'll be called up all the sooner. Besides, Dawe is right. Obviously, they can't put you on the case because the killer asked for you. Someone's going to die. There's nothing you can do about it.'

Lister was right, of course. The lesson of history is that there never was a disaster – from the introduction of the wooden horse into Troy (beware Greeks bearing gifts), to the need to arm against Hitler, to the collapse of the world financial system in the early twenty-first century – that someone, or several someones, hadn't warned people about in specific detail. Be assured that, if you discover incontrovertible proof of the imminent invasion of Martians, you would be best advised to save your breath.

And don't imagine you'll be famous after the event you prophesied takes place, or that history will vindicate you: ask Brooksley Born, Roger Boisjoly, Katsuhiko Ishibashi, John O'Neill and, perhaps most poignantly (considering the general tone of the story I'm telling you), Father Georges Lemaître, Catholic priest and professor of physics at the Catholic University of Leuven.

'I have a proposal,' said Lou, 'though it's only that. It's drastic, I suppose. It has its dangers.'

'Yes?'

'Frankl talks a lot about the defiance of the human spirit, but I wonder if it might help to take this a bit more ... at face value.'

'Again,' said Aaron. 'Yes?'

'You said that therapy hasn't helped in the past.' She smiled in a way that would have caused anyone else but Aaron to shiver, just a little, with desire. 'And perhaps not now either.' If she was expecting a demurral and a compliment, and I don't say she was, she didn't get it. 'And the drugs aren't helping much anymore.'

'Why don't you just get on with it?' A pause. 'Sorry.'

Another smile from Lou.

'I was thinking. Why don't you *do* something? Why don't you *defy* ... answer back? Perhaps that would break this deadlock of yours.'

'Meaning?'

'Start by writing to the Church. It sounds silly when I put it like that. I mean, why not write to the Archbishop of Westminster. He's head of the Catholic Church here. Complain to him directly.'

'Why?' It was clear to Lou that Aaron was not at all pleased at this suggestion.

'Confront him with what happened. Make him – make *them* – react back to you. Don't suffer in silence. Turn things out, not inside.'

'What sort of response?'

'An apology?'

'I don't want an apology.'

'Receiving a "sorry" can be surprisingly helpful.'

'For who? If they really understood what they've done, they'd announce the immediate dissolution of the Catholic Church, and then each one of them would have to tie a millstone around their necks and throw themselves into the sea.' He smiled. 'Even I think that's unrealistic. How would anyone survive having accepted they were the exact opposite of everything they claimed their life to be about?'

They sat in silence for some time.

'What if, instead of writing to the Catholic Church complaints department for an apology, you demanded compensation?'

'I don't want their money.'

'Then what *do* you want?'

Aaron started to reply, then stopped. Another silence, short this time.

'Are any of the priests or nuns who taught you still alive? If so, why don't you go and talk to them?'

He looked at her, at first as if she was asking a truly absurd question and then with the expression of someone presented with an answer that was so obvious he was amazed he hadn't seen it before.

'Some priests were aware that particular instances of abuse had occurred. A few were courageous and brought complaints to the attention of their superiors. The vast majority simply chose to turn a blind eye.'

> Commission of Investigation Report into the Catholic Archdiocese of Dublin, July 2009

'No one [in the Vatican] thinks the sexual abuse of kids is unique to the States, but they do think that the reporting on it is uniquely American, fuelled by anti-Catholicism and shyster lawyers hustling to tap the deep pockets of the church. And that thinking is tied to the larger perception about American culture, which is that there is an hysteria when it comes to anything sexual, and an incomprehension of the Catholic Church. What that means is that Vatican officials are slower to make the kinds of public statements that most American Catholics want, and when they do make them they are tentative and half-hearted. It's not that they don't feel bad for the victims, but they think the clamour for them to apologise is fed by other factors that they don't want to capitulate to.'

> John L. Allen, Jr, Vatican correspondent for the *National Catholic Reporter*, 2003

CHAPTER 9

CONFESSION

It was one o'clock in the morning, and Father Thomas Lloyd was eating sardines on toast in the vast and gloomy kitchen of the rectory of St Edmund's Church in Abingdon, a place not a hundred yards from the Victorian building in which Aaron had received the worst beating of his life from Mother Mary Frances and a mere thirty yards from where the sadistic old bitch was buried. Burial in the otherwise full cemetery was a privilege accorded only to people with a special reputation for holiness.

As he was about to begin his meal, one which he realised at some guilty, deep level he was not as thankful for as he ought to have been, there was a hard rap at the door. Although it was unusual for there to be such a late caller, it was not unknown for someone to fetch him to a deathbed or a tormented soul to come looking for the peace of mind only God could grant. Still, he was no fool and was wary. He walked out of the cavernous kitchen and switched on the light in the barely less sepulchral cavern of the hall.

'Who is it?' he called out, ill at ease.

'Is that you, Father Lloyd?'

Who else would it be in the rectory of the church at this time of night? was what he wanted to say. Immediately, he accused himself of the sin of the lack of charity. 'Yes. Yes, it is.' To make amends, he opened the door immediately. The man on the

Confession

stoop was not an alarming sight – five nine, perhaps, and thin.

'Come in out of the rain.' He ushered the man inside and gestured him through the hall into the kitchen. The abundance of mahogany gave an unpleasant brown quality to the light. 'Let me take your coat.'

Draping the man's coat on the hat stand, he turned to get a better look at his visitor. Many years of ministering to the soul-distressed made him alert to the despairing and the desperate. His visitor did not seem to be either. The man looked at the uneaten plate of toast and sardines.

'I'm sorry. Please finish your meal.'

Father Lloyd was tempted, but not for long. He would offer this sacrifice up to God, aware, of course, that God would realise it was not all that much of a renunciation.

'No. I've rather gone off the idea.' He gestured for the man to sit. 'Tell me your name and what I can do for you,' he said softly.

'I'd like to make a confession.'

'I see.' A pause and a sigh. 'Well, there's no doubt you've come to the right place, Mr—?'

'Gall. Aaron Gall.'

'Are you from around here, Aaron?'

'I used to be, a long time ago.'

'Is that so, indeed? I've been away and back a fair few times, but I've spent near half my life as a priest at St Edmund's. You must have been here during my away years.'

'No,' said Aaron. 'You taught me – my class – religious instruction when I was a boy.'

The priest looked worried. It didn't look good or feel right to forget a parishioner.

'Help me. I'm an old man, and my memory isn't what it was.'

'The old primary school, just before it moved.'

'My God, that's a fair few years.'

'I was eight or so the last time I saw you. It wouldn't be reasonable to remember me.'

'I was only here a few months the first time, waiting to go to Birmingham.'

There was a silence – an odd one, uncomfortable for the priest. 'So, what brings you out tonight?' he said at last.

'You remember Mother Mary Frances. She's buried in the churchyard here.'

'So they told me.'

'They?'

'The Sisters of Mercy.'

Another pause.

'So. This isn't a visit on the sudden, then.'

'No.'

'What is it you want, my son?'

Aaron smiled quietly and spoke softly. 'I'm not your son, old man, and this isn't a visit.'

Father Lloyd was too old and experienced in the ways of those overstretched by life not to realise something unpleasant was up.

'So, what it is, then, Mr Gall?'

'A reckoning, I suppose you'd call it. You see, the last time we saw each other, Mother Mary Frances beat me for some time in your presence because my workbook was untidy.' Gall, all strange tranquillity until now, searched the priest's face for signs that he remembered now, even after all this time. 'You don't recall, do you?'

The priest straightened up and his mouth shifted down a little at the corners. They stared at each other.

'Funny, that,' said Gall at last. 'I mean, peculiar. To me,

Confession

it's not a memory, although I wish it were – and not even a very bad one. To me, it's still happening inside. I can see you now, just the way you were that day, the odd face you had on you when she went about me. I could see you didn't care for it. You really don't remember? That's odd. In a bad way. You know, I always assumed that everyone remembered – all the other kids – because it wasn't as if it was common, a beating like that. But probably they've forgotten, too, like you. It makes me wonder if even that evil bitch ever thought about it again.'

The priest said nothing.

Aaron smiled. 'Would you agree, old man, that she was an evil bitch to beat a child for something like that? What do you think? I really am quite interested.'

'Things ... attitudes were very different in those days.'

'Were they? I suppose they were, you're right. But they didn't feel different to me. Some things don't change. Fear, for example. Terror. The power of a blow delivered by an adult to a small child. The force of the blow, according to Newton's law of motion, has, in fact, always been the same, since the beginning of the universe. The laws of motion ordained by God are, curiously, not at all different anywhere at any time. Eternal values. Constant. Never changing. But I suppose science isn't your thing. How about the word of God? Who so shall offend one of these little ones, it were better for him that a millstone were hanged about his neck and that he were drowned in the depth of the sea.'

Aaron watched his face carefully. He was shocked by the echo in the priest's expression of that from all those years before. Later, he regarded this shock as peculiar. Why wouldn't he look the same under such pressure? He was the same person, after all.

'I can see,' said Father Lloyd at last, 'that you feel wounded by what occurred. I'm sorry that I can't remember. It was a long time ago – though clearly not for you. The punishment as you describe it sounds very wrong – very – for an error of such a nature.'

'I see,' said Aaron.

'But your quoting of scripture is a misunderstanding – although an understandable one. The words you have missed are most important, most important.'

'I thought,' said Aaron, reasonably, 'that I had them exactly.'

'No,' said the priest, almost grateful. 'No, you do not. The words are precise. Jesus says it would be better he were thrown into the sea than cause one of these little ones to fall into sin by setting a bad example. It's not the same now, not at all. Though it's a mistake easily made.'

Aaron looked thoughtful. 'Now, that's very interesting, Father Lloyd – you see, because I'm a man of numbers, so to speak, so I'd always taken those words at face value.'

To his surprise and considerable relief, because there was something very unsettling about the man before him, Father Lloyd began to sense that he was getting through, that the man had come, without realising it, for understanding, and not just to upbraid him and the church he loved.

'But,' said Aaron, 'I'm not sure I understand what you are saying, what it means to …' He searched for the word.

'To fall into sin?'

'Yes.'

'What Jesus was talking about was any occasion for a weak person to do something sinful – the term "child" shouldn't be taken too literally – causing someone to commit a terrible sin is what's worthy of having a millstone

Confession

tied around your neck and being cast into the sea. It's not what it appears. I'm not saying – I'm not at all saying – that what happened to you all those years ago was not wrong. But the judgement by Jesus concerns not being the means of drawing the innocent into sin, of not causing them to stumble. It's not really about hurting children, as such.'

'Right.' Aaron considered for a moment. 'So, in a manner of speaking, and I exaggerate to clarify things, you could say that by chastising me for slovenliness – a sin, I accept that – Mother Mary Frances, admittedly in an extreme and unloving way, was trying, wrongly, to prevent me from falling into sin.'

Father Lloyd was not entirely a fool. He realised he was being treated scornfully.

'What do you want, Mr Gall?'

Aaron stood up, or so it at first appeared to Father Lloyd, for how else was a person to grasp the sight of a man growing in stature before his very eyes, broadening, widening, lengthening and transmorphing into a creature of hair and claw and snout and teeth. And eyes!

Other than the sound of stretching and growing and Aaron's faint moan of pleasure at his ecstatic metamorphosis, the only other noise came from the puddling of urine on the floor below Father Lloyd's seat.

'What I want,' said Wolf Aaron, 'is to tie a millstone around your neck and drown you in the depths of the ocean.'

Had anyone been passing the graveyard of St Edmund's Church at midnight and had unusually acute night vision, they would have witnessed a sight as curious as it was terrifying: a large werewolf dancing delightfully over the recently dug-up grave of Mother Mary Frances.

He was leaping and pirouetting, gambolling and

frolicking about between the gravestones. He was throwing the bones of the ten-years-deceased nun up into the air, now catching them in his teeth, now juggling an array of thigh bones, femurs, of humerus and ulna, true ribs, false ribs. The proximal phalanges of her hand – the ones that made such painful contact with his head so many years ago – he gargled noisily then spat out over the graves like so many lemon pips. Her skull he raised up into the night, watching the moonlight play in the holes that were her eyes. Then he tossed it into the air, let it drop on to his arcing foot and despatched a volley with her cranium at a vaguely goal-shaped section of the graveyard wall. It shattered like blown glass.

The werewolf Gall bowed to an invisible crowd. 'A quality goal, by a quality player.'

Have you ever driven to the end of a busy road and realised that for the last half-mile you've been daydreaming and have made no conscious effort to avoid crashing your car into the innocents walking by, casually assuming that the other people mooching along in their two tons of death-dealing metal are paying attention to what they're doing? So has everyone. So who's been doing the driving while you were giving your Oscar acceptance speech, or telling your employer to fuck himself, or considering which one of a dozen shining knights you will allow to talk to you of your beauty and their unworthiness?

(The unrelenting banality of your daydreams, by the way, makes me want to puke.)

Neuroscientists even have a name for the guardian angel driving your car while you're away with the pixies in charge of these two tons of motor car: they call it a daemon, a sort of safety feature added to your brain by the divine creator

Confession

after He realised that his mud-based creation was utterly incapable of making its way through the day without being lethally distracted by some self-deluding fantasy. It was this astonishingly capable soul-servant that drove naked, blood-covered Aaron Gall back to the Finchley Road. And it was sheer luck that enabled him to walk unseen into his flat at 3 a.m.

When he woke up the following afternoon, he was unable to remember anything after the moment when the late Father Lloyd asked him what he wanted. He also had a truly vile taste in his mouth, caused by the fact that, during the night, his newly acquired wolfy instincts had impelled him to lick himself entirely clean of the blood and guts and brains of the old man which had covered him from head to foot.

While Aaron was not a vegetarian by conviction, he rarely ate meat. This might explain why he spent much of the remains of that day yarking into the toilet bowl. On the other hand, even a passionate carnivore might well have found it difficult to keep down eight pounds of raw flesh devoured in less than five minutes.

His explanation for the black-out and the projectile vomiting? A nasty stomach bug. What other explanation could there be? Perhaps in the fugue state that had blacked out the last five hours since he remembered knocking on the door of Father Lloyd's house, he'd visited a curry house and eaten to excess. Of course, not even the notion of excess could account for such a vast amount of partially digested meat.

But if his desperate guess was implausible, where did that leave the truth?

So, the next time you think of yourself as being in

SCORN

control of your bovine viper of a brain, remember that it's only your soul-fix auto-pilot, the good Lord's ghostly duct tape, that's keeping you out of prison, keeping you alive.

'The Blessed Cardinal Newman is only one in a tradition of saints who have spoken with great ferocity about the horror we should have for sin: "The Catholic Church holds it better for the sun and moon to drop from heaven, for the earth to fail, and for all the many millions on it to die of starvation in extremest agony, as far as temporal affliction goes, than that one soul, I will not say, should be lost, but should commit one single venial sin, should tell one wilful untruth, or should steal one poor farthing without excuse."'

Timothy M. Dolan, Archbishop of New York, a Pastoral Letter on the Sacrament of Penance, 17 March 2011

'One cannot really be Catholic and grown-up.'

George Orwell, 'Extracts from a Manuscript Notebook' (1949), *The Collected Essays, Journalism and Letters of George Orwell*, vol. 4 (1968)

CHAPTER 10

SIN

'What does it mean?' demanded Geoff Dawe, head of the Murder Squad and the cop who had been so hostile to Scrope and Lister a couple of weeks earlier in Paddington. He'd arrived at the presbytery a few minutes after Scrope and Lister, and was referring to two words on the wall of the kitchen just above the body, written in what was presumably the victim's blood:

NO SENSELESSNESS

'I'm thinking, sir,' said Scrope, mildly insolent, in the practised way of the public schoolboy towards his superiors. All three turned back to the body. Father Thomas Lloyd was lying spread-eagled, mostly naked, with an enormous tear where his chest and abdomen should have been. Beside him on the floor lay the remains of a liver, a heart, a lung, and several other bits and pieces they were not qualified to identify.

'Is that a spleen?' asked Lister.

'No,' said the pathologist, examining the body. 'It's the tail of the pancreas.'

'Never mind that,' said Dawe. 'What in God's name did this?'

'No idea,' said the pathologist. 'If it wasn't for the

Sin

circumstances, I'd say it was an animal. But it would have to be a pretty big one.'

'And,' said Lister, 'one able to write three-syllable words.'

'Did he use a knife?'

'Probably not. He could be trying to confuse the wounds.' He pointed to a set of three parallel cuts on the face, deep. 'The only time I've seen anything like that before was a victim attacked with a sharpened ... uh ... you know, one of those little hand-fork things for digging weeds.' He looked up. 'It's going to take hours, the autopsy.'

'No preliminaries?' asked Scrope.

'No.'

'Was it a break-in?' asked Dawe.

'No forced entry,' said Scrope.

'Time of death?' They all looked at the pathologist.

'A guess.'

'Between one in the morning and three.'

Dawe looked at Scrope. 'Is that odd? Would it be someone he knew?'

'Not necessarily. He was a priest, after all. He couldn't very well tell someone who'd turned up demanding confession to keep him from eternal damnation to fuck off and come back in the morning. Could easily have been a stranger. Even a very odd one.'

Dawe looked around, dissatisfied. 'Any idea about the clue?'

'I'm still thinking, sir.'

Dawe grunted softly, in a way that he hoped communicated his feeling that, if they couldn't say something useful about the words written on the wall, then what was the point of the two of them?

SCORN

'I'm going to talk to the scenes of crime officer.'

'You should thank me,' said Lister, when Dawe had gone.

'Yeah?'

'For not making you look bad about the clue.'

'You got it, then?'

'Yep.'

'What took you so long?'

'You can say that, but is it true? I think we should both write it down on a piece of paper. Then we'll know if you're lying.'

'I know what it means. I just don't know what it *means*.'

They muttered together for ten minutes. Then Dawe came back.

'I was talking to the housekeeper. She only comes in for a few hours a week, but she used to be nearly full time when there were four priests living here. Apparently, no one wants to join the ministry anymore. Though she says they were on a shortlist for a Pole or an African.'

'No one saw or heard anything, but there must have been a hell of a racket.'

'The nearest house is a hundred yards away.'

Dawe looked at the words on the wall and waited.

'It's a sort of crossword joke,' said Scrope. '"Senselessness" is an answer to a clue, not a clue itself. It's supposed to be the hardest clue ever devised: E13. The answer to the clue E13 is "senselessness" because it has thirteen letters and what it then needs you to do is take "sense less" – as in "take away" – "ness" which leaves you with "E". So that gives you "No E". That's the clue.'

'So what does it mean?'

'Nothing – not on its own. He's going to make us wait.

Sin

Every time he kills someone, we'll get another part of the clue.'

'So we just wait?'

'He's having us on. I don't think we should be drawn into this too much. He's clever, and he won't be telling us anything useful. He'll just pretend to.'

'But he might give something away.'

'It's possible. Hard to say. He thinks well of himself, that's for sure. I'd be careful myself of relying on this stuff.'

Dawe was mollified by all this. He'd expected Scrope to play up his importance, to demonstrate his superiority of intelligence and education.

'All right. I don't need to tell you, when the press get a hold of this, the shit's going to hit the fan. Watch out for them and get the report in tomorrow morning. We'll talk about it then.'

'Chief.' The scenes of crime officer called from the other side of the room. 'You need to see this.' He was supervising two cops who were moving a hideous brown wardrobe approaching the weight of a small car. 'Slowly!'

Dawe strode over and, without thinking, put his shoulder into helping the two men shift the wardrobe. Scrope and Lister followed, just as automatically standing by and watching them work. Groaning and screeching in protest, the wooden leviathan shifted away from the wall. Another clue was scrawled behind it.

ALAS THE STONE OF SCONE REMOVED BY EBENEZER IS THERE BY THE ACTIVE VILLAGE.

'I thought you said he was going to make us wait for clues,' said Dawe.

'So you know the answer?'

'No.'

'Neither do I. So what makes you think he isn't making us wait?'

'I thought you were supposed to be brilliant at this stuff.'

'Brilliant enough to know he's raised his game.'

Lister laughed. 'Don't you mean he's raised *your* game?'

Scrope smiled. 'I stand corrected.'

'Can you smell anything?'

'Such as?'

'Dogs. Unwashed dogs.' Lister called over to the scenes of crime officer. 'Did the victim have a dog?'

'No.'

'Unwashed priest, perhaps,' said Scrope.

Lister walked over to the corpse and sniffed the dead man's armpits. Scrope wrinkled his nose.

'Well?'

'Disembowelled bodies smell pretty bad. But I could smell soap. Whatever the odd smell is, it's not the late Father Lloyd. Odd.'

The scenes of crime officer approached.

'We're going to turn him over. Mind out.' The two policemen watched as, with almost tender care, the body was carefully lifted and moved on its front.

A pause to take in what they saw.

'That's odd,' said Scrope.

The body had been left lying on a pad of salt and a packet of fish fingers.

'I forgot to mention …' said Dawe, '… the first victim, Father Malone – the killer left the same stuff under his body, too.'

*

Sin

When the newspapers and television learned of the murder of Father Thomas Lloyd, joy was unconfined. In the light of events the week before, involving the murder of a priest by two French extremists, journalists, as if with one heart, yearned for it to be a domestic terrorist crime and looked forward to perhaps weeks of blaming the government or the police for scandalous inaction or complacency. Dreamed of demands that Something Be Done to prevent further attacks, calls for more police with guns, a more alarming colour of warning. There would be interviews with I-told-you-so entrepreneurs of every stripe, man-in-the-street Q&As. (Q: *Are you alarmed about the alarming rise in terrorism?* A: *Yes, Victoria/Jeremy/Kirsty, I am very alarmed.*)

Sadly, their hopes were dashed. It turned out that the murderer seemed to just be your garden-variety nutcase, not an Islamic terrorist bent on destroying civilisation. Interest faded pretty quickly.

This may surprise you, given the hideous nature of the injuries involved, not to mention the issue of cannibalism. You're right to be surprised. But, wisely, the cops decided to keep the details of the murder away from the media, in the hope that they would catch the perpetrator before the juicy particulars leaked out. After all, they reasoned, how long could an anthropophagus, homicidal, grave-violating maniac stay off the radar? Once he was caught, the public would be shocked but could no longer be encouraged by the sensationalist scaremongers in the media to *blame*.

But however briefly connected to the possibility of terrorism (otherwise, it might never have got beyond page three of the *Abingdon Herald*), Father Lloyd's death was initially widely reported. As a result, the amnesiac Aaron was appalled to discover that the priest he'd gone to see a few days before had been murdered within hours of his leaving him in perfect health.

Shock was followed by alarm. He realised that he was morally obliged to contact the police but also that he was placing himself in some jeopardy by doing so. Was this concern for his own interests shameful, given that the life of a human being was involved?

Alas, Aaron had grown up in the West Midlands at a time when the police there had become renowned for an interrogation technique which involved putting a gun to the head of a suspect and inviting him to confess or risk having his brains splattered all over the walls. Of course, this kind of thing was no longer allowed, partly because of a rigorously determined policy of rooting out corrupt police officers but mostly because a new law had been passed requiring that all interrogations be recorded on tape. Given this, his alarm about his closeness to the crime, and his hazy recollection of how the meeting had concluded, Aaron's hesitation may not have been admirable, but it was certainly understandable.

After an hour or so, he did the right thing.

Three hours later, Scrope and Lister were in his flat, giving Aaron what felt to him like the third degree but which to them seemed routine, given the fact that they had, of course, googled him (*Linking both the theoretical and engineering aspects of physics at CERN, Professor Aaron Gall is best known for his development of stochastic cooling techniques* ...). Reasoning that such a person was unlikely to be either a killer cannibal or stupid enough to bring himself to the attention of the police, what they realistically hoped was that he could tell them about Father Lloyd's state of mind just before he died and, if they were exceptionally fortunate, that he might have seen something useful.

But Aaron had nothing helpful to say. Still, for all their entirely understandable, completely wrong assumptions about Aaron's involvement, Scrope and Lister were good enough at their jobs to give Aaron's tree a little bit of a shake.

'Ten o'clock,' said Lister. 'A bit late for a visit to an old teacher, isn't it, Professor?'

'Yes, I suppose. But I'd passed by the place a few times over the years and not gone in to see him. I realised that, if he was still alive, I might not have another chance, so when I saw on the board outside that he was still parish priest there and that the light was on, I thought—'

'And he remembered you after all that time?'

'Not at first, of course not. To be honest, I don't think he remembered me at all. It was a long time ago. But we happily agreed to pretend, and we just chatted for half an hour about the things he did remember – other teachers, the odd pupil who stuck in both our minds.'

'And how did you part?' asked Scrope.

'Oh ... I can't remember really what we said ... Oh, sorry, you mean the tone? Friendly. Though I think he was relieved to get back to his supper, to be honest.'

Both policemen registered that this was the second time that Aaron had used that phrase. When people being questioned went on about their honesty it was often a sign that they were not being entirely frank.

'Father Lloyd never hit you when you were at' – he looked down at his notes – 'St Edmund's?'

Aaron looked surprised and amused.

'Not at all. Father Lloyd was the gentlest of people. He never laid a hand on anyone.'

It was a relief finally to tell the truth. And it helped.

SCORN

The thing about telling the truth is that it is so true. But while Aaron's unease faded, Scrope was a good enough cop to keep going.

'When you say that he never laid a hand on anyone …' He let the question hang. Aaron smiled again, sure of his position, safe for now.

'Not *that* either.'

'Do you know a Father Seamus Malone?'

'I remember him from a very long time ago. I wouldn't say I knew him.' He looked at Scrope.

'He also died in …' – a pause – '… violent circumstances. Could you tell us where you were on the night of the eleventh last month?'

To his surprise, Aaron had to resist a strong impulse to laugh, an urge he would not have had under such circumstances only a few months before. Indeed, he would have been as terrified as middle-class people usually are when questioned by the police about a serious crime in which they might be implicated.

'I'll need to check my diary on my phone.'

He did so. 'Nothing that day. I would have been here.'

'No visitors that evening?'

'No.'

'Phone calls?'

'No idea. But you can check, I suppose.' He gestured at the phone. 'And tell where I was. I'm always surprised at how easily people can tell what they were doing on the night of whenever. I couldn't be sure where I was a week ago, to be honest.'

*

Sin

On their way back, Scrope and Lister stopped at the KFC in Swiss Cottage and set about a bowl of Brazilian Barbecue Bites.

'What do you think?' asked Scrope.

Lister stared at his unfinished meal.

'Tastes like it was left over from last week's carnival.'

'I meant, what do you think of Gall?'

'Oh. Seems straight enough.'

'Probably.'

'But?'

'No *but*, not really. But let's dig a little more. It's not as if there's much else to go on. He didn't look very well. Horrible colour. Try his doctor. There might be something we can use to get a warrant to take a look at his car.'

At the same time, Aaron was staring sightlessly at the results of a search on the death of his childhood bugbear. Oddly, or perhaps not, there was very little on the web. Malone had been murdered before the events in France so, given that the police had managed to keep the gory details of his death out of the news, he was merely a dead old white man and as such not very interesting. There had been so little fuss that the papers had yet to make a connection with the murder of Father Thomas Lloyd and the exciting prospect of a serial killer. Admittedly, terrorism had downgraded sequential murderers in the parade of menaces to society, particularly if the victims were old men, but there was still plenty of mileage to be had from the idea of a killer with a plan. But, for the moment, the dots remained unconnected. Aaron continued to stare at the screen for quite some time.

Of course, although he could not be sure that he was responsible for murdering Father Malone, he thought it was highly likely. Malone would have died for a number of reasons, worst of which was giving Aaron twelve strokes on his backside with one of the ropes in the gym (yes, the ones dangling from the roof, about the thickness of a man's wrist). His offence? Talking in line, a crime which, not that it mattered, had been committed by someone else.

On that occasion, his memory loss had extended to twelve hours before and after the day of the killing. On the morning after the night in question, he had woken up naked in the shower under a powerful stream of water that might have been washing over him for hours. There was no sight of vomit either. But perhaps he'd done that somewhere else. The mysterious cockiness he'd had to suppress when he was talking to the two policemen had vanished, replaced by a blizzard of fears about his sanity.

Unable to relax, he went for a long walk, finding himself in the pleasant grasslands of Regent's Park, where he wandered for some time, barely noticing the other people there or even where he was in the park. He was brought back to earth by a scream, then another and another, quickly building to a howling, raging din. He was standing outside the zoo. Inside, the animals were going crazy with fear.

Later on, the unprecedented events were reported on the national news, the chief excitement being the escape of a terrified gorilla. Alas for the media, the animal made it only into the zookeeper's area, where he was shot with a tranquilliser gun. While the drugs worked their way into his system, the gorilla consoled himself by drinking five litres of undiluted blackcurrant juice before falling into a deep sleep. Once Aaron had left the scene, the hysteria died down quickly and all returned to normal.

'A Catholic missionary priest has become the first victim of Ebola to die in Europe. He contracted the disease in Liberia while looking after patients. Two of his fellow workers at the hospital who tested positive at the same time have since died in Liberia from the virus. All belonged to the Order of San Juan de Dios, a Catholic humanitarian group that runs hospitals around the world.'

Daily Telegraph, 12 August 2014

'A Christian Brother was also involved in a shocking incident that began when a 12-year-old boy accidentally defecated on the floor in the sports dressing room. The Brother came on the scene and some of the excrement ended up on his shoes ... He told the boy to lick the excrement from his shoes and he did so.'

The Ryan Report, The Commission to Inquire into Child Abuse in Catholic Institutions in Ireland, 2009 (The Commission was blocked from naming abusers by a legal challenge from the Christian Brothers)

CHAPTER 11

AN ECUMENICAL MATTER

'What can I do for you, Father?'

Archbishop James Gillis, Catholic Primate of All England, looked up from his desk at the young deacon in front of him. He was not sure about Father Peter North. It was not so much that he looked like an underdeveloped twelve-year-old, nor that he came from an ancient and still wealthy Catholic family that could name two members hanged, drawn and quartered in the shameful executions that followed the Gunpowder Plot. Gillis was not without awareness of his own faults. He had come clean to his personal confessor, Father Matthew Sanchez, that, having been born himself in a house in Cork without running water or electricity, he felt a certain resentment of his over-privileged new assistant. He was not proud of this, but it took some time to face up to it in the confessional.

Needless to say, he felt better for asking God's forgiveness. People who refused to listen would never understand the deep relief of facing up to the accumulated nastiness of being human, the often small but ugly detritus of day-to-day living that sooner or later clogged up the joy of being alive, a joy that only the sense of being truly forgiven could offer you.

The thing was, he needed Father North rather badly. Annual vocations to the priesthood had been in

An Ecumenical Matter

the mid-twenties for the last decade. More to the point, although there was no doubting the intensity of the faith of these priests, there were questions, one might say, about their astuteness. North, however, was a young man of the highest intellectual calibre, a quality the archbishop very much required. He was in the process of writing a vindication of the teachings of the Church, and he knew very well the scrutiny this would bring from the Vatican, who were always fearful in case something controversial might inadvertently be said, or something that might be construed as critical or unnecessarily clear. Clarity in Catholic ecclesiastical writing was habitually avoided: it raised the possibility of painting yourself into a corner, doctrinally speaking, from which it might be difficult to extricate oneself if it upset the Congregation for the Doctrine of the Faith, the office that, as the so-called liberal press never tired of pointing out, had replaced the Inquisition.

North, with his double first in physics and European literature, was the nearest thing to a guardian angel of the kind he so very desperately needed. But he suspected North of intellectual pride, and worse, that he looked down on him and his writing. He had a suspicion that, underneath the thoughtful-sounding questions and artless observations, Father North was, in some complicated way, mocking him. As a result, he was often more short-tempered with the young deacon than he felt was fair. He struggled not to be unchristian, but wasn't always successful.

For example, the question 'What do you want, Father?' was spoken with tightly repressed irritation. Father North acted as if the question had been asked with heavenly sweetness.

'It's about the Father Greg Reynolds business.'

'Who?'

'Reynolds. The Australian who's been arguing for the ordination of women. It's just been confirmed that he's been excommunicated by the Holy Father.'

'What else did he expect?'

'Indeed, Your Grace.'

'So?'

'I was wondering if it was ...' He hesitated. 'I was wondering if it was wise.'

'Wise?'

'Yes, for the Holy Father to excommunicate his first priest – first anyone – for arguing in favour of women's ordination. It might look ...' He trailed off. He had been revising the section of the archbishop's chapter on the ordination of women – not a very long chapter, it should be said. This was not an area of difficulty, intellectually speaking, because there was no ambiguity concerning the position of the Church on the matter. Even to discuss it was a grave sin. The chapter in question was a restatement, not a discussion.

'It doesn't matter to the Church about how things *look*. We are not a multinational corporation in need of better public relations. We're not protecting our brand. We are the word of God incarnate on earth.'

'Yes, I see that, Your Grace. But still, is it wise to excommunicate a priest for arguing – one presumes sincerely, if wrongly, of course – that women should be considered for the priesthood, but not a priest who has ...' – he grew more uneasy – '... who has sexually assaulted a child in contravention of the sixth commandment?'

'Adultery? What are you talking about?'

'The Emeritus Pope Benedict when he was a cardinal

An Ecumenical Matter

described the actions of priests having congress with children as a sin against the sixth commandment. In the same document, he confirmed that discussion of the ordination of women was a similarly grave sin.'

'Are you sure?'

'Quite sure. I can forward the relevant document if you'd care—'

'No, I suppose I can see what he was driving at now you've pointed it out.'

'Yes, Your Grace.'

'Anyway, to answer your question about this person.'

'Greg Reynolds.'

'*Greg*.' He said the name as if it were in itself a clear signpost to spiritual malfeasance. 'Priests who have committed grave sins against minors are not excommunicated because, in my experience, they invariably repent and beg for forgiveness. As such, they can be punished, but not expelled from the grace of God. Did our friend *Greg* repent?'

'No, Your Grace.'

'There you are, then. Soliciting children is a grave sin. Arguing for the ordination of women is also a grave sin. Reynolds has not asked for forgiveness, and he has been excommunicated. If he had repented, he would not have been. If a priest did not repent for soliciting minors, then he would be excommunicated, too. I would have thought that was clear to anyone – except those who make an effort not to understand. As for former Father *Greg*, he is now free of the Church to which he once gave an unbreakable oath of obedience and is at liberty to pursue his spiritual shipwreck in whatever manner he so chooses.'

'But, Your Grace, would it not be better to be more circumspect about allowing questions of sin concerning children and sin concerning the role of women in the Church to be so easily associated? Isn't it a mistake to give such easy opportunities for misunderstanding to those who regard us with malice?'

Archbishop Gillis smiled with a certain satisfaction at having caught out his too-clever-by-half deacon.

'Wiser than the pope, Father North?' mocked Gillis. 'Forgive an old man's memory. What's the precise definition of the sin of pride?'

North smiled awkwardly. 'An excessive love of your own excellence, Your Grace.' He tried to make light of it. '*Mea maxima culpa*. I merely meant—'

'The queen of all vices, Father,' said Gillis, unwilling to avoid tormenting him. Being a man who knew how to examine his conscience, he recognised that he was definitely committing a sin of some kind by taking so much pleasure in doing so. But, he reasoned, we are none of us perfect.

The buzzer on his desk intercom rasped, hoarse and grating, as if conspiring to discourage any attempt at a reply.

'There are two policemen to see you, Your Grace.'

'Vilnius was taken over by the Germans on 24 June 1941 and the killing of the Jews began almost immediately. In 1941 Mother Betranda initially sought to help the Jews by gaining the support of the Vilnius Catholic leadership, but they rebuffed her efforts out of fear that Nazis would destroy Church property and kill any Christian found to be aiding Jews. Acting on her own initiative, Mother Betranda then took in 17 members of a local Zionist group, and hid them within the grounds of her monastery. When several of her nuns objected, Mother Betranda reportedly threatened them with expulsion from the monastery and excommunication from the faith. After leaving the convent, the members of the underground maintained close ties with Mother Betranda, who visited them in the ghetto, and (along with other Dominican nuns) helped them obtain weapons, and brought them their first hand grenades.'

The Wartime Rescue of Jews by the
Polish Catholic Clergy, Mark Paul (ed.)

'At a time when the heads of the major nations in the world faced the new Germany with reserve and considerable suspicion, the Catholic Church, the greatest moral power on earth, through the Concordat, expressed its confidence in the new German government. This was a deed of immeasurable significance for the reputation of the new government abroad.'

>Cardinal Michael von Faulhaber in 1937, reminding the Third Reich of the benefits of the Church signing an agreement with the Nazi government in 1933 (This constrained the previously vocal criticism of clergy in exchange for guaranteeing the rights of the Catholic Church in Germany. Bishops taking office were required to take an oath of loyalty to the German Reich)

CHAPTER 12

CLASS WARFARE

'Scrope?' said the archbishop, after the introduction had been made. 'Are you a Buckinghamshire Scrope?'

'Yes.'

Gillis turned to his deacon. 'A very great Catholic family, like your own, Father North. Perhaps you know each other from Downforth?'

'I was at Ampleside,' said Scrope. He did not like to apologise for his upbringing, not being the sorry type, but it was hard to say a sentence like that in a way that was not either ingratiating or boastful.

'Really? Well, I was at the Clontarf Industrial School for Boys.' Gillis was aware that this was said with sinful pride but decided to absolve himself. Putting these rich types in their place was probably not even a venial sin. It was good for them.

'Well, perhaps we should discuss these dreadful crimes. Please hold nothing back, Inspector Scrope. We must look this evil right in the face and see what it is. I understand that you have details not reported in the newspapers.'

'We do, though I can't stress how important it is that things don't go beyond this room, Your Grace. It's vital we keep some of the specifics secret. We've already had half a dozen cranks claiming they're the murderer. As long as we can keep some of the facts of the case closed, they're easy to spot. And it keeps the perpetrator in the dark as well.'

'Of course. As priests, we're used to keeping secrets.'

This was meant to be light-hearted, but it reminded Scrope of the thing he had most hated about his upbringing: the dark confinement of the confessional and the deep terror he had felt from the very first time of having his soul exposed in all its revolting vileness. Sitting in the confessional, which always reminded him of two coffins on their ends facing each other, he would always be trembling, throat dry, terrified.

Bless me, Father, for I have sinned. And what sins they were! He had taken his mother's and father's names in vain. He had used profane language. But worst of all was the sin he could never bring himself to utter. Purple of stained soul, black fires of hell, roasting and burning him for what he had done and what he could not name. And so he did not. He confessed, but not that. Never that. And so each time he failed to declare this terrible act he committed a further sin, and then another, and each time he took the pure body of Jesus into his mouth having not purified himself he added another and another, until he knew that his soul was covered in so many spots of livid, bruisey sin that his soul was entirely black and he was meat for the eternal forces of hell. All he had to do was name the sin. But he could not, and never had.

Between them, Scrope and Lister detailed the insults to the bodies of the two murdered priests, the very silence of the enormous room seeming to listen as they spoke. The archbishop became increasingly white. Oddly, the young priest appeared absolutely fascinated, his face wincing and grimacing with all the stretchability of a particularly curious seven-year-old being told about a Tyrannosaurus rex.

Class Warfare

When they finished there was a long silence.

'And people,' said the archbishop, at last, 'think that there's no such thing as the devil. I don't suppose this could be some kind of satanic cult?'

'We won't rule it out, but we think it's unlikely.'

'Why?' The question was out before Father North could stop himself. The archbishop looked at him ungenerously.

'I hope you understand, but there are certain things I can't readily go into.' In fact, Scrope could have told them about the clues, but the archbishop no longer had authority over him other than the authority of memory, and it was in rejecting this memory that he had reasserted something he thought he no longer considered important: he was resisting his faith again.

'But you can tell us something?' said the archbishop.

'I can say that the man who did this is unusually well educated. No disrespect to the academic attainments of Satanists everywhere, but he genuinely doesn't fit the profile.' He forestalled further presumptuous questions from the archbishop by quickly moving on.

'In fact, we also came here to ask for your help.'

'Of course. Whatever we can do.'

'Both bodies had been laid over a small pad of damp salt.' He paused. 'And a packet of fish fingers.'

'We were wondering,' said Lister, 'if the salt rang any bells in terms of symbolism, beyond the one of repentance or sorrow, something you might pick up on that we wouldn't. He's clearly making a point, even if he's not doing it clearly.'

Another silence. Again, like that of an enthusiastic schoolboy, Father North's face, a semaphore of helpfulness, swayed into his superior's eyeline, but was ignored.

SCORN

'Salt as a symbol of a quality that's lacking or been lost – *when salt loses its flavour, how can its saltiness be restored* – could that be relevant?'

'We'd thought of that,' said Lister, with a certain impatience at the idea that they would not have.

'Nothing springs to mind. I'd need to think.'

By now, Father North's eyes were almost bulging with the desire to speak. Archbishop Gillis sighed, and looked at him. 'Do you have any suggestions, Father?'

'Ah, yes. I was wondering about the salt. I mean, it doesn't entirely fit, but in Mark, there's a passage about those condemned to hell being salted with fire. And I seem to remember something about an orthodox tradition where those in the act of repenting the most serious sins have to drink salt water before a priest. It's dreadfully obscure, though.'

'That might be just up his street. Aside from being a murderer,' said Scrope, 'the sin of pride is very much his weakness. He admires his own intelligence.'

'I hope you don't admire it, Inspector,' said Gillis.

'I think it's important to give the devil his due.' He turned back to North. 'Anything else?'

'Well, the problem is' – he was enjoying himself now – 'that salt symbolises both good and bad elements. It gives flavour, for example, and to lose flavour, spiritually speaking, is a very bad thing. But the association is the sin of blandness, of being lukewarm. I can't see how that fits these circumstances. In the Old Testament, bodies were rubbed with salt to symbolise truthfulness. Eating salt together binds people in a promise. I'd like to do some reading, if I may?'

'Thanks.' Lister handed him his card.

'And the fish?'

'Same thing, really. Let me think. It seems too obvious to point out that the fish is a symbol of Christianity. By using a packet of fish fingers, he avoids the dignity of the real thing by using something cheap and manufactured.' He thought again. 'Of course, it might not be religious. It might be a joke.' He looked at his superior. 'A horrible one.'

'Meaning?'

'"Luca Brasi sleeps with the fishes."'

Both Lister and Scrope smiled appreciatively. Both enjoyed the fact that they'd underestimated the young man.

'Well?' said an understandably irritated Gillis. 'I'm sorry if I'm slow.'

'Not at all, Your Grace,' said Father North. 'It's a mafia phrase that means a body has been disposed of in the sea.'

'How in God's name do you know that?'

'It's not what it seems, Your Grace. It's a line from *The Godfather*.'

The archbishop stared at him.

'A film.' He paused. 'By Francis Ford Coppola.'

His superior kept on staring. 'I'm perfectly well aware of that.'

'It's also a line in the *Iliad*, if I remember correctly,' said Scrope. 'When Achilles kills Lycaon, he throws him in the river and says, "Lie there now among the fishes."'

Lister was pleased to join in with the bullying. 'And in *Moby-Dick*, Stubb says something like ... when the water bearer drowns as with the fish we sleep. Something like that, at any rate.'

*

SCORN

When Scrope and Lister had gone, Gillis turned to North.

'I am glad, Father North, that we were both here to listen for a change to the details of the dreadful abuse handed out to priests. Those who hurt children have no place in the Church. But you should remember that, throughout history, it is the *Church* that has been persecuted relentlessly.'

As they drove back to Paddington, Lister and Scrope were unusually silent. Only Scrope said anything: 'Compulsive geologist succumbs to stress.'

Two days later, Scrope received an email from the archbishop's office detailing the connections between the two murdered priests. There were two facts of interest, the lesser one being that, for ten years, they had worked in the same vast diocese that stretched from Plymouth to Oxford. More important was that the second victim had given religious instruction briefly at St Edmund's, which in turn had sent its brightest boys to the Salesian Grammar School in Oxford. It was here that the first victim, Father Seamus Malone, had been a teacher of physical education for seven years.

'I think we might have the beginnings of a story,' said Scrope to Lister.

Lister looked at him, nodding thoughtfully.

'Anal fissure.'

'I can't think what took you so long. What about that warrant on Gall's car?'

'Not a chance.'

'Why?'

'Because, in the magistrate's view – and, frankly, it's one that I share – there's not a shred of evidence to justify doing so.'

A moment's pause.

'The Taliban don't put up with any nonsense about evidence.' He sniffed. 'I suppose you think that's in poor taste.'

'No, you make a fair point. Say what you like about the Taliban, at least they know how to make the trains run on time.'

Aaron was so quickly receding as a suspect that Lister almost called off his visit to Lou Bettancourt. But he was, in truth, a meticulous person.

'Well, you know, Officer …' Lou pretended not to remember his name. To put him in his place, thought Lister.

'Detective Sergeant Lister,' he replied affably. He put his card on the coffee table.

'I don't think I'm going to answer your questions about my patient. I'm sure you understand.'

What Lister was sure about was that she didn't care much whether he understood or not. This was pretty rare, in his experience. It was a truth universally acknowledged in the police force that the middle classes were generally terrified of the police and would shop their grannies without a moment's hesitation once a cop asked them a question. Gall's doctor had been so spinelessly co-operative he would have loaned Lister his credit card if he'd asked him to. He liked Lou's insolence. Along with her sexy scruffiness, she was hard to resist.

'Look, Ms Bettancourt, I can understand you want to protect your patient. But he's not a suspect, he's just a witness. The only one we have in a terrible murder we've good reason to believe might not be the last.' The line between witness and suspect was one which the police encouraged the public to believe in, on the grounds that it made them more likely to incriminate themselves or their friends.

'Given that Mr Gall's been suffering from a mental illness …'

'His doctor shouldn't have said anything.'

'Perhaps, but he did. All we need to be sure of is whether his evidence is reliable. I'm not exaggerating when I say that a life hangs on this. What I'm worried about is the life of an innocent person and whether I have to waste valuable time trying to eliminate Mr Gall when you can do it for me. And, I should point out, it's for the good of Mr Gall as well.'

How carefully Lou had been dragged along the line between the different siren calls of clashing moral obligations. He'd got to her, but she was made of stern stuff when it came to manipulation.

'Does Mr Gall suffer from delusions?' he tried.

'What I was meaning when I said I wasn't answering any questions about Mr Gall was that I wasn't answering any questions. But consider this, if you like: every time he arrives here for a session, having climbed six flights of stairs, it takes him a lot of minutes to get his breath back. He's not physically capable of murdering someone.'

Lister, trying to get her on his side, looked at her as if accepting, with the due scepticism of a copper, that she might be right and that he was beginning to come round.

'But his physical strength aside, what about Aaron Gall himself? Is he a man of violence?'

'Absolutely, definitely no.'

CHAPTER 13

A QUESTION OF MORALITY

Later that evening Scrope and Lister were ogling the wine list at the Gyngleboy and inclining to a bottle of the underrated Pampas del Sur 2008.

'You're not going to be tempted, are you?'

'It depends.'

'No, it doesn't. You get caught and it'll be prison.'

'I suppose I could talk to Dawe. He *might* go for it.'

'Too risky.'

'If I get more information than I give them, then it could save lives.'

'Yeah, I can't believe we're having this conversation again. You might save lives, maybe a lot of them, but if the wheel comes off you're fucked.'

The wine arrived and they sat in contented silence for a few minutes.

'You can almost taste the sun setting as the llaneros return from a long day in the saddle.'

'Gauchos – the llaneros are Venezuelan.'

'Just testing. I knew that, but did you?'

Another silence.

'On the back foot.'

Lister nodded, taking it in.

Another long pause.

SCORN

'Achilles,' said Lister after five minutes.

'What?' said Scrope.

'The answer to the clue: On the back foot. Back foot means heel. Theon was a warrior killed by Achilles.'

Scrope sighed.

'It wasn't a clue, you fuckwit, it was just an observation about us being on the back foot.'

He paused, savouring the opportunity. 'Besides, you're confused – Theon was a first-century commentator on Homer not one of Achilles' victims.'

'Fuck you, motherfucker.'

'Pope Francis again raised the clergy sex-abuse crisis, by consoling clergy in New York for the suffering the scandal had caused them. Francis told members of religious orders and diocesan priests that he was aware they had "suffered greatly" by having to "bear the shame" of clergy who had molested children. He thanked them for their faithful service to the church in the face of the scandal.'

Daily Telegraph, 25 September 2015

CHAPTER 14

MEN AND WOMEN

The place where Lou Bettancourt treated her patients was no airy Hampstead drawing room with a couch, full of the symbolic bric-a-brac of ancient civilisations. It was a room on the sixth floor of a clapped-out terrace on the Camden Road which she rented by the hour, sharing the house with an oddball collection of colour therapists, chakra balancers and even, on Tuesdays, a shamanic healer. She was curious about the healer, wondering if what he did was as ridiculous as it sounded and thinking that it would be interesting to challenge that assumption, but had been put off this admirable willingness to confront her prejudices by the fact that he charged even more than she did.

Aaron made his way up a staircase that could have been part of a set for an adaptation of *Oliver Twist* and reached the sixth floor to discover her lying on the landing, pale as a china cup, clearly in terrible pain.

'My God, Lou,' he said, kneeling at her side.

'I tripped. Fucking lino,' she gasped.

'I'll call an ambulance.'

'No. It's just painful. It'll pass. Just help me inside.'

'It might be broken.'

'It's not broken,' she said, cross. 'Help me up.' Taking her hand and then her shoulders, he eased her on to her good leg, but even though the pressure was light on the injured one, she cried out. 'Ow! *Scheisse!*'

Holding on to Aaron, she was able to reach into her pocket and take out the key to open the door. Hopping and flinching, he eased her on to the moth-eaten but soft chair in which she held court. Lou leaned back and closed her eyes. He sat down and waited.

'Just give me five minutes.'

The five minutes turned into twenty.

'I think it's time to call an ambulance.'

'No ambulance,' she said peevishly.

'Listen to me, you bad-tempered madam, you don't know if it *is* broken or not. And you could have torn a ligament or something, which is just as bad.'

'I'm not going to hospital.'

'Why not?'

A pause.

'I'm afraid of them.'

Another pause.

'Perhaps you should see someone. I noticed the colour therapist from downstairs was in.'

'Fuck!' She cried out in pain. '*Dumme Hündin!*'

The whiteness of her skin deepened.

'How in God's name are you going to get downstairs?' He gave her a moment to let this sink in. 'I'll carry you.'

'Don't be ridiculous.' Irritated, but also dismissive.

'You don't think I can?'

'I weigh more than ten stone.'

'More than eleven, I'd say.'

She gasped, but whether in pain or annoyance was hard to tell. Not even the strongest, most confident modern woman is entirely free of the judgements of the patriarchal past. 'We'll both fall.'

SCORN

'Then let me get an ambulance.'

'No.'

He sat and stared at her. Lou, now a deathly white, closed her eyes and lay back on the chair.

Aaron Gall walked over and picked her up easily, as if she were the insubstantial heroine of a romantic novel of the kind that Lou would never be seen dead reading. He carried her, open-mouthed, across the room and opened the door, using his elbows. He moved over the landing and started down the stairs as if he were taking a small child to bed. Within a few steps, her initial and entirely sensible feeling that this absurd attempt was certain to kill the both of them was replaced with a most surprising feeling of being, in all senses, in safe hands.

With a graceful strength and sureness of step, Aaron swept Lou down the six flights of stairs, opened the door and carried her out into the bright sunlight.

'Where's your car? You *do* have a car? OK. If we have to take a taxi, you're paying.'

Of course, as Aaron strode along the pavement, easily carrying the voluptuous Lou, they were already noteworthy, and there were many smiles and much romantic fluttering as Aaron stepped into the road to hail a black cab. This proved difficult. The drivers who passed were wary of the sight of a woman being carried. What if she was drunk and threw up in the cab?

Finally, he saw one stop for a Pooh stick of a lunch mummy, walked directly in front of the astonished woman and said, 'Excuse me, this is an emergency.' He stepped into the cab and gently eased Lou on to the seat.

'Where to?'

'Granary Street,' she said weakly. 'The one off Pancras Road.'

Men And Women

It was five minutes away. In ten, he'd carried her inside, paid the driver and returned to settle her down in bed.

'Someone should be with you.'

'It will be fine.'

'Let's not start that again.'

'My husband's in Bilbao.'

'There has to be someone else.'

'It'll be …' She stopped, seeing the look on his face. 'It'll be too embarrassing. I'll just have a sleep. Please.'

'I'll give you two hours. Then I'll wake you up and we'll see.'

'There's no …' Another look. 'Thank you.'

He delivered painkillers and a glass of water and went into the front room and took a copy of *The Power of Defiance* by Viktor Frankl from the bookshelf and sat down to read.

'Dear Bishop Gregory: I intend to relinquish my chairmanship of the National Catholic Review Board ... Our Church is a Faith institution. A home to Christ's people. It is not a criminal enterprise. It does not condone and cover up criminal activity. It does not follow a code of silence. My remarks, which some bishops found offensive, were deadly accurate. I make no apology. To resist grand jury subpoenas, to suppress the names of offending clerics, to deny, to obfuscate, to explain away; that is the model of a criminal organization, not my church ...
Sincerely, Frank Keating'

> Frank Keating, Catholic layman, letter of resignation, 2003
> (He resigned as chairman of the Church-appointed panel investigating sexual abuse by priests. Keating is a former FBI agent, US attorney and governor of Oklahoma)

CHAPTER 15

THE RIGHTEOUS BROTHERS

After Aaron had shaken the dust of the Church from his feet on the day he finally left the Salesian College School for Catholic Boys, he had rarely thought about his lost faith again. Its effects were still in there, stored in some toxic sump in his soul, but they were so deeply buried, wrapped up tight with rivets of heart steel and the sealing wax of misery, that for years it seemed, barring the once-a-month burst of inexplicable rage, the mysterious depressions and the untreatable skin condition, that he'd emerged in more or less one piece.

Granted, these unacknowledged symptoms (*it's just the way I am*) led to the long trail of broken relationships with women, and the children he'd had by two of them. Being divorced these days, even twice, and not getting on with your children was hardly unusual, hardly a sign of a deep-rooted psychosis.

Now he was thinking rather differently about the one true faith. For example, he was wondering how it was that the Catholic Church was far and away the most successful organisation in the history of mankind. Surely you didn't outlive the Romans, the Merovingians, the Templars, the Hapsburgs – even those ideological mayflies fascism and Stalinism – without knowing a thing or two nobody else knows.

SCORN

But the problem was that most of the priests he'd been educated by were quite stupid. Even the ones who weren't entirely dim were very far indeed from the kind of creature you would need to create and sustain such a powerful and successful organisation as the Catholic Church across two thousand years. In his search for an answer to this question of Catholic exceptionalism, Aaron now spent considerable time reading at the British Library and scanning the internet for evidence of the unknown Napoleons of the Faith, the Otto von Bismarcks of the magisterium, the Gladstones of the shoes of the fisherman. He was in no way attempting to be supercilious when he googled 'great minds of the Catholic Church', to find scant pickings in terms of those whose talents could even begin to explain the unique power and the matchless glory.

For the first time, he read Thomas Aquinas, a thinker revered by philosophers, and not just Catholic ones, in the hope there might be some answer there. He reasoned, more like a physicist than a philosopher, that if the Church regarded him as the greatest of all theologians, greater than Plato or Buddha, then he wouldn't have to read *all* Catholic theologians. He just had to read Thomas Aquinas.

He tried hard, to be fair, but this was difficult because of his basic belief that you could talk of a distinguished theologian only in the same breath as you might talk of a distinguished astrologer – and his emerging animal side made his patience even less elastic than before. Thomas Aquinas's arguments for the existence of God as first cause of everything depend upon the supposed impossibility of a series having no first term. But Aaron knew this was rubbish. Any mildly competent mathematician could tell you there was no such impossibility. Every five-year-old knew the series of negative integers ending with minus one proves the contrary.

He thought about this for a moment, realising that this rash assertion was the wolf talking. All right, probably not a five-year-old. And, to give him his due, Aquinas was born before the emergence of scientific methods of reasoning. More fertile grounds for blame were to be found in his claim that heretics should be burnt at the stake on a second conviction for blasphemy. As was often the case (always the case?), this cruelty was defended by many contemporary historians on the grounds that we should not attempt naively to place the liberal principles of modernity on a man born in the violent furnace of thirteenth-century Europe.

'Ha!' shouted Aaron loudly. 'How about judging him by the standards of a man born in the violent furnace of Middle Eastern society in the first century, who made it abundantly clear that you should do good to those who hate you, turn the other cheek, and forgive seventy times seven!'

Unfortunately, he did this shouting in the British Library and was told to leave immediately or the police would be called. It alarmed him that on being confronted by the assistant head librarian, who was, after all, only doing his job, for several seconds he found himself fighting an impulse to disembowel him and eat his liver.

Thirty minutes later, he was trying to settle himself down by means of a walk in Regent's Park, this time carefully avoiding the zoo. After ten minutes of deep breathing, he was calm enough to return to the matter of how the Church had survived for so long.

Not even the Jesuits, with their reputation for almost supernatural intellectual craftiness, really lived up to close examination. Aaron knew some Italian from having had half a dozen Italians in his department, as well as five years chairing a joint committee responsible for sending muons to the Gran Sasso laboratory in Abruzzo. It was enough, dictionary in hand, to make his way through *La civiltà cattolica*, the Jesuits' two-hundred-year-old journal on Catholic thought, a magazine supported by numerous popes as an intellectual bastion against liberalism. Some of it was interesting; some of it even impressive. It needed also to be acknowledged that cultural magazines of all kinds tended to look lame after a couple of decades. But a great deal of it was deeply dull, and there were any number of articles that were utterly poisonous in their hatred, deranged anti-Semitism being only the worst example.

In short, there was still nothing to explain to him why the Catholic Church was still there. Even if it had been created by brilliant minds in the past – and there wasn't much evidence for this – it certainly wasn't populated by them anymore. He'd discovered that Pope Benedict, always being praised for his eminence as a theologian, had responded to a complaint about the Harry Potter books by condemning them outright, without having read them. He'd also expressed the view that teenagers dancing at festivals were alienating themselves from Christ by becoming absorbed in solipsistic hedonism. Not even the priests who had brought him up, beaten him occasionally and harassed him repeatedly for dumb insolence, men who were narrow-minded and often ignorant, would have said anything so foolish.

It didn't make sense, any of it. Certainly, the spate of stories about sexual assault and the relentless determination to cover them up at any cost were apparently endless. But while they had an effect, it wasn't all that significant.

The Righteous Brothers

There was shock, all right, but it didn't seem to go anywhere. Pregnant young women mistreated in institutions run like prisons then having their babies removed and sent abroad – *disgraceful!* Children in Catholic reformatories being called by numbers not names and being obliged to make leather straps studded with threepenny bits, with which they were then beaten – *horrifying!* Arrests at the Vatican bank after decades of financial scandal – *deplorable!* And then nothing. If the Scientologists or Mormons had done even a hundredth of this stuff, they'd be banned in every country in the world and all their leaders would be in prison. Something deeply odd was going on.

He wondered if it was because there was just too much atrocity to take in, and it was too weird to believe that it had really happened. Aaron liked to think that, if mobile-phone cameras had been invented a hundred years earlier and even a tiny fraction of the cruelties visited on the children of the faithful had been filmed, then the world would have been ready to build a prison the size of the Large Hadron Collider to contain the wicked of the Catholic faith.

Perhaps that was what had saved the Church: it was camera shy. It was an odd thing about the Nazis – they liked a selfie, liked to film themselves and provide a chromatic memory of what they were so that, down the ages, there will always be a living image, better than a million words. But the faith acted behind walls. The only witnesses were children. And words were all they had left – but words weren't enough, words were useless. Words in the mouths of children were straw in the wind. There were five volumes of words in the Irish government's report by the Commission to Inquire into Child Abuse – 2,600 pages of them. He hadn't read them all, these word maps of hell, and, for the same reason, hardly anyone else had read them either.

Guilt was what saved mankind – one of the priests was always saying that – and, for once, he agreed. So guilt was what Aaron was going to spread to the four winds. He'd teach the Catholic faith about guilt all right. He was going to make Catholics guilty about something it was worth being guilty about. He was going to make them ashamed to go outside, except in the dark, ashamed to admit what they believed, ashamed to breathe. After he had finished with them, there would be millions of Catholics lining the roads, crawling on their knees and chastising themselves with whips of scorpions, crying out for forgiveness. The makers of hair shirts would be quoted on the stock exchange as millions bought two of them (one for Monday to Saturday and a particularly itchy and scratchy one for Sundays). Google would buy up the manufacturer of those spiked metal rings that penitents tied around their thighs. There would be a dearth of peas as demand went through the roof for the dried variety to insert in the socks of weeping multitudes, walking in agony for absolution for not protecting their children, or not protesting indignantly to their parish priest against the Church's refusal to act against those who hurt them. The roads into Mexico City, Paris and Munich would be jammed each morning with the faithful heaving a wooden cross to work, all to the furious honking of tardy Protestant motorists.

He'd teach ordinary Catholics, with their simple faith about atonement and penance, before he was finished. He'd mortify their flesh all right.

'External validity in sampling refers to the approximate truth of conclusions that involve generalizations. Put in more pedestrian terms, external validity in sampling is the degree to which the conclusions in your study would hold for other persons in other places and at other times.'

The Web Center for
Social Research Methods

'Pope John Paul II teaches that no matter how separated someone is from God, "in the depths of his heart there always remains a yearning for absolute truth and a thirst to attain full knowledge of it". He goes on to say that the splendour of truth "shines forth deep within the human spirit".'

Veritatis Splendor ('The Splendour of Truth') w2.vatican.va/content/john-paul-ii/en/encyclicals/documents/hf_jp-ii_enc_06081993_veritatis-splendor.html

CHAPTER 16

A THOUSAND WORDS

'Unless you see signs and wonders, you will not believe.' But as is usually the case with Jesus Christ almighty, he gets it half right just before the wheels fall off. 'What is half-truth?' asked Pontius Pilate, as the gospel according to John ought to have put it. The not-true bit of this sentence is that people require signs and wonders to believe – and it's not true because people believe any number of idiotic things without a concrete demonstration, let alone a miracle: homeopathy, Scientology, socialism, the efficiency of free markets, that women are much nicer than men, that you only use 10 per cent of your brain, that you can see the Great Wall of China from space, that an exception to a rule provides evidence to substantiate that rule, that $\sin z$ is a bounded function, and so on and so on. Where would this list of staggering credulity end, do you think? The far side of the moon, perhaps – you know, the one that isn't always dark.

So, people don't require signs and wonders to believe; they require signs and wonders because prurient marvels and sensational auguries for human beings are like whisky to a drunk, or shit to a fly. This is why, as the wiser among you will have worked out for yourselves, I've provided you with blood and guts to get you to continue with this book. It's not that you can't handle the truth, it's that you don't give a damn about the truth (though it's only fair to point out: you can't handle it either).

It's time to take a break from the deranged railings of an anti-Catholic cannibalistic werewolf and concentrate for once on dull facts, to take in some documentary evidence. So take a snort of Columbia's finest nose sugar, boost your flagging energies with a quick visit to Buttjizz.com, wake yourself up with a drink of ice-cold bottled water at 2,900 times the cost of something identical from the tap and consult your colour therapist about what shade of blue will get you best through the ordeal ahead as we confront the tiresome documentation concerning the Catholic world in a grain of sand.

If someone had made up Father Marcial Maciel Degollado, you'd condemn his creation as an improbable fiction, a crassly constructed, shamefully caricatured, ghastly cartoon designed in bad faith by a vile traducer of the Catholic priesthood. Alas, he was all too real. Father Maciel had a rap sheet of crimes that went back over fifty years, beginning with a charge for using morphine in 1956, a charge he escaped by persuading two of his seminarians to perjure themselves. Over the next thirty years, he sexually abused at least thirty boys, and repeated these offences on innumerable occasions. He might be called the Catholic Jimmy Savile – except, of course, that title has already been taken by Jimmy Savile.

It took many attempts by various victims to have Maciel's abuses investigated, victims who had grown up and were determined to see him held to account. Among them was a priest, a righteous brother, a faithful servant to the Church, Father Juan Vaca, who had been abused by Maciel for ten years. Vaca repeatedly wrote to the Congregation for the

SCORN

Doctrine of the Faith, formerly known as the Inquisition. Sadly, its previous enthusiasm for torturing the accused to get at the truth had fallen into disuse. The cardinal responsible for investigating such claims was Cardinal Joseph Ratzinger, later to become Pope Benedict XVI.

Vaca knew his complaint had been read, because he received a protocol number. Otherwise, there was no reply. He sent more letters and received the same response. More and more complaints were made by others as well, but Maciel had enormous influence in the Vatican. Most of all, he had the enthusiastic support of Pope John Paul II, who saw him as a great spiritual guide for young men intending to be priests. More than this, in the deeply traditional order Maciel had founded, the Legion of Christ, the pope saw a profoundly important bulwark against the soul-rotting power of individualism and liberal values. Maciel's Legion came to operate fifteen universities, and some 140,000 students are now enrolled in its schools. It is estimated to be worth 25 billion euros.

It is thought that Ratzinger wanted to take action against Maciel but realised the then pope would not support such an attempt and would have been outraged at any such claims made about a man he so profoundly favoured. So Ratzinger did nothing, thereby allowing the rape of children to continue without hindrance. In 1998, eight victims were finally able to file formal charges at the Vatican, to the effect that they had been repeatedly sexually abused by Maciel. The following year, Cardinal Ratzinger informed the victims that the charges had been shelved.

Then it became clear that Ratzinger knew the charges of multiple and repeated rape were true – when he became pope himself, he ordered Maciel to step down as leader of the Legion of Christ, an organisation that now had 124 religious houses all over the world. Well done, that man, I hear you say. Justice was done!

But that's all he did. Nothing more was demanded of Maciel, to atone for all his rapes of the children in his care, other than that he retire to a life of prayer and penitence. No apology was offered and no criminal proceedings were instituted. Shortly after his death in 2008, it was revealed that not only had Father Maciel embezzled large sums of money from the organisation he founded, but also that he had several mistresses and had fathered as many as six children. When questions from the public at large were raised about Pope John Paul's inaction over Maciel, his long-time spokesman defended the Holy Father against accusations that he had presided over twenty-seven years of shameful inaction on the issue of child abuse. The spokesman pointed out that John Paul had great difficulty accepting that any priest could commit such acts because of 'the purity of his thought' and that, in any case, neither the pope nor anyone else appreciated the seriousness of the crisis.

But you know who I feel sorry for in all of this, *mes amis de la boue*?

It's not the many victims of fiddling about by incontinent priests. No, indeed, the person I really feel sorry for is Richard Nixon.

And why is that, I hear from those of you who are still awake? (It's not just the flesh that's unwilling, is it? The spirit is pretty fucking disinclined as well.)

You know, everyone goes on about how the President of the United States is the most powerful man in the world. But consider what happened to poor old Nixon. Disgraced, hounded out of office in the greatest act of public humiliation in history, his name to live long in the annals of infamy, forty-five of his most powerful henchmen sent to prison – and all he did was approve a non-violent break-in to install a few microphones and photograph a few trivial files about someone no one had ever heard of.

John Paul II presided over a period of more than twenty-five years in which he not only ignored the body rape and soul murder of uncountable numbers of vulnerable children but also refused to listen to evidence against a victimiser whose crimes against humanity constituted a kind of blasphemous pantomime of drugs, fraud and the sexual assault of numerous boys. John Paul II, God's representative on earth, who looked away from these crimes – ladies and gentlemen of the jury, he is now a saint.

That's real power. That's why the Catholic Church has lasted two thousand years and why Tricky Dicky could only manage six.

But now that I have your inattention, perhaps we might go on to the case of Cardinal Hans Hermann Groër, thought to have molested as many as two thousand boys, who was allowed to retire from public life by the same pope (and an admittedly unenthusiastic Ratzinger). He died in good standing with the Church.

Too much for you? I think it is. If we went any further, let me be plain, we might never stop.

So now I return you to the storm and stress of Aaron Gall's quest for revenge as he discovers that the old adage about pride preceding a fall has, for him, a particularly painful epiphany. We find him in his flat, rolling around on the carpet, doubled up in pain. Staggering to the toilet, it takes

A Thousand Words

him half an hour to pass a bloody shard of bone the size and feel of a razor blade – a large splinter from Father Thomas Lloyd's marrow-sucked shin bone.

'The reaction of Pope Pius XII (1876–1958) to the Holocaust was complex and inconsistent. At times, he tried to help the Jews and was successful. But these successes only highlight the amount of influence he might have had, if he had not chosen to remain silent on so many other occasions. No one knows for sure the motives behind Pope Pius XII's actions, or lack thereof, since the Vatican archives have only been fully opened to select researchers. Historians offer many reasons why Pope Pius XII was not a stronger public advocate for the Jews: a fear of Nazi reprisals, a feeling that public speech would have no effect and might harm the Jews, the idea that private intervention could accomplish more, the anxiety that acting against the German government could provoke a schism among German Catholics, the Church's traditional role of being politically neutral and the fear of the growth of communism were the Nazis to be defeated. Whatever his motivation, it is hard to escape the conclusion that the Pope, like so many others in positions of power and influence, could have done more to save the Jews.'

www.jewishvirtuallibrary.org

'At the peak of Hitler's power, in 1941, an outraged Bishop Clemens von Galen, of Münster, forced the government to drop a plan for mass euthanasia of the "feeble-minded", the sick and the old. But criticisms of the assault on the Jews were made only in the most veiled and muted of terms. Until the very end of the war, Pope Pius XII never once attacked the Nazis by name. In contrast, he organised worldwide protests and forcefully condemned collaborationist clergy when the Hungarian Communist regime tortured Cardinal József Mindszenty in 1949.'

Charles R. Morris, reviewing
Constantine's Sword: The Church and
the Jews, by James Carroll (2001)

'What is more, the Church herself by reason of her astonishing propagation, her outstanding holiness and her inexhaustible fertility in every kind of goodness, by her Catholic unity and her unconquerable stability, is a kind of great and perpetual motive of credibility and an incontrovertible evidence of her own divine mission.'

First Vatican Council, Chapter 3, section 12

CHAPTER 17

A HISTORY LESSON

'What's this supposed to be?' asked Brother Gregory Melis. It was the fourth period on a Monday morning for 3 Alpha and so it was History. The question was being asked of a sullen boy of thirteen. 'I asked you a question, boy: what's this supposed to be?'

'My homework, Brother,' said Aaron Gall.

'I'm glad you were able to tell me that, because if you hadn't told me I might have thought it was something the cat dragged in.'

There was some laughter from the assortment of toadies and teacher's pets who thought they were unlikely to feel the weight of the Brother's sarcasm, and resentful silence from the rest.

'Why do we study history, Gall?'

A silence.

'Answer me.'

'So we know what happened in the past.'

Melis looked hard at the boy, who stared at some point located several yards below the floor.

'True enough, I suppose. Simple, bordering on banal, but true enough.' He turned and walked a little way to the front of the class, to make clear to everyone that he was making a point. He opened up his voice a little. 'But your answer obliges us to ask: how do we know that what

A History Lesson

happened in the past actually happened? Put your hand down, Fenton, it was, if not exactly a rhetorical question, then one so important that I intend to answer it myself.'

A disappointed member at the stupider end of the flock of pets dropped his hand with the speed of a startled anemone. Satisfaction all round from his rivals.

'The answer, as I'm reasonably sure Mr Fenton was going to point out, is *evidence*. Evidence is what we need. Evidence is what we require. And evidence is entirely absent, Mr Gall, in what I will call your essay, for want of a better word to describe a mass of undifferentiated text in which assertion – usually wrong, in any case – is followed by specious and unfounded proclamation, most of it ungrammatical, and with all of the difficult words – by which I mean other than "and" or "but" – as reliably misspelled as that fabled clock in Geneva is held to be accurate.'

At this point, Melis turned from the general to the particular and seemed to glide towards the boy for his summing-up.

'I know,' he said to Gall, 'that you are lazy. I cannot say for sure that you are stupid. But it is my burdensome task, as one of those charged with your education, to ensure that, in some way, by hook or by crook, I try to turn you, with your refusal to think for yourself, into one of God's most blessed creations, with at least a basic ability to reason, in order that you do not become the prey of every charlatan or trickster who wishes you to do this or buy that or otherwise persuade you to do that which is immoral or foolish. And so it is for your own good, Mr Gall. Look at me when I'm talking to you.'

Slowly, hatred blazing, Gall looked up at him.

'I say it is for your own good and the good of a society

that ought to be ruled by reason that you will spend ninety minutes in detention every evening until Friday, during which time you will work on an essay inspired by that most engaging of contemporary singers, Anthony Newley, and entitled: "What kind of fool am I?"'

There was a loud snigger from the far side of the room.

'Since you are so amused by the idea, Mr Fenton, why don't you join him?'

The story of how Melis became the murderous object of the werewolf's attention was, like Caesar's Gaul, divided into three parts. The second took place at a Mass some six months later to honour the Forty Martyrs of England and Wales, who sacrificed their lives for the Faith during the cruel persecutions of Catholics in the sixteenth and seventeenth centuries. It so happened that Aaron Gall was performing the service of acolyte to the priest saying Mass that day. This was partly due to his still-continuing belief in the faith into which he'd been born, but also because it entitled him to a badly cooked breakfast of sausage and egg, as opposed to a badly cooked breakfast of porridge.

So when the time came for the sermon, Gall was seated facing the congregation and Brother Gregory Melis in particular, who was in a pew at the very front of the chapel. Despite the fact that, in general terms, Aaron had pretty much deserved his punishment for an atrociously sloppy piece of work, and that Melis had given him a number of useful texts and very useful lines of inquiry to make up for the flippancy of the title he'd been given, at the time Aaron had burned with completely unjustified resentment at his punishment. But having been told that, if he didn't come up with something worthwhile, he'd have to repeat

A History Lesson

it until it was done properly, he'd put some backbone into the task. So much so that Melis had been obliged to revise his opinion as to Aaron Gall's lack of intelligence. It was, in short, an excellent piece of work, and he had said as much to the boy. How many of us can resist praise, even – especially – when it comes from those we dislike? Aaron was no exception, and had come to regard Melis with something like benevolence. And so he started to listen to what Melis had to say and allow the pleasure of ideas to work their magic, and not just the pleasure of numbers.

Since he'd arrived at the school at the age of ten, it had not taken the boy long to regard the school as a jail and the priests as his jailers. The fact that he had committed no crime made him increasingly resentful the longer he was locked up. Outward displays of rebellion entailed a hefty blow to the head, or the application of leather on arse (clothed, it should be pointed out – that was one form of abuse he was not subjected to). Not even the hard cases in the school – and given that it took the bulk of its day boys from Blackbird Leys, then, as now, one of the most violent council estates in the country, it was not lacking in tough guys – were ready to provoke the priests into responses that could be out of all proportion to the crime.

Rob Brinley went on to join the army and ended up in Northern Ireland in a unit which specialised in creeping up behind IRA players and blowing their brains out. But even he kept himself under control at the Salesian College, mostly on account of an early experience at the age of eleven. Only a few days after he had arrived, still with some playfulness in his soul, he had blown up a paper bag and exploded it in the dining hall. The priest in charge had taken him out behind the hall to a rarely visited shrine to

SCORN

Mary, Our Lady of Perpetual Mercy, punched him to the ground and given him a good kicking.

Complain? To whom? Rather like the clock manufacturer of legend who eliminated complaints about his timepieces by closing down the complaints department, the Catholic Church was not in the habit of offering small boys – or anyone else – a friendly pathway to accusing the agents of salvation of doing what was necessary for the redemption of souls. You can't open a door if the door has no handle.

A boy's soul is the devil's playground, and what is necessary is necessary. A leathery boot in the stomach is a merciful act when its absence leads to an eternity of fire and hideous torment. For those who did not want to end up behind the dinner hall on the receiving end of a boot in front of the Virgin Mary (not very successfully interceding with God for mercy towards sinners), there were only two realistic options: either accept without reservation that the Church was divinely inspired and its priests ordained by God to offer salvation to everyone, or go down the (still perilous) route of dumb insolence.

Gall had a talent for silent dissent, but one that involved a good deal of cutting off his nose to spite his face. He refused to work, not just in the matter of the improvement of his soul, but in any way at all. In mathematics and physics, he took little more than five minutes to do the forty minutes set aside for homework, with most of that devoted to ensuring that he never got more than four out of ten. His revenge consisted in deliberately constructing mistakes that were difficult for the teachers to unravel, making it frustratingly hard for them to mark his homework.

Whenever anything interesting came up in his classes,

A History Lesson

he would pay attention and absorb what was being said; whenever he was asked a question he liked to give elaborately confusing but wrong answers. When it came to all the other subjects, he preferred to shut down completely and enjoy confused daydreams about the school cleaner, a woman of advanced age and indeterminate shape hidden behind several layers of nylon overalls but who was the only female ever allowed inside the school.

When not doing this, his thoughts were of what a complete waste of time it was to study geography, history, English (especially), or indeed anything else other than physics and maths. It was Melis and his praise for his detention-enforced work that made Gall reconsider whether the study of history might be worth some effort after all. It was this unexpected conversion of Aaron to the cause of historical truth that led to Melis's horrible death some thirty years later.

'And so it was, boys, that just after St Philip Howard was born, His Catholic Majesty King Philip of Spain was his godfather and Queen Mary of England was present at his baptism.'

It was 6.30 a.m. and Aaron, dressed in the red cassock and white surplice of an acolyte, was kneeling at the side of the altar, facing the congregation of bleary-eyed boys and watchful priests. Up at the lectern, Father Brian Tooley was giving a sermon celebrating the death of one of the Catholic martyrs, who had given their lives for the Catholic faith in the face of the brutal, unrelenting and vindictive persecution of Elizabeth I.

'But let me tell you, boys, that for the first twenty-five years of his life, Philip Howard was not a good Catholic – not a good father, not a good husband, not a good man. He wanted to take possession of his birthright to the full – to be heir to the highest position in the land after the throne. If, to take that place, it was necessary to reject the Catholic faith, he would do so, and did, apparently without a second thought. His wife, Anne, however, was made of truer stuff: she refused to have anything to do with the new state religion created to serve the ignoble passions of a lustful king.'

Lust! A brief stir of interest fluttered over the drowsy boys. Their hopes for sex were to be disappointed, but now their second favourite interest was to be comprehensively indulged. Father Tooley pulled out an ancient print from under the lectern and displayed it to the congregation. It was a badly drawn picture of a naked man being held upside down by his ankles by two executioners. A third was in the act of raising a butcher's cleaver, preparing to bring it down heavily between the victim's splayed legs. His insides had already been cut out, and various bits of his gizzards, along with his penis, were being fried in a pan before his still-seeing eyes. Just behind this appalling scene, another Catholic, still conscious, was being cut down from a gibbet so that he, too, could undergo the same unhappy experience.

Father Tooley thrust the picture towards the now fascinated boys so that they could see in as much clarity as possible the sight of a man being cut in two, a pig about to go upon a butcher's block.

'This! This was the gruesome death Anne Howard was ready to endure for her Catholic faith.' A spasm of regret showered across the watching boys at the thought they might have been looking at a naked woman being tortured rather than a naked man, absorbing though this was. Truly a boy is slugs and snails.

The sermon unfolded at length, losing the interest of the

A History Lesson

boys the further it receded from sex and violence. Queen Elizabeth, Tooley informed them, had cruelly executed Philip's father because she believed that he was plotting to marry Mary, Queen of Scots, and put her on the throne. Then, with the death of ever more persecuted martyrs, Philip Howard could no longer remain the prisoner of heresy and joined his wife in determined opposition to the Protestant queen. Enraged by his opposition and vindictive to the last, Elizabeth had him tried for treason when he reluctantly found himself the leader of the Catholic laity in England and hid many priests in Castle Howard.

'He knew, boys, he knew that his conversion back to the faith would be punishable by death. And so it proved. Sentenced he was, to be hanged, drawn and quartered. But so repulsed were the people of England by his condemnation, Elizabeth grew fearful and would not sign the warrant for execution but imprisoned him in the fearful prison, the Tower of London, with a single servant and his dog for company. And then, with all the cunning of the serpent, she offered to restore all his property and privileges if he would attend just one Protestant religious service. He refused, and died in prison eleven years later. His wife, Anne, died at the age of seventy-three, having carried on serving the Catholic faith in England for the rest of her life.'

Father Tooley stood up tall and looked over his audience calmly and sadly. 'And England is still suffering, boys, suffering under a time of affluence and secularism and individualism, and a great undermining of Catholic faith and morality.'

Tooley sighed and climbed down from the pulpit to resume the Mass. Aaron, however, was looking directly at

Father Melis, who was sitting calmly in the front pew, the priest's expression one of mild interest. Aaron, by now nearly a year into his conversion to the virtues of historical rigour, was puzzled. Where was the look of contempt so easily shown in class when one of them offended against the laws of evidence? His bemusement was interrupted by a sharply hissed 'Gall!' from Tooley, who was waiting for him to move to his side and kneel for the remainder of the Mass.

'I'll talk to you later,' Tooley threatened, as behind them the congregation groaned and laboured into a hymn to the pleasures of suffering and martyrdom.

'Faith of our Fathers, living still.
In spite of dungeon, fire and sword.
How sweet would be their children's fate?
If they, like them, could die for thee!'

That night, in the municipal-swimming-pool-sized washroom, Aaron carelessly washed himself at one of the score of basins needed for a dormitory of eighty boys to clean themselves, and tried to make it past the vulture-faced priest known, for unexplained reasons, as Ginky.

'Come here, Gall!' Aaron turned, sullen-faced. 'Hands!' said Ginky. Aaron raised his hands palm upwards and then, in prescribed fashion, flipped them over. 'Neck!' Aaron turned to one side and bent his head to left and right.

Ginky considered his skin. Aaron stewed. 'Open your mouth!'

Slowly, in agony at the humiliation as the other boys looked on, Aaron opened his mouth, trembling with fury. Ginky leaned in and looked in Aaron's mouth. He was so close Aaron could take in the priest's body odour. It had

A History Lesson

been four days, perhaps, since the cleric had washed, and Aaron thought he was going to retch.

A few more seconds to make his point – that the boy was owned – and Ginky pulled back.

'Do them again. And this time try putting the brush in your mouth.'

In revenge for this, and in exchange for three stale 'chocolate bananas' (no chocolate in the 'chocolate'; no banana in the 'banana'), Aaron came up with the idea of getting one of his mates, the doodle-obsessed Jacob Guza (known to everyone as 'Knob') to draw a cartoon of Ginky in the process of being hanged, drawn and quartered. The executioners were in the act of holding him naked and upside down while cutting him in half with a huge saw between his legs. The executioners had pegs on their noses to avoid having to take in the hideous pong emerging from his scrawny, boil-covered body (signalled by a large number of wavy lines coming from his armpits). Next to them was another torturer holding his nose as he was about to put Ginky's wormy genitals into a frying pan.

'I do, incidentally, think that mockery, ridicule and even invective can sometimes be appropriate: I'd be in trouble if I didn't, since Our Lord used them, and so did many prophets, Fathers of the Church, saints, and apologists down the ages. They are useful to take people worthy of ridicule down a peg or two. The Pope, however, is never ridiculous. When he is wrong, things are too serious for that.'

> Dr Joseph Shaw, Tutorial Fellow in the Faculty of Philosophy, University of Oxford, 2014

'You kiss the arse of Luther, the shit-devil, look, my fingers are smeared with shit when I try to clean your filthy mouth.'

> St Thomas More, condemning William Tyndale for translating the Bible into English (Having fled England to escape More, Tyndale was denounced by the Vatican, found guilty of heresy, strangled and then burned)

CHAPTER 18

MANNERS MAKYTH MAN

In the middle of New College, Oxford, so called because it was new in 1379, there is a large mound covered in trees and bushes which is built over the largest cesspit in the world, one said to have gone unemptied for three hundred years. On this particular moonlit night at eleven o'clock it was occupied by two students, both of them about to lose their virginity. Over the young man's clumsiness we draw a discreet veil, except where his lack of skill touches on our story. The young woman's earlier hopes of bliss had, after fifteen minutes, declined to a resigned desire to get it over with.

'Ow!'

'Sorry,' said the young man.

A few minutes later, as she lay back and thought of nothing very much, she looked up at the almost full moon rising over the dark and looming walls of the ancient city and thought for a mad moment that she saw a large dog loping along the battlements that led deep into the exclusive heart of the college and its exquisite garden quad, where most of the dons had their lodgings.

This strange and impossible hallucination, for so she regarded it, stayed forever with the just deflowered maiden, to vex and trouble her otherwise rigid sense of the rational for as long as she lived.

SCORN

The werewolf Gall had risked the exposure of the battlements only because, when he started, the bright moon had been obscured by clouds. But he miscalculated the awkwardness of the climb and the unknowable arrival of a strong wind at fifteen thousand feet that cleared his cover in less than two minutes and left him exposed for a few moments as he made his roofy way to his ancient revenge on Father Gregory Melis, now asleep in his lovely room in the garden quad.

Because he was taking Mass at 6.30 the next morning in the Catholic chaplaincy in St Aldate's, Father Melis had taken an early night and was three minutes into a light sleep when he woke with a start to an enormous crash, followed by an unnatural shriek.

'Fucking cats!' he shouted.

It was a reasonable guess, given that the college's wheelie bins were stored three floors below the back window of his bedroom. But it was wrong in an unusual way. Had he been properly awake, he would have realised the cat would have needed to be the size of a tiger to have made such a racket.

The werewolf Gall had stepped on a loose slate and been de-roofed in a deranged scrabble of claws. He avalanched off the building on to, luckily for him, an industrial-sized dustbin below that broke his fall. Gall bounced off the plastic tubs and into the alley, where an actual cat was confronted by its worst nightmare: a 350-pound fox.

There was a loud knock on the priest's door and again, had he been more wakeful, he might have been alert to its bad-tempered resonance. Pulling his dressing gown around himself, he pulled open the door and started to speak.

'Yes, what is it?'

Manners Makyth Man

The werewolf, head bent to see below the door whose shape he filled entirely, growled softly.

'You probably don't remember me, Father, but you used to be my history teacher.' Before the astonished priest could say anything, the werewolf Gall raised both hefty paws to either side of his throat and said gently, 'One squawk and I'll snap your neck.'

He needn't have bothered. Father Melis had already fainted.

He woke up a few minutes later, his eyes opening wide as soup plates as he realised he was not waking up from a hideous dream. Terror left him unable to speak as the werewolf sat on his haunches a few feet away, contemplating him with the kind of anticipation a dog might show before a bone, if dogs had the patience to contemplate anything. The terrified staring of the priest and the quiet consideration of the werewolf went on for a full two minutes. Finally, Melis found his voice, cracked and whispering as it was.

'Get thee behind me, Satan!'

The werewolf yawned and made the odd, trilling growl of a large dog expressing mild protest.

'If you think insulting me is going to help your position, I'd think again. I told you – I'm an old pupil of yours.'

'What? I don't understand.'

'Aaron Gall.'

'What?'

'Aaron Gall. That's my name. I was a pupil of yours at Salesian.'

'I don't remember.'

Another doggy yowl – more irritable this time.

'Now you're really getting on my nerves,' said the werewolf.

'Gall?'

'Yes.'

'Aaron Gall?'

'Yes.'

'I don't understand. What are you? What's going on?'

'I was transfigured. I don't see what the problem is. You're a priest – don't you believe in transfiguration?'

'What are you talking about?'

'Transfiguration. A complete change of form or appearance into a more beautiful or spiritual state.'

Being mocked seemed to penetrate the priest's terror.

'I know what transfiguration is. There's nothing beautiful or spiritual about you. The devil ever threatened the holy in the shape of a dog.'

Another yowl.

'I'm not a dog any more than you're holy, old man. I'd mind your manners, if I were you.'

'I'm not afraid to die.'

'We'll see about that,' said the werewolf, leaning forward with a lippy grin.

'So, you're the thing that's been martyring priests?'

A yowling laugh.

'Brilliant, Father – no wonder you're the Hobsbawm Professor of Renaissance History at Oxford University.'

'How do I know you're Aaron Gall?'

'So you remember now.'

'I remember an intelligent but lazy boy whose ideas needed bucking up.' This time, the yowl was much lower in tone – a brooding sort of tone. 'Kill me and get on with it.'

'Talk first, judgement afterwards.'

'What judgement? I tried to help you. I never did you any harm.'

Manners Makyth Man

'Not physically.'
'How, then?'
'Not spiritually,' continued the werewolf.
'Then how?'
'Not that other distasteful thing.'
'Then what?' said the exasperated and fearful priest.

The werewolf moved forward. His hot and clammy breath blew in the face of the priest when he moved his enormous snout just a few inches from his face.

'You betrayed me.'
'How?'
'You betrayed all of us.'
'I don't know what you're talking about.'
'You are a man of intellect and learning. Your reputation is that of an historian of the most rigorous kind.'
'What are you saying?'
'Throughout your academic life, even when you were just a school teacher, you taught in the most exalted way what it meant to weigh the evidence. The aim of history, you told me, was to separate, in so far as it was humanly possible, what was true from what was false, to identify with rigour and discrimination the relationship between causes and effects – I remember your prose – "between the significant and the silly, to detect error".'

'I know what I mean by history, you devil. I also taught you to get to the point and not to waffle. If I must die, I don't see why I should have to listen to your jabber.'

Slowly, the werewolf leaned back on his huge haunches.
'Philip Howard,' said the werewolf at last, and waited.
'I don't know anyone called ... Oh, *St* Philip Howard.'
'That's the one.'
'What about him?'

SCORN

'Do you remember Tooley's sermon about him?'

'*Father* Tooley to you, you insolent maw worm.'

The werewolf raised his massive head, opened his jaws and let out what to the priest's ears seemed something like a groan but was in fact a laugh. Laughter did not come easy to the vocal chords of the family of dogs.

Once the sound had died down, Melis made a bolt for it, and not a bad effort for a man in his seventies. But the werewolf Gall was many times too quick for him and he was thrust on his back by means of a giant paw in his chest. The werewolf leaned into the priest's face again.

'Going somewhere? Now, just for being rude, I'm thinking of starting to eat you from the toes upwards. If I'm careful, I might get to your belly button before you die of shock.'

The werewolf felt a terrible tremor of fear flutter through the body of Melis. He felt, too, the man's effort to bring his terror under control. Slowly, he did so, breath by breath, taking some measure of command. *Not bad*, thought the werewolf Gall.

'Able to listen now?' said Gall.

A few moments. A hard swallow. The priest nodded.

Gall removed his right paw from his chest and sat back. 'Sit down.' The old priest got to his feet, thighs shaking, and walked over to the comfortable chair in which, only a few hours before, he'd taken a tutorial. A silence as the two stared at each other.

'How do I know you're Aaron Gall?'

For a minute or so, Gall spoke throatily of the place they'd shared, cheek by jowl, for two years (Melis had been just passing through before greater things to come). It was not far into this remembrance that Melis realised that the monster before him was, at least in this regard, telling the truth. The sources had been evaluated and found to be reliable.

'What do you want?' asked Melis at last.

'A trial,' said the werewolf.

'Like the trial you gave the others?'

'All right. Not a trial,' conceded the werewolf.

'A star chamber – that's the term you're looking for.'

'If you say so. I weighed you in the balance and you were found wanting a long time ago. But now's your chance.'

'And will anything I say make a difference?'

'You never know, Father.'

The wolf raised himself up. 'Getting back to Tooley and his sermon on Philip Howard. Do you remember it?'

'I must have heard it a dozen times, so *yes*, I remember it. Why?'

The wolf leaned forward.

'I do questions. *You* do answers. List the events.'

'What?'

'In order. I know your memory, Melis. Do it or, by God, you'll know what suffering is before you die.'

The helpless priest was finding recollection harder than usual, but Gall was right about his memory for detail.

'Howard was born in—'

The wolf slammed his paw on the carpet. 'Not Howard's life! Tooley's *sermon* about his life.'

Melis recast. 'It started ... I think it started with his baptism. Yes.'

'And who was present at Howard's baptism?'

'King Philip of Spain, Queen Mary—'

'Do better, old man. What did Tooley call them?'

'His Catholic Majesty of Spain and England.'
'And Queen Mary. What did he call her?'
'Sad. And tragic.'
'Good. Yes, that's how it went. And how did he describe her actions against her main Protestant opponents?'
'That 277 persons were executed.'
'In what time period, Father?'
'Four years.'
'He didn't say that she personally decided to burn alive 277 men and women.'
'It was 288.'
'What?'
'The number of Protestants executed was 288, not 277.'

The wolf growled approvingly.

'You don't disappoint, Father. Your love of truth corrects me. Except, of course, that "executed" doesn't do it for me. I think there's a better term, don't you?'
'Burned alive.'
'And this woman, Her Catholic Majesty Queen Mary. That lying scumbag Tooley, how did he say she died?'

Melis sighed. It was hard to say what it meant. 'Most piously, as she had always lived.'

'And these men and women that she burned alive were not mostly powerful or obviously a threat, were they? Isn't it the case, Father Melis, that they were as ordinary as a glass of water? Candlemakers, shoemakers, servants. Anne Askew was tortured so badly before she was burned for preaching that she had to be carried in a chair to the fire. And to teach her a lesson for arguing the justice of her case, they took an hour over the burning. Though, as you taught me to be strict and unbiased, it's only fair to acknowledge she probably only burned for fifteen minutes before she died. Remind me, Father Melis, what mention did Tooley make of this?'

The priest did not reply. 'Well?'

'Nothing.'

'And how did he describe the death of the Most Catholic Majesty who ordered this abomination?'

'That she died most piously, as she had always lived.'

'That's right, Father. Again, your scrupulous memory does you credit. And her husband, His Most Catholic Majesty Philip of Spain. Leaving aside the Inquisition, on account of the fact that estimates at the moment vary from a quarter of a million to a couple of thousand, how many Protestants did the chief defender of Catholic Europe murder in the Netherlands?'

The old priest, still vibrating with fear, did not answer.

'Would eighteen thousand executions, not including death by massacre and in battle, be fair?'

Still no answer. Without warning, the werewolf sprang forward and opened his jaws doggy wide, blasting a stream of wet, wolfy air into the face of the terrified man.

'Yes! Yes! It would be fair.'

The wolf leaned back.

'You're not just saying that.'

'No.'

'Not even a teensy-weensy slither of a reservation?'

'No.'

'And do you accept that not one word of what that perjuring, yarn-spinning liar said in his sermon was true? Do you accept that neither Howard's wife, nor anyone else, was ever under threat of execution just for being a Catholic, let alone in danger of being hanged, drawn and quartered?'

'Yes.'

'That Elizabeth I, so far from persecuting Catholics, did everything to avoid doing so, despite the fact that the pope had, in writing, specifically stated that anyone who assassinated her would be committing no sin?'

Melis seized his chance.

'There are some serious historians who argue that this was an exaggeration of the pope's position.'

'Do *you* think that?'

The air went out of the old man.

'Probably not.'

'Furthermore, weren't there numerous attempts on her life by Catholics, despite her clearly stated refusal to look into men's souls as to their religion but only to prevent the overthrow of the state and its lawful ruler?'

'There were many such attempts, that's true, but there were many servants of the queen who despised Catholics.'

'Point taken. But Elizabeth wasn't one of them.'

'No.'

'Was it, then, unreasonable of Elizabeth to regard Philip Howard with great suspicion?'

'He never tried to overthrow the Crown.'

'But his father did. Isn't it true that Tooley claimed that, in some way, Queen Elizabeth maliciously determined on his death because of a paranoid belief there was a Catholic plot to execute her and put Mary, Queen of Scots, on the throne?'

'Yes, he did,' said the old man wearily.

'And wasn't it the case that there was exactly such a plot?'

'Yes.'

'So, when the son of the man who wanted to cut her

head off reluctantly became the leader of the Catholic laity and started hiding priests loyal to the very depths of their soul to a pope who had declared it was no sin to murder her – was that unreasonable?'

'Not really.'

'And was her decision not to cut him in pieces and roast his genitals in front of him when he was still alive caused by her fear of public opinion?'

'Possibly there was some thought of that nature in her mind.'

'Tooley didn't say *possibly* – he was in no doubt. Were the public *repulsed* by his death sentence?'

'Some of them were, certainly.'

'So you agree with Tooley that her offer to restore all his privileges and wealth if he'd just go through the motions of a single Protestant service was entirely cynical.'

'Not entirely, but it wasn't just a question of going through the motions. To have attended a Protestant service at the time would have been a betrayal that would have gone shouting up and down the length and breadth of Europe. He refused out of deep conviction.'

'But still she let him live.'

'In prison.'

'With his dog and a servant.'

'I don't know where you got the idea he had a servant from.'

'I read it somewhere, I can't remember where. I'll concede, according to the strict law of evidence that there was probably not a servant.'

'If there's no evidence, then there's no probability.'

'Good. Then we both agree that, as an accurate account of the politics and events of the time, Tooley's sermon was

SCORN

a complete pile of camel shit from beginning to end.'

A pause.

'It was not history. No.'

'Fuck *history*, Father Melis. Was any of it true?'

'No.'

'And you knew that at the time, all the way through. You knew that the sermon, which was a statement of everything the Catholic Church claimed was the case then, and still claims is the case now as I speak to you, was in every way a pack of bloody lies. Did you know it was lies? Did you know that, then and now?'

'It's a complicated—'

'No, it isn't complicated, Father Melis. You knew what he was telling us was lies. You knew what the truth was. But you said nothing.'

'Father Tooley was—'

'Fuck Tooley! It's you I'm concerned with. Tooley was an ignoramus. You're supposed to be – no, I take that back – you *are* a man of the highest intellect, implicitly sworn as an historian and a man of God to tell the truth. You let them stuff our mouths with lies and you said nothing.'

'It wasn't—'

'You said nothing. You lied. You listened to lies and you said nothing. You knew the truth and you said nothing. Judas!'

With one swipe, the werewolf separated the old man's head from his body and launched it crashing against the far wall. It landed on the floor with an odd, dead thump. There was a strange silence and the growing smell, the terrible smell, of blood and shit. The werewolf loped over to the head, picked it up and stared into its sightless eyes. 'Behold,' he said softly to the room, 'the head of a traitor.'

Manners Makyth Man

Less than ninety minutes later, a now fully human Aaron Gall was emerging from the shower in his London flat, whistle-clean and smelling of soap. I cannot help wondering where your sympathies lie at this time, given that, when it comes to mankind, fellow feeling is such a staggeringly arbitrary quality.

To put it crudely (a good idea when dealing with the earthly), if you read the *Guardian*, we can be fairly sure that, in your view, poor Aaron is a victim, whereas if you subscribe to the *Catholic Herald*, there is a good chance that you threw this book at the wall around about page twenty-five.

(I realise that a reader of the *Catholic Herald* would almost certainly not have started the book in the first place, any more than a reader of the *Guardian* would, for example, subject themselves to a literary novel movingly dramatising the case in favour of capital punishment. A truth that rather makes my case about the weird empathies of humanity. My goodness, you people can be hard to like, though, as you'll see in time, I haven't given up. No indeedy!)

Nevertheless, from the tricky perspective of free will, even the reader of the *Catholic Herald* would have to acknowledge that Aaron had, as yet, committed no sin. The Church is very clear that no transgression is possible without a determination to do evil knowingly. When he emerged from the shower washed clean of the blood of Father Melis, he was as guiltless of the crime of murder as you or me (assuming this is not being read by anyone living on death row whose only other choice of fiction is a moving literary novel favouring the case for capital punishment.

A dripping Aaron was still under the influence of his protecting automatic daemon when he stepped in front of the full-length bathroom mirror and began to dry himself.

SCORN

Ever had a sudden moment of realisation, an epiphany of the truth that marked out a momentous line in the sands of self-knowledge between everything you thought was the case about the kind of creature you were and everything that was really true? Neither have I.

This is not to say I haven't realised the moment after making a profoundly unwise choice that I deeply regretted it – but that's for later on.

But let us not say that the moment of revelation to Aaron about what he had become was a mere line in the sand. Let's instead refer to it as a Grand Canyon or a Mariana Trench. It's odd, really, but one of the most peculiar aspects of the human soul – if one can really use such a grandiose term about something so meagre – is the enormous number of popular works of art devoted to the inspiring subject of redemption and change.

(By popular works of art, I mean to say the only art that ever tells you anything useful about people – as for *high art*, that pokey bum-wank, don't get me started.)

The huge number of films about the triumph of the human capacity for transformation is in interestingly inverse proportion to its almost complete absence in the real world. Let me be clear. I'm not a cynic – I grew out of all that long ago – so I don't deny profound change in the human heart sometimes happens: about as often as being struck by lightning or winning 640 million euros in the Big Fat One. So I readily acknowledge the possibility of spiritual and moral transformation. But almost certainly not in you. Or anyone else you know. Or have ever known.

But, staring into the mirror that day, it was if Aaron had woken up with a deep sense of terrible dread from a forgotten nightmare, only for it to return in all its

Manners Makyth Man

horrifying clarity in a single moment: the neck-twisting of Father Seamus Malone (a restrained beginning); the evisceration of Father Thomas Lloyd (getting into his stride); and the total-body horror-gutting and topping of Father Gregory Melis. And even more horrible a revelation was that, after his terrible acts of violence (and in the case of Father Melis, during), he had eaten an increasingly large amount of priest.

In vivid flashes, he relived the shending of bowels and debauching of bellies, the screams and the howls and the terror of dying. Stupid and clever alike, they pleaded and suffered, these priests who, after all, were just old men, and just like Aaron in one respect: they were also the victims of a One True Faith that boasted of its power to take a child of any kind and make it theirs.

But wolves do not take a forgiving view. Pitilessly, he blatched and balloted their guts, gobbled their chitlins and their glands, outraged their livers, insulted their kidneys. He crunched their ribs and chobbled their bile. Some begged for mercy, others accepted martyrdom, but nothing could stop the decortification of brains, the ablation of bowels, the squelching of thyroids. Munch! Munch! Munch!

Aaron looked into his mirrored eyes and remembered the transfiguration of his body and his soul, and in every detail the abominable acts that change had caused him to commit.

HAH!

A moment more, and then again.

HAH!

It was a huge and ecstatic yawp of delight, a bark of joy – intense, absolute and unconfined. Aaron threw his head back and howled. Can bliss threaten to overwhelm glee? Can exhilaration revel in happiness, bathe in enchantment? Hearing that yawp and howl, you would never doubt it could.

Aaron danced out into the living room, sank rapturously to his knees and, like any happy mutt, began to rub his back in ecstasy along the floor. Backward and forward he ground his hairy carcass into the roughness of the sisal warp, changing back and forth at will between wolf and man, laughing and howling as he felt the dreadful stain of *Vergangenheitsbewältigung* drain forever from his soul.

Not familiar with the term? Try using the internet for something other than prattle or pornography for once.

And as for Aaron: free at last, free at last. O Lord, free at last. Now he could transform at will. Unholy duality – Aaron and the wolf were one.

'Anybody can become angry – that is not difficult, but to be angry with the right person and to the right degree and at the right time and for the right purpose, and in the right way – that is not within everybody's power and is not easy.'

> Aristotle, Nicomachean Ethics, Book II, 1109a.27

'Carroll, an award-winning novelist, still feels his faith deeply; these are not the rants of an angry ex-Catholic.'

> Charles R. Morris reviewing Constantine's Sword: The Church and the Jews by James Carroll (an analysis of Catholic anti-Semitism)

'It is to San Francisco that you must go to have an idea of the number of secret and powerful organizations with which the Church of Rome hopes to destroy the schools, and every vestige of human rights and liberties in the United States. Almost all these secret associations are military ones. They number 700,000 soldiers, who, under the name of the United States Volunteer Militia, are officered by some of the most skilful generals and officers of this Republic.'

Charles Chiniquy, *Fifty Years in the Church of Rome* (1886) (The author was a former priest, and the book – part spiritual autobiography, part exposé, part paranoid fantasy – had gone through over forty editions by 1891. It combined scenes in which 'the Church of Rome' is made to look ridiculous with sensationalist charges of corruption and evil (twain.lib.virginia.edu/yankee/cycath3.html))

CHAPTER 19

BEHOLD, THE HEAD OF A TRAITOR!

Scrope stood between the decapitated head of Father Gregory Melis and his body some ten feet away and examined the two clues scrawled over the William Morris wallpaper on the wall either side of the window.

The one to the left read: EAT COYOTE POOP!

The one to the right read: III A FIX AGAINST THE GOSPEL.

Both of them were written in the blood of the victim, along with what looked like brains and small bits of finely shredded liver.

'What *is* that?' said Lister to the coroner after he had finished examining the head on the floor. Both he and Scrope vaguely knew him. He was a former army doctor who'd overlapped them for a couple of months in Baghdad.

'Offhand ...' said the coroner, having carefully examined the wall. 'Offhand, I'd say it was finely diced bits of liver.'

'Was he dead before his head came off?'

'No. That's what did it all right. But bloody peculiar.'

'Do you think so?'

'I mean peculiar even by the standards of a cannibalistic decapitation.' The coroner looked at Scrope and smiled slyly. 'I hear the cops all think you two are a right pair of supercilious cunts.'

'Can't say I blame them. So what's odd about the head?'

'It wasn't cut off, it was torn off.'

'That's difficult, right?'

'It's not possible.'

'So what are you saying?'

'I've never really given it much thought before. But a human being unaided by a specially designed head-yanking device couldn't do it. I don't even know if a bear or a gorilla could do it.'

'So we're talking about a bear or a gorilla who can write and has a grudge against Catholics? Or a man who can write and has a grudge against Catholics and controls an unusually powerful tame bear or gorilla?'

'I'm just telling you that the only time I've seen decapitation is in a couple of car accidents at high speed and a dozen beheadings when I was in Iraq. None of the wounds was like this.' He gestured at the neck of the corpse, all ragged flesh and sinew. 'They were *nothing* like this.'

There was a silence that had little to do with Lister having lost his tongue. 'Do your employers know that when you and Lord Snooty here were in Iraq, you were pretty notorious for your involvement with dismembered flesh. What do you think?'

'At the moment, we favour the Butler Did It theory,' said Lister.

Feeling he'd got the worst of the exchange, the coroner sloped off.

'What do you think?' said Scrope, indicating at the two clues as Lister came to his side. Lister considered them for a moment.

'The first one, no idea. The second, I'd say the Gospel is a cipher for "the truth". Another word for "fix" is mend

– it's got an "a" in front of it so I think we've got something like "amend the truth".'

'The numerals?'

'Don't know yet. And it might be that "amend" refers backward to the Roman numeral and not forward to "the truth".'

'I think you're right about it going backward, not forward. It's "amend the third of something".'

'Shit!'

'And what's the third article of the American Constitution?'

Lister groaned and an expression of mild pain crossed his prematurely lined but handsome face.

'Limitations on the compulsory billeting of troops in private households.'

'That's the third *amendment* to the Constitution. What the fuck did they teach you at Eton?'

'Fuck you, douchewhistle. Go on, then.'

'The third section of article three of the Constitution itself defines treason and its punishment. Father Melis was murdered because he was, in the eyes of the person who did this, a traitor against the truth.'

'You're sure it was a person?'

Scrope looked at him.

'Obviously not.'

'So why did you say it was?' asked Lister.

'I wanted to see if you thought it was.'

'Isn't there a Conan Doyle story about monkeys and murders?'

'Edgar Allan Poe. "The Murders in the Rue Morgue". A trained orang-utan did the killings.'

'I'm talking,' said Lister, victorious, 'about the Conan

Doyle story where an old man is transformed into a sort of human ape by eating monkey glands.'

'I stand corrected,' said Scrope, smiling. 'But here it wasn't a trained gorilla or an orang-utan or anything like it.'

'And you know this because?' said Lister.

'A hunch,' said Scrope. 'Can't really say why; I just find the improbable here more implausible than the impossible.'

'So you really think the idea that some highly literate monster did this is more plausible than that it was done by a man with a trained gorilla?'

'I do.'

There was a silence. 'The coroner,' said Scrope at last, 'has probably been blabbing about us. About what happened in Basra.'

'Is it a secret? I didn't realise.'

'Well, I'd hoped.'

'Really? Then you must be veeeeery stupid.'

Ten minutes later, as Scrope was about to leave the scene, his mobile rang. It was not someone he knew.

'I'd like to speak to Inspector Scrope.'

'Speaking.'

'I'm the man who murdered the two priests.'

A shocked pause from a man whose pride at always being cool was never less than sinful.

'Can I ask who's calling?'

Aaron laughed.

'Very droll. Now, just for a sec, I want you not to do the predictable thing and record this. Because you don't want anyone else to know what I'm going to offer you.'

'How do I know it's you?'

'Salt. And fish fingers.'

Behold, The Head Of A Traitor!

These details had not been released to the public.

'All right.'

'Just so you know, for the sake of your conscience, I stole this mobile from a drug dealer outside Hillingdon Library. The war on drugs is not going very well, is it? But it's a convenient source of phones if you want to keep out of the way of the police – so it really doesn't matter if you trace it.'

'You need help.'

'Of course I do. That's why I chose you. You *do* realise that, don't you?'

'What do you want?'

'To exchange information. I give you something, then you give me something.'

'And you think that's going to happen?'

'Oh, I agree it might not go down well with whatever the police have for an ethics committee. But think of it as the lesser of two evils.'

'I *will* catch you.'

'Yes, you will. When I want you to. You need to be clear about that. You need to be humble, Inspector. You're wherever you are in this investigation because I put you there. If you don't co-operate, there's nothing. If you do, then, in due course, you'll arrest me. Like I said: the lesser of two evils. Think about it.' The line disconnected.

Aaron had intended to talk for longer, but he'd suddenly felt the most intense stabbing pain low down in his gut. Having put down the phone, he raced to the loo and vomited violently for several minutes. In the horrible dunny mess in the bowl, one colour stood out: a bright red; within it, several shards of bone.

CHAPTER 20

THE HERE TODAY AND THE GONE TOMORROW

'To state the matter shortly, the Sovereign has, under a constitutional monarchy such as ours, three rights – the right to be consulted, the right to encourage, the right to warn.'

Walter Bagehot, *The English Constitution*, 1867

Every week, the prime minister of the United Kingdom has a meeting with the queen. It is a private meeting and the conversation remains a secret. This is the point of contact between the bureaucratic face of British politics and the magical. Nothing is barred from these discussions, it is claimed by the few politicians who have attended; it is open season.

Whether this is true – and if so, in what way – we shall see.

The prime minister present today was the queen's eighth in a reign extending back to the middle of the previous century. He was well-spoken and, but for one item of clothing, well turned out, in the way of someone accustomed to dressing well, rather than with the air of discomfort of someone dressed up so as not to create a bad impression. He was not overweight, but his face had the softness which speaks of an easy life, almost but not quite flabby. They shook hands. He nodded, diffident, but not overly.

'Another busy day?' asked the queen.

'Oh, yes, it has been. Sorting out the Council of Ministers meeting.'

'We had an interesting time in Northern Ireland, which was very nice.'

They sat. On this day, the meeting was in Balmoral and the room less pompous than the, in my view, vulgar formality of Buckingham Palace. The rug in front of the fire was a hideous yellow tartan, but most striking was the fire, an electric radiator you could find in bedsits and skips the length and breadth of the realm. The prime minister's elegant wife wouldn't be seen dead with such a debased contraption in her house. This difference distinguishes the aristocracy from the wealthy upper-middle class – to the truly well-born, good taste is a bourgeois affectation.

The prime minister had not attended one of these meetings in Balmoral before, and was struck by the personal details of the room – someone *lived* here. The corgis were wagging their way around the room and, on the table, arranged, admittedly, by a butler, were an odd range of periodicals: papers from *The Times* to the *Daily Mail*, and a startling contrast of magazines: two copies of *Hello!*, a copy each of *Field and Stream*, *The Week* and, oddest of all, *Majesty*, a monthly magazine devoted entirely to the family of the woman sitting in a cheaply covered granny chair wearing a pink jumper and pearls, and a tartan skirt that clashed with the rug.

He started to feel uncomfortable. Her Majesty seemed

to be looking disapprovingly at his shoes – a more racy than usual Italian pair with what he was now beginning to think an unhappily sharp point – an impression reinforced by a black corgi with a brown head who was lying at the queen's feet and also staring at the shoes, as if in harmonious agreement with his mistress about the ghastliness of his footwear.

'How did the meeting go, ma'am?' he asked, to draw her attention away from the shoes, which, in his mind, were growing to full winkle-picker status. He was referring to a meeting she'd had with the Secretary General of the United Nations the previous week.

'Oh,' she replied, slightly crestfallen. 'Unfortunately, he finished fourth.'

He was stunned for a moment. By the time he realised the meeting she was talking about was a horse race, she had moved on to fulfilling her constitutional obligation.

'Of course, the most worrying thing is the murders of these priests. With His Holiness coming on an official visit in August, obviously it looks terribly bad. Has the nuncio been informed of events?'

'Oh yes, ma'am. We've made particular efforts to do so. The officers in charge of the case have talked to Archbishop Gillis, and I understand they're in touch regularly.'

'If there was any question of His Holiness postponing ...' She let the suggestion hang in the air for a moment, then concluded: 'There isn't, I suppose.'

The prime minister shifted awkwardly and admitted there had been concerns, allusions, references to the possibility.

'Oh, dear. It would look bad, of course.'

'Yes, it would, Your Majesty.'

The Here Today And The Gone Tomorrow

'People might believe that it's all ancient history with the Catholic Church, but it's not.'

'I agree, ma'am. We're putting every resource into finding the person responsible.'

She looked at him thoughtfully.

'A little bird told me – as queen, one hears some very unusual things – that the police were keeping a great many details of these crimes from the press.'

'Ah,' said the prime minister. 'Yes, ma'am, that's true.' She looked at him. 'It's more the details. The very unpleasant details. The violence involved is extreme – very extreme.'

'I'm not a sensitive plant, Prime Minister.'

'No, of course, ma'am.'

Somewhat uncertainly and queasily – he was not a man used to violence – he set out in detail the mixture of eviscerations and trauma, not overlooking the half-eaten lungs, sexual organs and brains. When he had finished, there was a restrained silence. He began to fear he had gone too far, despite her wishes.

Finally, thoughtfully and calmly, the queen spoke. 'How dreadful.'

CHAPTER 21

THE PRESENTATION

Scrope and Lister were sitting in the main operation room of the murder investigation team to which they'd been assigned, maintaining a front of provocative loosey-goosey nonchalance solely designed to annoy the policemen and women staring at them with an equally studied rancorous loathing. On both sides, words were being muttered into ears.

'He's a wanker,' said Scrope, soft-voiced.

'I think you'll find,' corrected Lister, 'he's actually a dickhead.'

Scrope considered the correction. 'OK, you're right.'

At the back of the room, staring malevolently at Scrope and Lister, Acting Inspector Allan 'Serious Dave' Connor spoke under his breath to Sergeant Lenny 'Mr Angry' Bower. 'What a pair of grass cunts.'

There was no disagreement this time.

The door opened briskly and in walked Detective Chief Inspector Nathan Adebayo. He dropped various items on the desk at the front of the room and looked up. He raised his voice, but not by much.

'I'm not your teacher, and you're not my class. I expect hush.' The room settled down. 'Don't let me ask you that again. Right? The secondment of DI Scrope and Sergeant Lister is unusual, but then these are pretty unusual murders. I've heard rumours of tensions, for whatever reason. I've

The Presentation

chosen to ignore them because I can't accept that police officers, whether permanent' – he then looked at Scrope and Lister – 'or seconded, would indulge in something so unprofessional when the lives of people they are sworn to protect are at stake. Don't let me hear that rumour again.'

He spent fifteen minutes giving instructions, assigning and reassigning, reporting and being reported to. 'Before I get DI Scrope to take us through the material, I want to say something about what you're going to hear and you must treat it as confidential. By which I mean, if I trace a leak back to any one of you, they won't be downgraded to supervising special constables on Traffic or a Neighbourhood Watch scheme, they'll be charged with misconduct in a public office. A lost pension will be the least of their worries.'

He gestured to Scrope to take the floor. Scrope stood up and switched on his PowerPoint. A picture of a headless body flashed up on the screen.

'Fuck,' he said. 'Excuse my French.' He fiddled with his laptop for a few seconds and the right picture came up.

'What I'm going to tell you is going to be hard to accept, and not least because I can't, in all honesty, tell you in a clear way what it is you *should* accept. These are the facts as we have them, and the physical evidence. Nevertheless, no matter how strange what I'm going to show you is, the point is, we have to use it because that's all we've got.'

He turned to the screen, now showing a picture of the first victim. Using his new laser pointer, with which he was delighted, Scrope tagged a series of indentations along the huge wound in the eviscerated stomach.

'We now know these are teeth marks.'

There was a comic groan of horror from the watching Stasi, as Lister liked to call them. This is good, thought

SCORN

Scrope, they're turning their attention away from loathing me and to the case. Laughter unites.

'So we've got our very own Hannibal the Cannibal.' More laughter.

'Unfortunately not,' said Scrope. He flicked up another picture: a dissected liver.

'This is from the second victim, Father Thomas Lloyd. What you've got here is a bite radius. No human being has a jaw shaped like this, or with teeth this size or configuration.' He looked at the joker appreciatively. 'However plausible the theory – this isn't cannibalism.'

'It could still be cannibalism,' called out Lenny Bower. 'Just by an animal.'

'Strictly speaking,' volunteered Lister, 'only a creature from the same species can be a cannibal.'

Scrope looked at him sourly. 'Let's not worry about that. The point is that whatever's doing this is not human. So, last week, we got Constable Coates to ask around a couple of zoology departments.'

He nodded towards a slightly unearthly-looking policewoman sitting at the front, perhaps six feet tall, with marsupial eyes. 'Perhaps you could sum up, Constable?'

It seemed a good idea to bring in someone known to the squad and repair some of the damage done by that fuckwit Lister being such a bloody know-all with that camel shit about cannibals. The constable stood up. There was suspicion from the gathering – the implication of all this was that she had been holding out on them with outsiders – but it was balanced by fascination because of the strangeness of what they'd just heard.

'None of the scientists at the Oxford zoological department could identify the bite marks. They sent the photos

The Presentation

through to a Canadian expert, and he thought the closest could be some kind of wolf, though he couldn't say what kind. The size of the muzzle is far too big – wolves aren't much bigger than Alsatians, apparently. And though the bite radius is huge, the size of the teeth is comparatively small. The Oxford people said that the power of the bite was at the extreme end of the spectrum – more like a hyena.'

She looked at Scrope, who smiled – it was enough. She sat down.

'I hate to tell you that things get stranger, but they do,' said Scrope, flicking up an image of a large bite into Father Malone's ribs, then one into Lloyd and one into Melis. 'It's not that obvious to the naked eye, but each bite radius is bigger than the one before. Given the time frame, this means a growth rate previously unknown to science in a large mammal.'

'Or three different hyenas,' offered Serious Dave.

Scrope smiled, nodding with what he hoped was understood as flattering approval.

'Exactly so. Which leaves us with a suspect who is a very high-functioning lunatic with a profound grudge against Catholic priests who owns a small pack of appallingly ferocious yet biddable hyenas. He's managed to move around the south-east without anyone noticing, including through an Oxford college surrounded by forty-foot-high walls with about three hundred people wandering about and only one way in, which is guarded by two people.'

'Or he's a werewolf,' said one of the sergeants.

Not even those who laughed thought this was particularly amusing. Scrope smiled politely and considered this enough of an acknowledgement. 'We've put the rest of the forensics in a folder on the system.'

'That means you all read it,' said Adebayo. 'There will be questions.'

'If there's anything you want to add that isn't supernatural, just let us know, no matter how strange. Whatever's going on here, it's bound to be peculiar. So please don't be inhibited.'

'As it happens, Inspector' – it was Serious Dave – 'I've got a suggestion. I mean, it's seriously out there, but it's better than the werewolf theory.' A ripple of mockery went around the room.

'Please,' said Scrope. 'Anything is welcome at this stage, Inspector.'

'Acting Inspector,' corrected Serious Dave. 'Wouldn't want to claim any credit I didn't deserve …' A pause. '… *Inspector* Scrope.'

The resentment that Scrope had been congratulating himself on easing flapped back into the room. Serious Dave coughed, the fuck-you chirpiness plain as he faced the judgement of his jury of colleagues, bound together by the first commandment: there shall be no bullshit of the Fancy Dan variety. Boasting was permitted, but not showing off of a kind that implied innate superiority. That kind of thing was the preserve of grass cunts like Lister and Scrope. In short: no poncing.

'When I joined the force' – he screwed up his face as if his experience on the actual job, unlike some people in the room, ranged back to the very limits of memory – 'about *fifteen* years ago, I was on traffic duty on the M25. Every couple of weeks, the blokes from the Clangers …' He looked at Scrope, all helpfulness. 'That's what we in the force call the fire brigade, *Inspector*.'

Scrope nodded his gratitude.

The Presentation

'They used to use this pair of mechanical jaws to cut the roofs off cars. I saw one of the new ones last year and it was very easy for one man to carry around – electric power, rechargeable. I know it's pretty wild, but it works just like a jaw. You could rig up teeth on the inside. I don't know if you can change the size of the jaw, but I don't see why not. The perp could have killed them with a knife or some kind of blade then used something like that to disguise the real cause of death.

'Accuse me of being off my hinge,' he said – self-mockery was as important a skill to a copper as the art of interrogation – 'but then, a nutter is what we're dealing with.'

'It may be an unusual idea, *Acting* Inspector' – the very slightest of inflexion, neither too cowardly or too aggressive – 'but it's the best theory we've had yet.'

He turned to Lister. 'Look into it would you, Sergeant?' Lister grimaced. 'I'll hand you over to Sergeant Lister to summarise what we've got on the killer.'

Lister stood up. Everyone there knew his rank was only temporary – he'd joined up three months after Scrope, and by then the fast-track scheme for ex-soldiers had been suspended temporarily to appease the deep hostility to it from the Police Federation.

The temperature in the room dropped a few degrees. If his inevitable promotion was an insult to career police, his presence as an ordinary copper somehow doubled the injury. Not that Lister ever made the slightest effort to understand their grievance when it came to him. This didn't mean he failed to understand it; in fact, he even sympathised. Their resentment was not only understandable, it was rational.

When Scrope tried to tell him to be more agreeable, his

reply was always the same: 'I don't blame them for being pissed. I'd be just the same if I were them.'

'Then try being a bit more graceful.'

'Why should I apologise for what I am?'

'No one's asking you to apologise.'

'Yes, you are. I'm over-privileged. It's true, absolutely. But so fucking what? I don't remember being consulted about being born into a wealthy family. It was definitely no conferring when it came to going to Eton – no "Daddy, in the interests of social justice, I'd prefer to go to Hackney Down Comprehensive for the Criminally Insane and get the shit kicked out of me every time I open my fucking mouth." The longest relationship of my life was with a girl born in a Middlesbrough tower block. She left me because I was a cunt, not because I was a snob. I'm not apologising for what I am to anybody. So you can fuck off.'

Lister got to his feet and took over the clicker. He brought up pictures of each of the victims.

'Obviously, we looked for anything they had in common besides being priests, with the expectation, it would be fair to say, that murders of such brutality would come out of something pretty serious – revenge for some kind of major offence, perhaps that they were all involved in some sort of sexual offences against children. Then we'd have a motive and a connection. Unfortunately, as far as we can tell, Church records don't have a single reference to offences of that kind by these priests.'

One of the sergeants, a woman, chipped in. 'Isn't the Church pretty notorious for covering up that kind of thing?'

'Absolutely. But they claim that even rejected claims of touching up kids would still be on the files. They showed

The Presentation

us the records of some priests not involved in this case, photocopies with the names redacted.'

'"Redacted"?' called out another cop. 'I only got a D in English.'

'It means "tenebrate", "in-camerise", "crepuscalate", "en-dinge" or "adumbrate". No? How about "blacked out"?'

'A regular fucking Stephen Fry, aren't you?'

'Why don't the two of you grow up?' said Adebayo. 'Or, if you can't do that, take it out behind the bike sheds. Afterwards. Get on with it, Sergeant.'

'So, at any rate, the claim that none of them had a record of abusing children looks firm enough. We'll keep an open mind. It wouldn't be all that surprising if there'd been no official complaint on one of them, but that all three seem clear means that the sexual abuse motive doesn't stand up – at least, not yet. The best break we've got is that all the victims served in the same area in the same ten-year period. Two of them, Malone and Melis, were teachers, which started to look interesting – but Father Lloyd wasn't, unfortunately.'

'Did either of the teachers work at the same school?'

'It's possible. Malone was a peripatetic for years, a sort of permanent supply teacher. One of the papers in his file is missing, but the first page shows him in eight different schools. They're trying to track down the diocese records to fill in the gaps, but that's going to take a few more days at least. If we can link the two of them, it'll really help. At the moment, all is crepuscular and en-dinged.'

He smiled, clearly mocking himself, which eased the wariness from some in the unit. Not all of them shared the dog-for-cat hostility of Serious Dave and Mr Angry.

The women, in particular, were drawn to his easiness and refusal to apologise.

When they were sixteen, Connor and Bower's career choice was between pounding the beat and burglary. But now the Daves and the Angrys in the police force were on the way out. Everyone had a degree these days. They were the Arapaho and Cheyenne of the job market, watching, bewildered, as their once unchallenged prairie of on-the-job training filled up with nurses, bank clerks, housing managers, branding strategists, all smugly trundling past in their degree wagons, astride their BA ponies. Nobody learned on the job anymore. The copper was being out-evolved by the Law Enforcement Officer. Serious Dave and Mr Angry were resentful dodos and chippy quaggas, as uncomprehending of their passing away as the British walrus or the Norfolk damselfly.

'Please,' said Aaron Gall. 'You mustn't worry in the slightest about not remembering me. It was, after all, a very long time ago.'

'Still,' said the woman sitting opposite him in a Starbucks that could have been in Middlesbrough or Dar es Salaam. 'I'm really embarrassed, but I want you to know it has nothing to do with you. Five years ago, I'm sure I'd have recognised you. The name, too. But ...' She hesitated. 'I've been diagnosed with the early stages of dementia. I forgot my son's name the other day. So you mustn't think it's because I didn't care about you all.'

'Of course I don't. I'm very sorry to hear you're not well.'

'So, tell me about this project of yours. It sounds very exciting, a bit like that documentary ... What's it called? ...

The Presentation

No, don't tell me. *7 Up!*' she said, triumphantly, victorious over the looming horror.

'Yes,' he said, smiling as if he recognised the similarity and was a little self-conscious about it. 'It does a little, doesn't it? But, in a way, I want to turn the idea on its head – well, perhaps more on its side. I want to track down an entire generation of children from the same environment, not contrasting ones. I want to see what the years have done to a group of people who started out more or less together, and see what's happened to them.'

'Will it be for television?'

'No, I don't think so. I want to give time to everyone, follow their lives up and down, in detail, if I can. A book.'

In fact, he would not have recognised her himself, even if he'd parked himself opposite her on a long train journey. She had been perhaps twenty-three when she had sat to one side of the room as Mother Mary Frances beat him for his untidy work in general, and for failing to put a little tail on the circle of his number nine in particular.

Now she was a plump old woman who looked well enough. He remembered that the Inuit or some group of people or other had a word for the old that broadly translated as 'those shortly to die'. The only thing connecting the girl who watched on that day and the pleasant woman sitting across from him with her personality slowly evaporating was her red hair. It was much shorter now. Then it had been a crowning glory, streaming down her back in a beautiful stain of ruby filaments.

He could remember nothing at all about her after that day, but before then she had been a gentle and kindly presence who captured his gawping attention, the ogling little beast, because of her habit of sitting at his eye-level on her desk and crossing and uncrossing her legs in accompaniment to whatever lesson he wasn't paying attention to.

O women, beware the eyes of little boys as well as men – their incorrigible prurience is guzzled with their mother's milk. Only a strict regimen of guilt and shame has any chance of correcting their inherent depravity. You might discontinue wearing dresses for a start; button your blouses tightly at the top; wear your cardigans loose, and even looser still your Levi's. Do nothing, womankind, to fatten the eyeballs of these ungovernable lookers-on.

He was surprised by her height when she came into the coffee shop. He remembered her as being very tall. Which she would have been, of course, in his dwarf years.

'I'm sorry I can't be of much help to you – or any.'

'That's all right,' he said. They sat in silence for a moment. 'Did you hear about that terrible business with Father Lloyd?'

Her face went dark. 'Yes.'

'I understand they think the same person desecrated the grave of Mother Mary Frances.'

'It was horrible.'

'Do you remember anything about them?'

'Not Father Lloyd. I only met him briefly a few times, and not for long.'

'And Mother Mary?'

There was no reply for a moment. She took a sip of her tea and sighed very quietly. 'She was a very harsh person.'

'In what way?'

'She frightened the children. To be honest, she frightened me.'

'Really? Why?'

'For someone so cold – she could freeze you with a look

The Presentation

like no one else I ever met – when she became angry it was like an explosion or a volcano or something. I never saw anyone get so angry. You thought, *She's going to explode, to go off. Bang!*'

She sighed again. 'I remember, one day, she decided to take the children out to the woods because it was such nice weather. She chatted away to them, happy as a lark as she pointed out the different wild flowers – autumn hawkbit, borage and butterburs. I know you can only use the word "gay" in one way these days, but that's what she was that day, gay and happy. But the children just looked at her. You could see them thinking: *When is something terrible going to happen?*'

'I remember that, too, about her,' said Aaron. 'I remember one boy – can't recall his name – short, a bit fat. She set about him for some reason, really gave him a going-over. It was in your class, now I think about it, and Father Lloyd was there, too, about to give us our religious instruction.

'Do you remember? I remember,' he said.

She looked at him, fearful, and her mouth pulled down at each side in an almost imperceptible twitch. 'I do remember, actually. It was terrible, the worst thing I ever saw her do.'

'You'd have thought the priest would have stopped her.'

'Perhaps he was afraid of her, too,' she said, more distraught than sad. A silence.

'It would have been hard,' said Aaron, at last, 'for a young teacher like you to intervene, to go up against a woman like that. You shouldn't blame yourself.'

She looked at him again, this time bemused. 'I mean, that's how it was in those days. It would have been impossible even for an adult to intervene, to say, "Stop! Leave

SCORN

that innocent little boy alone and don't hurt and terrify him!" It wasn't just that I would have lost my job. It was going against your faith. The nuns, the priests – they *were* the faith. People today don't understand the power. They don't understand at all.'

Aaron stood up. 'Thank you so much for seeing me. I hope everything goes very well for you.'

The woman stood up, too, but she was shaking now.

'Good luck,' she said.

'Yes. Thank you. Good luck to you, too.'

'The Church becomes very feminised. Women are wonderful, of course. They respond very naturally to the invitation to be active in the Church. Apart from the priest, the sanctuary has become full of women. The activities in the parish and even the liturgy have been influenced by women and have become so feminine in many places that men do not want to get involved.'

> Cardinal Raymond Leo Burke on the Catholic 'Man-crisis' and what to do about it, 2015

'By virtue of their feminine genius, women theologians can take up, for the benefit of all, certain unexplored aspects of the unfathomable mystery of Christ. Women know how to incarnate the tender face of God, his mercy, which translates into availability to give time more than to occupy spaces, to welcome instead of excluding.'

> Pope Francis, 2014

'The door is closed.'

> Pope Francis declaring the ban on women priests to be infallible for all time, 2016

CHAPTER 22

THE BALL OF STRING

ALAS THE STONE OF SCONE REMOVED BY EBENEZER
IS THERE BY THE ACTIVE VILLAGE.

Scrope was going over the still-unsolved clue from the scene of the Abingdon murder for the squad, but it was a perfunctory effort. This was not out of snootiness, but because he thought of his abilities with these interesting waste-of-time amusements as idiosyncratic and of no significance. He knew plenty of intelligent people who would have been baffled by the crossword in the *Sun*, just as he knew gifted cruciverbalists who were as thick as a madwoman's custard.

He was also unconvinced that the clues were likely to be taking the investigation anywhere useful. He thought he was being played.

He finished his brief presentation. 'If anyone's got anything, please feel free.'

Surprisingly, it was Sergeant 'Mr Angry' Bower who spoke up, defensive and cocky at the same time.

'Ebenezer – it's slang for "E", for "ecstasy".' He put on a posh voice. 'The well-known psychoactive euphoric.'

A laugh from the other cops. Bower had shown he knew something Scrope didn't and managed to insult him in the

The Ball Of String

same sentence. Later, in the canteen – the real one, not the metaphorical one – the true coppers, endangered like the panda whose colours they echoed so famously, agreed with the compliment handed down by Allan Connor: 'Kudos, Sergeant Bower, kudos.'

Scrope could see Lister was about to needle Bower in response and shut him up with a narrowing of the eyes.

'Thanks, Sergeant. Very helpful.' He looked back at the screen. 'That gives us "Removed by E". Anyone any the clearer?' He waited for thirty seconds and was about to wind things up when the tall, slightly inhuman-looking officer raised her hand.

'Yes, Constable ...?'

'Coates, sir. I think I might know the answer to "the active village" bit. It just popped into my head.'

At first, she had decided not to explain this magical appearance, on the diplomatic grounds that it would be sure to raise the hackles of her colleagues. But then the disobedient impulses that had marked her life spoke. *Why*, they said to her, *should you apologise for what you are?* Tempted, she fell.

'I did *Hamlet* for my dissertation, and I do the *Guardian* crossword when I have the time.'

Together, this was too much for Serious Dave. He groaned softly enough to be heard. This sort of thing had to be nipped in the bud. Coates ignored him. 'If you remove the "e" from "active" you get "activ village".'

Scrope examined the screen to see what she was driving at.

'Another word,' she said, 'for "village" is "hamlet", yes? So it's not "active" anymore, it's "Act IV". It looks like a reference – at least I think so – to something in Act IV of *Hamlet*.'

Scrope gazed at the clue on the monitor.

'Yes,' he said softly. 'I think you must be right.' He looked at her and nodded his appreciation. 'I'm impressed.' He smiled. 'I don't suppose you have any idea what he's pointing to in Act IV?'

She looked crestfallen and Scrope immediately realised his mistake. 'Sorry. I think it's a brilliant insight. I'll trawl through it later.'

Serious Dave listened to all this with mounting apoplexy. *Fucking* Hamlet, *fucking dissertation, fucking* Guardian, *fucking, fucking, fucking, ARSEWIPING BULLSHIT.*

'She doesn't have a sense of humour, she's a woman.'

'Stow it, Connor,' said Adebayo. 'You and I will have a word later.'

Molly Coates recovered quickly and spoke in a softly forgiving voice.

'It's all right, sir, *Acting* Inspector Connor is absolutely right – if women had a sense of humour, none of them would have sex with him. They'd be laughing too hard.'

The ensuing huge cheer and round of applause made the young woman blush with pleasure. One of the men applauding was Sergeant Bower, who enjoyed seeing his pal humiliated almost as much as getting one over on Scrope. He took a rubber chicken out of his desk drawer and gestured towards Coates with it. 'I'd say you've earned a squeeze of the Cock of Justice.'

He squashed it twice to demonstrate its squeak. Much laughter and groans all round.

Coates smiled. 'I wouldn't want to squeeze it, Sergeant, but I know what I *would* like to do with it.'

More laughter, but this time even Connor joined in.

'All right, settle down,' said Adebayo.

The Ball Of String

*

Later, at the Gyngleboy, over a bottle of Cloudy Bay Pinot Noir, Scrope and Lister were discussing the day's events.

'I wonder why people say that,' said Scrope. 'That women don't have a sense of humour. I mean, Sally Garfield is a scream.'

'Mel Begosian was funny,' said Lister. 'One of the funniest people I ever met.'

'She was.'

'So why do you hear it all the time?'

'Actually, I think I can explain,' said Lister. 'Lots of women have a sense of humour. Obviously, some don't; lots of men don't. But what all women share, and it gets mistaken for not having a sense of humour, is that – and I know it's a pretty big generalisation, but it's true – they're gullible.'

'All of them?' said Scrope.

'Nearly all. That something is mostly but not universally true is the essence of a generalisation. I don't mean about sex, but that's just basic preservational biology – if they were as gullible about sex as they are about everything else, the average woman would be pregnant pretty much all the time. What I mean is, they'll believe anything you tell them about things in general. I mean, you could sell preference shares in a marmalade mine to Sally Garfield, and she won the Smith Prize.'

'Never heard of it.'

'It's a Cambridge Prize in Mathematics. More difficult than anything you've ever done, anyway,' said Lister. 'And, once, I persuaded Mel that I was Bob Monkhouse's illegitimate son.'

SCORN

Scrope laughed. 'Why?'

'I thought it was funny at the time.'

They didn't notice WPC Coates until she was sitting down beside them.

'What will you have?' said Lister, again struck by her looks, pleasing and ugly at the same time.

'Whatever you're having.'

'You didn't mention to the others that we invited you?'

'And be hated for being a teacher's pet? I'm not a complete idiot.'

'Well, we know you're not that,' said Lister.

She looked at him as if weighing him up. 'The clue wasn't that difficult.'

It was most certainly that difficult, but Lister realised he'd been put in his place, and a draughty one, too.

'As you've got a knack for this stuff,' said Scrope, 'we thought you might help us with the rest of the clue.'

'Sure, if I can.' She was neither cocky nor unsure of herself.

'We've been thrashing around a bit already. Quite a bit, actually. We need a fresh eye, so if you'd like to take us through it, maybe you'll get it, or nudge something we've been missing till now. Can't hurt.' He took a folded piece of A4 out of his suit pocket and smoothed it out on the table with the clue written in capitals at the top.

ALAS THE STONE OF SCONE REMOVED BY EBENEZER IS THERE BY THE ACTIVE VILLAGE.

'So, what we've got now is "Alas the stone of scone there by the Act IV *Hamlet*. M!"'

She looked over it for a moment.

The Ball Of String

'It feels like you're giving me a test,' she said.

'We're not,' said Scrope. 'You can't do worse than we have.'

She took out her phone and tapped away. 'Just to remind me. "The stone of scone,"' she read out, '"traditional block of stone used for crowning kings in Scotland, then England. Symbol of Scottish independence. Stolen by nationalists, recovered but returned to Scotland."'

She thought for a moment. 'Kidnap. Nationalism. Queen Elizabeth. Last monarch to be crowned sitting on it. Don't think so. Did you go through the Scottish angle?'

'Yes. Nothing.'

'Different kinds of stone. Rhinestone, gemstones, kidney stones, heart of stone, stepping stone, millstone, Rosetta stone – the same text in three languages.' She mulled. 'Philosopher's stone, standing stone. God!'

She stopped. 'OK, let's try "scone".' She tapped the phone again. Her face lit up. 'Instead of Scone the place, how about the cake? Stone cake? Sounds like a fairy tale, Rumpelstiltskin and the stone cake.' She scrolled on. 'Doesn't seem to be a stone cake. What's a scone made of?' More scrolling. 'Wheat, oatmeal, baking powder, no yeast.'

'Wait. Wheat?' said Lister.

'Yes, wheat. But we don't say something's made of wheat. It's made of flour.'

'Yes!' said Scrope. 'Stone and flour. Millstone.' He realised he'd taken the ball away. 'Sorry, you would have got there.'

'No. Maybe ... Who knows? You said it wasn't a test.'

'Right.'

They all turned with the same passion to the A4 paper. Scrope wrote the clue down again.

SCORN

ALAS THE MILLSTONE THERE BY THE ACT IV *HAMLET*.

'OK. We've got "millstone" and something that happens in Act IV of *Hamlet*.'

Scrope wrote down 'Alas'. '"Alas" means "grief", "sadness" and is nearly "a lass".'

'Ophelia – a lass – drowns in Act IV,' said Coates.

'OK, sounds about right,' said Scrope, and started writing. Coates turned to Lister.

'So we've got this: The millstone (there by the) Ophelia drowns.'

'Most plausible is: "There by the grace of God,"' said Lister.

'OK, that gives us: The millstone there by the grace of God Ophelia drowns.'

Five minutes of working through this got them nowhere. The silence was broken by Lister.

'What if it's "Thereby hangs a tale"?' He held up his phone to reveal he'd got the suggestion from Google. 'I think it's got something to do with hanging.'

Coates tapped quickly into her phone. So did Scrope – but he didn't need the web for the answer, just the reference. He'd heard the answer many times in chapel as a boy. 'The Gospel according to Mark, verse 9: "It were better for him that a millstone were hanged about his neck and he be drowned in the sea than he should offend against one of these little ones."'

A few minutes later their glee had diminished.

'We're not really any better off,' said Lister. 'It was perfectly obvious he was killing them because they'd abused children.'

'Except that they hadn't.'

The Ball Of String

'There's no *record* that they had. Not the same thing.'

A long silence, broken by Coates.

'It doesn't have to be sexual abuse, does it? I mean you can't say: *I had a good education because nobody raped me.* Isn't *not* raping children setting the bar a bit high?'

Neither of the two men said anything: it was such a shamefully good point.

'A relative of mine had a teacher at school. Not a priest; I'm a know-nothing C of E. This teacher was sarcastic to her all the time about everything. The other kids picked up on it and made her life miserable. She's never had any confidence in herself. I mean, she's not mad or anything, or depressed, she just always jokes about how stupid she is. The teacher never touched her, nothing at all like that. But he helped to ruin her.'

'Enough to justify killing in revenge?' asked Scrope.

She looked at him.

'He *ruined* her.'

'She's right,' said Lister.

'I agree,' said Scrope. 'We've been looking at this through the wrong end.' He looked at Coates. 'I take my hat off to you.'

'Do you have a hat?'

'I do,' said Scrope. 'Several. Just not with me.'

'His favourite,' said Lister, 'is one of those pointy ones with bells on it.'

For a few minutes the three of them bathed in a mutual glow of satisfaction. Scrope left, not because he particularly wanted to, but because when Molly went to the loo Lister had told him to fuck off home.

Lister was disconcerted when, half an hour later, Molly said she had to go. Outside, he tried again.

SCORN

'My car's just around the corner. Can I give you a lift?'

'I don't think that would be a good idea.'

'Why? I promise you I'm able to take no for an answer.'

She smiled pleasantly. 'I can see that you might have considerable experience of being turned down.'

He smiled, too, though the sensation wasn't entirely welcome.

'All right. Fine. I'm going down in flames.' He opened his arms and gestured her gently away.

She waved down a taxi and smiled at him. 'I enjoyed this evening. Really.'

'Then why?'

She looked at him and sighed.

'Because being teacher's pet is bad enough, without being teacher's bitch.'

The door shut and the taxi left Lister behind.

'Wow,' he said softly.

The next day, Scrope went to see Chief Inspector Adebayo to go through the clue and its solution.

'Outrageous,' said Adebayo, referring to one thing.

'It is, isn't it?' replied Scrope, referring to something else.

CHAPTER 23

PROFESSIONAL STANDARDS

Aaron Gall sat in the ugly but only mildly uncomfortable chair opposite Lou Bettancourt. They were looking at each other silently.

She looked unusually sombre. What she was about to say was clearly very serious.

'I'm afraid I can't see you anymore.'

Aaron smiled. This was odd, for two reasons. One was that he was smiling at Lou Bettancourt's decision to stop treating him; the other was that his smile, for the first time in many years, had a hint of joy about it.

CHAPTER 24

SOME DAY I'LL FLY AWAY

'Police are appealing for information in connection with the theft of a sparrowhawk snatched in a raid on an aviary in the garden of John Freeborn, 65. Police are mystified that the thief left behind much rarer and more valuable birds of prey.'

Richmond and Twickenham Times

'Only for bad food is there no forgiveness.'

Jewish proverb

Aaron was sitting back in a chair at the dentist's waiting to have his gob full of fingers and tubes and a nasty, horrible, shrieking drill. He was also considering the verdict of the dentist: that his teeth would need another ten hours of appointments to deal with the long-overdue renewal of the eleven fillings in his teeth, most of them very ancient indeed.

'A pity you had so many sweets when you were a child. Basically, your teeth are as hard as the hob of hell, as my old dad used to say. Unusually so.'

Aaron took the rebuke resentfully.

Some Day I'll Fly Away

'If you'd been brought up in a school where the porridge tasted like cold sick and the sausages not only looked like dog turds but, for all I know, tasted like them as well, I doubt you'd have been able to turn down the Refreshers and packets of Dip Dab that was all they sold at the tuck shop. It was that, or be too hungry to get to sleep.'

Later, down with the hygienist and still in a bad mood, he was spitting the vermillion carnage from her scrapings and diggings into the small porcelain bowl when he noticed lots of small pieces of hair in the dried blood. The hygienist looked at him suspiciously: the only other time she had seen anything like that was with neurotic teenage girls with a habit of chewing their own hair. However, the look in Aaron's eyes deterred her from saying anything.

'If you'd like to lie back, I'll give them a bit of a polish.'

The chair eased backward, but Aaron kept on falling, falling, into the distant past.

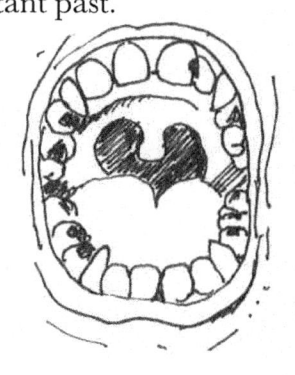

'It is well known that humour, more than anything else in the human make-up, can afford an aloofness and an ability to rise above any situation, even if only for a few seconds.'

Viktor E. Frankl, Man's Search for Meaning

I inquired from prisoners who had been there (in Auschwitz) for some time where my colleague and friend P had been sent.

'Was he sent to the left side?'

'Yes,' I replied.

'Then you can see him there,' I was told.

'Where?'

A hand pointed to the chimney a few hundred yards off, which was sending a column of flame up into the grey sky of Poland. It dissolved into a sinister cloud of smoke.

'That's where your friend is, floating up to heaven.'

Viktor E. Frankl, Man's Search for Meaning

CHAPTER 25

THE DISTANT PAST

It was Tuesday morning in 3 Alpha, with Father Vincent McTeague, universally known as Flintstone – because of a vanishingly distant similarity to Fred, but mostly because it was believed that his head was full of rocks and that you could strike up a fire with them, using his soul for sparks. McTeague was a hard man, even compared to other hard men from the Land of Saints. It was also universally held by the boys that any Irish priest must, by definition, have been brought up on a farm, in a bog so hideous that even life as a bastard in black was preferable.

As it happens, I can confirm that, while McTeague's soul was figuratively formed from a mixture of bog-water, pig-shit and putrid potatoes, his actual fleshly body had been born in Dublin in a comfortable lower-middle-class semi-detached on the Malahide Road, just opposite Plunkett's, a newsagent's owned by a descendant of St Oliver Plunkett, who was hanged, drawn (disembowelled and castrated while still alive) and quartered by the English at Tyburn in 1681 – the last Roman Catholic martyr to die in England for his faith.

It is worth recording the final words of the Lord Chief Justice as he sent the unfortunate Plunkett to his death: 'The bottom of your treason was your setting up of your false Catholic religion, than which there is not any thing more displeasing to God, or more pernicious to mankind in the world.' This judgement, in my humble opinion, is in the finest traditions of English justice – like the sentence itself, harsh but fair.

Today, McTeague was teaching about the matter of beatification, an early stage of the process leading to a declaration of sainthood. In particular, McTeague was inspired by the recent announcement that Pope John XXIII, dead a few years, had been so designated. In the strict interests of fairness, it should be pointed out that the late pope had been a man worthy of admiration in many ways. He'd done impressive work during the war, saving a great many Jews by, among other things, providing false certificates of Catholic baptism. One of his first acts on becoming pope was to eliminate the description of the chosen people as 'the treacherous Jews' in the Good Friday Mass.

'Now,' said Flintstone McTeague, 'we already have confirmation that Pope Pius intervened to miraculously save the life of a nun dying of an internal haemorrhage. When one of the sisters put a relic of the recently deceased pope – a finger, I believe – on her stomach, the dying nun had a vision of Pope Pius in her sleep. And when she woke up, she was cured!'

McTeague was fortunately too carried away by the story to appreciate that there was not much excitement in response from the boys in his class. But they soon perked up when Aaron raised his hand and asked a question.

'Yes, Gall,' said Flintstone.

'If Pope Pius decided to intercede with God to perform a miracle to save a nun, why didn't he stop the slag heaps in Aberfan from collapsing on the junior school in the town and killing over a hundred children?'

The Distant Past

What word to describe the silence that followed? Let me be perfectly clear that none of the watching boys had the slightest interest in the theological question so foolishly raised by Aaron. What electrified them was the nature and severity of the hideous consequence that would surely result. A beating? A hanging? A burning at the stake?

The boys were not to know that at the time of that terrible disaster the headmaster had given a speech to the priests at supper regarding the mysterious ways of a loving God vis a vis human suffering that echoed Aaron's question. It was rather moving, actually, to be rigorously fair. (Fairness is a quality, I'm sure you've gathered, on which I pride myself.)

Given the deep dislike that existed between himself and the headmaster, a man he regarded as a communist sympathiser because he had not taken a belt to one of the fifth-form boys for sending away to the Chinese embassy for a free copy of Mao's *Little Red Book*, McTeague thought it best to be on his guard and wait until time, as it surely would, gave him the opportunity to teach Gall a lesson he'd not quickly forget. His face was dark with rage, but he confined himself, for now, to words alone.

He walked over to within a few feet of the boy. 'Have you ever heard of St Catherine of Siena, Gall?'

Aaron was now very deeply regretting what he'd said. You'll see from this that the emergence of the werewolf many years later only added to his capacity for impulsiveness. It did not create it entirely.

'No, Father.'

'Of course you haven't, boy. Well, St Catherine was out one day tending to victims of a plague, and this holy and loving and compassionate work obliged her to wipe the weeping wounds of those infected, to wipe their pus-emitting boils. On one occasion, she was so revolted by the sight and smell of the slimy green putrefaction oozing from the pustules of one plague-ridden person that she recoiled for an instant. *But!*'

Here, McTeague turned from the shaking Aaron and looked murderously around the room at the enraptured, those who were not Aaron's pals, still hoping for something violent.

'But here is the point. She convicted herself of not loving Our Lord enough, of letting her human nature, quite understandably, overcome her calling by focusing on the grossness of the illness and failing to see Christ in this poor afflicted person. She directly proceeded to wipe the pus from the person's wounds and weeping boils, then she rinsed out the rag in a basin, and then *drank the water in the basin as a penance for what she considered her sin!*'

He turned back triumphantly to Aaron. 'That, Gall, you sneering little heathen, is the kind of person who is allowed to criticise the pope. So!' He turned again to sweep the entire class with his triumphal rage. 'Any pus-water drinkers in here? Have a go at it, attack the pope. Go on, I dare you!'

No one dared. He turned back to Aaron.

'So, boy, got anything to say for yourself?'

'Yes!' said Aaron, standing up defiantly and shouting out with deranged courage. 'I've had to spend the last three years listening to you, you fucking old lunatic, and I'm not going to stand for it anymore. Come on if you think you're hard enough!'

Of course, he didn't actually stand up and say this. Although he was already starting the slow process of going

The Distant Past

mad, you'll remember from his conversations with Lou that he was never, in fact, suicidal. He only imagined this heroic defiance.

'Well?' demanded McTeague.

'No, Father.'

'No, Father, indeed,' said the priest.

St Oliver Plunkett was of the opinion that, once Irish Catholic priests could be weaned off their habit of drunkenness, they would all be saints. This view would not have been shared by Aaron and his friends, who had spent many years in the presence of sober Irish priests without very much evidence of the presence of heroic suffering born out of heroic love and heroic joy that is the Catholic hallmark of sanctity. Perhaps if they'd been drunk more often they might have been kinder.

Students of coincidence may be interested to know, for reasons that will become clearer as I tell this story, that, after he was sentenced in Westminster Hall, St Oliver's agonisingly disambiguated body was initially buried in two tin boxes. The head eventually found its way to Drogheda, whereas the rest of the body ended up in Downforth Abbey, the school where George Scrope would one day be educated. Various other bits of the martyr were taken as holy relics to France (the left upper arm), Germany (a small piece of backbone), the United States (samples of blood-soaked cloth) and Australia (a foot).

Feeling uneasy, are you? That there's just a little too much scorn here, a touch of the know-it-all sneer-artist at the expense of those with a simple faith? Is there too much here in the way of *de haut en bas* disdain?

If you *are* uncomfortable, then I suggest you get someone to hit you around the back of the head, or arrange for a man with intense body odour to slip his hands around your genitals. Then imagine calling out to the ordinary faithful for help to protect you from the humiliating blow and the stinking caress. But the ordinary faithful do not respond. The ordinary faithful are praying. The ordinary and simple faithful are looking the other way, as they have always done. Now decide how *de haut en bas* the condescension feels.

Two footnotes to all this:

At a cost of most of a week's pocket money, Aaron commissioned Jacob Guza (Guza's vengeful caricatures were now so popular with the boys that 'chocolate bananas' didn't cut it anymore) to draw a cartoon of McTeague holding a half-eaten rotten potato in one hand and a nearly empty bottle of whisky (VAT 69) in the other. His mouth (missing several teeth) was wide open, and he was singing, 'Dinah, Dinah, show us your leg', all the while up to his ankles in a particularly fetid-looking bog in which were floating a large number of turds, dead cats, and so on. On the bank, St Catherine was mortifying her sinful flesh by drinking from a large bottle labelled 'Puss'. It should, of course have been spelled 'Pus' but, alas, with the commercial success of his drawings, Jacob spent more time doodling than paying attention to his lessons.

The second footnote should put the heroic moral indignation expressed by young Aaron concerning the terrible death of so many children in Aberfan in a slightly different light. Only a few weeks later, he was telling the following joke:

'What's black and goes to school?'
'I don't know, what's black and goes to school?'
'A slag heap!'

'This is, perhaps, the most fundamental lesson of our study: ordinary people, simply doing their jobs, and without any particular hostility on their part, can become agents in a terrible destructive process. Moreover, even when the destructive effects of their work become patently clear, and they are asked to carry out actions incompatible with fundamental standards of morality, relatively few people have the resources needed to resist authority.'

Stanley Milgram, Obedience to Authority, 1974

CHAPTER 26

FORGIVE THEM, THEY KNOW NOT WHAT THEY DO

Alone in her retirement flat in Headington, Teresa Tandsby finished watching *Coronation Street* and wondered, not for the first time, why she was wasting her time on something that, at heart, she regarded as spiritually unworthy and banal. On the other hand, she reasoned, this was generally true of most things on television: there weren't enough wonderful wildlife documentaries or science and arts programmes on BBC4 to make up for the soul-debasing reality junk, infantile daytime quiz programmes (not *Countdown*, though) and insulting Channel 4 dramas about sleazy working-class layabouts.

She particularly resented these. She came from a respectable working-class family who believed in education and good manners. Even those who always watched *Coronation Street* seemed to have forgotten that being working class didn't mean having an innate inability to read a book or have a conversation without shouting. The idea of an ordinary working person on the television having any spiritual life was now incomprehensible, unless they were a bigoted nutcase or a Bible-quoting serial killer. Why did the lives of people on TV have to be so *thin*?

The truth was, the awfulness of the gogglebox was not

Forgive Them, They Know Not What They Do

the cause of her unease. The conversation with the former pupil had stirred up memories she had by no means forgotten, however deeply they had been buried. Whatever the doubts and irritations about her faith that had afflicted her over the years, she remained a devout Catholic, deeply proud of the fact that her family, stretching back to before the Reformation, were believers (her wealthy son had spent £11,000 having a genealogist trace the family back to a ploughman living in Hungate in 1384).

But the beating that Sister Mary Frances had handed out to the fat little boy with the untidy workbook – she remembered that all right. True, she hadn't thought of it for a long time, but the memory triggered by her visitor came back too vividly, the way the smell of her granddaughter's lemon essential oil took her back, in an instant, seventy-five years, to her mother's kitchen, helping her dissolve the artificial lemon capsules for a lemon meringue pie.

She'd taken slaps and hits on the palms with a ruler from the nuns who taught her, but hadn't everyone? None of them was as vile as Mother Mary Frances but, even by her ferocious standards, the beating she handed out that day was horrible. Teresa knew she should have intervened. That old monster had punished children before in front of her, and she hated it: watching it, being made to be a part of it.

But to go against her was to invite yourself into the old nun's rage, and she had been too young and too inexperienced to stand up to it. No one had ever stood up to them in all her life. Not her mother or her father. The priest who was there, Father Lloyd, was nice enough, but he did nothing. So what was she to do, going against the word of God ... *thou art Peter and upon this rock I will build my church ... I give you the keys of the kingdom ... Whosoever you exclude on earth*

SCORN

will be excluded in Heaven ... he who rejects you rejects me ...

But it was also the woman herself who was paralysed by the nun's depthless rage at a harmless and forgettable little boy. Its pointlessness terrified Teresa, made her a child again and amazed her into the inert. She knew it had been a sin. The following day she confessed to her parish priest about her terrible sin of omission and was coldly warned about her pride in judging one whom God had called to holy orders. And so she had never been forgiven, because she could not bring herself to confess a second time and feel again the touch of priestly hostility, cold as space and as eternal.

And she wasn't forgiven now either.

Aaron Gall, all werewolf in his fur and teeth, stood silently behind her. As she went to switch off the television and pour herself a glass of wine, the werewolf reached quietly either side of her head with his enormous paws with their awkwardly prehensile thumbs, and twisted sharply with half the power in his arms. There was a sharp crack, but there must have been little pain, if any at all. Aaron understood that she was one of the injured, too.

Afterwards, Aaron Wolf went to the kitchen, found a multi-pack of crisps then returned to the front room and sat down in the comfortable chair. It wasn't really big enough for him. He tore open each crisp packet and poured the contents in one gulp down his throat. With greater difficulty, he also drank the fortunately already open bottle of wine.

Eating over the body was not lack of courtesy. The fact of the matter was that his huge body required vast amounts to keep it growing. He had decided that her death would be enough, that there would be no anthropophagous devouring of guts and brains. But he was unsure whether

Forgive Them, They Know Not What They Do

to leave his habitual clues. Each death brought the policemen closer, even if he had gone out of his way to be deeply obscure and, within limits, misleading. By simply leaving a clue, he would be tying her death to that of the priests and, given what she had in common with Lloyd, giving them a dangerously specific lead. As things stood, her murder, for so he accepted that it was, would be interpreted as exactly that. There would be no reason to connect her death to the others, and therefore he would give himself more space and time.

On the other hand, these deaths – *her* death – they were supposed to have a point. They had nothing to do with anything so banal, so inadequate, as revenge. So he ate more crisps and drank more wine and pondered.

'I, Anthony Blair, reared in the Protestant religion but now by the grace of God brought to the knowledge of the truth, sincerely and solemnly declare that I firmly believe and profess all that the holy Catholic, apostolic and Roman Church believes and teaches, and I reject and condemn whatever she rejects and condemns. I promise and swear true obedience in all that concerns the primacy and infallibility of the Roman Pontiff.'

Oath taken on Conversion to the Catholic faith

CHAPTER 27

THE BLAIR PROBLEM

It is easy to despise politicians, and, as a creature which loves what's easy as a bear loves buns, that's pretty much what you do. Is it wrong to be so ready to go with the flow of facile contempt? After all, just because something is easy to do doesn't make it wrong to do it.

Consider Anthony Charles Lynton Blair, former prime minister of the United Kingdom. Aaron had been watching a documentary about his life on the BBC and, as he talked in that odd, more-in-sorrow-than-in-anger voice of his about something or other, Aaron found that his feelings about the former prime minister were oddly complicated. Just like everyone else in the country, he felt a bemused loathing for a man he had once voted for and liked – admired, even. The answer to the question concerning that loathing usually involved something to do with his assertion about the presence of weapons of mass destruction in Iraq as a basis for the war – for *all* his wars, *Blair's* wars. He was loathed because he was a traitor to socialism. He was loathed because he was a warmongering, Bush-supporting cunt. Because he lied.

But Aaron knew that wasn't it, that there was something else about him. After all, his other wars were really rather good wars. It was Blair who put a stop to so much slaughter in the Balkans. It was because of Blair that men like Charles Taylor and Slobodan Milošović, men who'd brought hell itself to earth, were dragged from thrones built on the mutilated corpses of men and women and children and made to account for their malice. Surely not even the most pious socialist can really regret the snapping of Saddam's neck. And who brought peace, after all, to the festering swamps of hatred in Belfast?

In the first ten minutes of watching Mr Blair talking thoughtfully away, Aaron felt an unwelcome emotion: he began liking Tony all over again. There were flashbacks on the programme that made him laugh. Thanked for the present of a sweater by George W. Bush, the president joked that he knew Blair had picked it out himself. 'Picked it out?' said Blair, 'I *knitted* it.' Hard to dislike that kind of thing. The personality profile of delusional, narcissistic, American-lap-dog, warmongering cunts doesn't usually contain a self-deprecating sense of humour.

It wasn't much of a coincidence that Archbishop James Gillis, Head of the Catholic Church in England, was watching the same programme. Unlike the werewolf, his feelings about Tony Blair were not at all mixed.

On the television, an old-fashioned CRT the size of a small cathedral, Tony was being interrogated by Jeremy Paxman, an interviewer who these days alternated between two expressions: one as if he were going to explode with rage and the other as if he wished he were dead.

'Mr Blair,' he said, leaning forward, 'I'm not sneering when I say that I don't really understand why someone who supports gay marriage, who supports legislation on the rights of women to have access to abortion, who, as we know from your biography, practises contraception with an unspecified device and, as I understand it, believes that

The Blair Problem

women ought to be allowed to become priests — why — well, why have you decided to actually become a Catholic?'

Tony took in a deep breath and clasped his hands together — sorrowfully, thoughtfully.

'Hah!' exclaimed the archbishop, looking triumphantly from the TV to Father North. 'A bloody good question. Well done, Paxo.'

On the telly, after a few skilfully muttered phrases to give himself time (*You see, the thing is, Jeremy*), Tony started his reply, adding a few pauses and false starts to give the impression that his answer was spontaneous.

'I had been going to Mass for a long time ... It's difficult,' he said, still thoughtful, still sorrowful, 'to find the right words. I felt this was the right path for me. There was something not just about the doctrine of the Church, but of the universal nature of the Catholic Church, that ...' He smiled, giving up the possibility of explaining himself. 'As I said, it felt right.'

The longing-for-death expression on Paxman's face began to shift towards irritation.

'Of course, Mr Blair, the nature of faith is inevitably difficult to explain, but I think it's plainly the case that the Catholic Church is not just a place where people go together to *feel* faithful.'

'Yes, Jeremy, yes!' said the archbishop.

Paxman began to show some enthusiasm for his task. 'The Catholic doctrine that you — I don't know if *dismiss* is the right word; it's more like *ignore* — is as fundamental to Catholicism as any notion of mystical faith of the kind you seem to be talking about. The pope has authority, the Church demands obedience to that authority, and that authority is unequivocal. You can't just ignore this as if it were optional, can you? The new pope has made it perfectly clear, for example, that it is the gravest of sins to even *argue* for the ordination of women. You are, aren't you, obviously and straightforwardly in direct opposition to every one of its central tenets, with the exception of your having a belief in God. So, I ask you again, Mr Blair, what possible explanation can there be for you deciding to join a religion, all of whose beliefs you reject?'

A slightly impatient but forgiving smile from Tony. 'Not all.'

'Not all, but *most*.' The spectrum of Jeremy's exasperation was beginning to show red. The archbishop's delight increased.

'Yes, Jeremy, yes! We have a word for people like that in the Catholic Church – we call them *Protestants!*' he shouted.

Just as a skinhead is always prepared with a shiv, a sharpened comb and a Stanley knife, Tony pulled together his collection of tics and grimaces. The first, along with the carefully controlled but faintly impatient exhalation of breath, was a slight rolling of the eyes (*I am obviously trying to be clear on this and yet you wilfully misunderstand*). Then there was the slight rise of the eyebrow and the regretful smile with a little moue of *Forgive them, they know not what they do.* Finally, the sacrificial smile of saintly duty: the cross of being right must be taken up (*Let this cup pass from me*) and borne to the place of sacrifice.

'Ever since I began preparations to become a Catholic, Jeremy, I truly felt – and you may not *choose* to believe this – I felt I was coming home. This is now where my heart is, where I know I belong.'

'Well,' said Paxman, pausing to reload. 'I can see, because you keep repeating that it *feels* like you're part of

The Blair Problem

the Church, but I don't understand how you're part of it in the light of the fundamental difference between you and the authority of the Church you claim is your home.' A glint of malice came into the interviewer's eyes. 'A *home* apparently so important to you that, in your recent autobiography, the word "Church" appears in the index once, under the name "Church, Charlotte, popular singer".'

Tony's smile said this was a joke he was blokeish enough to accept, but also suggested it was somehow a cheap shot to which he had magnanimously turned the other cheek.

'Yes, but Jeremy' – not so much sorrow now but gentle firmness: *I've laughed at a joke at my expense, but now we must be serious* – 'I truly believe that the Catholic Church is a huge force for good in the world and that the pope stands for many fantastic things. And, of course, I understand why some are fearful of conceding change because, perfectly reasonably, they are concerned that to concede *some* ground will lead to conceding everything. I understand that concern, but actually, we need an attitude of mind where rethinking and the concept of evolving attitudes becomes part of the discipline with which you approach your religious faith.'

'Discipline!' shouted the archbishop. 'Discipline! You sack of shite!' He turned to the astonished Father North. 'Forgive me, Father.' Then he went back to shouting at the television.

'So, Mr Tony bloody Blair, you talk about discipline as if you're going to correct popes, whose wisdom and erudition as theologians makes your vapid posturing look like the camel manure they are. By God, I can't believe it. The pope who's done all those *fantastic things* has made it clear in the line of two thousand years of Catholic thinking by those in the office directly descended from Jesus Christ that homosexual acts are an intrinsic moral evil and that even the inclination to homosexuality is an objective disorder against natural law. And now you, Tony Blair, are going to put him and the apostles right? My God, I long, I *long* for the days when I could have set fire to you a dozen times for your blasphemy.'

The archbishop stood up, unable to contain himself and fearful for what he might let slip in front of Father North, and almost ran towards the door. But he turned back and left a parting gibe for the television: 'And there wouldn't have been a merciful garrotting before any of them!'

Lister and Scrope were sitting in their preferred car park next to the A40. Unusually, the interior lights were on, because Scrope was reading a thick report on the cause of death of Father Thomas Lloyd. Lister was staring vacantly out over the car park. Even when Scrope uttered a loud bark of amusement, he didn't seem to notice.

'Listen to this,' said Scrope.

'I'm thinking,' said Lister.

'No, really, listen. What makes you think that Dr Shah employs a typist to transcribe his autopsy reports from tape recordings who isn't really as engaged with her job as she might be?'

'I'm still thinking,' said Lister. Scrope ignored him and started reading aloud.

'"There is massive trauma to the abdomen and upper extremities, with multiple tearing wounds consistent with the bite wounds of a large predatory mammal. There are three separate bites to the rib cage, left of the median. How about a cup of tea, then?"'

The Blair Problem

This had the desired effect: Lister started giggling, which provoked Scrope to do likewise. This went on for some time. Eventually, they both settled down. Then Lister started again, and it was several minutes before they regained their composure. Neither of them said anything for a while, but whatever thoughts had absorbed Lister had now dispersed.

'Did you see Tony Blair on the telly yesterday?'

'Yeah,' said Scrope. 'The last fifteen minutes, anyway.'

'He's a strange man.'

'Really?' said Scrope. 'He seemed all right, I thought.' A pause. 'Basically.'

Lister looked at him. 'What?' said Scrope.

'Your tone.'

'What about it?'

'You're not talking about the *Newsnight* programme, are you?'

'No.'

'You've met him.'

'Several times.'

'Why didn't you mention it?'

'I don't have to tell you everything. You're not my fucking wife.'

'Actually, I'm sort of like your wife. So why?'

'Why what?'

'Why not tell me?'

'I don't know. I just didn't. I don't like name-dropping, all right?'

'So, what was he like?'

'All right. He was a bit leery – Alice told him I'd been in Iraq and Afghanistan.'

'Who's Alice?'

SCORN

'My sister-in-law. She knows Cherie.'

'Oh, that Alice. *Fucking hell!*'

The cry was so loud that a startled Scrope looked around to see if they were being attacked.

'What?'

Lister was excited but alarmed.

'Last night, you know, on *Newsnight*, the Tony Blair thing, in the lead-up to the interview, they did a bio.'

'And?'

'Just a minute.' Lister took out his phone.

'You're a fucking slave to that thing,' said Scrope. 'You're always at it – tap, tap, tap, like a demented woodpecker.' Lister was not paying attention.

'Let's try this again,' he said, at last. 'The clue. "Eat coyote poop!"'

He turned to Scrope. 'All right, a coyote is a kind of wolf.'

'Too easy. A red herring.'

They both giggled at this.

'Could be a mind fuck. Probably … given that brain banging is his style.'

'Well, I've always admired your talent with the obvious – ogle the web.'

'Fuck you, motherfucker.' Nevertheless, Lister thumbed away on his phone. They spent twenty minutes going back and forth, discovering the surprisingly rich complexities of coyote coprophagy, furry scat, bony scat, territory marker scat (twisted and spiral). The dangers of heartworm to dogs from eating coyote shit. They moved on. Peter Coyote. Again nothing. They discovered an inexplicably large number of golf clubs with coyote in the name. Anagrams: toe coy; coo yet; oocyte (a female gametocyte that develops into an ovum after two meiotic divisions). No joy. A kind

The Blair Problem

of immigrant smuggler. A kind of firefighter. Another irritating half an hour. They gave up and moved to 'poop' on its own. Poop deck (ten minutes). Poop – a constellation in the southern sky (five). Then they just gave up. Giving up was part of the process. They discussed an assortment of trivial things. Their current favourite joke (Question: What's brown and sticky? Answer: A stick). This was also part of the process. Then back to 'coyote'. Ten minutes, no joy. Lister stopped thinking and let his thoughts wander. Fortunately, also his eyes. On the list of alternatives – very tiny – at the bottom of the search list he saw: Coyote Ugly. It was a famous New York bar and a not very good film.

He took 'ugly' over to the clue and moved it around. Ugly poop.

An electric signal moved down his spine. Ugly poop. Ugly poop.

Eat ugly poop.

'What's the poop?'

Scrope looked at him. A beat.

'Rumour. "Poop" is another term for "rumour".'

'In the bio that started *Newsnight,* they mocked Tony Blair because he belonged to a terrible pop group called ...' He opened the palm of his right hand to Scrope so that he could finish. Scrope groaned.

'Ugly Rumours.'

'"Eat coyote poop" means "eat ugly rumours".'

'Fuck! He's going to eat Tony Blair.'

'I vow to change nothing of the received Tradition, or to permit any innovation therein ... Accordingly, without exclusion, we subject to severest excommunication anyone — be it ourselves or be it another — who would dare to undertake anything new in contradiction to this constituted evangelic Tradition and the purity of the Orthodox Faith and the Christian Religion, or would seek to change anything by his opposing efforts, or would agree with those who undertake such a blasphemous venture.'

Papal oath

'Actually, we need an attitude of mind where rethinking and the concept of evolving attitudes becomes part of the discipline with which you approach your religious faith.'

Tony Blair, 2009

CHAPTER 28

THE HOLY FOOL

Upstairs, in Tony Blair's tastefully decorated bedroom – Farrow and Ball, Staffan Tollgard – the great man was sitting on an elegant and very expensive Møbler Papa Bear chair, while across from him on the bed, the werewolf Gall studied him carefully with a sort of bemused ferocity. The werewolf had been in the bedroom for nearly ten minutes and had found the conversation unexpectedly fascinating.

The former prime minister of the United Kingdom had emerged from his en suite bathroom (Marks and Spencer pyjamas and a La Myse dressing gown, courtesy of the Burj Al Arab hotel in Dubai) to discover an eight-foot werewolf waiting for him. All things considered, Aaron had to concede, he took it rather well. He didn't scream or urinate on the carpet (Blenheim's Wilton, Cayman Islands edition, £250 a square metre).

Blair stood there, still as a stump.

'What are you?' he said at last, his voice barely a whisper.

'Funnily enough,' said the werewolf, 'I was going to ask you the same question.' He growled, a light-hearted rumble. 'Later, perhaps.'

On hearing a werewolf actually speak, Blair's face, already white, drained to a shade rarely seen in the natural world.

'Can I sit down?'

'Your house,' said the werewolf. 'Do what you like.' He smiled, not an easy thing for a werewolf to do or for an observer to interpret. 'As long as you don't call out or try to leave.'

Blair, keeping his eyes on Gall, moved to the wing-backed chair and sat down rather heavily, as if his nerve had suddenly given way. 'We're not going to be interrupted, are we? The consequences could be unfortunate.'

Blair shook his head.

'Cherie is in Edinburgh presenting the Woman Lawyer of the Year Award.'

'I don't care,' said the werewolf, immediately rather regretting his rudeness. 'My apologies, Mr Blair. I'm rather tense. Though not as tense as you, I imagine.'

'Perhaps you can explain what the problem is and we can go from there.'

'I wouldn't try to manage the situation, Mr Blair. It won't do you any good and it will only get on my nerves. I have questions.'

'And what if I don't have answers?'

'Not a tactic I'd pursue.' The werewolf cleared his throat. 'I want you to answer the following questions to the best of your ability.'

'If I can.'

'You're doing it again.'

A pause. Blair said nothing for a moment.

'Is this about Iraq? Because, you know, I think we need to move on and concentrate on Syria. Isn't that what you should be concerned about?'

The werewolf shook his muzzle. 'You just can't help yourself, can you? I don't give a fuck about Iraq and I don't

The Holy Fool

give a fuck about Syria either. I've come here to ask you some questions from the catechism.'

'What?'

'The catechism is a text which contains the fundamental Christian truths formulated in a way that makes Catholic doctrine easier to understand. I quote, of course, though, strictly speaking, it doesn't say "easier to understand", it says "following their understanding". Not really a good example – of clarity, I mean.'

'I meant I don't understand what you want,' said Tony Blair. 'I know what the catechism is.'

The wolf tried to purse his lips to make a mocking sound, but this is almost impossible for someone with a muzzle.

'You may know what it is, the catechism, but I'm terribly curious to discover if you know what's in it. But then – what am I saying? – you must – because you joined the faith as an adult, a decision that must have emerged from many years of deep thought and consideration.' The werewolf smiled, though an inexperienced observer might not have thought so. 'Why *did* you, by the way, join the Catholic Church?'

Tony Blair looked at him, his eyes full, as was only to be expected, thought the wolf, of strategy and calculation. He sighed and cast his eyes down a little, as if in a mixture of reluctance and embarrassment to speak of such private and difficult matters to a hostile stranger.

'I had been going to Mass for a long time. As time went on ... It's difficult to find the right words. I felt this was right for me.' He looked away, down and back again, and shrugged almost imperceptibly, as if revealing a depth of emotion he was struggling to keep hidden. 'The truth is, there was something ... *something* about the doctrine of the Church, of the universal nature of the Catholic Church.'

'Ah,' said the werewolf, 'most interesting.'

An acute observer might have detected a brief twinkle of something from Tony Blair, as hard to fix for certain as the buried gleam of the fin of a golden carp in an ornamental pond of unusual depth and murk. But perhaps, thought werewolf Aaron, this was unfair. How could a politician be anything but tenebrous, and why shouldn't a man faced with an eight-foot werewolf calculate the effect of what he was saying?

The werewolf cocked his head to one side and considered Tony Blair carefully, a movement that had the effect of making Aaron, for the first time, appear almost benign, if someone with a head the size of a coal scuttle and teeth like splinters could look agreeable. He opened his mouth and a trilling sound emerged, one so expressive in dogs that people often believe their beloved pet is talking to them.

'Is that the ploy?' said the wolf. 'Simple sincerity and ever so slightly awkward candour?'

'You expect me to be at ease with you looking at me as if I were Little Red Riding Hood?'

'That seemed entirely sincere.' He paused – a wolfy smile. 'But not entirely wise, perhaps.' He cleared his throat. 'Or perhaps very wise. It gets exhausting being fair-minded. No wonder people don't care much for doing it.'

He coughed in doggy fashion, a harsh and barking sound, his throat not fettled for so much chat and natter. 'It's not easy,' he continued, 'being impartial. My new interior life is not in the way of being over-endowed with balance and fair-mindedness. Apologies for being sneery, and for the foul language.' Another hacking cough. 'Actually, while

The Holy Fool

I have you here, and there not being much chance of a return match, so to speak …'

Blair flinched at that.

'It wasn't strictly true, about the war, I mean. So, tell me – and you might as well be straight – as no one's going to be quoting me, why were you so bent on going into Iraq?'

Tony Blair leaned back. This, at least, was familiar ground. 'We could talk all night.'

'No, we couldn't.'

'Very well, you have the advantage over me.'

'I do.'

'I'll tell you what I've said to others who've asked the same question. I'd taken the view that, y'know, we really needed to remake the Middle East. And, in the end, you're going to have to go through, I'm afraid, this long and drawn-out and, yes, sometimes bloody period of transition.'

He looked at werewolf Aaron, simple, direct and honest. And, this time, his honesty, whatever the calculation also involved, was, thought the werewolf, not in doubt. Tony Blair could see that his honesty could itself be seen by the creature in front of him, and thought it best to press home his advantage. 'You see, the thing is that people are deeply critical of, and I understand their criticism, and that's genuine, but it is surely also the case …'

'You're doing it again,' interrupted the wolf.

'Doing what?'

'Managing the situation. Managing me. I said I was interested but I'm not that interested. We should get on with why I came here. I want to know what you understand about the One True Faith into which I was born and which you selected for yourself. You see, I look at you and the faith you've so carefully chosen, and I don't understand.'

'Just.' A pause. 'Don't.' Another pause and a cough. 'Understand.'

'The thing is—'

'Do you have lemons?' asked the wolf.

'Um ... I suppose. I'm sure we brought some back from Amalfi last week.'

'Ah,' said the werewolf enthusiastically, '*I limoni di Amalfi* – the *prince* of lemons.'

'Yes, they are rather—'

'Stop trying to distract me. I'm going to ask you those questions now,' interrupted the wolf. 'If I don't get the answers I like, then I'm going break your bone casings and suck out the marrow. Then I'll gobble your liver. And when I'm finished and you're still alive and bawling, I'm going to slurp down your testicles – and to do those slippery bollocks of yours justice, I'm going to squeeze those lemons all over them.'

Tony Blair stared at him, mouth open. His eyes moved quickly towards the door.

A pause and a wolfy chortle. 'You're thinking of making a run for it, aren't you? Go on, then.'

Tony Blair sat back.

'The catechism is a complete summary of what Catholics throughout the world believe and contains the infallible definitions of those beliefs set down by the popes and the magisterium of the bishops in a way that is both inviting and challenging.' The werewolf cleared his throat. 'I quote, of course.' Another wolfy attempt at a smile.

'But you know all this already, being a man of grasp and intelligence who took this decision as an adult, who chose the One True Faith and was not merely born into it. Let's start with an easy one. Explain the difference between

The Holy Fool

a venial sin and a mortal sin.' The wolf leaned forward and opened his eyes wide with malevolent expectation.

'The ... Well, I've never actually—'

A growl from the wolf warned him to get on with it.

'The ... ah ... venial sin is ... um ... a sin which is ... while important ... is venial, which is to say—' He swallowed hard.

'Not so important?' offered the werewolf helpfully. Tony Blair looked scared, he thought.

'A mortal sin,' continued Tony Blair, 'is a sin that, if not confessed and forgiven is ... very serious indeed.'

'Yes, that's right,' said the werewolf encouragingly. 'It is serious, but for a man of your intellectual grasp and as someone who *chose* the faith, may I ask you what would happen if, say, you committed a mortal sin and then I, for example, ate your heart?'

Tony Blair's eyes bulged a little.

'I'll have to hurry you.'

'One would go to hell!' blurted out Tony Blair.

'Yes. But why? What *is* a mortal sin, Mr Blair?'

Blair was too terrified, understandably, to speak.

Aaron sighed. 'Look, I realise this must be very stressful, and I want to be reasonable, so I'm going to give you this one. Let me tell you. It must be *serious*. You must know what you're committing is a serious sin and know it fully. You must have decided consciously to commit that sin. You understand?'

'Yes.'

'You agree?'

'Um ... I agree that it seems like a very clear account of the Church's position.'

'You joined a Church that doesn't have *positions*, Mr

Blair. It is the One True Faith, and any time the pope definitively decides a question of faith and morals, he acts infallibly and for the whole Church. The condemnation of worshipping false gods as a mortal sin deserving of eternal damnation is not a *position*. Your opinion is not invited. Have you worshipped false gods, Mr Blair?'

Tony Blair looked startled.

'No!'

'Have you committed adultery, Mr Blair?'

'Me? Absolutely not.'

'And do you accept without question that adultery is a mortal sin? A sin that, if unconfessed and unforgiven, guarantees your spiritual shipwreck and an eternity of damnation in hell? After all, you knowingly, willingly, joined a Church in which, when the pope teaches infallibly, all Christians are obliged to believe what he teaches.'

Tony Blair stared at the wolf.

'By the way, you do believe in hell, don't you, Mr Blair?'

'Um ... I'm not sure I believe in a fiery place where the damned burn and are tortured through all eternity – but in a not entirely clear way I ... Yes ... I suppose I do.'

'Now we're getting somewhere,' said the wolf with relish. 'And do you unwaveringly affirm Pope John Paul II's condemnation of abortion, that it always constitutes a grave moral disorder? It is a mortal sin and infallibly so, and you must have knowingly accepted that when you became a Catholic. Because, why else would you become one?'

'Well.'

Again, the werewolf noted Blair's anxious glances at the door, and a slow movement of his buttocks forward in his armchair. A long, low growl stopped him mid-glance and mid-shuffle.

The Holy Fool

'Look,' said Tony Blair reasonably, 'I don't know all the answers. Look, there are a great many good and ... and *great* things the Catholic Church does, and ... and there are many, many fantastic things this pope stands for.' He smiled as if uncertain, troubled and thoughtful. 'But, you know, I think what's very interesting is that, if you went into any Catholic church and you did a poll of the congregation, you'd be surprised at how liberal-minded people are.'

The werewolf looked uncertain, thoughtful himself, as if Tony Blair's words had magically had some effect.

'You really think so?' he said dubiously. But was there a persuaded hopefulness in the flint in his wolfy eyes and the jauntier angle of his enormous muzzle? 'You think they'd take a different position?'

Tony Blair, for the first time, felt the warp of the situation bend towards him. 'Yes, you know, I really think so. You have to, and people do over time, they really do rethink many things, many things. Now, my view,' he went on, easing back in his seat, 'my view is that rethinking is good. So,' he said, brightly, 'let's carry on rethinking.'

'You might be right, you know,' said the werewolf, still thoughtfully.

'Well, you know, I believe there's a growing appetite in the Church – the congregation, I mean – for a change in attitude, a belief in evolving attitudes, where changing your mind becomes part of the discipline with which you approach your religious faith.'

'So you think that, in time, the pope's infallible assertion about, say, abortion and homosexuality being both gravely disordered and an intrinsic moral evil, you think ...' Whatever a hopeful werewolf sounded like, Tony Blair sensed the buried optimism reaching out to him, as so many had reached out to him before. 'You think that the pope could see things in a more *nuanced* way?'

'In time, slowly. I don't know, is the honest answer. I don't know.'

'So you truly believe that the pope could really recant the Church's unyielding statement of the unchanging will of God that certain actions – abortion, which you've personally defended; homosexuality, which you've also defended; the ordination of women priests, which you've also defended ... You really believe that, one day, the Holy Father and magisterium will change their minds and state that no longer will abortion, homosexuality and the ordination of women priests be a deep and eternal offence to what it means to be truly, authentically human. That could happen?'

'In time, it's possible, but, after all, as my wife Cherie says, and she's a cradle Catholic: the Church doesn't belong to the priests and the bishops.' The werewolf nodded thoughtfully, hopefully. Tony Blair eased a little the tense muscles of the exquisite buttocks so famously eulogised by the former Mrs Murdoch.

Then a sound. The werewolf is alert in every cell, as only predator or prey can be. Tony Blair is merely puzzled at the very muffled crump. The wolf flicked his ears around, a lizard's tongue tasting the air for sound.

Could be a shot. Let's kill him as we must and get away, said the wolf.

But I have so much more to say and hear, said Aaron back. *It's almost certainly a firework going off half a mile away. Happens every night.*

'Almost certainly' will get us killed. Eat him now – and just a token chew, so we can be on our way.

No! It was just a firework. This is a chance I'll never get again.

The Holy Fool

Decision made, wolf and Aaron were together now as one.

'I'm amazed,' said the wolf. 'Truly amazed.'

'Well,' said Tony Blair, holding down a huge feeling of relief, 'I can't say any of these things for sure, but I believe it's possible. I mean, when I first tried to abolish Clause Four of the Labour Party's absolute unwavering support of the nationalisation of the means of production, people said I could never ...' He realised this sounded awkwardly vain. 'It could never be done.'

'To them, it was an infallible doctrine without which socialism could not *be* socialism.'

'Exactly so.'

The werewolf nodded thoughtfully, acceptingly. A silence; a connection formed between the two of them. This was a man, after all, who had learned to shake hands with the murderers of Sinn Fein and the mad bigots of Unionism, who had become liked and trusted by them, and liked them in return. After Martin McGuinness and the Reverend Ian Paisley, a werewolf was perhaps not such a stretch.

The werewolf stood. He seemed even taller than before. 'You can get up.'

Feeling that thirty years' experience had saved his skin, a little cautiously, Tony Blair got to his feet.

'You know, Mr Blair, I feel I've had to change my mind about you, even though your joining the Catholic Church was a blow in the face – a blow to me, to every child fucked and fondled, to every child frightened into accepting the absolute authority of the sick dreams of old men, to my mother, who had to wait two months for her parish priest to give her permission to have her diseased womb removed, to Galileo, to all the rest of the dead souls murdered by the One True Faith. But I can see that the Church is right to say that no man can sin who doesn't understand the nature of the sin he's committing. Even the pope says you have to understand. And you clearly understand absolutely nothing. So I'm going to explain it to you very simply, what the faith is. And we won't need catechisms – nothing ecumenical, no encyclicals. No, we need to start with the basics. With first principles.'

Then the werewolf fetched Tony Blair the most enormous blow to the side of the head, sending him staggering to the floor with a dreadful thump.

It's been said that, the moment after being struck, every man's face takes on the same expression: the face of Jesus just as he was nailed to the cross. Eyes wide, mouth gaping in pain and horror and fear, Tony Blair tried to stand up, his legs unable to support him. The werewolf nodded his head, appreciating the situation. 'You know what Mike Tyson said, Mr Blair? Everybody has a plan until they get punched in the mouth.'

The wolf leaned forward until his nose was almost touching Tony Blair's and he could feel his doggy warm and wet breath on his cheeks. A smile from the wolf and then, softly: '*Now*, you understand.'

The wolf stretched his long and hairy back, all the time keeping his eyes on Tony Blair. He winked at him. 'Can't believe it, can you?' He eased himself back on to the king-sized mattress by Savoir (Mongolian cashmere, horsetail from the Shetland Isles).

'See, the general view of you is that you're a self-serving, warmongering cunt. But, you know, I don't think that's it at all. Does it matter? Not sure. So I can either kill you

The Holy Fool

now, or you can give me an answer to a question that really puzzles me. And if you can do that, then I'll let you go.

'And it's this. Tony, I feel as if I'm standing in front of a sworn vegetarian, a prince among vegetarians, a fruitarian even. And what this person so deeply committed to not eating meat has done is joined the National Rifle Association and declared that he has finally come to his spiritual home. And this is the really interesting bit: he still deeply believes that meat is murder.

'So, the thing is, if you can explain within the next five minutes what the fuck is going on in your head, then I'm not going to kill you. I'm just going to give you a good kicking, like the one a priest gave my friend Pete for exploding a paper bag in the refectory.

'Tony, I'm going to count to three, and then you're going to start talking. And, in five minutes, you'll be alive or you'll be dead.'

'One.'

Tony Blair stared. Eye panic. Tongue dried.

'Two.'

Brain hammering. Thought terror.

'Three!'

CHAPTER 29

TO SERVE AND PROTECT

There has been considerable negative comment about the £250,000 annual cost to the taxpayer for protecting a former prime minister nobody likes anymore. But most, however reluctantly, concede that it's right that an elected servant of the state whose past service made him a likely target for assassination should have his life guarded at the expense of the public purse. The implications of not doing so are curious, certainly.

There were more pressing, but still complicated, questions for Scrope and Lister. How was Tony to be warned? A call to Adebayo received an astonished but also perplexed response. He asked the certainly redundant but understandably human question as to whether they were sure, and on being given a not entirely respectful reply promised to deal with the problem.

Scrope and Lister waited, excited and tense, but also curiously deflated: they were sitting in a car park of a Burger King next to the A40, while an unprecedented drama they'd unearthed was being played out somewhere else.

'Blair's probably not in London,' said Lister. 'Probably not in the UK.'

'What if he is?'

'What can we do about it?'

'We can go there.'

'You know where he lives?'

'Connaught Square. I've been there.' A pause, then awkwardly, 'Twice.'

The ride to the Blairs' London residence was a blast. They hit almost ninety miles an hour on dual carriageways over White City, horn blaring out a siren-like warning by means of a button in the dashboard they'd never had a remotely convincing reason to use before. Because Tony Blair probably wasn't at home and, in any case, his protection was someone else's responsibility, they felt that there was lots of excitement to be had but not much risk. The hit of adrenaline was the most intense either of them had experienced since one day in Basra, although that was an experience that went very far beyond anything they ever wanted to endure again.

Having turned off the siren as they approached the Blair residence, Scrope's BlackBerry went off – whimsically, the theme tune from *Hetty Wainthropp Investigates*. It was Adebayo, telling them the Anti-Terrorist Squad was on its way. Given that Blair was unlikely to be present, the chance of the killer being about to murder him at that precise moment seemed remote. With the ATS arriving imminently, both of them felt that the chances of being involved in anything dangerous were satisfactorily small. When they entered the square, their complacency took a knock: the Blair house was burning with lights.

'For crying out loud,' said Lister miserably.

'What?'

'Look at the skylight in the roof.' It was clearly open, not to be expected at nine o'clock on a bitterly cold night.

'Shit!' said Scrope, and accelerated to the front of the

house. They double parked and got out, Lister cursing everything from his own stupidity in taking so long to solve the clue to the freezing rain and the incompetence of the Anti-Terrorist Squad.

Scrope held up his warrant card to the CCTV, hoping not to have to ring the doorbell. No response.

'Fucking typical,' said Lister, as he pushed the bell. After ten seconds, there was a buzz from the speaker.

'Can I help you?'

'We're police,' said Scrope, holding up his warrant card again. 'There's a threat to Mr Blair's life. Let us in.'

'I'll have to come down.'

'Then get a fucking move on.' He took his hand off the intercom buzzer.

'Why didn't you tell him to check that Blair is OK?'

'Because you only end up doing duty on celebs if the wheel's fallen off your career once too often. Six months ago, one of Blair's jokers left his Glock in the bog of Starbucks on the Edgware Road. Now, we're involved – best to do it properly.'

'I really don't want to die protecting the life of Tony Blair.'

'You should've thought of that before you opened your big gob in the car park, then, shouldn't you?'

The door opened slightly and a woman in uniform peeked out at them.

'Warrant card.'

Scrope raised it to the door.

'And the other one.'

'Fuck me!' said an exasperated Lister. He had to search three of his pockets to find it. Satisfied, she opened the door. Behind her was another uniformed officer, with his semi-automatic drawn.

'So what's going on?'

'There's a skylight open on the roof. Is that normal?'

'No,' said the woman, alarmed.

'We think there might be someone in the house intending to kill Mr Blair.'

At this, the officer with the gun started back and looked upstairs. As he did so, his gun went off and a bullet cracked into the wall about an inch from Lister's ear.

There was an appalled silence. Scrope was the first to speak. Lister looked like he might never talk again.

'I'm arresting you,' said Scrope, 'for negligent discharge of a loaded weapon. You do not have to say anything, but it may harm your defence if you do not mention, when questioned, something which you later rely on in court. Anything you do say may be given in evidence. Put on the safety and give me the weapon.'

Mouth open, the policeman did not respond except to look at Scrope. The slightly flickering corners of his mouth rehearsed disgrace, dismissal, the death of future hopes and the death, also, of any respect.

'Shouldn't we leave this till later?' said the policewoman.

'No. Give me the weapon.'

Lister reached over and took it. The policeman, still in shock, let it go easily.

'You stay here,' Scrope said to the disarmed cop. He turned to the woman. 'Where's Blair?'

'In his bedroom, I think. On the top floor.'

'Can you find out for sure?'

'No. We'll have to go room by room up the stairs.'

'I think you should hand over your weapon to me. That would be best.'

'No.'

'Have you ever shot anyone with that thing?' said Lister.
A hesitation.
'No.'
'Well, I'm very anxious not to be your first. I think you should do as Scrope asks. He knows what he's doing.'
'I'm fully trained in—'
'OK. We don't have time for this. Take us up.'

CHAPTER 30

DON'T DO ANYTHING FOOLISH

'Tony, I'm going to count to three, and then you're going to start talking. And, in five minutes, you'll be alive or you'll be dead.'

'One.'

Tony Blair stared. Eye panic. Tongue dried.

'Two.'

Brain hammering. Thought terror.

'Three!'

The door burst open and Lister, Glock handy, ran into the bedroom.

'Drop your ... Fuck me!'

Lister had seen a fair few hideous sights in his time, so the sight of one of the most famous politicians in the world lying terrified on the carpet, one side of his face a bright scarlet red, would have been nothing. But a wolf the size of one gorilla standing on the shoulders of another, howling at him in astonishment and fury, was too much unreality to accept.

In the moment, as Lister froze, the werewolf reached across and grabbed Tony Blair as if he were the weight of a ballerina who'd been dieting for a month on a homeopathic soup made from the shadow of a pigeon that died of starvation. With all his strength, the werewolf hurled Tony Blair at Lister and sent both of them haxdy-daxdy into the corridor, throwing the bodyguard to one side as she fired twice – TKCHEU! TKCHEU!

'Fuck!' howled the wolf in agony as he slammed the door shut and turned the key. 'Fuck! Fuck! Fuck!' Then he took three great steps into the middle of the room, leapt up to the skylight fifteen feet above, pulled himself through, and was out on to the roof and gone.

CHAPTER 31

UGLY RUMOURS

There is no adjective in the English language with a sufficient resonance of stillness to do justice to the silence that followed.

Scrope reacted first. 'Don't say anything to anyone about anything until we've talked together privately. Is everyone clear?' The guard and a still whey-faced Blair nodded. 'The AT Squad will be here soon. I'll stall them for a bit, and you can get yourselves together. But say nothing.'

Ten seconds later, Scrope was on the landing outside, holding ajar the fire door that led to the Blairs' upstairs rooms. After two minutes, he saw a balaclava-covered head dart around the corner of the floor below.

'This is Detective Inspector George Scrope. Who's down there?' he shouted.

There was a brief pause and then a reply.

'Who's up there shouting out who's down there?'

Another brief pause and a smile from Scrope.

'Is that you, Capek?'

'My God, it *is* Lord Snooty,' shouted up a delighted voice. 'Is the faithful Butthead up there with you? Hang on, I'm coming up.'

'No, you aren't.' The change in tone was striking. 'Look, sorry, Bob, but I can't have anyone trampling over the scene. It's got to be clean, all right?'

'What the fuck are you talking about, Scrope? I need to check the target's OK. That's the job.'

Capek was absolutely right. But the longer Lister had to calm down Blair and the guard, the better. Besides, this was turning out to be fun, even with his brain turning cartwheels over what he'd just witnessed. It turned out that seven years' experience of fearing hideous dismemberment and death allowed him, just about, to cope with seeing a giant talking dog about to eat a former prime minister.

'You should have thought of that, Bob, before you turned up ten minutes too late.'

Another pause.

'OK, but it's not our fault. The fuckers told us to go to Connaught *Street*. Just let me up and I'll sign it off, and we'll be gone.'

A man in his mid-thirties, dressed in black with hair closely cut, cautiously emerged at the foot of the stairs.

'I wouldn't want to have to blow your head off, Bob, but another step and I'll take my chances. Still, I'm sure they'll give you a nice send-off. You know, a big wreath and a well-thumbed copy of *Readers' Wives* in the coffin so you'll have something to keep you busy in the afterlife.'

'Don't be such an unreasonable cunt, Scrope.'

'Can't help you, Bob. You have to stay there.'

'Why are you being such a wanker?'

'If you were in my position, I promise you, you'd do exactly the same.'

'Is he alive?'

'Blair? Yeah. A bit wan.'

'Let me come up and check.'

'What is it about "fuck off" that you don't understand?

Ugly Rumours

You arrived after the incident closure, so it's got fuck all to do with you.'

'What are you talking about? What incident closure?'

'You need to spend more time reading the law and less watching internet pornography, mate: arrive after the incident is over, and you've no jurisdiction. You should know that. But I'll cut you some slack and won't put it in my report.'

'You're making it up.'

'How the fuck would you know one way or the other? You're not coming up here, and that's all there is to it.'

'So, you're seriously telling me, if I come in, you're going to shoot me?'

'National security, mate.'

'You wouldn't.'

'Come up and try me, then.'

The bluff could only last so long. Capek stepped out into the corridor and said amiably, 'Put the fucker down, Scrope.'

Scrope did as he was told and, smiling, showed that his hands were empty. Then he walked back into the bedroom and spoke to Tony Blair.

'You've probably heard this already, and I don't have time to be delicate: say absolutely nothing of any kind in any way whatsoever about what happened until we debrief you. Clear?'

Once it was clear to Capek that Blair was safe, to Scrope's relief, he quickly went back downstairs to organise a search of the building and the grounds, and to brief the police who arrived just after them to search the wider area.

An hour later, in the enormous hall of the Connaught Square house, Capek had just finished standing his men down when he was approached by the bodyguard who had nearly blown off Lister's head. He was desperately trying to find out more about the man he'd almost killed, and his boss. Maybe the arrest was a bluff. Maybe he was going to be fired for gross misconduct. He started on Capek with a few pleasantries, then got to the point.

'Chief, what's he like?'

'Scrope?' said Capek, both thoughtfully and cheerfully. 'He's a cunt.'

'And the one with him – his sergeant. What about him?'

'Lister? He's a cunt as well.'

There didn't seem to be too much malice attached to this judgement.

'What sort?'

Capek considered for a moment.

'Not bad, for cunts. Posh boys, but good at their job, I suppose.' By now, he realised that the bodyguard was more than just curious, he was clearly a bit desperate. For a soldier like Capek, this was irresistible. 'I mean, they're all right in a fucked-up kind of way.'

'What do you mean?' This didn't sound good. Capek put his finger to his nose, hamming it up.

'In Iraq, no one called them Scrope and Lister. They called them the Butchers of Basra.'

CHAPTER 32

THE BUTCHERS OF BASRA

'Sit down.' It was friendly enough, but there was a louche unease about both Scrope and Lister as they did as they were told. 'How are you?' asked Colonel Browning.

'Fine,' said Scrope.

'Does that mean we can go now?' asked Lister. He was ignored.

'I want the two of you' – he looked as if he were deliberating on what was the right word – 'to accompany a delivery.'

'What sort of delivery?'

'A cash delivery.'

'No, thanks,' said Scrope. 'Besides, it's against British law to pay bribes.'

'Perfectly true. But it's not against the law to deliver them,' said Browning. A silence. 'You're quite sure you won't go?'

'Very quite sure.'

Browning seemed to think this reply was not very significant.

'You need to go out with a column to drop off the money over here.' He stood up and pointed to a map of Basra city. 'There's not much action here, and we've chosen a route which should be pretty quiet.' He looked at both of them. 'OK?'

'Is that an order?' said Scrope.

'Does it have to be?'

'If it's not an order, we don't want to go. It looks dangerous.'

'Wasn't that why you joined up?'

'I joined up,' said Lister, 'because I wanted to learn a reliable trade.'

Browning smiled and sat down.

'This is off the books, understand?' he said.

'Does that mean we get paid in cash?' asked Lister.

'And I very much want you two keeping an eye on the package, so to speak, because a previous package went missing. I'd like to remind you at this time that the review over that fucking fiasco at the Al-Kabir mosque comes up in two weeks.'

'That wasn't our fault.'

'*I* believe you, but will the review board? If it wasn't your fault – and I know it wasn't – but if it wasn't your fault, then it has to be somebody else's fault, someone higher up than you and therefore more important. I think it's unreasonable to ask me to stick my neck out for you if you won't do the same for me.'

A soft sigh from Lister, silence from Scrope.

'I told you – it's on reasonably peaceful roads to a pretty stable part of the city. It's not about defending anything, it's just that I want someone there so they know I'm watching and they keep their fucking hands off.'

'*They* being?' said Scrope.

'You know ... *them*.' Browning smiled. 'The Iraqis are going to be in a much better mood to drop their boycott on working with us if this goes through, so there are British lives at stake. The Yanks are pretty frustrated with our lack

The Butchers Of Basra

of progress in Basra. Fucked off, in fact. And who can blame them? This will help to get them back onside.'

At five fifteen the following morning, Scrope and Lister watched as Browning squabbled with a very young lieutenant who'd been dropped in with the dozen British squaddies at the last moment.

'My lads haven't been trained on ACAVs,' he said, pointing at the huge armoured personnel carrier and the pair of amiable-looking Americans crewing it.

'I don't fucking care,' said Browning. 'They know how to open a fucking door, and that's all the fucking training they need.'

'I can't agree, sir. The men are used to Land Rovers and I—'

'Which are fucking useless if an IED goes off. The Yanks have loaned us an ACAV, and that's what we're using.' He looked at his watch. 'Sunrise is at 5.41, so get a fucking move on.'

The watching squaddies, enjoying seeing the lieutenant scraped, got on with loading the heavily armoured carrier.

The thirty-odd Iraqis that made up the bulk of their column were travelling in six Humvees they'd further strengthened by getting local metalworkers to weld on bits of armour from an assortment of IED-destroyed allied tanks. The result was Mad Max ugly but reassuring – they had a reputation for being much less easy to penetrate than the standard version. The Iraqis themselves were too young-looking for Lister's taste. Still, they could have been fighting since they were fourteen. Then the package they were to deliver turned up: it was a clapped-out Fiat Ducato, looking like a delivery van for a waste-disposal firm on its last legs.

'Don't look at me,' said Browning. 'That's how it turned up last night. Fair enough, really. Inconspicuous.'

'Not in a column of seven armoured vehicles. For all the protection they'll get in that thing, they'd be better off on a bicycle.'

'Look, they insisted. Anyway, you're in the ACAV, so what's it to you?'

Scrope walked around to the back of the van.

'What's this on the door?' he shouted. Both men came round to have a look. 'The rear door – it's welded shut.'

'I told you, someone fucked off with the last package. They sealed it up before it got here. Their drivers. Not my problem zone.' He looked at his watch again. 'Sun'll be up in a bit. Better fuck off.'

The borrowed American transporter was already carrying one more soldier than it was designed for, but they just managed to squeeze Lister in. Scrope didn't mind swapping the entirely enclosed safety of the ACAV for a seat in the front of the Iraqi Humvee. He liked to see where he was going, and the local smiths had a good reputation for their modifications to the armour. He felt better where he was.

As the journey went on, he became more uneasy. The young Iraqi captain in the Humvee spoke good English and there wasn't any need for Scrope to speak Arabic, which he did, adequately. It became clear after a quarter of an hour that the Iraqis not only looked inexperienced, they were. Given what they were up to, it felt dangerously odd that what had them most excited was that one of them had got hold of a copy of *Pirates of the Caribbean* on DVD and was going to show it to everyone on his prized possession – a sixty-inch flat screen he'd liberated from Saddam's palace overlooking the Shatt al-Arab river. But sending inexperienced troops into a dodgy area might be just what it usually was – a fuck-up common to all military organisations at all times.

Enclosed in the AVAC with the platoon of 1st Mercians, Lister was enjoying listening to the easy flow of men, most of whom had been together for years. One of the squaddies was cheerfully telling the others about a letter from his mum detailing the scandal involving a Member of Parliament who'd been caught sending photographs of his penis to a young local woman.

'It's fucking outrageous,' claimed the delighted soldier. 'Here I am, risking fucking life and limb for fucking queen and country, and he's living the good life in Barnsley, sending pictures of his cock to his constituents. It's just not right – that should be me.'

It also turned out that the uneasy-looking lieutenant wasn't the only newcomer. Attention turned towards a soldier who, while also looking about fourteen, had the manner about him of a Year Nine hard case. The other soldiers were keen to see whether it was a bluff or not.

'Hey, Booth.' The boy looked at him, unimpressed. 'If you catch the Big Red One today, is there anyone you want us to give a message to?'

The boy looked thoughtful for a moment. 'Yeah,' he said, 'tell your mother it was the best sex I ever had.' There was a brief, astonished silence and then a huge eruption of laughter and cat-calling at the soldier who'd tried to wind him up.

Once the glee died down, attention turned to Lister, someone the corporal clearly knew about. The corporal casually wondered if Lister knew a captain he'd been under

for a few months in Afghanistan who'd been at Sandhurst.
'Who says I was at Sandhurst?'
'Weren't you?' said the corporal slyly.
'OK, I was.'
'This captain. Guy Alexander. Ring any bells?'
'Yeah,' said Lister. 'I was with him at Sandhurst for six months.' He laughed, partly admiring, partly mocking. 'A right fucking weirdo.'

This was the source of much jeering delight. If it was a test, he'd passed.

'He fancied himself as a real badass,' said the corporal. 'His biggest regret was that he couldn't light up a tree line with napalm.' Lister laughed – *Apocalypse Now* had been the house film at Sandhurst.

'His only real ambition was to get Command to let him fire off a Javelin. At seventy thousand quid a throw, 'course they kept telling him to fuck off. So Colonel fucking Kilgore keeps at it, and Command keep telling him to go and fuck himself. Until, one day, we're taking so much damage from Talib mortars up in the hills he decides to fire one off. So we set it up and he calls Command and, to his surprise, they say he can fire, but it's his decision, subject to review.

'Well, that puts a crimp in his swagger. So after some faffing about waiting for another puff of smoke to confirm they're still there, he chickens out and tells the gunner Shaky Keane to stand down. So Shaky says, "I can't sir, it's armed. We either fire the fucker or throw it in the bin."

'To be fair, Alexander starts cackling away and tells him to fire – I mean, what the fuck else can he do? So it's mobiles out, and off it goes with a fucking great bang. Then it hangs in the air for a second, then the booster cuts in and then WHOOOOF – it seems like fucking ages, because you can see it heading for the hills and there's a big orange splat and it's about four seconds before the boom tumbles down the hill. And it's high fives from the ANA and dry sherries all round. Fucking brilliant!'

This was clearly one of the group's much-loved war stories and was received throughout by the squaddies like a bunch of jazz enthusiasts listening to a Miles Davis track, relishing all the tiny improvisations and minor improvements.

'Sarge,' said one of the squaddies, 'tell him your theory.' He turned towards Lister. 'Our company sergeant's got an A level in economics.'

The company sergeant smiled, awkward about his claim to academic fame in front of Lister. On the other hand, he was proud of his theory, whatever it was.

'Please,' said Lister, smiling.

'Well, it's just that it seems to me,' said the sergeant, 'that, every time we're about to let off a Javelin at £70,000 a throw, why don't we just offer them a Jag to fuck off back to Pakistan instead. Throw in a few thousand Minis and Vauxhall Vectras, and Helmand would be like fucking Knightsbridge.' Cheers and laughter. 'And, besides being cheaper, think what it would—'

WHOOMPH!

'Shit!' Scrope watched the ACAV being snatched upwards as if it had been grabbed by a child mistreating his toys. A second later, another explosion hit the Fiat, cutting it in half. The front of the van bounced onwards, tyres blazing, cabin scoured of men and seats. Scrope couldn't help noting the lone, undamaged air freshener with a blue tassel swinging back and forth from the rear-view mirror.

Then the clattering rain of pebbles and sand obscured

his line of sight. The Humvee stopped, brakes squealing. Scrope was out. After a brief silence, he could hear a woman scream. Then it was the Iraqis shouting and dispersing all around him as he headed past the smoking two-thirds of the Fiat and to Lister's AVAC. Then the shooting – God knows whose – near and far. Crack! Crack! Crack! Crack! Crack! Crack! Crack! Crack! Crackle! Crackle! Crackle! Crackle! Crackle! CHUNG! Pop! Pop! BANG! An RPG exploded in the road about twenty yards away. 'Fuck!' Dropping down, he moved through the dust and smoke. As he came to the AVAC, the twin back doors burst open and the squaddies started falling out, coals from a sack, weapons up and dispensing. Then Lister emerged and tripped, to be caught by Scrope.

'All right?'

'Can't hear you. Ears fucked! Their officer's unconscious – banged his head.'

CHACK! CHACK! CHACK! CHACK! CHUNG!

The Iraqis opened up with the .50-calibre. Ting-a-ling! Ting-a-ling! *Who the fuck is playing triangles?* thought Scrope.

'Now I can hear fucking bells,' shouted Lister.

'EYES ON! EYES ON!' shouted the corporal. 'OVER THERE! NO LEFT, FUCKING LEFT!'

Ticka ticka ticka. DWOK! Pling! BANG!

'FUCK, EYES ON!'

'MURDER HOLES! MURDER HOLES! FOOKIN' ELL!'

'OVER THERE. RIGHT. UP ONE FLOOR.'

Taka taka taka taka taka taka taka!

TING! TING! TING! Ting! Ting! Wok! Wok!

'SHIT!'

Lister and Scrope crouched behind the battered AVAC

The Butchers Of Basra

and looked around for something to shoot at. TICK! TICK! TICK! WOOMPH! As Scrope looked around, heart patter patter, someone in his head began to sing.

'And the auld triangle
FOOKIN' 'ELL!
Goes jingle jangle
Triangle
Jangle.'

Ting-a-ling! Ting-a-ling! Ting-a-ling!

'Fucking playtime,' he heard Lister shout. Sixty yards away, two heads emerged from a side street, gawping. Combatants or nosy fuckers? He fired twice at the wall behind them, and they vanished. Then three more out of a side street behind a pile of tractor tyres. Crack! Crack! Crack! Wok! Clatter! Clatter! Chang! Chang! Chang!

'Jingle jangle, the auld triangle.'

Scrope drew a line on the tyres. Just looking, just looking. *Jingle jangle of the auld triangle.* Poka! Poka! Poka! PING! Then he saw one of the men with a pipe or something. Tried and sentenced. He raced over to the Humvee with the .50-calibre machine gunner and pointed it at the tyres. Chack! Chack! Chack! Chack! Chack! Chack! Chack!

A fine mince of rubber burst upwards and then a slash of red against the dirty yellow wall. Ting-a-ling! Ting-a-ling!

Ah, thought Scrope, *not triangles ... bullets hitting the lamp posts.*

Scrope dropped down and ran towards Lister, then was violently jerked to a halt. Shot! Shot! Have I? But it was just the leg of his trousers snagged by a jagged piece of steel from the Fiat as he ran past the shattered delivery van.

'Fuck!' He reached down, saw he was cut by the metal

jag. 'FUCK!' He dropped his rifle as he tried to untangle himself. Kneeling down, he was suddenly aware of someone looking at him from a few feet away, behind a pile of rubble. He was an Iraqi but not a soldier. The man raised his rifle and Scrope thought, *Where did he get a .303?* The man hesitated as if unsure what to do next. The noises of battle went on, but someone had thrown a thick glass bowl over the two of them.

Then the man gasped as if deeply impatient and annoyed at his lack of action, bowed, as if suddenly overwhelmed by the need for forgiveness, going down until he looked like someone performing a particularly slovenly bow to Mecca. Then the back of his head not so much fell off as slipped down the side of his neck and on to the tarmac.

Ten yards away, Lister was kneeling, head tucked into the butt of his rifle. He did not look at Scrope but lowered the gun, looking oddly surprised. Then he turned around and started firing back across the street.

Lister stopped talking. Molly waited for him to finish, but he seemed to think he was done.

'Well, obviously, you got out alive. But why are you called the Butchers of Basra?'

Lister looked at the anxious young woman.

'Oh, right. Got lost in there somewhere. For the next thirty minutes, things were pretty bloody but, finally, a couple of Challengers arrived. That's a tank.'

'I know what a Challenger is.'

'They blew a few things up and then it just stopped.'

She stared at him.

'Once it was all clear, we tallied up and went over to the Fiat. The explosion had snapped the welds open on

The Butchers Of Basra

the back and one of the doors was off its hinges, and there was this incredibly intense smell of roasting meat. Anyway, a couple of Iraqis were told by their captain to open it up. Scrope and me were both thinking, *Time we weren't here*, but we didn't move. Once they'd grabbed the door, the whole thing basically fell off, and there it was – a dozen goat carcasses smoked and burnt.'

'That was the bribe?'

'Of course it wasn't.'

A pause.

'Sorry. The Iraqis Browning was working to keep happy claimed it was a screw-up. They claimed it was the wrong van. Some civvy welder sealed up the meat-delivery van meant for a temporary hospital on the old rifle range.'

'That's why you're the Butchers of Basra?'

Unfortunately for Molly, her relief was a little too obvious. Just as his reaction was a little too extreme.

'Sorry to disappoint you.'

'Meaning?'

'I take it back. There's nothing at all insulting about you thinking I was a war criminal.'

'I didn't think that.' This came out so forcefully, it would have been hard not to conclude this was exactly what she'd been thinking. A higher form of life than your muddy human being – a Catholic saint, perhaps, born out of heroic love and heroic joy – might have been detached enough to accept that the word 'butcher' in such a context might give even the most trusting girlfriend the shivers. But trust between lovers is a funny old thing.

'What was I supposed to think?' she said, crestfallen, appealing to his sense of fairness. 'Suddenly, the station is full of coppers going on about someone you and Scrope

SCORN

being called the Butchers of Basra.'

'You could have asked the question in a different way.'

'I don't understand.'

'As if,' said Lister, not as mildly as it sounded. 'As if you thought there might be a reasonable explanation. Of a kind, as it happened, that was actually the case.'

A pause, looking for a way out.

'All right. I'm sorry.'

'Apology accepted, and I don't mind at all that I had to beat it out of you.'

'Well, you always go on about what a tough guy you are.'

'What?'

'OK, that came out wrong. I just meant that you give the impression.' She hesitated – *Don't say the wrong thing.*

'The impression that?'

'Nothing bothers you. That it's all the same to you – everything. You just told me you were blown up and that you killed someone standing in front of you and you saved your friend – and all the time where this was heading was a stupid joke. You could have put my mind at rest in a few seconds.' The best form of defence is attack.

'It wasn't a joke, it's what happened. You asked me to explain, and I did. It wasn't funny, it was either a fuck-up that killed four people or we were screwed by the Iraqis as a ... Fuck, I can't think of the word ... A ...' He waved his right hand in exasperation.

'Ruse?' she offered.

'Diversion.'

Silence for a moment.

'The rumour was that, while we were slugging it out in Al Hadi, they were delivering the money in a taxi.'

'That's it? Another joke?'

The Butchers Of Basra

'What do you expect? Tears?'

'You were blown up and you killed someone – that hasn't affected you? You don't want to talk to me about that stuff?'

'That's what I did for a living. Kill people. It was something I volunteered for. That's what soldiers do. It bothers some, but not most, of us. I mean, you're a cop. Don't you mind getting other people into trouble? That's what you do – you destroy people's lives. I don't see you weeping about it. I killed a lot of people and I lost sleep over it. But not because I was sorry for them. It was because it was intense – utterly, totally, incredibly, amazingly fucking intense. So you can't sleep. And not intense good or intense bad, just intense like nothing you can imagine. Do I miss it? No. Do I regret it? No.'

But this wasn't entirely true. No bad dreams, or anything to speak of; no bad conscience, because what choice did he have? But it still came back to him from time to time: the terrible moment before he shot the man pointing his rifle at Scrope.

Poor old Molly. He was being unreasonable and unkind. But what he couldn't say to her is that the man he shot wasn't a man. He was probably no more than thirteen, and there was a good chance he was too scared to pull the trigger. But Lister couldn't take the risk.

So what was there to say?

CHAPTER 33

SECRETS AND LIES

'So, Scrope, what's your opinion?'

Dawe and Adebayo had arrived within a couple of minutes of each other and were standing in Blair's bedroom, clearly very unsettled, while the bloodstains guy was working on one of a trail of blood spots that now stained the carpet. One of the bodyguard's bullets hadn't missed, after all. Scrope looked at Dawe, apparently uncertain. 'About all this,' prompted Dawe, gesturing around the room. 'I mean, you saw this thing, whatever it was.'

'Yes.'

'And?'

'And I don't know.'

'It couldn't have been a disguise of some kind?' said Adebayo.

'A disguise? No.'

'It looked like a wolf, according to Mr Blair.'

'Wolves are quite small, no bigger than an Alsatian, apparently. This thing was about eight feet tall and it was standing on its hind legs. And it could talk.'

'You heard it?'

'I heard it swear when it was shot – and through the door. Mr Blair confirmed it could talk. If I'd only seen it myself, I'd be checking into the Priory or having myself sectioned, but all four of us saw it. And the only plausible connection between what happened here and the death of the priests is that they're all Catholics.'

'I thought you were, too. A Catholic, I mean,' said Adebayo. 'I thought that was why you were on the case.'

'Partly.'

'OK, partly.'

'You can't unjoin the Church, Chief Inspector. They regard you as theirs until after your last breath. I'm here because that thing wanted me to be.'

Dawe groaned in exasperation.

'How in God's name are we going to keep this out of the papers? Can you imagine – "Werewolf Eats Prime Minister".'

Scrope grinned politely.

'I wouldn't use the "W" word. Mr Blair can probably be relied on to add this to all the other unspeakable secrets he must be keeping locked deep in his soul. Can you keep the bodyguard quiet?'

'We'll take her in for a debrief and put the fear of God into her,' said Dawe. 'It's an official secret from now on. I'll sort it out. No one here says anything about this to anyone – not until I've had time to think up a lie that works.'

'What if the thing won't let us?' said Scrope.

'Meaning?'

'He's going somewhere with this, and he knows how to play us, and when. Presumably, he was going to kill Blair tonight.'

'But he gave you a clue.'

'It was only luck that Lister got it in time. OK, brains as well, but we weren't meant to solve it until it was done.

SCORN

If he'd eaten a former prime minister – that wasn't going to stay quiet. He's opening this out, and it's pretty obvious where it's going.'

'Just as a matter of curiosity, how did you get this number?'

Scrope's mobile woke him at six the following morning. It was the wolf.

'Oh, I'm a person of many talents.'

'I believe you.'

'I'm flattered.'

'But I'm not.'

'By me? I thought I'd made my admiration very clear.' The werewolf laughed. 'After all, you're my chosen one.'

'A bit insulting, I thought, giving me a clue and then banking that I'd solve it, but not in time to stop you.'

The werewolf sniffed.

'*Mea maxima culpa*. I'll strive to be less cocksure in future. Maybe that's how you'll catch me.'

'Your conceit?'

'That's an ungenerous way of putting it. But don't think of it as an insult to you, think of it as my nature. *For some men life loses its flavour when life itself cannot be risked.*'

'Not really a man, though, are you?'

'I suppose not. Anyway, I can't stop to chew the fat. I just wanted to reassure you that, while it stings a bit, the bullet more or less just broke the skin.'

'These clues are just camel—'

The phone disconnected.

'The belief in a worldwide conspiracy of Jews, Masons and Protestants was not one that Mussolini shared at the time [1925], but in the next years the Pope's Jesuit emissary Tacchi Venturi would employ all his powers to persuade him to see the world in these terms ... The dictator relied on the Pope to ensure Catholic support for his regime, providing much-needed moral legitimacy. The Pope counted on Mussolini to help him restore the Church's power in Italy ... Pius XI hailed Mussolini as a man sent by Providence.'

David Kertzer, The Pope and Mussolini, winner of the Pulitzer Prize, 2014

'Dachau Concentration Camp became the centre for imprisonment of clergymen who opposed the Nazi regime. Of a total of 2,720 clerics of various denominations recorded as imprisoned at Dachau, some 2,579 (or 94.88%) were Roman Catholics. Of those priests, 1,034 died in Dachau and 1,240 survived.'

Various sources

'When I took off Schwarzhuber's boots and his jacket to clean them in his office and he stood there in his vest, he looked like nothing. They were nobodies when they weren't in uniform. They were nothing, nothing!'

Hellmuth Szprycer, *Hitler's Holocaust*, PBS, 2000

CHAPTER 34

NOW HEAR THE WORD OF THE LORD

'The thing is, Your Grace,' said Superintendent Dawe, 'we're concerned that the person responsible for these murders might regard the state visit of the pope in August as an opportunity to pursue his grudge against the Church.'

Dawe was more intimidated by the sepulchral vastness of the room than he'd expected, and even more so by the impossibly dignified man in front of him, recently declared a cardinal by the new pope and dressed in keeping with such an honour. That he was robed so formally was not primarily from vanity – although there was a little of that, perhaps – but in order to intimidate, in particular, that fellow Scrope into treating the Church with more gravity. Hence the not strictly necessary formal simar, a cardinal's version of the cassock made from virgin lamb's wool and trimmed in scarlet silk, and with a mozzetta shoulder cape lined with watered purple noile. To finish, the pectoral cross suspended from a cord in co-ordinated green and gold, and his so recently bestowed cardinal ring, the size of a toy saucer.

He could have worn a zucchetto, a charmeuse skullcap shot with vermillion silk, but personally he found them rather affected.

While he was put out that Scrope seemed not even

to notice his habiliments, it was satisfyingly clear that his superior officer was properly impressed by being in the presence of one who, in all humility, had been gifted by God with an authority that led all the way back to Jesus and his apostles.

'So you're suggesting I should ask the Holy See to cancel what is only the second official visit by a pope in history? This is extremely serious, Inspector, I dare say, almost unthinkable.' He looked at Dawe somewhat suspiciously. Cardinal though he was, and, to be fair, a great critic in his day of the Irish Republican Army, he had an Irishman's innate suspicion of the motives of the English state.

'I appreciate that, Your Grace.'

'I wonder if you do. For the Holy Father to cancel a pilgrimage to the faithful, even under a significant threat – how do you think it would be taken by his detractors, of whom there are many? We are not afraid of sacrifice, Inspector.'

Dawe could endure one failure to accord him his true rank, but not two. '*Superintendent.*' The cardinal looked at Dawe with what Scrope later described to Lister as withering indifference, though, truthfully, his expression was something more impressively disdainful than mere human words could capture.

'I'd need to see all your evidence, and I mean *all* of it, before I could possibly consider even discussing it with the Holy Father.'

'I see.'

'Whether you see or not, *Superintendent*, that's my position.' The cardinal looked at him, daring him to argue.

'The problem is, Your Grace,' said Scrope, all soft and respectful, 'for reasons we can't go into, this is also a matter of *national* security. To go into the evidence would mean we would be liable for prosecution under the Official Secrets Act. We're trying to do the right thing by the Church and the Holy Father. What we all want is to keep him safe from a very serious threat.'

The cardinal turned his cardinal's gaze on Scrope.

'If you wish me to consider this, I must see the evidence. If you will not provide that evidence, and you think the threat is serious enough, then you must withdraw the invitation and do so publicly. There's always the danger that there's some mad person who will do something, but the Holy Father takes the view that to make an armed distance between the pope and the people is a greater madness. So it's up to you. One or the other.'

Driving back to Paddington with Lister, Scrope wondered if Cardinal Gillis was bluffing. It didn't seem plausible that he'd keep a warning like this to himself but, bluff or not, there wasn't much they could do. There wasn't anything you could call evidence that showed convincingly that the thing was intending to eat the pope. As to declaring that some sort of translupinised man-creature was at the heart of it – that was obviously a non-runner. Not even an organisation that officially believed in the devil as an actual living presence was going to swallow that one. Oddly enough. Indeed, Scrope had a hard time believing in it himself, and he'd seen it.

He and Lister kept asking themselves and each other in what way they could be mistaken. Even when they talked to the bodyguard, they started by asking her to tell them exactly what she'd seen, and then to tell them again, and then again after that.

Tony Blair seemed to have no trouble recounting his

experience in detail, although he took the point readily that he should say nothing about the events of that night. When they confirmed this with him, just to be on the safe side, he said, 'Alastair Campbell always used to warn me not to talk about religion – "We don't do God," he'd say.' He smiled. 'So I'm hardly going to mention I was attacked by a werewolf.'

He paused for a moment. 'After all, I've never said anything about the time I was kidnapped by aliens.' He said this with such a straight face that, for a moment, he caught them out. There was a silence, then they all laughed together, like the old public school boys they all were.

CHAPTER 35

SOUR GRAPES

BIRD THEFT FROM PRIVATE COLLECTION

'During Tuesday night a sparrowhawk was stolen from the aviary of a local collector in West Wycombe. Police were baffled that the bird stolen was not rare, while many valuable and exotic species were left untouched.'

Buckinghamshire Free Press

'It looks like Warren has killed someone else. Possibly.'

They'd decided to give the werewolf the first name of the singer who'd written 'Werewolves of London'. It seemed apt, though even this lackadaisical pair had debated whether this might be unseemly.

You don't think it's flippant?

Offhand glibness is part of our cultural identity.

'Possibly?' said Scrope.

'The MO is different. It's a woman. He snapped her neck but, afterwards, there's no damage to the body.'

'So why do you think it's Warren?'

'Because he left a clue on the wall.'

They hadn't released the evidence of the clues to the press and TV.

'A copycat? Someone blabbed and he found out about it.'

Lister shrugged. It was, of course, possible. 'She is a Catholic, though.'

'Where?'

'Oxford. Headington. The Oxford Stasi were just treating it as a run-of-the-mill murder except for the clue. Molly Coates picked it up.'

'She seems to have her wits about her.'

'Yes.'

'When did it happen?'

'The twelfth.'

'Before Blair. Got the clue?'

Lister handed him a piece of paper. Scrope thought about it for a couple of minutes.

'It's him.'

'Why?'

'The more clues someone sets, the more you get used to how their mind works. Hard to disguise, even if you want to. He doesn't want to. He wants us to find the bodies. We'd better go and have a look.'

An hour and a half later, they were standing in Teresa Tandsby's front room. It was entirely undisturbed, except for the writing on the wall.

'What was it done with?' asked Scrope. Lister riffled among a file. 'A red magic marker. Nothing unusual – get them in W. H. Smith's.'

They looked silently at the single clue written on the wall to the left of the window.

OPEN THOSE BUNS, BOYS, AND
FRISK THOSE SPHINCTERS

Sour Grapes

'What do you think?' said Scrope.

'Easier than usual. "Frisk" means "search". Buns is another name for a roll. So he wants us to search the toilet roll, probably.'

It took a great deal of unravelling, nearly half the roll, before they found the piece of paper with the real clue.

**BERKS! ON TRUMP'S BACKWARD EGO
NOTHING CAN LIVE**

'How did he get it in there?' said Scrope. 'I mean, without making it obvious it'd been tampered with?'

'I'll ask him right after he tells us how he turns himself into a werewolf.'

'You know what? You can be very undermining sometimes. I was making a point. He couldn't have done something so delicate with great big hairy paws. So I'd say that means he can change back and forth at will.'

'I stand corrected.'

Lister went back to examining the piece of rice paper hidden within the toilet roll.

'Why do I have this overwhelming feeling,' said Scrope, 'that Warren is pissing us about with all this crossword shit?'

'Why, then?'

'I don't fucking know.' He laughed but said nothing.

'What?'

'Perhaps it's just animal high spirits.'

Lister thought about this.

'I'm sorry I asked.'

They turned their attention back to the clue.

'Are we the berks or the people who voted for him?'

'Dunno. Try "backward".'

'Probably refers to "ego". Gives us "oge". "I" backward? Nothing springs to mind.'

'Look at the words that make sense backward: "on" gives us "no". "Live" gives us "evil".'

'Promising.'

'"No evil" – see no evil, hear no evil, speak no evil.'

'Even more promising.'

They spent five minutes going round the houses.

'We can eliminate "backward", possibly, as it's done its work. "Ego" probably means "I". That gives us … "Berks! No trump's I nothing can evil."'

'Trump's eye, perhaps. Trump refusing to see, hear, speak evil.'

'I wouldn't say he'd refused to speak evil, exactly.'

'Fuck, it's got nothing to do with Trump. It's an anagram of "triumps".'

'"Triumps" isn't a word.'

'Brilliant. Why don't you call the crossword police and we'll get them to add crimes against intellectual rigour to his charge sheet. OK, so we've got "Berks! No triump(h)s nothing can evil." Put it in ogle.'

Lister thumbed.

They looked at the result mournfully.

'We are very stupid and deserve to die.'

The Google result declared: 'The only thing necessary for the triumph of evil is for good men to do nothing. Edmund Burke.'

'I think of those in religious orders and some of the clergy in Dublin who have to face these facts from their past, which instinctively and quite naturally they'd rather not look at. That takes courage, and also we shouldn't forget that this account today will also overshadow all of the good that they also did.'

Catholic Archbishop of Westminster,
Vincent Nichols, 2009

'Any cleric who seduces young men or boys ... shall be publicly flogged and disgraced by spitting in his face, bound in iron chains, wasted by six months of close confinement ... and never again allowed to associate with young men.'

St Peter Damian, Letter 31:38 to Pope
Leo IX, AD 1049

'A nation that kills its own children has no future.'

Pope John Paul II, 1996

CHAPTER 36

I AM A SMOOTH MAN BUT MY BROTHER, HE IS A HAIRY MAN

'So, brother dear, how are you?'

Aaron shrugged, despite the fact that his brother was three thousand miles away in Chicago.

'Not too bad.'

'Meaning you *are* too bad but don't want to talk about it, or you are in fact mired in stodgy, lukewarm mediocrity?'

'Stodgy, lukewarm mediocrity sounds about right. And you?'

'Magnificent! I never cease to count my blessings.'

Aaron laughed. 'Delighted to hear it.'

They swapped the usual stuff – wife, ex-wife, children. But Aaron felt a surprising need to talk about events, even if in a roundabout way.

'The parish priest at St Edmund's died.'

'Where?'

'St Edmund's – the parish church to St Edmund's Primary.'

'Oh, right. So another bastard in black bites the dust. Why do you care? More to the point, dear brother, why should I?'

'He was murdered.'

I Am A Smooth Man But My Brother, He Is A Hairy Man

'Really?' Now he was interested.

'Horribly.'

'Even better.'

'Whoever killed him ate some of him: brains, liver, heart.'

Nat laughed.

'My God! Imagine all the toxic residues in a priest's kidneys and lungs. Yeeuuch!' A pause as they both laughed. 'Odd thing to do, though, eat a priest.'

'Very odd,' said Aaron, smiling. 'He also dug up the grave of Mother Mary Frances and threw her bones all over the cemetery.'

'OK. That is unusual. And some would say extreme. But then they didn't know the sadistic old bitch. Here's to him, the mad fucker.'

'Did she go for you at all?'

'Me? God, yes. Didn't you know?'

'Know what?'

He grunted, a sound of surprise and confusion.

'I suppose not. At the time, Mum told me not to say anything to you. You were only five or something. I suppose she didn't want to frighten you with something like that.'

'Like what?'

'I just assumed they said something later. Obviously not.'

'Now you're being irritating.'

'Keep your hair on. Well, remember when I fell off Trevor Munsie's motorbike when I was nine? I told you about that, didn't I?'

'Endlessly.'

'OK. So I broke my left arm and, obviously, they X-rayed it, and the doc told Mum I'd broken the little finger of my left hand recently and asked why she hadn't brought me in. This was news to her, so she backed me up against the wall and threatened to break all the other fingers if I didn't spill. So, scared shitless as I was, I told her. Sister Mary Frances had caught me talking at the back of the class and brought me out front and hit me six times with the edge of that fucking great big ruler she always carried around with her. It hurt like hell – I was up at night crying for weeks afterwards.'

'Why didn't you say anything?' He knew the answer before he had finished asking the question.

'I thought I'd get into even more trouble for admitting I'd done something to be beaten for. Anyway, nobody was stupid enough to report a nun. Who would you tell, anyway?'

'She broke your finger for talking at the back of the class?'

'I didn't know it was broken. I was ten years old. After three weeks, it stopped hurting. It never even crossed my mind to report her. She was a nun, for God's sake.'

'So, what did Mum do?'

'She was furious, but she was too afraid to confront her, so she complained to the archbishop. Three months later, he wrote back a shitty letter saying that they'd investigated the matter thoroughly and that Sister Mary Frances was a deeply respected member of the Church, admired and loved by all, and that I must have been lying to cover up some wickedness or other. So that was that.'

There was a long silence.

'Did she take it out on you later?'

'Funnily enough, not really. She just completely and utterly ignored me, cold-shouldered me in everything.

I Am A Smooth Man But My Brother, He Is A Hairy Man

Didn't speak to me or acknowledge my existence till I left at the end of the year. Must have been a crucifixion for her. I've that satisfaction, anyway. Too risky even for her – she had to swallow it all. God, it must have choked her like hot ashes to see me every day for a year and not be able to give me a bloody good hiding. By the way, send me a carton of Jaffa Cakes, will you?'

'Oh, right.' A short pause while he wrote a reminder. 'Very peculiar that someone would wait four years to take out her revenge on your eight-year-old brother. You have to be impressed by a hatred like that, wouldn't you say?'

Nat was taken back, a little, by the odd tone – the humorous coldness of it. 'What do you mean, revenge?'

Cool and measured, Aaron told his brother about the beating given him by Sister Mary Frances for not putting a tail on his nine.

'What a fucking cunt,' said Nat when he'd finished. 'Why didn't you tell Mum and Dad?'

'Why didn't you tell them when she broke your finger? I was ashamed for being so disgustingly untidy ... No, just for being disgusting. I remember staying awake all night once because she warned me that, if I died in a state of sin in the middle of night, I'd go to hell and burn for all eternity. I remember, just after that, going to confession and having to make up some sins because I was eight years old and hadn't done anything. What sort of sins can a fucking eight-year-old commit?'

'Did she hit you again?'

Aaron, whose voice had started to rise, calmed right down. The effect was disturbing.

'Oddly enough, no. But I spent two years in hell waiting for it, knowing it could be for nothing at all. So she didn't have to.'

Nat sucked his teeth loudly in sympathy. There was the sound of a door slamming and a woman calling out.

'Look, gotta go. You won't forget the Jaffa Cakes?'

'Possibly.'

'And a jar of Branston Pickle. Can you believe it's in the gourmet section at Wisma – $15 a pop?'

CHAPTER 37

WHEN IN ROME

'Do what you want and pay the price.'

Spanish proverb

At about 2 a.m., Aaron felt a pain in his stomach, and it swiftly began to get worse. No antacid ever made would quieten this particular agony. He got up, went into the locked cupboard in the front room and removed a dustbin bag the size of a pillow case.

Reaching inside, he took out a fistful of hair of varying shades and textures and began to eat.

'Mortal sins are shown in large letters like these: MORTAL.

One MORTAL SIN is enough to send your soul to hell for all eternity.

KILLING SOMEONE ...

COMMITTING AN IMPURE ACT ...

EATING MEAT ON FRIDAYS.

Father S. J. Wilwerding, Examination of Conscience for Boy and Girls

'In all the disputes which have excited Christians against each other, Rome has invariably decided in favour of that opinion which tended most towards the suppression of the human intellect and the annihilation of the reasoning powers.'

Voltaire

CHAPTER 38

HEART TO HEART

'Britney Spears!'
   'What about her?'
   'She's the answer.'
   'To?'
   'PRESBYTERIANS PUNCHED MY BABY.'
   'Oh. Yes. Miles away. Sorry. You're right.'
   'I know I'm right. I don't need you to tell me I'm right. I worked it out.'
   'Fine. I don't really care, except to say it's shameful that you took so long.'
   'What do you think of Molly?' Lister's tone, more hesitant than usual, was not lost on Scrope.
   'Who?'
   'Coates.'
   'Um.' Scrope tried to sound apologetic. 'Remind me?'
   'You know who she is.'
   'It's true, I was just having a lark.'
   'Well, don't.' A pause. 'And?'
   'She's intelligent. Good at her job.'
   'Is that all?'
   '*All?* For my father, being good at your job was a sign of spiritual excellence. You could be a sack of shit in all respects, but if you were good at your job – well, it was a redeemer.'

SCORN

'I'm not asking your father. And I don't want to employ her.'

'OK. She's clever and witty. I can see why you'd find her' – he chose the word carefully –'alluring.'

'What's that supposed to mean?'

'I mean, someone with coarse tastes might find her looks unusual.'

'You think she's unattractive?'

'Leaving aside the fact that what I think is irrelevant, as it happens, no, I don't. Her looks are unconventional.'

'You *do* think she's unattractive.'

It was not in Scrope's temperament to be evasive on such things. He regarded euphemism as a sign of weakness or dishonesty. But he didn't like being pressed either. 'She's striking, and I don't mean unattractive. I've told you what I think. Now fuck off.'

'I think she's beautiful.'

'Then that's all that matters.'

'She thinks I'm a snob.'

'Are you?'

'No.' A pause. 'Yes.'

'Do I detect some ambiguity here?'

'She thinks I talk down to people.'

'Her?'

'Other people.'

'Do you?'

'You know I do.'

'Then stop.'

'You aren't any better.'

'But it doesn't bother me.'

'So it's all right to be a snob?'

'No, of course not.'

Heart To Heart

'You just said you were one.'

'But I didn't mean it. I was trying to be sensitive to a gibe that everyone aims at us, whether it's true or not.'

'So you don't think I'm a snob?' said Lister, and Scrope was both a little surprised and surprisingly touched by his need to be reassured.

'Definitely not.' A pause. 'But then I'm not really qualified to judge. Perhaps we should ask Molly. Oh, you did.'

'Perhaps we *are* snobs.'

'Speak for yourself.'

'Molly said we both were.'

'She knows you, but she doesn't know me, so I don't give a toss what Molly says. Do you look down on her because she's socially inferior to you?'

'No.' A pause. 'My mother's family would, but they're middle class. And my oldest sister.'

'But not Charlotte?'

'No. Absolutely not. She's married to a builder. Her children are the children of a builder. She doesn't look down on them, does she?'

'I didn't think you liked her.'

'I don't. She's a cow. She's just not a snob.'

'So why does Molly think you are?'

'We. She meant the two of us.'

'You did point out to her that treating members of one social class as if they were all exactly the same is pretty much the definition of snobbery?'

'No. Because being a smart alec didn't seem appropriate at the time. Having the last word while you're trying to get off with someone … It's not going to work, is it?'

'So, you didn't defend yourself? You don't think being pathetic is at all unattractive?'

'She has me at a disadvantage.'
'Which is?'
'I think she's wonderful.'

At this point, stopped at a traffic light, Lister reached into the cubbyhole behind the gear lever, brought out a stick of chewing gum and quickly unwrapped it before popping it into his mouth.

'Yeucch!'
'What?'

Lister turned to Scrope and breathed at him.

'It's spearmint. I asked for the peppermint one. I fucking hate spearmint.'

Scrope turned his head away, as if something important had struck him.

'Could you pull up?' he said to Lister. 'I feel like a walk.'
'Your flat's three miles away.'

Lister stopped the car. Scrope was out of the door before he'd finished. 'See you tomorrow,' he said, and was gone.

The vials of Lorenzini are a network of jelly-filled canals in the head of a shark which enable it to sense distress from the electrical contractions of the muscles of an injured fish. There are people who have something like the vials of Lorenzini in their souls, people who can sense the wounded with brutal sensitivity. Scrope, eyes down and pale, moving slightly oddly, gave away his anguish to a Shepherd's Bush evil-doer mooching around in the small park in the middle of the road, looking for strugglers.

He allowed Scrope to move some fifty yards into the deserted dark of a side road, where he could be sick without humiliating himself in front of others. Scrope had been in hideous places full of terrible people many times, but only when he was strong himself, armed to the teeth and ready with others for what was coming his way. But now he was vulnerable and on his own, and he'd walked through a door from his normal world of the competing strong into the vile Mordor of the fragile. Unable to carry on, Scrope leaned against a wall and began to retch, huge belches of pain, empty barfs of raw indignity.

'Are you all right, mate?' said the thief, hard on his shoulder, his skilful right hand fluttering inside his coat to feel for the juicy wallet.

'It's OK. I'll be fine. Thank you,' gasped Scrope, as another spasm of retching shook his astonished body. The thief, seeing himself alone and the man dry-heaving in front of him so lost, began to consider the pleasure to be had from indulging in a little physical revenge on someone whose mohair coat and voice revealed how much nicer life had been to him.

Scrope was far too gone to pay attention to the muffled groan as the thief was lifted into the air by huge and hairy paws. For a moment, the thief struggled until the werewolf snapped his neck as easily as if he were a chook intended for that night's dinner. And like a chook, he shivered for a moment and was still. As gently as you like, the thief was laid out on the other side of the garden wall while Scrope retched on.

After a few minutes more of dry heaving, the need to vomit began to subside. Exhausted, holding on to the wall for support, he turned around.

Wolf Aaron, eight feet tall, stood on his haunches, looking at him, full of lupine curiosity. Scrope barely reacted, too exhausted to do much of anything. The werewolf smiled.

'Mint,' he said, after a moment. Then another sniff, longer and more considered. '*Spear*mint. And fear. Interesting.' He regarded Scrope as benignly as a friendly dog. 'So what put the heebie-jeebies into you, Inspector?'

Scrope closed his eyes as if he was going to be sick again, panting softly all the while.

'None of your fucking business.'

The wolf sniffed, almost as if he were considering the smell of the rebuke. 'No, I suppose not. Still, not very gracious, considering I saved your wallet, if not your skin.'

Whatever had been threatening to engulf Scrope seemed to have decided to give up. He looked at the wolf.

'Meaning?'

'Look on the other side of the wall. There.'

Scrope shuffled to the low garden wall and looked over at the dead man with the oddly angled neck.

'Who's he?'

'He was just about to turn you over. Luckily for you, I just happened to be passing by.'

'You killed him? Seems a bit harsh.'

'Perhaps. Wolves aren't very good at agonising. It's one of the many things I like about being one. The soul of a wolf, Inspector, is exquisitely unchristian. Besides, you've killed a fair number of people yourself without the benefit of due process. And worse, so I hear.'

'What do you want?'

'A word,' said the wolf. 'That's what I want.'

'Go ahead.'

'Oh, not here. I've risked a bit too much already. There's an entry just up there. Nice and dark. After you.'

The two of them made as strange a sight as you like, walking towards the small alley between two condemned

Heart To Heart

houses, the one exhausted, the other moving jauntily, if awkwardly, on his hind legs, dropping to all fours only as they vanished into the dark passageway. A young woman looking out of the window as she closed her curtains caught a few seconds of this oddest of couples before they vanished into the shadows. She was startled, certainly. How could she fail to be? But the sight of them was brief, and she reasonably chose the simplest explanation: what she saw was not an eight-foot werewolf ushering a slumped man into a dubious hiding place but someone taking a late-night walk with his unusually large dog. The standing upright was hard to explain, but not *that* hard – some sort of doggy trick. In a few seconds, she wasn't sure exactly what she'd seen.

'So,' said Scrope, leaning back against the wall for support. 'What do you want?'

'Why must I want anything in particular?' said the wolf. 'You and me, we're bound up together for the duration. It amuses me, does that help?'

'Why are we bound up together?'

'Frisking for compliments?'

'Clarity.'

'That's for me to know and you to find out.'

'You're waiting for something?'

'Am I?'

'I would have—'

'What do you make of Tony Blair?' interrupted the wolf. A silence.

'You want to talk about Tony Blair?'

'Indulge me.'

Another pause.

'Considering the circumstances, I thought he was quite

impressive. Not many people would take something like that in their stride.'

'You don't find that odd? Someone taking in their stride being confronted by a werewolf intent on eating him with a couple of lemons?'

'"Odd" implies there was something wrong with his reaction. I take it you mean "mad"? No, I didn't find it odd. I told you. I found it impressive.'

This time, the silence came from the werewolf. Was he upset? thought Scrope. That would be bad.

'Yes,' said the werewolf, at last. 'It was impressive. But – and I don't mean to be unkind – I also think it was odd.'

'We'll just have to disagree.'

'Wolves aren't just bad at having a conscience. They don't much care for disagreement either.'

Another silence.

'But I'm not a wolf, of course.'

'What are you, then?'

'Hard to say, given I've only got a sample of one to go on.'

'How did it happen? If you don't mind me asking.'

'I don't mind you asking, as long as you don't mind me not answering. That really would let the cat out of the bag, if you don't object to me mixing my metaphors, so to speak. But I wasn't really asking what you thought of Blair that night in particular. I meant to ask you what you thought of him in general.'

'I've met him twice before. He didn't remember.'

'Not very flattering.'

'I don't see why. He meets a lot of people. Our two conversations never got much beyond … To be honest, I can't even remember.'

Heart To Heart

'I didn't mean that either. I meant, what do you make of him as, say, the politician who sent you into two wars in general and that unfortunate business in Basra in particular.'

'I was a professional soldier. Going to war is what I did for a living. Complaining about it always struck me as a weird thing to do.'

'You thought the war was justified?'

'I made a point of not being dishonest by claiming I had a right to a view.'

'So, you've no opinion on his wars?'

'Both of them were fucking disasters, incompetent strategically and unutterably stupid in the way they were fought. But that's got fuck all to do with whether they were a good idea or not.'

'But you're not saying they were sensible wars to start with?'

'I'm not saying one way or the other. Of all people, I gave up the right when I took the money and the chance to do something extreme.'

The wolf sighed. 'Anyway, enough about what you think. Let's talk about what I think. After you nearly blew my head off the other day and it struck me that this business might end badly from my point of view—'

'That didn't occur to you when you started eating people?'

'Not as much as you might have thought. Perhaps it's a wolf thing. At any rate, getting shot, even though it was just a nick, made me think. I started out with something particular to say – but now, though less important, I find my adventures have given me something else to pontificate about.'

SCORN

'Tony Blair?'

'Yes. I think he's a very interesting person. An important person, or rather an important *character*. See, I'm not entirely sure he's a person in the normal way of these things.'

'He seemed perfectly all right to me. He has a sense of humour – not, in my experience, ever true of the madly weird.'

'You know, I agree. We're getting somewhere. Because you're completely wrong.'

'Am I?' said Scrope. 'You have the advantage over me when it comes to brilliant arguments, on account of the fact that you've got such big fucking teeth.'

'I apologise, Inspector. I appreciate there's a certain power imbalance between us but, I give you my word, no harm will come to you here, unless you do something stupid. Are you going to do something stupid?'

'No,' said Scrope.

'There we are, then. I appreciate there's something of the sentimentality of playing football in no-man's land about all this, but I don't see why we have to dislike each other personally. Or am I wrong?'

Scrope thought about saying something smart but decided not to.

'No. A truce it is. We're not actually going to play football, are we?'

'Very droll. I want to tell you what I think about Tony Blair. I don't know why. I suppose being a lone wolf is rather lonely. And these days I tend to give in to my impulses more than I used to.'

There was a distant tinkle of broken glass and a passing siren. 'Ah, the sounds of the city,' said the wolf.

Heart To Heart

By now, Scrope's eyes had become used to the dark and, in the diffused and dirty tango of the neon lights, he could begin to make out the enormous head, the dark twinkle of the werewolf's eyes, the light steam coming out of his mouth and hairy nostrils.

'I thought about Tony for a long time,' said the wolf. 'I carefully considered the "he's a warmongering cunt" theory, and I have to say I rejected it completely. I was also attracted by the notion that he's completely mad. I really did almost decide that, in a very individual way, he was in fact barking.'

The wolf took in a deep breath and blew it out in a long stream, like a smoker toking his last gasper before giving it up for good, resigning himself to the nicotine patch and the unsatisfied longing.

'But it won't do. I mean, what's so fascinating about the man is that, for years, he was incredibly successful and yet, in the end, everything he achieved collapsed into total and utter failure. He was bright, courageous, likeable, determined, and yet everything went tits up. How could he have generated so much disaster?' A pause. The werewolf looked at him.

'You tell me. You're the one pontificating,' said Scrope.

'I'll tell you. He's not a cunt or a madman. What I think he is – and I've thought a lot about it – is that he's a fool.'

'Right.'

'You're not impressed, Inspector Scrope? You should be. I don't mean that he's an idiot, or anything like it. Have you ever heard of the Holy Fool?'

'Yes.'

'Of course you have. What was I thinking? Tell me what you understand by the term.'

Scrope shifted awkwardly. 'Someone considered foolish by most, but who, underneath his apparent lack of wisdom, has a capacity for seeing things clearly.'

'A little thin, Inspector Scrope. But I suppose we can't know everything.'

'And you do?'

'Justly rebuked. Of course, when the idea popped into my head, I looked it up. A Holy Fool is someone who God chooses to grant a vision of things that, though derided and mocked, grasps the real nature of the world that is utterly obscured to those who rely on knowledge or reason.'

'Wikipedia?' said Scrope.

'Partly,' said the wolf.

'It can be very useful.'

'There we are, then. You see, Tony masks his holy foolishness from the rest of us because he's articulate and charming and intelligent, where your conventional Holy Fool lives in rags and speaks in tongues and denies the riches of the world and the power of the mighty.'

'Not at all like Mr Blair, then.'

'A little obvious, perhaps, but fair enough. Lovely carpet in his bedroom, though, didn't you think? My paws practically drowned in its softness.'

'I wasn't barefoot myself, but I know what you mean.'

'You must put away coarse dismissals of the man who loves Sea Island cotton and Italian lemons and the friendship of the mighty. I'm convinced, myself, that Mr Blair sees them as ordinary people just like everyone else; it's just that they happen to have much more money and power. His generosity is real – he likes to give everyone a fair shake: hail fellow, well met. But, inside, he's not hungry for power or wealth.

Heart To Heart

'Inside, he sincerely believes in his own goodness, and that unshakeable belief guides him against everything solid, every fact, every reality. To Tony, Rupert Murdoch isn't a bad man, not once you see things from his point of view; as for flame-haired newspaper editors on trial for conspiracy, he once shared a drink and some happy banter with them, and he won't turn his back on them just because they're in a pinch. Gerry and Martin? Political killers aren't pantomime villains once you get to know them and share a rueful joke or two.

'He doesn't just think the best of *himself*, he thinks the best of others, too. That's what makes him a fool, a deep and unsavable and horribly dangerous idiot who'll always bring disaster and failure wherever he goes. You know what brought him into Iraq? He and George Bush thought that they needed to remake the Middle East. He actually said that: *remake*. And now he's going to remake the Catholic Church as well.'

The wolf snorted. 'Who knows? Perhaps he is just mad, after all.'

Scrope felt able to stop using the wall to keep him from falling over and slowly stood up straight.

'Then why don't you just let him get on with it? Give him a few years, and maybe the Vatican will look like the Middle East.'

'No, it won't. He's powerless against the Church – unless he can get the Americans to invade, I suppose. But he's sent a powerful signal that the Church is acceptable, if only he can sprinkle some Tony Blair magic over its more regrettable beliefs. So I'm going to fuck him over good and proper for betraying us all.'

There was a low grumble from the wolf that sounded

something like laughter. 'You know, I really needed to get that off my chest. Thank you, Inspector Scrope.' A pause, as he regarded the unsteady policeman. 'You should tell me what's eating you. I might be able to help.'

'You might not think Tony Blair is mad but, clearly, you think I am.'

'Suit yourself. I offered.'

There was a scuffle just outside the passageway and a slurred voice. 'That you, Baldo? Got some one-hit wonder from that cunt Nas. Fuck, it's dark in here.' There were three clicks of a lighter and the sparks to go with them. The flame revealed the white face and bad teeth of a junkie, staring at a werewolf looking at him from about eight inches away and with a head the size of a large bucket.

'Aaaaaaaggggh!'

The junkie dropped the lighter and ran in the direction of the high street as fast as his poor wasted muscles and arthritic knee could carry him, screaming all the while. 'Werewolf! Werewolf!'

Light-blinded, Scrope could again see nothing, though he could feel the hot, wet breath of the wolf on his face.

'Pity we couldn't finish our talk. Time I wasn't here. Sorry, can't have you following.'

The wolf gave him a sharp kick in the shins. Scrope, crying out in pain, went down like a sack of hammers.

And, with that, the werewolf turned out into the street and loped down the road in the opposite direction to the terrified junkie, slowly and pleasurably changing back into Aaron as he went.

'The Pope by the divine assistance is possessed of that infallibility which God willed his Church to enjoy in defining doctrine concerning faith or morals.

So then, should anyone, which God forbid, have the temerity to reject this definition of ours confirming papal infallibility: let him be anathema. (That is, condemned to eternal fire with Satan himself to mortify his body.)'

Vatican Council, Sess. IV, Const. de Ecclesia Christi, Chapter IV (1870)

(433 bishops voted for the doctrine of infallibility; 2 voted against)

'Pope Nicolas I (858–67) adopted 115 forged documents claimed to be by Roman bishops of the first century. For what purpose? The forgeries gave the impression that the early church had been ruled by papal decrees and were the will of God. The forgeries still appear in The Code of Canon (Church) Law revised under the supervision of Pope John Paul II in 1983 which set virtually no limit to the exercise of power by the pope. These forgeries are not curiosities of the time but have had an abiding impact on the history of the church.'

The Catholic Church, Hans Kung, pp. 82–3 (edited for brevity)

(Hans Kung is a theologian and remains a priest 'in good standing'. He was theological consultant for the Second Vatican Council but later rejected the doctrine of papal infallibility in his book *Infallible? An Inquiry* (1971). As a result, in 1979, he was stripped of his licence to teach as a Roman Catholic theologian)

CHAPTER 39

HOLY CHARISM

'The supreme triumph of reason, Father North,' said Cardinal Gillis, 'is to realise when to stop thinking.'

This satisfactory rebuke – satisfactory, that is, to the cardinal – was delivered as the result of a conversation over dinner between the Head of the Catholic Church in England and his private secretary, in which the latter had, at first in a roundabout way, asked his superior what changes the new pope might make to faith.

'You assume that he'll make any changes.'

'Of course not, Your Grace,' replied North, carefully but with a glint, thought Gillis, of stubbornness in his eyes. 'But it's impossible to deny that expectations of – what can one call it, reform? – that they exist.'

'Call it something else, Father.'

'Of course, "reform" is the wrong word. What could I call it?' He paused, mischief in the air. 'Ongoing clarification, perhaps?'

'Very good, Father North.' The cardinal was amused but not deceived. 'I wonder if you took up the wrong vocation. Perhaps you should have been a politician, or – I heard the term on the radio the other day – a brand manager.' North nodded a graceful acceptance of the mockery.

'Nevertheless, it's clear that there is anticipation of important change.'

'From deluded liberals who know as much about the Church as they do about right and wrong. The way they go on, you'd think the Holy Father was about to replace the Ten Commandments with Eight Recommendations.'

'Very good, Your Grace.'

'Ah, flattery. You really should think about taking up politics.'

North smiled, making a point of not showing offence.

'But even the Church has to acknowledge politics. With respect, it's not just the liberal media who expect change – the faithful also, I think.'

'Then we'll see how faithful they are. "And some seed fell upon stony soil and sprouted quickly, but when the sun rose they withered, because their roots were shallow." The pope is the servant of the truth of God, not the expectations of men and women. It's the nature of truth that it simply is: whether you like it or not is utterly irrelevant.'

'So you think nothing will change?'

'What I think is also utterly irrelevant. God chose the pope through the power of the Holy Charism. He speaks through him and through the promise to his predecessor given by Jesus Himself: whatever you forbid on earth will be forbidden in heaven. And whatever you permit on earth will be permitted in heaven. *That*, Father North, is the truth, and nothing can change it. Like or don't like: irrelevant. What the pope shuts, no one else can open, and what he opens, no one else can shut.'

Satisfied that he had boxed North into a corner, the cardinal took a sip from his bottle of Sauvignon Blanc – £33 for a case of six from a Tesco's bin-end clearance. No one could, now or ever, accuse Gillis of bling. He took wine with his lunch on roughly two days a month as an act of

Holy Charism

celebration of the generosity of God.

He sat back and contemplated the young priest.

'But, for the sake of argument, and in the expectation that you won't argue that he'll abolish God or allow the ordination of women and therefore oblige me to hand you over to the Inquisition — what do you think could be changed? As our Holy Father's spin doctor, what advice would you give him to satisfy the universal thirst for a revision of God's laws?'

Father North, for all his intelligence, did not perhaps have the experience of life to sense that something of a storm was brewing out of the cardinal's deep frustration at the world and its tireless condemnation of his faith.

'Your Grace, speaking merely hypothetically, I can think of one matter that could be debated.'

'Ah, celibacy,' said the cardinal, apparently with good humour. 'I do believe I can hear the sound of Bryant and May extra-long matches rattling in the box with the longing to burn you at the stake even as we speak. Go on.'

Father North smiled mischievously.

'You're teasing me, Your Grace. After all, you know much better than I that the rule of celibacy is an ecclesiastical convention, not a doctrine of unchanging faith. In principle, it can be changed by the pope at any time. Before he became Pope Benedict, even Cardinal Ratzinger said as much.'

'"Before" is the most important word in that sentence, Father. Becoming pope is not a promotion granted for merit and faithful service. To become pope is to become the chosen of God. Before they became pope, both of them were, like me, merely proud men dressed in a little brief authority. What they say *after* they become pope, when they have been utterly changed by God's grace, is the beginning and end of it. What Cardinal Ratzinger said once he became Pope Benedict was that celibacy must be *strictly* adhered to.'

The cardinal sat back and took another sip of his wine. 'But, of course, you're right. The matches must go back in the box. It *can* be a matter for discussion. Is it something that appeals to you personally, Father?' More taunting.

North raised his left eyebrow as if astonished at the very notion.

'Marriage is an honour, Your Grace, that I dream not of.'

'The Church must adapt, the Church must alter, the Church must change.' The cardinal's taunts had changed from something that looked like teasing to the sneering panache of a popular comedian. 'But tell me something, Father. Tell me why the Church has survived for two thousand years. Do you know?'

North had a formidable intelligence, but he had never had to duke it out with a man who used to be referred to by the seminarians in his care as 'God's bouncer'. He had overstepped the mark.

'No?' said an exultant Gillis. 'Shall I tell you? The thing is, I don't know why the Church has survived for two thousand years. What I do know is that it *has* survived.

'Now consider our enemies.' He smiled. 'The Romans fed us to their lions and their crocodiles, burned us, crucified us. And then it bowed to us. It put us at the centre of that empire. And we're still there at the centre of the turning world, but where's the Roman empire now? Gone with the wind. And where is communism, Father? Come and gone. Fascism? The same. And Luther? Lutherans

Holy Charism

have moved with the times, Father; I believe a woman is head of the Lutheran Church. But when the head of the Lutherans speaks, no one reports it on the news. The world's media are readier to report a small earthquake in Peru in which no one was hurt than report the position of the Lutherans on anything. But when the pope speaks, all the world still listens.'

He did not give poor old North time to answer, looking at him as if the poor creature was every apostate who ever lived all rolled up into one. In fact, North was starting to resemble a victim of shell-shock about to have a poem written about him by Wilfred Owen.

'But I can see you're thinking that the moral authority of the Church is no longer at the centre, that we're crippled by all this talk of paedophiles and cover-ups. Well, just look at the reality of it all. When the pope arrives in a country it is, Father North, news everywhere. The news reports everything he does and does not do. All of it matters to the world, all of the time. And not because he is likeable or not likeable or any of that nonsense, just because he is the pope, the successor all the way back to Peter receiving that charisma from God himself.'

He was in full flight now.

'Napoleon, Stalin, Hitler, Mao – vanished. Movements of every kind, winds-of-change ideas, they come and they go, and we remain. Empires and tyrants and saviours of every kind – we've outlasted them all. And after three hundred years of liberal delusions about happiness and self-esteem, what do we have as a result? A modern world fanatical with trash, fervent only about money and looks and a freedom that's worthless, the freedom of ghosts. Depleted selves, all utterly miserable and lost.

'It's coming to an end, let me tell you, Father North. Even though they don't know it yet, people are looking for an authority that tells them what they need to hear – a pope that offers them freely the majesty of a relationship in eternity with God almighty.'

He looked at Father North with exasperated disbelief.

'And now, when, whether they know it or not, all eyes turn to observe the pope, what do you want to do? Bow down before the modern world just as it's about to die of a stroke in front of us? That's the threat to the Church, not these false idols that babble about freedom and happiness and deliver neither. Who else will redeem them? Right-wing politicians? Actors? The beautiful? The free market? Socialism? A mobile phone? A holiday in the sun? Trash, all of it, and proven trash.'

Of course, poor Father North was very far from believing that the Church should bow down before liberals and progressives and their shallow notions of freedom and happiness. But he was in the right place at the wrong time. He was the closest Gillis had to someone who did.

'Do you know when I realised just what a terrible mistake it was to listen to anyone but the Church? It was revealed to me when I was giving a confession to an old woman on Easter Sunday a year ago. Do you know what had eaten away at her faith, Father North? Do you know?'

Father North did not know.

'It was that, all her life, she'd been told by the Church that if she ate meat on Fridays she would be tortured in hell for all eternity. Now, do you think, Father North, the Church should have threatened those who ate meat on Fridays with hell for all eternity?'

North was horrified to discover that something in his

Holy Charism

chest was trying to shout: *Yes! The Church should ordain fire and brimstone for those hounds of hell who eat flesh on a Friday!*

'No, of course it shouldn't,' said the cardinal. 'Why on earth would God punish someone for all eternity for eating bacon, for goodness' sake? It always was idiotic, and it always will be. But we should never have said so. And why, you ask me, Father North? I'll tell you why. One day, the Church says it's not a sin anymore, that you can stuff your mouth with sausages and steak and chops on holy Fridays to your heart's content. After all that fear and certainty about the loss of God forever, now we've changed our minds, now it's just fine. Not even the teensiest-weeniest bit of a sin.

'Now, you tell me, Father, how a good Catholic woman like the one in the confessional can be taking anything we say seriously after terrifying her for sixty years and then one day telling her it doesn't matter at all. That's what change does for you, Father North. Good reform, bad reform – it doesn't matter. Change destroys. Reform and die. Fixity is the source of all our strength. Fixity means we will live, and everyone and everything else will fail. A few centuries from now, we'll see the Reformation and the Enlightenment for what they were: little local difficulties.'

Gillis walked over to the door, then had one last thought and turned back into the room.

'Goodnight, Father North, and I hope you'll sleep badly, as you consider the one single idea that alone will preserve the Catholic faith and all the eternal souls of mankind that are in its trust.

'Change nothing. Allow nothing to be changed. Do not allow anyone to change anything.'

'The Dublin Archdiocese's preoccupations in dealing with cases of child sex abuse (at least until the mid-1990s) were the maintenance of secrecy, the avoidance of scandal, the protection of the reputation of the Church and the preservation of its assets. All other considerations, including the welfare of children and justice for victims, were subordinated to these priorities.'

> The Murphy Report into the sexual abuse scandal in the Catholic archdiocese of Dublin, 2009 (www.justice.ie/en/JELR/Pages/ PB09000504)

'I have sinned by pride in my abundant evil, iniquitous and heinous thought, speech, pollution, suggestion, delectation, consent, word and deed ...

I have sinned by sight, hearing, taste, smell and touch, and in my behaviour, my evil vices.'

> Confiteor (I Confess) Paenitentiale Vallicellanum II

The Suppression of Heresy by The Institution Known as the Inquisition

'*Far from being inhuman, [the inquisitors] were, as a rule, men of spotless character and sometimes of truly admirable sanctity, and not a few of them have been canonized by the Church. There is absolutely no reason to look on the medieval ecclesiastical judge as intellectually and morally inferior to the modern judge.*'

Catholic Encyclopedia (www.newadvent.org/cathen/08026c.htm)

CHAPTER 40

THE TORTURE CHAMBER

Aaron arrived in the early evening at Westminster Cathedral and hid in the trees that protected the two tennis courts from the houses on Morpeth Terrace. (I want to be scrupulously fair – unlike some people I could mention but won't – and point out that these were for the benefit of the pupils at the school that occupies the same site, and were not for the cardinal's personal use.) From this shelter, he was able to scope the vast residence of the cardinal and see what was what.

I like to think I am a creature of considerable subtlety, but I'm going to point out something here that may seem a little crass, a touch on the nose, as it were. Given that neither is likely to come on the market in the near future, it is difficult to say which is worth more, this central London residence or the fifteen-thousand-square-foot mansion in Madison Avenue occupied by the Archbishop of New York.

Not all Church properties are in such prime positions, and priests and cardinals must live somewhere, after all. The One True Faith is an organisation that needs organising. It must have offices and computers; it must have cars for its priests to move about in. It must pay pensions and health benefits. But what, precisely, is it that stops the

The Torture Chamber

Vatican from selling these goldmines in the capital cities of the world?

In fact, I understand why it doesn't. Grandiose moral gestures are a moral trap, you see. The sin of pride stalks every apparent act of generosity. Think of the danger to the Church's very soul from the moral vanity that would ensue from selling such succulent parts of its portfolio and giving the money to the poor.

But it's just a fraction of all they have, I hear you say. Yes, but where will it stop if they do start? For two thousand years, the Church has been mistaken about almost everything. Its talent for always being in the wrong is the Catholic faith's greatest genius.

Aaron waited until dark and then made his move. It was not quite nine o'clock in the evening when the cardinal went to take confession with Father Sanchez – who was, poor man, lying stuffed in a wheelie bin next to the kitchen with his neck broken as Gillis opened the door of the confessional in his private chapel.

For those unfamiliar with the confessional, think of two single wardrobes stuck together, connected by a small but veiled opening so that the one confessing can speak and listen as they kneel to admit their sins and have them absolved on earth and in heaven.

'Bless me, Father, for I have sinned,' intoned the cardinal. 'It is one week since my last confession.'

'Please continue.' Aaron, hidden in the deep shadow of the confessional, began to cough to disguise the fact that it was a long time since he'd been in a confessional, and that he didn't know how one ought to address a cardinal come to unburden his soul before God.

'Your voice is very hoarse, Father,' said a concerned

Cardinal Gillis. 'Are you unwell?'

'Just a sore throat, Your Grace, and a bit of a cough. Nothing a Lemsip won't cure. Please continue,' he repeated.

The cardinal considered his outburst at dinner. 'I have been unnecessarily harsh on a colleague.' A pause. 'And, on another three occasions, I spoke uncharitably of others. Mind you, that Tony Blair would drive a saint to anger.'

'And you're no saint, Your Grace.'

'What?' Gillis was more puzzled than offended. A pause. 'No.' He laughed softly, but awkwardly. 'Very far from it.'

Aaron wondered why the cardinal failed to smell a rat – he was no fool. But then, what was he to think? That his confessor had been kidnapped, snuffed out, dumped in a bin and replaced by a werewolf? We see what we expect to see, take the reasonable, sensible but wrong explanation over the implausible. Bizarre, but true. As it happened, the cardinal's nose wrinkled a little at the smell of wolf but, not being familiar with that whiff, he put it down to his confessor's well-known laxity with soap.

'Fair enough, Father,' said Gillis. 'But it is a sin, nevertheless, whatever the provocation.'

'Go on, Your Grace.'

'I spoke unkindly to another, and—' Aaron interrupted him with a deranged series of coughs and a sneeze loud enough to wake the dead.

'Are you sure you're well enough to continue, Father?' asked Gillis.

'Oh, I'm all right, Your Grace. Its bark is worse than its bite.'

'Your voice. It's very deep. You don't sound like yourself.'

'To be honest, Your Grace, I truly don't feel like myself.'

'We should postpone this until you're well.' Aaron heard

The Torture Chamber

the booth creak as the cardinal started to get off his knees.

'No, no, Your Grace. I really am better than I sound. What if you should die tonight?'

Although this seemed a gratuitous overplaying of his hand, it was a joke which the cardinal was inclined to be amused by. During his childhood, after all, he had been asked to consider this question every day of his little life. Besides, it would have been a strange feeling indeed to leave the confessional halfway through one's penitence. It was something that simply never happened. And there was, for once, something serious he wanted to ... if not confess, exactly, then to discuss. He knelt back down.

'I was too strict with rules, boundaries and discipline with regards to Father North on two occasions. And I was too *lax* with rules, boundaries and discipline with regards to Father North on three occasions.'

'I see.'

'And, last Sunday, I allowed trivial matters to dictate my spiritual schedule.'

Aaron was intrigued. 'I don't understand, Your Grace.'

The cardinal was accustomed to telling his sins in the way he saw fit, not explaining them. But he was now determined merely to get it over with, and forgave his confessor his peculiar behaviour on account of his illness.

'I postponed a meeting on Sunday afternoon with the Association of Catholic Mothers against the Ordination of Women.'

'Never heard of them,' said Aaron.

'I put them off so that I could watch Chelsea against West Bromwich Albion.'

'Entirely understandable, Your Grace. I'd have done the same myself.'

'I wonder, Father,' said Gillis, 'if it might not be wise to see a doctor.'

'Thank you for your concern. A good night's sleep will do it, I'm sure. Anything else?'

'Yes, Father, as a matter of fact. This dreadful business about the murder of priests.'

He paused. This was hard.

'I've been examining my conscience. Or, rather, it's been examining me.'

This is interesting, thought Aaron. *Just keep quiet*, he instructed the wolf. *Let him talk*.

'I've been wondering if I've been defending the indefensible.'

A pause.

'In the matter of those clerics who have offended against children, I know I should have been harsher with those who committed such a dreadful – truly dreadful – sin. But they all wailed about how sorry they were, and begged for forgiveness, and promised they would never do such things again.

'It repelled me – be clear about that – but it ...' He stumbled. For a moment, it was impossible to find the words. 'I did sin. I wanted to believe them, that they repented, because I knew, or half knew, what damage it would do to the Church to hand them over to the police. I knew it was an evil not to have done so. Or I know it now. I was not equipped to deal with the difficulties of the situation. But it was wrong; I know that now.'

A beat.

'Then ask for forgiveness, Your Grace,' said the werewolf. 'After all, we are all human; we are all sinners.'

There was another long pause, the intense silence only

The Torture Chamber

faintly impressed upon by the low breathing of the cardinal as he tried to find the words.

'Yes, that's very true,' he said at last. 'I was in that terrible position so few people ever experience, though they think they know the answer. How easy it always is to do the right thing for people like that! I was in that terrible position where I had to choose between one evil – a terrible evil, terrible – and one that, in my heart of hearts, truly, I believed to be even worse.'

This was a surprise for Aaron. He spoke before he could stop himself.

'Worse?'

'When it comes to having to choose between the greater and lesser of two evils, which one should you choose?'

Aaron could feel the cardinal inviting him into his conscience.

'The lesser of two evils, of course,' the cardinal said at last. 'All theologians are agreed on that.' A silence followed. Then, suddenly … 'Father, I am a sinner.' Aaron never expected to hear such an admission with such – not enthusiasm, that was not quite the word – such relief, such a deep sense of reprieve.

'God has seen, in his infinite generosity to such a sinful creature as I, to make me, in all my inadequacy, a guardian of the faithful … in all my weakness …' He stumbled again, a footstep in the wrong direction. 'I know I must protect the faithful from suffering in this world. I accept that. But a much greater guardianship, far more important than the suffering even of a child in this world – this is hard for the world to understand – is the infinite suffering of an unsaved life in eternity.'

The wolf was not much interested in explanations. The

wolf was interested in flesh. Aaron just about kept him under control.

'When I came across clerics who had' – he hated to speak the words, and then remembered how Father North referred to it – 'offended against the sixth commandment with a child, I was horrified, appalled, of course.'

This time, Aaron could not restrain the wolf.

'Thou shalt not kill?' he said, genuinely bemused.

The cardinal was somewhat surprised that his confessor did not know the order of his commandments. But, after the first flush of irritation at having been interrupted while so deeply unburdening his soul, he remembered that Father Sanchez was unwell.

'The sixth commandment is,' said Gillis as gently as possible, 'Thou shalt not commit adultery.' He laughed jovially. 'I believe you might be confusing it with the Protestant order of the commandments.'

'Ah, yes,' said Aaron. 'The effect of the Night Nurse, Your Grace.'

'Of course, of course,' said the cardinal. 'But if God gave it to us priests, sinful and weak as we are, to protect that child not just in this life, whose pain is just temporary, however appalling, but for all eternity – aren't we obliged to choose to protect that child and all the faithful in the eternal life to come, rather than in the brief and passing present, however terrible?'

He seemed to require an answer, an agreement to go with him to wherever this was going.

'Yes,' said Aaron, back on top for now. (*Let me devour his toecakes*, called out the wolf. *Let me crunch on his sweetbreads and wet my whistle on his chyle.*)

'But then, you realise that, if people see, openly and

The Torture Chamber

publicly, that a small number of priests have offended grievously in this terrible way, then how can the faithful, and the many, many souls either just coming to an exploration of the faith, or just new in the faith, how can they ...

'Well, these little ones need protecting. Every Catholic must heed the words of Our Blessed Lord: "Whoever causes one of these little ones who believe in me to stumble, it would be better for him to have a great millstone hung around his neck and to be drowned in the depths of the sea." Jesus is demanding that I protect the Church so that it can save people – save children – for all eternity.'

He stopped. His desperate desire to explain had run its course. The silence from the other side of the occluded window of the confessional seemed to judge him harshly. Was it possible his actions might not be forgiven? The horrible consequences of such a rejection stilled his breath. What if his penance from Father Sanchez was to reopen a case or report it to the police?

Odd, isn't it, how even a little guilt can make an impossible event like this seem, for a moment, plausible? I can't, of course, be sure, but I'm prepared to bet my shirt that such a penance has not been, and possibly never will be, uttered in the darkness of the confessional.

In his half of the confessional, Aaron was taking a deeper breath. If the time for talking had come to an end, then so had the time for listening.

'He's all yours,' said Aaron out loud.

'No one except the Catholic Church talks about lust anymore. Desire and passion as wonderful things in and of themselves have replaced the notion of a disordered and unsatisfiable hunger. And yet, who cannot accept that acting on the desire for sexual relations with children, for example, represents a disordered craving? Intelligent theologians of the Catholic Church have tried to describe lust in other ways, as the spirit of a company or a nation or a political movement – anyone in the grip of the hunger for nothing less than everything. But just as we need lust as a term for more than sex with little boys and girls, we need it to describe something even broader than the kind identified by the Church. The Church is not hypocritical just because it denounces paedophilia as a sin of lust while it strives to cover it up. It is duplicitous because it more than anyone lusts inordinately down to the very bottom of its soul. Its lusts are spiritual and moral lusts. It lusts for control of every act and thought. It lusts for possession of the human soul. Lust is at the very heart of everything it does – the priestly paedophile has simply extended that lust into a craving for the flesh of boys.'

Louis Bris, The Wisdom of Crocodiles

CHAPTER 41

CRIME AND PUNISHMENT

'What did you say, Father?' There was no reply, just some strange noises and an overpowering musty smell.

'This is your penance, Your Grace!' shouted Aaron gleefully as he began to change into his lupine alter ego with an ecstasy of stretching sinew. His omohyoids bulged, his galea aponeurotica swelled, his sternocleidomastoids erupted, his nasalis fattened to the size of an enormous glute. With a delighted howl, the werewolf burst out of the top of the confessional like a deranged jack-in-the-box. Eyes wide, lit with coals of fire, he stared down at the terrified cardinal. He yawned and growled, a high-pitched, doggy yelp, like a spaniel about to eat a favourite treat.

'Your sins are not forgiven, you, you wretch! And I sentence you to spend the rest of eternity being given one up the perforation with a red-hot poker, with time off on Sundays, giving blimpies to Adolf Hitler. Oh, and two Our Fathers and a Hail Mary!'

The astonished and terrified cleric barely heard a word as he gawped at this hideous visitation. But he was not too overcome to lose the power of self-preservation. Impressively quickly for a man of his age, he was out of the confessional and over to the door. And, unfortunately for the werewolf, he had gone upwards in the confessional box but not outwards, and was now, for a moment, trapped. He barked in frustration as it took three blows, restricted as he was, to smash his way out of the cabinet of sin.

By the time the werewolf was free, the leader of the Catholic faith in England was through the door and a fair way down the corridor. The werewolf bounded out of the room, staring wildly about for his prey.

'Come here, Your Grace. I want to chastise you.'

But the cardinal wasn't listening. He rushed on. 'Help! Help!' he cried.

Unfortunately, the two full-time members of staff had retired to their basement flat at the back of the building and could hear nothing, and Father North was in his bedroom, listening to the Velvet Underground on a pair of Dr Dre's.

'Help! Help!' But no one came.

Gillis was not unmanned by panic. Seeing the size of his tormentor, he turned into a corridor at ninety degrees, and then another. Realising he might lose his prey in the vast old building, the werewolf sprang forward with absolute determination to finish the job.

Unwise. He was almost on the old man, his muzzle a fraction away from biting him on the heel, when the cardinal turned into yet another corridor the werewolf had not anticipated. In his rubber-soled shoes, the cardinal was able to change direction easily, but paws were not made for polished lino. With a cry of astonishment, the werewolf, paws and nails scrabbling for a hold on the shiny floor, went careering straight on and crashed into a cupboard. It collapsed under his weight, showering him with mops, a Dyson fetching him a fearful clout on the head.

The werewolf left out a yelp of pain and anger, but

was up in a fraction, scraping and clawing for a grip, and back on the hunt, darting into the corridor down which the terrified cleric had fled.

But there was nothing. Not a sound. Not a sight. The Primate of All England and Wales was gone.

The eyes of the wolf narrowed, and his claws retracted. He raised his great muzzle into the air and sniffed long draughts of ecclesiastical atmosphere – odour of stale testosterone, biscuit-dry sweat of single males, scent of indignation and regret, odour of longed-for sanctity, niff of judgement, perfume of self-loathing, smell of hate. If the dog's nose can identify 300 million smells, the werewolf knows a billion more. The werewolf can smell a history, a life, whether you are male or female, what concerns you have or are going to have, whether you are pregnant, and not just that you are frightened but what exactly it is that frightens you.

The cardinal could not hide from a conk like that, even in the best-constructed panic room. Built by Cardinal Vaughan in 1903, the residence of the Cardinal of Westminster has an unusual feature known only to a very select few, kept secret not to hide its purpose but rather to protect the Church from accusations of unchristian paranoia. Cardinal Gillis, a man from a long line of victimised Catholics, had at the last minute dived into a priest hole built a hundred years ago into the large marble fireplace in the Throne Room. The fear that, one day, the priesthood might yet again be cruelly persecuted in England by the wicked – that day had come.

Sniffing delicately, the werewolf, now on all fours, now on twos, tasted the air high and low for the aroma of priest. He could sense something was not quite right.

There was the smell of primate all right, but suddenly cut off and very distant.

By now he was at the top of a great stairway leading down two floors, enormous green pillars to either side and, running its length, a long red carpet edged by dappled marble. It reminded him of one of the great cinemas of his youth, and it pleased him to think that, on the landing halfway down, just out of sight, there might be a pretty young woman in a nylon uniform holding a tray of overpriced ice creams. Down he came, sniffing and listening for anyone coming to the cardinal's aid, loping off the great staircase and over the marble floor of the hallway, with its ugly dappling that looked like a slice of uncooked black pudding, and then into the Throne Room itself.

It was a grand place, ballroom-sized, all gold and vermillion. He was a little surprised to see that the Throne Room did indeed possess a throne, though it disappointed him. It was ostentatious enough, with its velvet padding and elaborate carving in what looked like gold leaf. But he'd hoped for something on a dais with a canopy the size of a four-poster. If you're going to have a Throne Room, he thought, you ought to go for it.

Here, the contradiction of the smells was greatest. The cardinal had been here only moments before, but was not here now. The faint base-note smell of cardinal suggested he had not left either. He was hidden in a place where, for all its size, there was nowhere to hide. The werewolf moved forward, tasting the air with his enormous tongue – the Primate of All England was being stalked to the sound of slurping – as he made his way across the enormous room, the sound of his progress maximised by the click-clack of his claws on the parquet floor.

Crime And Punishment

Gradually – sniffing, clacking – he made his way to the great fireplace, over which hung a portrait of the pope. The werewolf growled at the picture. 'Blah!' He stared at the fireplace. It was clear that the cardinal was behind it, but it was not at all clear how he'd got in or, more importantly, how he could be winkled out. The werewolf placed both paws on the surround and began to feel around it, intoning all the while.

'Little pig, little pig, let me come in.' There was no reply. 'Not by the hair on my chinny chin chin,' said the wolf. 'Come out, come out, Your Grace, and let's talk about this.'

'Get thee behind me, Satan!' called out the cardinal, realising he'd been run to ground.

'You'd like to think that. It wouldn't occur to you that I might be the hand of God, even if a bit sinister, like.'

'Don't worry, worm. I know a demonic presence when I see one.'

Flicking his ears back and forth, moving his great head from side to side, the werewolf was able to sense exactly where the sound was coming from. It was cleverly disguised as an ornament to the fire, but his wet nose could feel the slight flow of air emerging from the space behind the fireplace. He felt over the area with his paws but could sense no lever to pull, no button to press.

'You won't get in here, you murderous gobshite.'

The trouble, thought the werewolf, was that the cardinal was probably right. He sat back on his haunches and gave a great yawn of frustration. He bent his head close to the ornament and could see several finger-sized holes for breathing. He could block them up, but there would presumably be others, and it would take too long, anyway.

SCORN

'While I'm having a think,' he called out to the cardinal, 'I was just wondering what you need a throne for.'

'I've got nothing to say to you.'

'Do you *rule* there, from your throne? It's a bit odd, don't you think?'

'Shut your great hairy gob.'

'I mean, you can't really see Jesus with a throne, can you? He's not really that bloke, is he? The throne type, let alone the Throne *Room* type. To me, it seems wrong. Is it comfortable? Why isn't it bigger?'

'God is not to be mocked,' said the cardinal.

'I'm not mocking God. I'm mocking you. It's your throne, not his. My kingdom is not of this world. Thrones, palaces, magnificent stairways – they're of this world. Anyway, there's one other thing. Aren't you at all interested in why I've come to suck the marrow out of *your* bones in particular?'

There was a silence.

'Because I'm Head of the Catholic Church in England and Wales?'

'That barely has anything to do with it, Your Grace, merely a sort of coincidence. I want your liver in my cavernous entrails for another reason entirely.'

'Boastfulness is the devil's sin.'

'I wish you'd stop calling me that.'

'Ha! The truth hurts.'

'The reason you're here is altogether less to do with symbolism and more to do with your own satanic malfeasance.'

'What are you talking about?'

'I'm talking about the fact that, for ten years, when you were the headmaster of one of the richest Catholic schools

Crime And Punishment

in England, you covered up the rapes and sexual assaults of the children in your care by half a dozen priests. Or am I thinking of someone else?'

The silence that followed was like that after a heavy blow.

'Well?' said the werewolf.

'I made a mistake,' said the cardinal, at last.

'A *mistake*?'

'A terrible mistake. I was too insensitive and clumsy in the way I handled people.'

'You discovered that one of the priests had been beating boys for his sexual gratification for years before you arrived.'

'I suspended him from teaching immediately I found out.'

'And sent him to work as a parish priest in the north. Why didn't you call the police?'

An agony of silence, then a frustrated cry.

'Things were different then. I was wrong, but there's been a change – a big change – in how we respond nowadays. If anyone comes with a complaint like that now, I've made it very clear – very – that they go immediately to the police.'

'They go to the police?'

'Or we alert them ourselves.'

'But you know, Your Grace, I don't understand. When I was a boy, we were told that masturbation was a mortal sin – die with it unconfessed and you'd get to burn in hell for all eternity. Jesus said that anyone who hurts a child should be drowned with a millstone around his neck. But you're saying, if you take a rectal temperature of a nine-year-old boy and then beat him on his naked arse for your pleasure, you only get sent to Workington?'

Again, there was silence. The werewolf raised himself up to his now gargantuan height of nine feet and kicked the outside of the priest hole with a most ferocious blow, which seemed to shake the entire palace. Although not even his size twenty-five paws could take on six inches of marble, the kick did cause one of the fireplace decorations to fall off, revealing a small air hole. He put his right eye up against the hole and tried to see in. The old priest, the product of many a youthful fight in the streets of Cork, realised what he was doing and jabbed a skinny finger through the hole and into his eyeball.

The wolf jumped back. 'OW! OW! OW!' he screamed, shaking his enormous head and clutching his injury with a vast paw. For a few moments, he walked around the room, cursing and swearing, stifling it so as not to give away how much it hurt. After a minute, he went back to the air hole and began whispering spitefully.

'When the police finally investigated what had been going on, just after you became cardinal, they discovered that another five priests had been abusing Christ knows how many boys during the years you were overseeing their spiritual and moral education. If you'd punished the first one as he deserved, and as your God commands, the boys would probably never have been harmed.'

'I didn't know anything about it, I swear.'

'I didn't say you *knew* anything for sure. You didn't want to know. That's how everyone deals with it.'

'That's a lie!'

'No, it isn't. The police uncovered records which showed the school, and that means you, knew about some of the offences committed by your monks.'

Crime And Punishment

'That's not true.'

But now the werewolf had an idea and stepped away from the fireplace.

'Isn't it the case, Your Grace, that you offered a woman who was molested by one of your monks fifteen hundred quid for therapy while persuading her not to contact the police, a bribe which, fortunately, she turned down. Your monk got six years, which took into account the fact that he'd done the same to three other women.'

As he accused the cardinal, the werewolf held up his enormous right paw and stared intently at the middle one of his five claws.

'But then, of course, I suppose you were only doing as you were told by a Vatican directive of 1962 written by Cardinal Joseph Ratzinger, later to become Pope Benedict XVI.'

'What?'

'What me no whats, Your Grace.'

To the cardinal's astonishment, the werewolf began to sing like a bottom-of-the-bill crooner in a third-rate music hall:

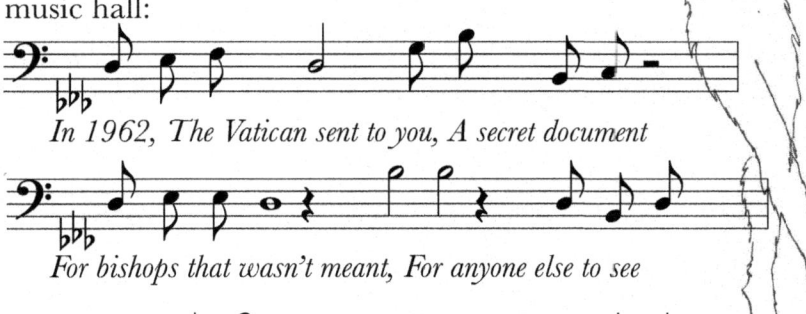

In 1962, The Vatican sent to you, A secret document

For bishops that wasn't meant, For anyone else to see

Saying excommunication, Is what would happen to you, If anyone else should view

Your judgements against a priest, For fondling a child or a beast

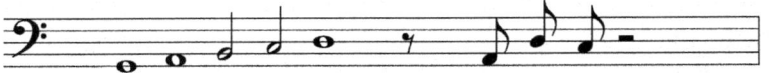

And that this revolting violence, Should be held in perpetual silence,

Signed Cardinal Ratzinger, Who on sin was prone to linger

A priest who was very strict. And later Pope Benedict.

The wolf finished his (hideously out of tune) song and began to cackle with mad laughter, then held up the middle claw of his right hand. Staring at it intently, he began to strain, as if trying to pass an immense stool. Slowly, the middle claw began to grow, a time-lapsed satanic spear of asparagus. The werewolf watched with orgasmic pleasure as the claw became a digit, the digit a member, the member a limb, the limb an extremity. Four feet long, it was only as thick as a child's finger and had four joints, but it was as hard as the hob of hell. And, at the end, a wicked pointy nail as sharp as a knife.

'Ah!' said the werewolf in his ecstasy, wiggling his new appendage this way and that, delighting in its hinged and steely springiness. He darted forward to the marble fireplace and, with his hideously long appendage, went Tap! Tap! Tap! And Scratch! Scratch! Scratch!

'You know the document I'm talking about, don't you, Your Grace?'

Crime And Punishment

'That's not true, you lying henchman of Beelzebub! The cardinal's directive said such things were a grave crime and that if a person knowing about it failed to denounce such a priest they would incur excommunication!'

'Balls, Your Grace. Nobody *knows* these things for certain, except the children they're done to, and we know what happens if they try to talk. It's your usual trick of always having an obfuscating, gimlet-eyed get-out clause. No one but the Vatican could describe the rape of a child as an offence against the commandment that thou shalt not commit adultery.'

'Go to hell, you horrible bastard.'

'Oh, you've changed your tune. Where's all your sorrow for the children you failed to protect?' This clearly hit home. Another silence.

'I know I let them down,' said the cardinal. 'But I never thought a priest could hurt a child in such a way.'

'But you *did* know eventually, and you had years to ensure the children in your care were protected, but you obeyed the document and kept it secret to defend the Church instead.'

'There's been a complete change in how we respond to these things nowadays. Standards were very different at that time, in all walks of society.'

'So you keep saying, Your Grace. How about applying the standards of an earlier time?'

'Meaning what?'

'Well, let's say the standards of around AD 32 – you remember? If you hurt one of my children, it were better that you had a millstone tied around your neck and you were cast into the sea.'

'Even the devil can quote scripture!' shouted the

cardinal. 'My apologies about these dreadful acts have always been heartfelt.'

'We shall soon find out, Your Grace, because, in a few minutes, I'm going to be gobbling up your heart, and I'll be able to taste if there's any real remorse in your aorta and your ventricles.' He made a series of lip-smacking noises of anticipation.

'Go to hell, you soot-eyed fleabag. It'll be a cold day in hell before you winkle me out of here.'

'Will it now?' And, with that, the werewolf bent the first phalange of his cubitinous claw and poked it into the largest of the breathing holes. Inside the priest hole, some three yards square, the cardinal, having sensibly switched off the low-level emergency light, heard the scraping entrance of the hideous digit and turned it back on again. He let out a terrible cry of disbelief and horror as he saw the werewolf's hideously extended finger with its horrible scales like a vulture's claw wiggling backward and forward as it obscenely inserted itself into his private space, its multiple knuckles and collateral ligaments allowing it to bend and twist and arch this way and that as the talon on the end attempted to hook its prey.

The cardinal scrambled back, but there was no space to hide from the talon searching him out, twisting and tapping, now on the floor, now on the wall. Tap! Tap! Tap! Scrape! Scrape! Scrape! And then the single claw hovered in the air and made a come-to-me gesture, a policeman signalling to a naughty boy to attend and receive punishment. Transfixed with horror, the poor cleric backed against the wall, eyes wide, as the finger moved towards his chest and pointed, as if it had eyes, directly at his heart.

Crime And Punishment

'Into thy hands, O Lord,' he cried, 'I commend my spirit!'

And then, with a venomous thrust, the werewolf stabbed the cardinal with such malice and contempt that his talon snapped against the concrete wall as it emerged from the primate's back. With a terrible scream, the cardinal arched and bucked in agony. Then, as if the very electricity of his soul had been cut off, he slumped and fell to his knees, his lifeblood streaming from back and chest on to the concrete floor. Outside, the wolf, eyes shimmering with delight, paused for a moment to savour the coming death.

Then, with a vigorous panache, he drew out his talon in one majestic, withdrawing splatter from the cardinal, from his refuge and breathing hole. Slowly and with satisfaction, he examined the enormous finger dripping with magisterial gore.

He looked around the vast room with its greens and golds and smelled the air in celebration. After a moment, he walked over to the throne and began to write on the gold leaf around the back of the seat. When he'd finished, he looked down appreciatively at his work for a moment. Then he raised his finger in the air and concentrated intently until it shrank back into his paw, as if it had never existed. He dropped on to all fours and left the room.

In the kitchen, he was surprised and somewhat irritated to discover what experience and instinct told him was a priest – although he was wearing pyjamas – examining the inside of a large fridge while wearing earphones, which, judging from the ubiquitous Chikey! Chikey! Chikey! beat was the kind of music the wolf regarded as rather unseemly for someone having taken Holy Orders.

(In fact, Father North was listening to the White Stripes'

'My Doorbell', from their seminal 2005 album.)

He considered trying to give him a heart attack by tapping him on the shoulder. But, given the young man's age, this seemed unlikely. *Why not*, he thought, *just snap his neck?*

Perhaps he had already had enough of death that night. Or perhaps there still remained something of the compassionate human being of old in the wolf. Kill. Or don't kill?

Wolves were not made for uncertainty. At that moment, Father North, having decided on a chicken leg, turned around. It is not perhaps so hard to understand why he failed to react at all in any observable way. No scream of terror, no panic-ridden rush to escape, no evacuation of the bladder or the bowels. There are, perhaps, certain unrealities too extreme to be comprehended even by the reptilian reflexes of the most primitive recesses of the brain. He just stared at the enormous werewolf, frozen in time and space. The werewolf looked back, contemplating murder, but something – his inner man again – held him back for a moment.

Then he decided. Very slowly, he leaned forward, his mouth and terrible teeth slowly opening. He gently placed his jaws around the chicken leg the stunned cleric was still holding. There was a moderately loud slurp, and the werewolf let go, leaving behind a bone completely scoured of meat.

He padded over to the kitchen door, turned the knobby handle with some difficulty and loped out into the night.

*'Just as the bees come swarming from a hive,
Out of the Devil's arse-hole there did drive
Full twenty thousand friars in a rout,
And through all Hell they swarmed and ran about.
And came again, as fast as they could run,
And in his arse they crept back, every one.'*

Geoffrey Chaucer, *The Canterbury Tales*,
The Summoner's Prologue, 1387

CHAPTER 42

POST-TRAUMATIC STRESS DISORDER

'What was it?'

'What was what?' replied Lister.

'That *thing* in the kitchen,' said a pale-faced and dark-eyed Father North.

'We think, probably, it was a man in a costume.'

'That was no costume.'

'Well, Father, you saw it, not me. But what else could it be?'

A pause.

'I don't know.'

'It was probably a very expensive kind of costume. We've talked to the people who make these high-end party outfits for trustafarians with too much money and the like. The mouths open, the eyes move.'

There was a loud crash of hammer on marble, then another one. Forensics had failed to work out how to get into the priest hole, so the scenes of crime officer had decided to use brute force.

'And the light was poor in the kitchen. And you didn't see him for long.'

'I saw him.' Another hideous thud on the marble fireplace. 'I saw him for long enough. I looked into his eyes.' Another crash. 'I saw his tongue. It was no disguise.' Two more appalling thuds, North wincing as if they were hammering his soul.

Post-traumatic Stress Disorder

'Perhaps we can talk later?'

North looked at him. 'Yes.' Another flinch.

As soon as North turned to leave, Scrope signalled Lister to come over to the throne to examine the clue written in what they presumed was the cardinal's blood.

'I don't think we're going to be able to keep the lid on the werewolf stuff for much longer. The vicar wasn't buying it.'

'Did you tell him to keep quiet about it?'

'Yes,' lied Lister. 'But I haven't finished with him yet. He's pretty spooked.'

'He's an educated man. Or rather, I should say he's an educated priest. Clever. He's going to be pretty careful about what he says when it comes to devils.'

'I thought the Catholic Church believed in devils?'

'These days, they like to stress the spiritual rather than the physical nature of evil.'

'They don't believe in devils?' Lister sounded shocked.

'I wouldn't go that far. It's just that talking about them as if they had real tails and pointy ears goes down a bit medieval. It would look bad for a priest like North – I'd say he thinks he's above all that. Twist his arm. He'll keep it quiet.'

He turned back to the throne and its scratchily written clue.

FIRST THE GOOD NEWS: OPENING PRESENTS A PASTY DOUCHE

'What do you think?'

Lister considered for a moment.

'I'd say "the good news" is a reference to the Gospel.'

'And the first Gospel is the Gospel of Matthew.'

'We need a number.'

'See one?'

SCORN

'No.'

Another hefty crash, and the sound of collapsing marble.

'I think we're in, Inspector,' called out the scenes of crime officer. The two men walked over to the fireplace, but Lister held Scrope back a little so they could not be heard as they waited for the rubble to be cleared.

'Are you all right?' asked Lister softly.

'All right?'

'Coping satisfactorily with the business of living. Because you've been remarkably quiet for the last week. You're pale. You look sick.'

'Just a bit tired. Not sleeping.'

'Have it your own way.'

The men at the fireplace were having difficulty shifting a broken slab of heavy marble hanging from the top of the fireplace.

'And how are *you* coping with the business of living?' asked Scrope.

'Molly's being a bit of a pain.'

'Because?'

'You know, those little jibes, where if you call them out they claim you're being oversensitive.'

'Such as?'

'Jokes about how she's selling out.'

'You're paying her to be your girlfriend? I didn't realise you were that desperate.'

'The odd thing is that, normally, I wouldn't put up with all that stuff. Why should I apologise for existing?'

'So, why are you?'

'I haven't apologised,' said Lister defensively.

'I mean, so why are you putting up with it?'

'Other than this one admittedly incredibly irritating

Post-traumatic Stress Disorder

habit, I really like her a lot. I mean, fair enough, her life has been a lot tougher than mine.'

'Everyone's life has been a lot tougher than yours.'

'That's not true. Five tours in Iraq and Afghan nearly getting my bits blown off on a dozen occasions.'

'You chose to do that. Nobody made you.'

'Fuck off. I was ready to sacrifice my life for queen and country. I've paid my dues.'

'You signed up because you wanted an adventure. Just like me. Just like everybody else.'

'That's not what the *Sun* says. The *Sun* says I'm a fucking hero, me. I did my bit.'

'Yeah, you're inspirational. So what are you going to do about Millie?'

'Molly.'

'Sorry.'

'I'm going to have to say something to her.'

'Something like "How would you like it if I kept going on about how working class you are?"'

'Possibly not that.'

'Why? It's true, isn't it?'

'I don't want to scare her off.'

'I understand that there's a special charity that helps wounded veterans look for their spines. Get a hysterectomy while you're at it. You should give them a call.'

'Perhaps *you're* suffering from post-traumatic stress disorder. That's why you can't sleep and you're all white. You could get invalided out on a pension. Good money, that. You could live in Ibiza and spend the rest of your life sunbathing and crying about what a tragic figure you are.'

'Tragic? At least I don't have to pay someone to be my girlfriend.'

'That's not what I hear.'

'Yes?'

'Rumour is you're frequently seen in Soho exchanging money for comfort.'

'That's a damned lie! You know what those chuggers in Soho are like. I thought she was collecting for Oxfam.'

'Chief Inspector!' The call was loud, scared and excited. The scenes of crime officer was shining a torch into an ugly, toothy gap in the fireplace. Scrope took the torch and pointed it into the dark.

Cardinal James Gillis, supported by the restricted space, was slumped on his knees, head curled downwards on to his thighs like the most demoralised of penitents, his blood spread out to touch all sides of the floor, black in the cold torchlight.

The forensic examiner, who'd been outside making a call, returned and gave Scrope a bollocking for going near the body before he examined it. Scrope retreated to the throne with Lister. For several minutes, both of them mulled over the clue on it.

'It's not a verb, it's a noun.'

'What is?'

'"Opening presents a pasty douche". It doesn't mean opening the fireplace "reveals" a pasty douche. It's a joke. "Presents" means "gifts". And when do you open gifts?'

'The twenty-fifth of December. So it's chapter twenty-five of Matthew's gospel.'

'Doesn't ring a bell. You?'

'No.'

Lister went on his phone for a few seconds. 'The parable of the ten virgins?'

'Unlikely.'

Post-traumatic Stress Disorder

'The parable of the bags of gold?'
'Don't think so.'
'The sheep and the goats?'
'Possible. Give me the gist.'

'Judgement day,' said Lister. 'Good sheep on God's right, sinful goats on his left. Jesus asks those about to be judged if they helped him when he asked. They claim they didn't recognise him. Jesus says he was present in anyone poor or sick or in need who asked for their mercy. He says, whatever you did not do for one of the least of these, you did not do for me. He sends the goats who didn't help those who asked for mercy to eternal punishment.'

Lister looked. Scrope's face was contorted by the effort of thinking.

'Your mouth looks like a chicken's bottom when you do that.'

'Could be,' said Scrope, ignoring him. 'A bit vague. And a bit too easy. He'll want us to work harder than that.'

'How many chapters are there in Matthew?' Some more tapping from Lister. Thirty seconds later: 'Twenty-eight.'

'We'll have to look at verse twenty-five in each chapter, see if one of them bites.'

'What about "a pasty douche"?'
'You're joking, right?'
'No.'

'"Pasty" equals "white". "To douche" means "to wash something" – usually in a medical sense of washing out an infection. Whitewash. We'd better have a look at the cardinal's past, see what he's been hiding. I'll drive – you can look him up.'

'What about the priest in the wheelie bin?'
'Oh, right. Just collateral, I'd say. Still, you never know.'

CHAPTER 43

THE GENERAL SYNOPSIS

WEEKLY SUMMARY CASE 7831/M52A/88

It's now thirty-four days since the murder of Cardinal James Gillis, and there has been no activity from the unknown perpetrator since that time, the longest period of inaction since the attacks began. Given the seniority in the Catholic hierarchy of his last victim, the UP may simply have stopped – he may have achieved his aims and so there is no reason to continue. What those aims are is becoming clear, though not unambiguously so. Recently discovered documents reveal that Teresa Tandsby was employed as a primary school teacher at St Edmund's at the same time as Father Thomas Lloyd was a religious instructor. The headmistress of the school was the late Mother Mary Frances, whose body was disinterred by the UP just after he killed Father Lloyd.

Enquiries at the convent where Mother Mary Frances was Mother Superior (the Poor Deirdres of Perpetual Mercy) showed a record of unblemished respect for her, bordering on saintliness. However, further interviews with former pupils reveal a woman feared not only by the children but by their parents as well. She was not often violent, it seems, but was subject to sudden and unpredictable rages

The General Synopsis

against a small number of children that were so extreme they were remembered with surprising detail, given the age of the witnesses at the time and the decades that have passed. When asked, the current Mother Superior of the Poor Deirdres of Perpetual Mercy expressed complete disbelief and considerable indignation that such a respected cleric could be defamed in this way. She said that she had known Mother Mary for many years and she was a kind and much respected figure, something attested to both by other nuns and the parishioners. However, I'm persuaded that the UP responsible for these crimes held a particularly strong grudge against Mother Mary Frances, presumably for the punishments she inflicted on him personally.

However, nothing we have discovered about Miss Tandsby or Father Lloyd suggests that either of them were violent towards the children; in fact, rather the opposite. Our working presumption is that they must be involved for more subtle reasons – possibly the UP asked for their help and was refused.

The next link in the chain is that both Father Seamus Malone and Father Gregory Melis taught at Salesian College in Cowley, a working-class suburb of Oxford. Presumably, this was where the killer met them and, for whatever reason, conceived a sense of having been wronged by both of them. Naturally, we cross-checked those boys who attended St Edmund's Primary with those who went to Salesian College – about eight miles away – but this proved a less useful lead than we'd hoped – nearly half of all the boys from the primary school went on to Salesian College, as it was the only Catholic school in the area. In addition, many of the records from both schools have been lost, St Edmund's having moved to a new site thirty years ago and Salesian College having closed down.

Although witness statements reveal that boys were subject to a certain amount of casual violence from the priests, neither Malone nor Melis seems to have been involved. While neither was remembered with any great affection, nor were they particularly disliked, as were a number of other priests at the school. The obvious question is whether they were involved in sexual abuse – inevitably, something more secretive – but this was universally dismissed by the witnesses who'd been pupils there. They were very clear there was only one such priest, all of the witnesses identifying the same man. With the few exceptions of some who remembered their time at the school with affection, most were either unenthusiastic or hostile about their experiences – one former pupil describing it as being a 'sterile cesspit'.

Apparently, the strict rules of the place ensured that no priest or boy was ever likely to be on their own very much. Revealingly, the one paedophile priest was the head of pastoral care and he had several private rooms he alone had the key to, as well as a reason to be alone with his pupils. There isn't the slightest evidence that either Malone or Melis was involved in any sexual activity with children. The witnesses we spoke to who had encountered them found the idea either objectionable, if they were still practising Catholics, or implausible, even if they were not. Whatever is motivating the UP in his attack on Catholic priests (and one lay teacher), it does not seem to be related in any way to sexual misdemeanours.

We continue to cross-check possible suspects, but the loss of records has been a major factor in denying us useful leads. The records administrator for the Catholic Church

The General Synopsis

in England is, however, doing as much as he can to help a team of three officers to try and track down any documents that may be missing rather than lost. He's clearly mortified by the ineptitude of his predecessors, so there's no question of any reluctance here on the part of the Church authorities. Turning up new records remains one of our last hopes. Had they been complete, I think there's a good chance we would have isolated a suspect by now.

Otherwise, forensic clues have revealed some human DNA, but those samples match no records. The 'clues' left by the UP at the site of the crimes initially seemed to be potentially useful, but my considered view is that they constitute more of a narcissistic mind game than anything else.

Conclusion

We are undertaking an extensive case review and, where records are available, continue to question witnesses and potential suspects who attended both schools. In addition, we have the team searching for missing documents. To be frank, the case has reached something of a dead end. Although there is no evidence to support the theory that the UP will make an attempt on the life of the pope during his upcoming official visit, I continue to believe that such an attack is plausible. I find it hard to believe that the UP is intending to hide his motives, given his extreme methods. In my opinion, he is waiting to take action of the most extreme kind in order to ensure that, when he decides to make his intentions clear, there will be universal attention. Why stop at a cardinal when the supreme pontiff is about to enter your territory of his own accord?

– George Scrope, Inspector

SCORN

What Scrope avoided was any mention of wolves, or that he and Lister had decided, in the light of the discovery, to go back over their list of physically past-it or sick middle-aged men from the Salesian school, men who might be harbouring a grudge but whose physical condition had ruled them out.

The trouble is that this involved nearly all of them. Reasonably, but of course entirely wrongly, it seemed obvious that such a violent desire for revenge must be rooted in a sexual assault, probably a great many. O lamentable *assume* that makes an *ass* out of *u* and *me*! They concentrated their attention on those with whom there was a likelihood of their having been fondled by the school's only known paedophile. As it happened, he had been a careful collator of records of the boys he had counselled in his time – and Aaron was not one of them. To the back of the queue he went.

CHAPTER 44

A TOUCH OF CLASS

'I have a friend – more an acquaintance, really – who can't have sex with any woman with a Northern accent.'

David Lister was lying in bed, staring up at a naked Molly Coates, sitting astride his waist just enough to cause her pussy lips to peep out discreetly from her dense though carefully defined ginger pubic hair. Molly's expression, the one that caused this provocative statement, turned chilly.

'Why are you telling me this? You've got a problem with who I am?'

'Me?' he said. 'No. I was wondering if you had the same kind of problem as my acquaintance. With me, I mean.'

'Obviously not.'

'Not *as* obviously – but the way you were looking at me just then, I'd say you have a problem all the same.'

'What do you mean?'

'Well, the thing is,' said Lister, 'when I had my eyes closed a minute ago ... well, they weren't, and I was watching you watching me, and I thought – it's not the first time I've thought this, to be honest – I thought: *she finds me unacceptable, you know. This girl. She looks down her nose at me.*'

'You think I'm an inverted snob?'

'Why "inverted"? Why not just a snob?'

Suddenly, Molly eased to one side and, without even thinking about it, put her left hand to cover herself between

SCORN

her legs as she did so. She stepped off the bed and, putting on her T-shirt, went over to the comfy chair (an heirloom of indeterminate age and very nearly indeterminate shape that had come down to Lister from his great-grandparents). She curled up in its arms as if fastening herself into armour made of floppy chintz.

'Is that what you think of me?' she said at last. Then she looked away.

He was reminded of one of those squid or jellyfish things he'd seen on a nature programme which, when they are threatened, shift a whole range of colours up and down their entire bodies in beautiful waves of red and violet and all the colours in between. Here, the colours were shame and resentment, guilt and defiance.

'It's hard to change the attitudes you were brought up with,' she said.

Lister looked thoughtful. 'I suppose my acquaintance would say the same thing.'

'We're not the same.'

'OK. Why?'

'Because I've got something ...' She paused, knowing she needed to watch what she was saying. '... Something to be resentful about, and your friend hasn't. I take it he was born with a silver spoon up his arse, and this isn't some stupid trap you've set me.'

'No. A silver spoon was involved, definitely. And now that I think about it, there's a real possibility it was up his bottom. Like I said, he's just an acquaintance.'

She took, if not a deep breath, a heartfelt one.

'My father was born in a village that didn't have running water or electricity. He left school when he was thirteen, but he's one of the cleverest people I know. Always thinking,

A Touch Of Class

always interested. A really sweet and thoughtful person. You want to know about the hidden injuries of class – he's the walking wounded.

'The day I got into university, he was so proud I thought he was going to have a stroke. I never saw joy like it. He thought the world of people with an education. He was so smart, but he didn't have an ounce of confidence. He was always talking himself down. I hated it. I hated him sometimes, because of it. And when I met you, it all came back, just bursting out. And the more I liked you, the angrier I got. Happy now?'

She looked at him – hopeful, daring and annoyed.

'Well,' he said, 'I am, actually.'

'Because now you understand me?' This was more the annoyance than anything else.

'That was sort of the point. To understand you.'

'Even if you understand that I hate you?'

A pause. 'Ow,' he said.

'Nothing personal – I don't *hate* you, I hate you.'

'Right, I think I'm clear on that.' Another pause. 'But not really.'

'Have you read any Marx?'

He hesitated, wondering whether to embroider.

'A bit. A dummies' guide.'

'There's a dummies' guide to Marx?'

'No, actually, but that sort of thing. It was a comic. It was pretty good, as it happens.'

'Well, the fact that I think you're lovely—'

'You do?' He was surprised at just how delighted this made him.

'Of course. Didn't I just show you?'

'I thought it might just be physical.'

'Don't flatter yourself.'

'Really?'

'Of course, physically. But I like you a lot.'

'You never give me that impression, to be honest.'

She sighed – some sorrow, some exasperation.

'It's hard to give you compliments. You're so fucking cocksure about everything. I thought it would make you unbearable.'

He thought about this.

'I promise you,' he said at last, 'that nothing nice you ever say to me will make me more nauseatingly self-confident than I am already.'

'I'll think about it. But the trouble is that you've got everything.'

'I wouldn't say everything.'

'I would. Money, power, networks. The confidence that everything can be shaped to do what you want it to.'

'OK. All right. I agree. All that stuff is fair enough.'

'That's good of you.'

'But I didn't join. They made me.' She laughed. 'It's not my fault, any more than it's your fault that you keep racing pigeons and know how to wear clogs and eat dripping.'

'Watch it.'

'Why do *I* have to watch it? Why shouldn't *you* have to watch it with *me*?'

'Because eating dripping is a short cut to an early grave.'

'And eating Stilton isn't?'

'Do you really want to go through the statistics of class and death rates? Because you'd lose.'

'Probably.'

'Besides, I've never eaten dripping. I don't really know what it is.'

A Touch Of Class

He laughed.

'Funnily enough, I do. I ate loads of it in Afghanistan. In the early days in Helmand, the supplies of food were pretty erratic. We had a corporal whose dad was a butcher in Accrington. He called it mucky fat. It was nice, though.'

'So you still eat it on your caviar sandwiches, then?'

'Oh, for Christ's sake. Just shoot me and be done with it.' He pointed to the side of his skull. 'Right there, just next to the scar I got fighting to preserve my class interests in a shithole somewhere north of Musa Qala.'

With an odd mixture of nervousness and determination, she smoothed down the front of her T-shirt.

'You know,' said Lister, 'I never really thought of myself as a type before.'

'We're all types,' she said, sniffing.

'And what type are you?'

'A stereo*type* – a working-class heroine with a chip on her shoulder. I'm worse than you.'

'Surely not.'

'But it's still true. I might be me, Molly Coates, the peculiar, totally not quite like anybody else redhead—'

'More ginger, actually.'

'... *Redhead*, who is not like anyone who's lived before me or after me. But no one is an individual in the way most people think they are. Just as big a part of me as whether I like talking to myself or sitting in the dark on my own is that I'm just as many things that aren't personal. I'm made of economics – we had no savings, no money-fat. I'm made of sociology – if I went home with a tit job, no one would think I was a half-wit. I'm made of politics – if I said I was voting Tory, it would be the same as going into a golf club in Virginia Water and announcing it was all right to have sex with children.'

'Lots of working-class people vote Tory.'

'Not in Macclesfield they don't.'

'I don't give a damn about any of that.'

She gasped with irritation.

'But you should. It's what I *am*, just as much as my charming but slight lisp and my *first-class* degree in political science and my *fabulous* bosom.' She cupped her breasts and pursed her lips like Marilyn Monroe in a pin-up. 'Look, saying you don't care about class just makes you look stupid.'

'Thanks.'

'Sorry. Look. The person, David Lister, doesn't care. I know. But David Lister, the type — it's just a part of who he is. It's like saying the flesh on your bones wasn't made from grouse and Eton Mess and Châteauneuf du Pape.'

'Over-rated, in my opinion.'

'Shut up! I'm made up of mushy peas and dripping. Even though I've never had dripping and I can't stand mushy peas.'

'No, *you* shut up! If we're going down the route of lame metaphors, the muscles we share are exactly the same, no matter what we ate while we were growing up. We're people, not products.'

'We're people *and* we're products.'

'Not true.'

She laughed, not dismissively, but like someone letting out a secret.

'You remember the other day, when you were talking about your nephew?'

'Which one, Tarquin or Jolyon?'

'Oliver.'

'Oh, him. What about young Olly?'

'You mentioned in passing that he was going out with a Sainsbury's girl.'

'OK, so?'

'It was an hour before I realised you didn't mean he was going out with a girl who worked in Sainsbury's, you meant someone who was going to *inherit* Sainsbury's.'

For a moment, he didn't realise what she meant. Then he began to giggle, and Molly joined in. He looked at her, eyes full of mischief. 'You're right. Our love is impossible.'

Outraged, she ran from the comfy chair and jumped on him, hitting him on his head and chest and stomach. Eventually, both of them laughing, he grabbed her wrists and stopped the punishment. They looked at each other, a long, lover's stare.

'Feel better now you've got that off your chest?'

She eased her wrists away from his loosening grip and pulled the T-shirt over her head, straightening herself and pointing at her breasts.

'I don't have a chest – I have booosums.'

Later, exhausted and sweaty, they lay in each other's arms for nearly half an hour without talking, the light failing.

'You know,' she said at last, 'just because I'm a completely pathetic female, still totally the prisoner of the false consciousness of romantic love, it doesn't mean I'm a pushover. Your class – I don't say *you*; that remains to be seen – you think you're entitled to everything that's worth having.'

'Aha!' he said. 'Ah, the E-word. I was wondering how long before we got to that.'

'You can say it as if it's tiresome to bring it up, but the

SCORN

fact that it's a *dreadful bore*' – she inflected the insult with a mildly posh accent – 'doesn't stop it from being true. Or are you saying there is no such thing as a class, of the kind you so blatantly belong to, that gets the lion's share of the cake?'

'I'd just like to point out that it's a generalisation, and a pretty big one.'

'There's nothing wrong with truisms,' she said. 'Truisms get that way by being true. And the thing is, you're getting worse. You think because you wouldn't dream of going into a factory cleaner's house and taking what you fancy from his fridge that you aren't still a bunch of robber barons. You might not be ready to steal his pot noodles and his tinned macaroni, but then, you don't want them.'

'My God, does the Police Federation know you're a communist?'

Molly laughed.

'I got my *Marxism* from my sociology teacher.'

'There's a surprise.'

'But he was wrong about one thing – he was sure the upper classes were on the run. In his day, they thought they'd seen the last of prime ministers from Eton. Actors and writers from up north were everywhere. Fashion, music – full of people who were as common as muck. He didn't realise you had the money and the power to adapt. The Cabinet is full of people you went to school with, isn't it?

'But you aren't just taking back what you used to own. You've decided you want everything we have that's worth having. In the sixties and seventies it was all Michael Caine and Twiggy and Bowie. But Chris Martin went to Sherborne and James Blunt went to Harrow.'

A Touch Of Class

'It's true. That Damien Lewis bloke, he was three years below me.'

'Lily bloody Allen went to Bedales.'

'Really?'

'Radiohead went to Abingdon School. Thirteen thousand pounds a year.'

'How the fuck do you know all this?'

She laughed. 'I'm writing a dissertation for my sergeant's exam.'

'What the hell has all this got to do with being a policeman?'

'Woman.'

'Sorry.'

'Things are changing, even for the police. Do you know what the worst one is? Simon Cowell, Darth Vader of Bland, godfather of everything rotting the soul of the proletariat – he went to Dover College.'

'OK, that *is* sinister.'

'You're going to hoover up everything, like one of those giant trawlers scraping the seabed. The next Dizzee Rascal will come from Harrow. Some chinless wonder from Winchester will be the next Wayne Rooney. Within five years, Henrietta Cholmondeley from Cheltenham Ladies College will win *X-Factor*.'

'To be honest,' he said, screwing his face up, 'I don't think many of the upper classes watch *X-Factor*.'

'I said you'll *win X-Factor*. I didn't say anything about watching it. Pretty soon, you'll have stolen everything from the working class except poverty, obesity and sucking off kerb-crawlers.'

'Jesus! All right, I give in.'

She looked at him and laughed, a lovely sound.

SCORN

'In that case.'

Then she kissed him. And this time there was something in the kiss wholly unlike anything she'd offered before.

"'No, I did need to address it [her experience of Catholic institutional child abuse] because, as I said before, when things crop up, smell, times of the year, there is a flicker of what has gone past and what you missed. Time, childhood that was taken away, can never be returned. I was entitled to a life and, even though it happened so long ago, those memories will always be with me. I won't ever, I don't think, forget them, even when time passes."

The witness eloquently articulated the views of most of the witnesses (albeit the too few witnesses) whom the Committee has heard.'

> Mr Justice Seán Ryan, Irish Government Commission to Inquire into Child Abuse, 2009

CHAPTER 45

A BLAST FROM THE PAST

'Air, hellair, Chumley-Warner,' said Acting Inspector 'Serious Dave' Connor, in what Lister silently acknowledged was a passable imitation of an upper-class Hooray Henry calling out to an acquaintance at Ascot or Henley. 'I don't suppose there's the slightest chance of Lord Snooty turning up for a spot of work, is there, old chap?'

'I don't know for sure, Biffo,' replied Lister. 'About the same chance as your faithful dog Gnasher turning up for his weekly worming tablet.'

Despite himself, Connor thought this was quite funny. 'You wouldn't by chance be referring to Sergeant Bower, would you?'

'I'm afraid I would.'

'Never mind. I'm sure he'd see the funny side of it. By the way, Gnasher's owner is Dennis the Menace, not Biffo the Bear.'

'I know,' said Lister. 'But I have a lot of respect for Dennis.'

Taunting one another in the workplace has always been a feature of the once exclusively male professions. Now that justice is being done and these bastions have fallen to the right demands of fairness and equality, this kind of teasing – sometimes affectionate, sometimes merciless – is on its way out of the ecosystem of acceptable working practices. Insults at work will become the dodo, auk or Steller's sea cow of the working world; verbal offence during the daily grind will be replaced by the pursed lip or the cold silence, gone with the wind, like navigating by the stars, Morse code, or making jam.

In the spirit of admiring each other's insults, Connor nodded towards the glass walls of Chief Inspector Adebayo's office. Over the weekend, five sayings had been etched into the glass.

'Look. Must have cost a fucking fortune.'

One of the etchings declared:

> THE BEST WAY TO PREDICT
> THE FUTURE IS TO CREATE IT

'You're the one who's good at crossword clues,' said Connor. 'What the fuck does that mean — if you want to get a conviction, the best way is to make up the evidence?'

Lister considered carefully. 'Could be. I'm not saying I disagree, but is it wise to make it official policy?'

The one next to it read:

> BE LIKE THE FOUNTAIN THAT OVERFLOWS,
> NOT LIKE THE CISTERN THAT MERELY CONTAINS

'Wrinkled old retainer,' said Lister, after a few moments' thought.

'What?' said Connor.

'Bollocks,' said Lister.

Connor looked puzzled for a few seconds, then worked it out. 'Very good.'

SCORN

There was a certain moment of appreciation that passed between them. Another one of those football matches in no-man's land.

'Look, I gave your boss my written statements two days ago,' said Connor. 'I thought they were urgent. We shouldn't be hanging around on this. I mean, what else is he doing? We've been busting a gut on these interviews. If he's got something, then he should be sharing it. If he's got fuck all, then what the fuck is the delay?'

During the conversation, the pair of them had been moving to Scrope's office. Lister opened the door. 'Thank you for your contribution, Inspector. I'll let Inspector Scrope know of your concerns, and I'm sure he'll get back to you when he's got nothing better to do. Goodbye.'

He shut the door silently behind him. What really worried Lister was that Connor was right. Warren the wolf was running rings around the pair of them and, whatever he said, Scrope had been notably distracted these last couple of weeks. He'd looked at Connor's report on the thirty or so men he'd interviewed who'd attended both St Edmund's Primary and Salesian College, and at least two needed a detailed follow-up by Scrope himself.

It wasn't that they represented a great opportunity for a breakthrough, but finding out Warren's identity was their only serious hope of stopping him. Someone among this group of his fellow pupils might have a clue who Warren was, or might even be Warren himself.

As a matter of routine, whenever Scrope was out, Lister made a point of scanning his desk for anything that might be useful which Scrope might have forgotten or not have any intention of telling him about. Lister liked to keep himself informed. But there was nothing of much

A Blast From The Past

interest except a message – 'Jonathan Massing called' – and a number, followed by 'URGENT'.

Lister considered this for a moment. Could be personal, he thought. Could be he's holding out.

He went over to his computer and tried to get it to come back to life. An arthritic buzz indicated it was trying. While he was waiting, he rang IT.

'I asked you to look at my computer. Every time it goes to sleep, it takes five minutes to come back on.'

'We've been snowed under a bit. Could be a couple of days.'

Lister thought about some cruelly aimed abuse, but the price of sounding off would have been weeks of non-attendance. He tried emotional blackmail.

'Look, the lives of innocent people are on the line here. I'm crunching searches by the hundreds,' he lied. 'This is really slowing me down. I wouldn't make a fuss otherwise.' This was also a lie. 'Any chance of speeding this up?' he added in his most placatory tone.

There was what sounded like a guilty silence.

'No,' came the reply.

By now, the computer had wheezed back to life. It took a couple more minutes fucking about before Google presented itself and, with a quick look to check Scrope hadn't turned up, he typed the name Jonathan Massing into the search box. He was clearly not a vain man – his stub on Wikipedia was basic in the way typical only of those not written by the subject: *Jonathan Massing, Navy Captain (retd), the 3rd Baron Frilford.*

Of the slim remaining factual pickings, the only one of any use was that he'd been educated at Downforth at the same time as George Scrope. It was nothing, then, to

SCORN

do with the case. It was slightly odd that Scrope had never mentioned him in all the times of hideous boredom they'd endured in Iraq and Afghanistan waiting for something horrible to happen. But it wasn't that odd. He wiped the search memory and decided to get on with some work – but only after he made himself a deadeye on their Fracino espresso machine, bought the previous month off eBay for a knock-down bid of £525.

Just as he was sitting down to enjoy the result, Scrope arrived, looking better than for some time. It didn't last. As soon as he read the note from Massing, he went a strange grey colour.

'You look as if you could do with a coffee,' said Lister.

'You offering?'

'Obviously, I'm offering.'

'A redeye would be nice.'

The door to the office opened at the same time as a redundant knock. It was Connor.

'Did you have a chance to look at my summary of the witness statements?' he asked.

'Oh, yes,' said Scrope. 'You're right, we should talk to whatshisname ... Aaron Gall, again. And his brother.'

'The one in the US?' asked Connor. 'I fancy a trip to Chicago.'

'Sorry. We need cutbacks to pay for the glass walls and the etchings on Chief Inspector Adebayo's new office. You'll have to confine yourself, for the moment, to checking he hasn't been in the country recently.'

'Yeah,' said Connor, mockingly disappointed. 'But Aaron Gall lives in Finchley. I've been to Finchley.'

'I think we should talk to the brother before we book your flight to O'Hare. We might be able to eliminate him

A Blast From The Past

and save you the trouble of a long and arduous trip.'

Lister, who'd been pretending not to be much interested, was as alert to this as Connor.

'We?' said Connor.

'You and me, yes.'

'Shouldn't that be you and I?' asked Connor.

'Yes,' said Lister, looking up at Scrope. 'It should be you and I.'

Connor was clearly delighted, both at having corrected Scrope and at replacing Lister. 'When do you want me to arrange the interviews for?'

'This afternoon,' said Scrope.

Connor left, ogling Lister triumphantly. A short silence followed. 'The summary of the witness statements was damn good,' said Scrope. 'He's earned the right to do the follow-up. It's also diplomatic.'

'Perfectly reasonable,' replied Lister.

Another silence.

'How about that coffee?'

'Between I and you,' replied Lister amiably, 'You can fuck off and die.'

The message from Massing had been an unpleasant surprise. In the pecking order of his friends at Downforth, Massing had been his second or third best, depending on the year, the term even. For eight years, they'd lived in the same school house, played in the same teams, talked and laughed together, had the occasional physical fight, got into trouble together. They had been brothers in arms.

But with school friends, though, it was pretty much the rule. You lived with these people twenty-four hours a day, shared the most important time of your life with them, grew up with them. Then, the moment the school gates closed behind you for the last time, it quickly turned out they no longer existed. Not quite that, and not everyone, but almost.

In the case of Jonathan Massing, he had come to want that non-existence to include the memory of him as well. It never had, of course. No matter how deep the memory dungeon, he knew what had brought Jonathan Massing back out into the light from the black hole into which he'd consigned him. It was time to settle up.

'I shall observe this secret absolutely and in every way ... nor will I ever commit anything against this fidelity to the secret (of these proceedings).'

Oath sworn by the priest conducting an investigation into a complaint of indecent acts including 'any obscene act ... perpetrated by any cleric against pre-adolescent children or with brute animals'.

Crimen pessimum

'71. The term crimen pessimum ["the foulest crime"] is here understood to mean any external obscene act, gravely sinful, perpetrated or attempted by a cleric in any way whatsoever with a person of his own sex.'

www.vatican.va/resources/resources_crimen-sollicitationis-1962_en.html

'Out of the depths I cry to thee, O Lord.'

De Profundis, Psalm 130

CHAPTER 46

THE HOUSE OF DESOLATION

'Hello, Massy.'

It was three o'clock in a Starbucks on the Edgware Road. There were only about eight people in there when Scrope arrived, four of them Appled-up, the rest out of Starbucks central casting, with their phones lying ready for use next to their caramel macchiatos, like Old West desperados who'd given up whisky and gunslinging for flavoured caffeine and internet chat.

'Hello, Scropes.' Massing gestured for him to sit.

'I'll just get a coffee first.' He didn't want one; in fact, he definitely wanted not to have one. But he couldn't sit down as if he'd just popped in for a moment on his way somewhere more important.

'You look well,' said Massing when he came back. 'Very.'

Poor Scrope was stuck for a reply. Massing smiled. 'Don't worry. I look about as well as the average fat, bald alcoholic is likely to.'

'Things not so good, then?'

'Not so good.'

But after the grim start, things got better. There were adventures to be recounted with mocking disrespect for one's own part in them, catching up on people you'd liked or disliked, those who'd come to nothing who everyone

The House Of Desolation

thought would walk through life, and those who barely anyone remembered who'd unexpectedly medalled and podiumed in business, TV, politics and law.

'I was driving into town a few weeks ago when I saw this enormous poster for *Superman Lives*. There he was, with his face eight feet wide – spotty little Jeremy Fenton.'

'Yeah, I remember him.'

'I caught that shit Harwood trying to shove his head down the toilet the day after he arrived. So I gave Harwood a fucking good hiding and told him to leave him alone. He was a nice little lad, Fenton. He'd give me his cakes after that. Now's he's a Hollywood sex god. I suppose you're wondering why I wanted to see you.'

Not for the first time in the conversation, Scrope didn't know what to say.

'Old friends catching up?'

'After all this time?'

'I don't know, Massy, tell me.'

Massing looked down at the table for a while and then back at Scrope, as if he were about to make a difficult apology.

'You remember Harvey?'

'Ugly Harvey?'

'What charitable little chaps we were. Yes, Ugly Harvey.'

'He's not a sex god as well, is he?'

'No. Still not blessed in that regard. He's a High Court judge now, so I don't suppose anyone calls him Ugly anymore. Anyway, I ran into him at the Lansdowne. I don't *belong*, I was just there for an engagement party. I was just leaving and pretty tired – a bad night – but I'd always liked him well enough. He was always so cheerful. I couldn't understand why. Anyway, we were going through the usual stuff and, suddenly, he starts talking about Minty.'

Some creature in Scrope's stomach, sensing a terrible threat, clenched and raised all its spines to protect itself.

'He's just as positive and cheerful now as he was then, Ugly Harvey, and he goes on about what a great music teacher Father Minty Brennan was, how he persevered with him on the piano, even though he had such a dead ear, how he gave him a love of music he never lost. He plays every day still. And he said we all owed him our thanks for how much he cared, that when he came to the school it was all muscular and philistine, and by the time he died he'd given it one of the finest school orchestras in the country.'

'True enough,' said Scrope.

'And, on top of all that, he was so sweet tempered.'

'That was true as well.'

'He was, wasn't he? I never saw him angry. I don't think he ever punished anyone. He used to be practically in tears if he had to hand out a bad mark.'

There was a silence of a kind you could not have defined unless you'd been present. 'And yet my life turned to shit because of him.' He looked up at Scrope again with an odd, desperate kind of hope in his eyes. 'See, I couldn't bear it. What Harvey said – it was making me mad. I mean it, Scropes, really dipso. So I had to talk to you, because' – he paused – 'well, you know about Minty.'

The creature in Scrope's stomach braced itself.

'I know we never talked about it, you and I,' said Massing. 'Ridiculous, but I knew you were copping it from Minty like I was.'

Later that night, Scrope thought how odd it was that you could open the door on hell in the middle of Starbucks, the

The House Of Desolation

lake of fire pooling next to the comely smartphones and the faux artisanal cakes. He wanted to speak – shamefully, he wanted to protest – but what he had to say to distance himself from all this was terrible, too. And Massing, in any case, could not stop to listen after all the years of the unspeakable.

'It was a lesson – on a Sunday, I think – one extra to prepare me for my violin solo at Cheltenham, and ten minutes into Massenet's *Méditation* from *Thaïs* he put his hands between my legs and started squeezing me gently. Then he'd stop, then he'd start again. Then stop. Then start. I was so freaked I couldn't believe what was happening. I didn't know, I just didn't know. I can remember vividly – and this was weird – the smell of his breath. Those mints he was always chewing.'

'Spearmint.'

'Oh, I never smelled anything so strong, before or since. And the way he breathed, and the veins on his nose. 'Keep playing,' he said. 'Don't stop.' He was so gentle and softly spoken. And then he undid my trousers and he got down on his knees and he pulled them down, and my pants. And then I stopped and he stood up and took away the violin. Then he turned me around, and I nearly fell over because of the trousers round my ankles, and you know. I didn't know what he was doing behind me but, God, it hurt – he just kept on and, in the finish, I was crying so much that he stopped what he was doing. But then I realised I had blood running down my legs and into my underpants and trousers. Then he told me that no one could know what had happened because people would be horrible to me if they found out what I'd done. They'd blame me because I was so beautiful. They'd all agree it was my fault, and my parents had paid good money for me to come to the school. He was terrified – I mean, that's what I think now – he was terrified of what he'd done. I couldn't think then at all. But I was twelve. He was a priest. What would I say? I didn't know what had happened to tell anyone.'

We ought to have as many words for different kinds of silence as the Inuit are supposed to have for different kinds of snow. We have a few, of course: 'awkward', 'difficult', 'angry', 'confused'; then there's 'respectful', 'disapproving', 'eloquent', 'hurt', 'guarded', 'intimate', 'comfortable'; there's 'deadly', there's 'pleasant', there's 'guilty', there's 'golden'. Perhaps we do, after all, have lots of words for silence.

But, however many there are, there isn't one for the silence that followed Massing's account of the twenty-five minutes in which his life – all of it – turned to shit. At any rate, whatever kind of silence it was, it was Massing who broke it.

'The thing is, Scropes, when Harvey went on about how much good Brennan had done for him, for lots of people, he kept saying how he'd never left anyone behind. Brennan ... If someone was lagging, he'd go out of his way to help, even if it was only a kind word. He kept saying he was a great, great teacher. And the thing is, he *was* a great teacher, he *was* kind. And so, as he went on, I started to think I was going mad.

'And so that's why I had to talk to you. Because you were the only other boy he used to rape.'

'One MORTAL SIN is enough to send your soul to hell for all eternity.'

Father S. J. Wilwerding, *Examination of Conscience for Boy and Girls*

'A harsh penalty [for priestly sexual abusers] may satisfy the demands of justice and respond to the outrage among the Christian faithful, but it may throw the offending priest into deep despair.'

Bishop Charles Scicluna, senior cleric responsible for the investigation of abuse at the Congregation for the Doctrine of the Faith, May 2002

'Growing up in duelling worlds — Catholic & secular — my relationship to my sexuality was constantly in flux. I used to pray every time I touched myself and I would cry myself to sleep, fearful of the wrath of God, guilty for my sins. It breaks my heart to think of children all over the globe experiencing the same shame. The poor children who don't know that they're normal, that it's okay, that they needn't be afraid of their own bodies.'

Caitlin Stasey, mid-twenties
herself.com

CHAPTER 47

MY OLD FRIEND

'My God, Jesus Christ!'

Lister was shaking his head, face grey, mouth gaping just a little, and then he was silent. But it was not a difficult silence this time; it was a shocked silence, an appalled silence. Then: 'I don't know what to say.'

Scrope looked shocked himself at this; oddly so, when he thought about it later.

'No,' he said. 'Sorry. I haven't explained this very well. Massing was wrong. I was never raped by Brennan.'

'Oh,' said Lister. 'Oh.' Then: 'Thank God.'

Scrope sighed, exasperated with himself.

'I'm not telling this very well.'

'So why did he think you were?'

'Because Brennan had been trying it on with me for weeks, touching my legs, leaving his hand on my lap and moving it about. And then he'd do this thing of slipping his fingers down the back of your shorts and, every time you'd make a mistake, he'd slip them down a bit further, and he'd smile and treat it as if it were a great joke. "Oh, if you make another mistake, my hand will creep a little lower," and he'd smirk, as if it was just a little joke between us. Massing opened the door of the music room once and saw me squirming away from him. Minty didn't notice him and he just shut the door quietly. That's where he got the idea.'

My Old Friend

'So what did he say when you told him?'

'Not much. He went very quiet. But I told him I believed him, of course, that Brennan was doing those terrible things, that he'd kept touching me up. But that Brennan just seemed to lose interest in me for some reason.'

'Because of Massing, I suppose. How did he take it?'

'I kept reassuring him that it meant I knew some of what he went through. That what other people thought about Brennan was all wrong.'

'Presumably he was grooming others as well.'

'I don't know. How could I? I mean, the thing is, what Harvey said was – I really hate to say it – it was, in a way, right. Outside of his desire for sex with a few boys, he was a kind of model priest. I don't think it was a front. He loved music, and he was a caring, helpful influence on dozens of boys.'

'As long as he didn't want to fuck them.'

'As long as that, yes.'

Another hard-to-identify silence.

'The thing is, I lied to Massing. I knew exactly what was happening to him.'

A pause. 'How?'

'I was there the day that Brennan did it to him – the first time.'

'Jesus.'

'I was outside. The music room was halfway down a huge covered staircase that didn't really lead anywhere except a room used for exams. No one went past it usually; you had to be going to the music room. And it was my turn for a lesson that day, right after Massing. I was freaking out when I got there – I wanted to be sick because I knew what he was going to be trying to do with his hands. I was pretty worked up.

'And when I got to the music room, there was this sign he had outside telling you whether you could come in or not. It said either "Wait" or "Enter". And it said "Wait," so I waited further down the staircase. I had to keep moving, I was so freaked. I was quite a way down the dark stairs when the door opened and Massing came out. I didn't want to talk to him, even though we were friends. He couldn't see me because he was already turning the other way, but I could see he was moving oddly. And the light at the door was very bright, and then I could see the blood on his trousers. And I just watched as he shuffled slowly up the stairs as if he'd shat himself.'

'Jesus Christ.'

'Then, and it was really, really odd, I just felt cold, as if something had drained out of me. So I went up the stairs into the music room and Brennan was there, and he was – I never saw anything like it, not before, obviously, but even since. He was frightened, really frightened, but he was also excited. And I could see from the way he looked at me he was not going to stop himself, he was just going to eat me up, no matter what. So I told him that I wasn't going to have a lesson that day, and that, when I came back next week, if he laid a finger on me, I'd tell. I'd tell what he'd done to me and what I saw when Massing came out of the music room.'

'So what did he say?'

'I don't know. I walked out. And the next week I went back and it was as if nothing had happened, and he never touched me again.'

Lister exhaled, not realising he had been holding his breath.

'Brave thing to do.'

My Old Friend

Scrope looked at him as if he were mad. 'I sold Massing out.'

'You were a kid.'

'I sold him out. You know how they found out about Brennan? A few years later, he tried pulling the trousers off another second former, and the kid ran off and told the headmaster.' Scrope smiled. 'You know what he did? He believed him. Didn't doubt the boy for a second. Even if he didn't *know* – they always know. Brennan was on the night train to Dublin before the day was out and was quarantined in a seminary in the middle of some God-forsaken bog by the middle of the next day.'

Lister refilled his glass. 'You were just a kid,' he said.

'So was the boy who told. He was just a kid.'

'What did Massing say when you told him?'

'I didn't tell him.'

CHAPTER 48

NEWS FROM NOWHERE

'It's funny. She should bring it up, I mean. She's completely right, I was thinking that the other day.'

'Thinking that I should dump her because she's common?'

Scrope looked at him, eyes narrowing. 'Yes, that's exactly what I meant.'

'All right. Tell me your great thoughts on the issues of class.'

'I didn't know about Simon Cowell going to Dover College – you're right, that *is* pretty sinister.'

Scrope went silent, grazing on a Burger King double Nevada Grande with chilli sauce, batavia lettuce and bacon. Lister was expecting him to continue, but Scrope just kept on staring at the traffic on the A40.

'Not going to tell me?'

'What? Oh. It sounds like you've had enough of the class struggle.'

'As long as you keep it short, you might come up with something useful.'

'Useful for what?'

'I'm taking a hammering here. My sense of entitlement is a lot more fragile than she thinks.'

'Show some backbone, you big fucking sissy! Stand up for yourself.'

News From Nowhere

'But she's right.'

'Since when has being in the wrong stopped you?'

'I don't want to sneer my way out of this one. She's got something, all right. I want her to like me ...' Lister's voice trailed off.

'Ah,' said Scrope, mocking. 'The awful daring of a moment's surrender.'

'Who said that?'

'What the fuck difference does it make who said it? She's right about you. You're used to having all the control, all the power, in everything.'

'Whatever my faults, I'm not a control freak.'

'Yes, you are. Me, too – don't get me wrong. It's just that we're not nasty, hard control freaks, we're laid-back, soft control freaks. You – by which I mean me – we'd never dream of *telling* a woman what to do, we'd just ease and charm our way into getting what we want. The thing about people with charm is that they can get you to say yes without even asking the question.'

'That's definitely someone else. Who?'

'You want to worry less about who said what, mate,' replied Scrope, 'and more about what's being said. Look it up, you lazy cunt.'

Scrope's attempt to ease tensions in the group by bringing Acting Inspector Connor with him to question the witnesses came to nothing, in the end. It turned out, you may think unsurprisingly, that his class loathing was more entrenched than could be cured by a single condescending gesture of goodwill. Connor had been so inflamed by the arrival of Scrope and Lister that he'd unwisely become involved in the latest of a long line of police scandals.

SCORN

It was alleged that a Cabinet minister, one closely connected to an attempt by government to bring about unwelcome reforms of the police force, on leaving Number 10 Downing Street late one evening, got into an argument over a locked gate. During this row, it was claimed that he called the officer in question a 'pleb' – short for plebeian, which for those of you who did not study Latin means a person of an inferior social class, a chav, a pikey, trailer trash, someone innately inferior to the person speaking. It was also alleged that, among other unflattering and abusive statements, he had said, 'You best learn your fucking place. I'll have your fucking job.'

Of course, Scrope and Lister had discussed this in the car while overlooking the A40 and, while certainly accepting that such disagreeable views were widespread among their social class, it seemed odd to them that a politician, of all people, would say something so usefully and specifically unacceptable in public in front of several policemen, a group notoriously hostile to those who in any way challenged their pay or status. Still, they agreed there was never any accounting for human stupidity, a view eight years in the army had done nothing to undermine.

To their fascinated delight, however, the police version of events started to unravel almost immediately, as rumours began circulating that, with the exception of one policeman at the centre of the allegations, nearly all the remaining, wonderfully specific, incriminating evidence against the minister had been either made up or carefully embroidered. What, in the middle of their glee, also deeply baffled them was that policemen who presumably had considerable experience of making up evidence would attempt to do so against such a powerful opponent, in a place where Lister and Scrope imagined there would be the kind of surveillance appropriate to it being a centre of government hated by Al Qaeda and ISIS and second only to the White House in terms of their focus of loathing.

Even odder was how very nearly the cops got away with their half-baked scheme. It turned out that the political nerve centre of the United Kingdom was covered by about the same level of technical surveillance as a radiator factory in Salford. The fact that most of the police were lying through their teeth was only revealed by a single low-quality CCTV camera operating at a considerable distance and without sound. It then emerged that Connor had been the author of an anonymous email sent to an MP in which he claimed that he was an ordinary member of the public who just happened to be passing at the time of the altercation and heard everything that took place and could entirely corroborate in exact detail the police version of events. In addition, he added, there were a number of tourists also present who heard the row and were clearly disgusted by the behaviour of the government minister.

The subsequent unsurprising discovery that there was a CCTV record of the event, however crappy, conclusively proved that there was no such bystander and no such group of tourists, disgusted or otherwise. No great efforts of detective work were needed to uncover the fact that Connor was the culprit – drunk at the time and having worked himself up into a spectacular fury, he'd used an email account registered in his real name to send the message.

On the day of Scrope and Lister's first interview with Aaron Gall about his brother, the soon-not-to-be-Acting Inspector Connor was sitting at home on full pay contemplating a charge of misconduct in a public office and the possibility (admittedly remote) of a potential life sentence, making up his defence by means of a history involving an abused childhood, a long-hidden mental illness and desperate alcoholism. All as far removed from the truth as his indignant description of the events outside Number 10 Downing Street.

'Adultery in the heart is committed not only because a man looks in this way at a woman who is not his wife, but precisely because he looks at a woman in this way. Even if he looked in this way at the woman who is his wife, he could likewise commit adultery in his heart.'

Pope John Paul II, Interpreting the Concept of Concupiscence, 1980

'Mulvey's essay ("Visual Pleasure and Narrative Cinema") also states that the female gaze is the same as the male gaze. This means that women look at themselves through the eyes of men. The male gaze may be seen by a feminist either as a manifestation of unequal power between gazer and gazed, or as a conscious or subconscious attempt to develop that inequality. From this perspective, a woman who welcomes an objectifying gaze may be simply conforming to norms established to benefit men, thereby reinforcing the power of the gaze to reduce a recipient to an object. Welcoming such objectification may be viewed as akin to exhibitionism.'

Roberta Sassatelli

CHAPTER 49

CARNAL KNOWLEDGE

Lister was reading a copy of the *Guardian* while lying on a sofa in his front room. The sofa could possibly have been more than ninety years old; it had taken the weight of four or five generations of Lister backsides. It was a sofa that could be owned only by the very rich or the very poor, by those who couldn't afford to care what other people thought or those who just didn't.

Suddenly, the door burst open. A screaming woman raced into the room, jumped astride the open-mouthed *Guardian* reader, tore the newspaper from his hand and threw it on the floor.

'Hey, mind my comic!' said Lister.

'Pay attention to me!' she demanded.

'Are you on something?'

Molly squirmed her knicker-clad bottom into his groin. This and a T-shirt was all she was wearing.

'I'm high on *you*, baby,' she crooned. 'Give your momma some lovin'.'

'I'd rather you didn't mention my mother in this context—' But her tongue was halfway down his throat before he could finish. She grabbed his right hand, leaned back, pulling aside the waistband of the maidenly white cotton pants she was wearing, and guided his hand inside.

'Haven't you decided—' His eyes widened. 'Oh my

Carnal Knowledge

God!' he exclaimed.

She laughed, delighted at his surprise.

'If the sisters found out what I've done, I'd be cast into feminist hell.'

'I want—'

But what he wanted, she never found out.

Forty-five minutes later, she was lying naked next to him on the sofa, though on top of his dressing gown. She did not share Lister's indifference to the vast population of backsides that had been there before.

Lister watched her looking down at herself with intense curiosity.

'Odd little thing,' she said.

'Not the word I'd use,' he said.

'I've never seen it like that before. I mean, not as an adult.' She looked at him. 'Why are men so cuntstruck?' She burst into laughter. 'I've shocked you.'

Somewhat embarrassed, he said, 'No, not at all. Surprised. You don't swear very much.'

'I wasn't swearing.'

'You know what I mean. Let me off.'

She smiled. 'All right. After being serviced so greedily, I'm prepared to be lenient.' A silence. 'Well,' she said, putting his hand between her legs. 'What's the secret of its power?' She lifted his hand up and inspected herself again. 'It really is an odd little thing.'

'Ah, the power behind everything,' he said.

'How?'

'I don't know how. But, put it this way, I don't think it was just Helen's face that launched a thousand ships and burned the topless towers of Ilium.'

SCORN

'Do you think I'm beautiful?'

'Yes.'

'I think I'm funny-looking – like my pussy.'

'You are beautiful,' he said, very softly. 'I never met anyone so incredibly, amazingly, wonderfully lovely.'

She closed her eyes and leaned her head back.

'Keep talking. Lay it on with a shovel, even if it's not true.'

'It *is* true.'

'That's it, that's the idea.'

'Marry me.'

Molly opened her eyes wider than at any time since she was a child.

CHAPTER 50

Q AND A

As Aaron Gall sat opposite the now reunited pair of cops who'd come to talk to him, he was feeling a curious, not to say dangerous, mix of emotions. It was something like the moment before having one too many where the small voice of reason and sobriety could still be heard through the emerging racket of the irresponsible drunk. Aaron the wolf had almost taken over Aaron the man, the depressed man, the sober scientist man, the man covering his inner pandemonium with many layers of coldness and caution and reserve. Wolf Aaron was not at all alarmed by the presence of two policemen, one of them someone he had very carefully chosen as his opponent precisely because of his intelligence.

But there was enough of Aaron the man to decide that the only sane way to proceed was to create an impression of feebleness convincing enough that they would never begin to suspect him of eating his way to the pope. But if they didn't suspect something, why were they here? This was Aaron the man's worry.

Aaron the wolf, on the other hand, took the view that, if they suspected anything, they'd have turned up with lots of guns. Aaron feared his own growing recklessness, while also delighting in it, but he knew that he was losing his old self and that an utter indifference to consequences was wonderfully, dangerously, taking over his soul.

Scrope and Lister sat, utterly at home, on the new leather couch in the basement flat, which was pleasant enough, if a little dark. They had reassured him – he was not, of course, convinced – that these were routine enquiries, background loose ends, that sort of thing.

'Do you remember Father Seamus Malone? He was the first victim.'

'Not much. He never taught me or anything.'

'Do you remember any incidents between him and any of the pupils?'

'Sorry, no, to be honest. All I can recall is a few sermons at night prayers about sin. How each venial sin stained the soul a little – a purple colour, I seem to remember – but that they added up until your whole soul would become black and hateful to the sight of God. But, to be honest, it could have been someone else. There's a lot of sin in the faith. Pretty hard to isolate one example, really.'

'So,' said Lister, 'you don't remember any problems. Did he ever hit the pupils?'

'No. I'm sure of that. I'd remember.'

'Your brother, Nathaniel, went to the same school?'

'Yes.'

'The one who lives in Chicago?'

'I don't have another brother, so yes.' This unnecessary provocation was down to the wolf.

'Are you aware if he had any problems with Father Malone?'

'No. He's four years older than me.'

'You haven't talked to him about them? The murders?'

'The murders? Yes. Of course.'

'On the phone?'

Q And A

'Yes.'

'Has he visited the UK this year?'

'No.'

'You're sure?'

Aaron smiled. 'Am I my brother's keeper? Why don't you ask him yourself?'

Aaron could see that his provocative tone had raised their interest in him. Unwise.

'Do you remember Mother Mary Frances?'

'Who could forget?'

'When you found out her remains were removed from her grave and thrown all round the cemetery, almost certainly by the same person who killed Father Malone, how did you feel about that?'

'I thought it was extraordinary.' This word struck both policemen as odd.

'Extraordinary?'

'As in "grotesque". Didn't everyone?'

'You disliked her?'

'If disliking the sadistic old bitch was to make for a suspect, then I'd have thought everyone she'd ever taught was in the frame.' Aaron smiled again. 'Isn't that a police expression – "in the frame"?'

'I believe so,' said Lister. 'Her obituary painted the portrait of a much respected member of the clergy.'

'If by "respected" you mean "feared", then yes. Everyone was terrified of her, even the parents.'

'Did she punish you at all?'

'No more than anyone else. Don't get me wrong, she didn't hit people on a daily basis or anything. She specialised in sudden epic bursts of temper once every six months, but out of nowhere and for no obvious reason. I remember one kid getting a twenty-minute beating in front of the rest of the class because he didn't write a tail on the end of his nine.'

'Sorry. A tail?'

'Yes – the loop of the nine is supposed to have a little tail on it. Well, this kid kept forgetting. So she went berserk. I'll always remember her face: dark red, as if there was black in it, and these little white spots in the middle of her cheeks.'

'Seems a bit harsh,' said Lister.

'It does, doesn't it?'

'You don't remember the name of this little boy?'

Aaron looked at Scrope with a faint smile, but one meant to insult. A long pause.

'I do, as it happens. He went on to Salesian College, too, did Knob.'

'Sorry?'

'That was his nickname. He was unwise enough to tell someone his surname meant "knob" in Polish.'

'And his real name?'

'Why should I tell you? If anyone deserved to be dug up and scattered about it was Sister Mary Frances. Nobody likes a sneak.'

'If your friend—'

'I didn't say he was a friend.'

'All right. If your former schoolmate did dig up the late, unlamented sister, then there's a good chance he was involved in some way with the brutal murders of people apparently innocent of the kind of brutalities she was responsible for. I'd have thought that—'

'Jacob Guza. The brilliance of your argument has convinced me to do my civic duty. That's Guza with a z.'

Q And A

'Do you know how we can contact Mr Guza?'

'Sorry.'

'Is there anyone else you still keep in touch with who might remember him?'

'Sorry. I don't keep in contact with anyone, not from that far back. Except my brother.'

'Would he know?'

'Not a chance. In those days, my brother hardly ever spoke to me, let alone anyone I knew.'

'Anyone else you remember?'

'Capable of extreme violence, you mean?'

'Seems like a good place to start.'

Aaron looked thoughtful for a moment – followed by a helpful recollection. 'I can remember one kid.'

'His name?'

'Michael – Mick. Hales. But he's not your man.'

'Because?'

'The old bitch adored him. A real golden boy. And he lapped it up. A couple of years before she retired, she discovered the concept of *esprit de corps*. So she put a chart up on the wall showing who demonstrated the most *esprit de corps* every term. It was always Mick Hales. Me, I was always last. Besides ...' A malicious laugh from Wolf Aaron.

'Besides what?' said Scrope.

'He went on to become a brigade commander in the IRA. Presumably, he managed to find some use for his talents at building team spirit. He was blown up by one of his own bombs in an accident just before the Good Friday Agreement.'

They talked for nearly an hour, about Gall's life at Salesian College and how well he knew the priests from there who'd been murdered. Malone? *Barely ever talked to him. Brother Melis? In his class for a year. He was all right.* Not violent? *No.* Anything else? *You mean touching up boys?*

'If you like.'

'No. Violence and sin was their style. There wasn't much of that stuff at the camp. That's what we used to call it, as in "concentration camp".'

'Was it that bad?'

'Don't know. I was never in a concentration camp.'

A silence. Clearly a dead end.

'Were you aware of any kind of sexual abuse?'

'It was a small school in a crowded suburb. You were never on your own because there wasn't any space. That's how they liked it; they could keep an eye on us. I heard stuff about one priest who liked to fondle little boys, but he just disappeared back to Ireland when someone complained.'

'Do you remember his name?'

'No.'

'The name of the boy who reported him?'

'Sorry.'

In short, Aaron took them around the houses. As they sat in the car after the interview was over, they considered what they'd learned.

'Damn all there,' said Lister.

'If that.'

'Bit of a weirdo.'

'I never met a Catholic who wasn't.'

'You included?'

'Me especially.'

'The Congregation for the Doctrine of the Faith is currently examining how to help the bishops of the world formulate and develop, coherently and effectively, the indications and guidelines necessary to face the problems of the sexual abuse of minors, either by members of the clergy or within the environment of activities and institutions connected with the Church, bearing in mind the situation and the problems of the societies in which they operate.

This will be another crucial step on the Church's journey as she translates into permanent practice and continuous awareness the fruits of the teachings and ideas that have matured over the course of the painful events of the "crisis" engendered by sexual abuse by members of the clergy.'

www.vatican.va/resources/resources_
lombardi-nota-norme_en.html

'You're not supposed to fuck the children.'

Mia Farrow

```
                    'crisis'
                    'crisis'
'crisis' 'crisis' 'crisis' 'crisis'
'crisis' 'crisis' 'crisis' 'crisis'
                    'crisis'
                    'crisis'
                    'crisis'
                    'crisis'
                    'crisis'
                    'crisis'
                    'crisis'
                    'crisis'
```

CHAPTER 51

A SURPRISING TURN OF EVENTS

'I shouldn't really ask, but how have your' – Lou paused – 'I'm not sure about the word … confrontations … with the priests gone?'

Wolves know fear, and now, recalled to life, so did Aaron. He felt that his face froze so clearly that she must see straight through him and make the connection.

'I've decided to stop.'

'Yes?' She was curious.

'What you said before about letting things lie. You had a point.'

He tried smiling to underscore the compliment, but Lou was not so easy to flatter. It was in her nature to get answers as a matter of course. She did not have casual conversations that stopped and then started somewhere else.

'I'm not sure – I mean, given how well you are now – that I was right?'

'You were. Absolutely.' He'd calmed down a little. 'I only needed to talk to two of them, and then I realised something.'

'Yes?'

'People don't change. I mean, sometimes they do, but not often, not really. It was what you said. People did apologise in a guilty way, pretending not to remember very much. But at the end of the second time I had this sudden, very clear sense that, if I could turn back time and they were in charge again, thinking what they still thought in their heart of hearts, absolutely nothing would be different. So what was the point? It doesn't matter to me. That's what I discovered. It doesn't matter to me whether they're sorry or not.'

He smiled, easy now that he'd managed to come up with something true, as far as it went. 'So I stopped. Besides, I'm feeling like a new man.'

Lou leaned back, thoughtful, and as she did so her lovely breasts, with their startlingly deep-brown nipples, rose out of the foam which lazily flowed down their curves, reluctant to let go. She raised both arms up into the air in surrender.

'Look,' she said. 'I've shaved under my arms to please you. Isn't that pathetic?' She turned to one side, causing her breasts to shake fetchingly, put one hand behind her head and put the index finger of the other to her lips like a forties pin-up. 'What do you think?'

He smiled. 'Adorable. But don't shave on my account. I like hair.' He smiled again. 'In fact, I *demand* you grow as much as possible.'

'So masterful,' she said, fluttering her hand in front of her face as if to waft cooling air over her fevered brow. 'It's terrible, though, the murder of those priests.'

Fortunately, she sat back into the bath as she said this, and closed her eyes. *How could she not see?* he thought.

'Yes,' he said. 'But, to be honest, I wasn't that bothered. I didn't feel anything at all. Is that terrible?'

Lou opened her eyes and looked directly into his. *She will see. She must.*

A Surprising Turn Of Events

'I think it's only human.' Then she looked down at the water between his legs. His erect penis was standing up from the surface, Godzilla from the deep.

'Oh my goodness,' she said. 'I swear it's getting bigger.'

'All the better to eat you with, my dear.'

She opened her eyes wide. 'Don't come near me with that thing.' She grabbed the loofah from behind her head. 'I have a sponge, and I'm totally preparing to use it.' She squealed with delight as he made a grab for her wrist, sending a huge wave over the edge of the bath to dash its creamy foam all over the blue-tiled floor.

CHAPTER 52

VIVAT! VIVAT REGINA!

The weeks passed, and there were no more attacks and no more clues. The days until the official visit of the Holy Father began to loom towards the watching policemen like a bleak mountain slowly becoming visible through the fog. Already terrified by the possibility of an assassination that would undo all the expensive good work done by the success of the Olympics, the attention of the hordes of journalists now assembling for the visit caused the various branches of government involved to become hysterical themselves. There were reviews, questions from the office of the prime minister, more reviews, veiled threats about Scrope being replaced (much to Lister's annoyance, no one thought his position was worth threatening), then not at all veiled threats. Scrope realised he was very close to being told to take a bottle of whisky and retire to the snooker room (funnily enough, in Lister's house in the country, there was both a snooker room and a revolver).

Aaron, of course, watched all this keenly. It didn't take much in the way of guesswork to realise that his carefully chosen policeman was living on borrowed time. A success was called for. It had to be a limited one, but a reminder all the same that Scrope was their best hope of making a breakthrough.

Early the next morning, the fierce and vulgar oranges

Vivat! Vivat Regina!

and reds of a London dawn filtered through the empurpling sooty particulates of cabs and bicyclist-murdering lorries. A woman slept. She was Elizabeth, the queen, second of that name since before the enormous werewolf standing at the foot of her bed was born. Unusually, this night, her sleep had been disturbed, uneven, her breathing shallow and irregular. Perhaps in some ancestral reaches of her brain the ancient fear of wolves was already warning her.

Werewolf Aaron stared down at the old woman: history itself, and not merely a person snoring and grumbling in her invaded sleep. Perhaps, he thought, she has the refinement to smell my hairy presence, the pea to her princess.

At eight o'clock precisely, there was a gentle knock upon the door. It opened and a maid entered, carrying a breakfast tray with a pot of tea, a bowl of Special-K and a couple of prunes (not the finest pruneaux d'Agen, but out of a tin). She placed the tray precisely on the table despite the dark and, as she had done for decades, walked to the first of two windows and pulled first one to flood the room with light, then the other.

She then turned to serve the royal breakfast.

Perhaps in the years since it was built in 1703 there had been a scream delivered with such piercing terror and distress in this room, but probably not. The bed was swimming in blood. On the wall above, in vermillion gore, there were written incomprehensible words.

Perhaps because of her disturbed sleep during the night, it was only now that Her Majesty awoke, with a start at this hideous sound. Then she began screaming, too.

Neatly arranged at the foot of the mattress, staring up sightlessly at their mistress, were the decapitated heads of four corgis.

SCORN

*

And now we must deal with a distasteful matter which, no doubt, given the likely intelligence of the sort of person reading this account, has been on your mind for some time. I will speak of it now.

It's hard to be a human being and also be intellectually rigorous, in pretty much the same way that it's hard to be a goldfish and operate heavy machinery.

(Is this the opinion of a friend? It depends on your notion of the word 'friend'. An honest answer is the sign of true friendship.)

And, after all, what would be culpable in a fallen archangel is admirable in a risen ape. It is a kind of ape, after all, that designed and built the Large Hadron Collider that launched this sordid tale of revenge and cannibalism. One should judge the capacity for reason in mankind rather in the light of the famous dancing dog – you don't expect to see it done well; rather, you are amazed to see it done at all.

As Sophocles, one of the brighter sort, remarked: To throw away an honest friend is, as it were, to throw your life away. But there are some people I am not and never can be an honest friend towards, except to vent at them my undying hate. Who are these, the most wretched of human beings, beyond salvation and beyond compare?

I do not call them members of a *profession*; I say rather word 'gang', 'prattle klan', 'jabber jezebels', 'middle-porch philosophers', 'trendfuck douchebags', 'runagate dribbly factulaters', 'shove-it-up-your-bucket-with-a-meat-hook bukkake candy bandits', 'cuntweasel concept mongers', 'good-idea fairies', 'pork pies and a bag of trout trash pedlars', 'loony left loony right and loony in the middle braindrizzling word crappers'.

Vivat! Vivat Regina!

I speak, of course, of the British Journalist.

I know what you have been thinking all this time: what of the fourth estate in all of this? Why has our guide and honest broker left them out? Well, now you know.

There were rumours, of course, pretty much from the start; then firmer rumours, then generalised admissions and denials from the Met. Then the hideous nature of the killings was officially announced, or unofficially or officially leaked, until the reports – just hints – of something even stranger than a mass-murdering cannibal made it out into the light of day. Then there were questions, demands for action, calls for heads to roll, for Something To Be Done. You know the drill.

When Plato pointed out that humanity's grasp of reality was like that of a chained man in a cave, able to see only shadows of the outside world cast on the wall and mistaking the shadows for reality, he got it brilliantly right. (You see, I *am* on your side!) The only change in mankind's dismal grasp of the way things are since Plato is that now, every hour on the hour, the village idiot turns up and shouts at the chained prisoner: 'Breaking news!'

The *Sun* was the first to print the story when news of the death of Father Thomas Lloyd leaked from one of its many paid contacts in the Met: HAIRY BEAST EATS PAEDO PRIEST!

Granted, this showed a certain lurid talent, along with a blatant disregard for the truth. Except for the day on which he walked away from Aaron's beating, Father Lloyd had been an exemplary member of the Catholic clergy. Nor was there, as yet, the slightest evidence that the murder was anything more than your common-garden variety form of violent cannibalism.

SCORN

The *Star* (Proud to Support our Armed Forces) was next to prick up its ears at stories of cannibalism and, when the rumours about the late-night visit to the Blairs' began to surface, they took their opportunity with both hands: WAS TONY NEARLY BALONEY?

But let's move on from the Soaraway *Sun* and the Stupendous *Star* to months later, when the *Telegraph* reported on that dreadful night at Buckingham Palace: DAUNTLESS QUEEN REPELS MADMAN DRESSED AS WEREWOLF: 'Her Majesty describes decapitation of corgis as "dreadful".'

The paper brown-nosed the Palace by eulogising the uniquely royal courage of a woman who was actually fast asleep during Aaron's entire visit.

There were, of course, other ways of seeing the issue: PROWLER IN CORGI RIDDLE AT PALACE MAY BE MENTALLY ILL PATIENT PREMATURELY DISCHARGED AFTER HEALTH CUTS.

I won't insult you by identifying the origin of that particular headline.

Or this one: PALACE CORGI KILLER ASYLUM SEEKER WITH LINKS TO ISIS.

Another paid leak from the Met concerning fears for the visit of the Holy Father gave the headline writers at the *Daily Star* a chance to shine in the battle of tabloid rhyming one-upmanship, as well as a chortling opportunity for gratuitous smut: IS LYCANTHROPE DOGGING THE POPE?

The *Private Eye* contribution was particularly controversial. Its front page was a photoshopped picture of the royal bed with the heads of the unfortunate corgis impaled on four elaborately decorated finials. They had crosses for eyes, and their tongues lolled heartlessly from their innocent little mouths. A policeman was standing by the window, staring out over the city of London with a pair of

Vivat! Vivat Regina!

binoculars, completely oblivious to the scene behind him: the queen sitting upright in her bed drinking from a china tea cup, saying politely to a Lon Chaney werewolf leaning over her: *Have you come far?*

The new pope and your narrator have at least one thing in common: a belief that in some examples of the very small there can be seen the entirety of the very large. Until I was obliged to give the gutter press more attention by far than I thought it deserved, I had always dismissed it as vulgar, base, disgusting and stupid. In short, they represented the very worst of humanity.

But I now see – and I arrived at this conclusion with the deepest reluctance – that their headlines demonstrate a wit, insight and intelligence that reveals an undeniable truth. If you want to understand the depth of human moral vanity, this can be readily seen in any newspaper of the left; if you want to see human nature at its complacent and self-serving worst, you can read any newspaper of the right. But for a true grasp of human nature in all its horrible, low-grade, mud-spawned vulgarity – containing, but not redeemed by, intelligence – you need look no further than the *Sun* and, in particular, the headline which did so much damage to the control of the case by the Metropolitan Police Force: DUNCES WITH WOLVES.

CHAPTER 53

THE UNTHINKABLE

All this was still festering in the background when, two hours after the dreadful discovery, Scrope and Lister could be found standing in the queen's bedroom, contemplating the most extraordinary sight in a couple of months of extraordinary sights.

'Of course,' said the queen's equerry, standing next to them, 'Her Majesty regained her equanimity extremely quickly. I don't mind telling you, she was very upset. But she's made of stern stuff, the queen. The poor maid, I'm afraid, may never be the same again.'

He sighed with anger and shook his head. 'I suppose it could all have been much, much worse, but, even so, this was a disgracefully cruel act. Disgraceful. What sort of madman would do such a thing?'

'You're right, Sir John, it could have been much worse. But while, yes, it was mad, the perpetrator is also making a point.'

'Meaning?'

'He has something to say. There's method here.'

The equerry sniffed.

'Well, I suppose you know best. You always were a clever little boy.' Scrope looked awkward at this, and more so at the look Lister gave him. The equerry nodded towards the message written above the bed in large, ketchup-red letters.

The Unthinkable

'I've no idea what that means.' He looked at Scrope. 'Do you?'

'We don't,' said Lister.

'Very well, George. I'll leave you to it. Drop in before you go, if you have time.'

After the equerry had left, Lister went over to one of the corgi heads that had been knocked on to the floor during the ruckus and moved it back and forth delicately with his biro.

'How come you know His Lordship?' asked Lister.

'Sir John? He's my godfather.'

'An interesting coincidence.'

'Not so much. I've got three of them.'

'I suppose it's a small world, yours.'

'I find it particularly laughable,' said Scrope, 'that you, of all people, are inviting me to check my privilege.'

'Who are the other two godfathers, then?'

'Shut the fuck up and get on with your work!'

'I wonder if Warren is changing in some way,' said Lister.

'Go on.'

'Whatever this is about, it's pretty fucking reckless, wouldn't you say?'

'I've been thinking the same thing.'

'No, you haven't. You just don't want to admit that I'm the one who should be in charge but I'm being overlooked because of my lack of influence with the establishment. Now I understand what Molly is saying about the hidden injuries of class.'

'For Christ's sake, don't tell Karla Marx about the godfather thing. She already looks at me as if she'd heard rumours I was planning to foreclose on an orphanage.'

'Karla Marx?' said Lister. 'She'd like that.'

'Well, don't tell her it was me who said it. Pretend it was your idea. I'm sure it wouldn't be the first time.'

'It pleases you to think so.' Lister contemplated the severed heads. 'Poor old corgis.'

The door opened and Chief Inspector Adebayo entered, looking both harassed and intimidated. He was clearly in an excitable state, but seeing the blood and the four heads in such extraordinary surroundings seemed to take the wind out of him completely.

'My God,' he said, at last.

There didn't seem anything either Scrope or Lister could add. Adebayo shook his head, as if to clear it of the bizarre horrors in front of him.

'To say I'm being leaned on is putting it mildly. Fucking redtops and their stupid fucking headlines! If I don't have something for the prime minister's office by lunchtime, we're all fucked. And by "all", I mean you two especially.'

The two men looked at their boss not with alarm but with a sort of mild curiosity. Adebayo was understandably irritated.

'It might not matter to you two comedians, but it bloody well matters to me. What have you got?'

'Nothing,' said Scrope affably.

'What about that?' said Adebayo, looking at the message on the wall. 'I thought you were supposed to be some sort of towering genius at this fucking bullshit.'

Scrope went through the motions of looking at the writing. 'No,' he said mildly. 'Nothing. Though you might be right, sir.'

'About what?'

'It being fucking bullshit. There's a good chance all this stuff' – he gestured at the clue on the wall – 'is exactly that.'

The Unthinkable

'Well, I suggest you find something, or by this time next week you'll be tagging insurance slags at Watford Gap. Call me the second you've got something. Understand?'

Scrope inclined his head in consent, but barely.

'Don't fucking nod at me, Scrope. Do you understand?'

'Yes, sir,' said Scrope softly.

'Geoff Dawe was right on the button about you two.'

After he'd left, neither of them said anything for a moment. To react as if concerned in any way would, of course, have been unthinkable.

'What's an insurance slag?' asked Lister.

'No idea.'

'I wonder what he meant by Dawe being right about us.'

Scrope started examining the tear along the neck of one of the murdered corgis.

'I think that was what that coroner who was in Iraq meant when he said we had a reputation for being a pair of supercilious cunts, though, from the way he said it, I got the distinct impression he was talking more about you than me.'

Scrope's phone rang. There was no caller identifiable.

'Hello?'

'Hi, there,' said Aaron. 'Get my message?'

Scrope signalled Lister to come and listen.

'I'm just looking at it now.'

'What do you think?'

'A bit hard on the dogs.'

'I suppose. On the other hand, the alternative would have been worse. Don't think it didn't cross my mind.'

'I see. You don't find that a bit outlandish at all?'

'Many would think so, but Her Majesty's government

has issued an invitation to the pope for a state visit – a man who symbolises the sick dreams of a long line of old men addicted to obedience and authority. Granted, when the invitation was issued it was to his predecessor, but *he* was a man with a long history of covering up the rape of children in order to protect the faith. My attempts at being outlandish are very amateur in comparison, wouldn't you say? You know, what I've come to love about the Church is that it never disappoints. There's always something more grotesque in the pipeline than you could possibly have imagined.'

'I still don't see what the queen's got to do with this.'

'We are all symbols, Scrope. We inhabit symbols, we eat symbols, we wear symbols. We're always being told she embodies England – and I agree. The queen has invited this pope, who also embodies so very much. She is going to honour this quintessence of all the measureless ill committed against me, my family and my friends. All in all, I'd say I've been very restrained.'

'So what do you want?'

Another wheezy laugh. 'You know, Scrope, some things are better left unsaid. But "thank you" isn't one of them.'

'You want me to thank you?'

'For saving your job. I got the impression from the papers that you were about to spend more time with your family.'

'Why don't you just stop?'

'There's no stopping now, Mr Scrope. You, me and the Holy Father – we're going all the way to the end of the line together.' The wolf paused, expectant. 'And the last stop is …?' he prompted.

'The last stop is the cemetery.'

The Unthinkable

'Delightful,' said the werewolf, and hung up.

It needed no discussion to understand that deciphering the words above the bed was of even more pressing urgency than usual. They looked silently at the message written in corgi blood.

FIRST OF ALL, TAKE THE BISHOP'S PRICK AND BUM TO SEE THE ARSE WARS AT MR CHICKEN'S HOUSE

'OK,' said Scrope, 'he's made one of them easy: "bishop's prick" must be "bishopric" and so I think probably "see" is ... He's telling us to look at something.'

Lister was already tapping away into his phone. At first, a search for Mr Chicken's house brought up a list of kids' cartoons, takeaways and a frat house in Chicago. He reduced it to Mr Chicken and, at number four in the list, was the website for Number 10 Downing Street.

'Oh, shit,' said Lister softly.

'What?'

'The last person to live at Number 10 before it became the official residence of the prime minister was a Mr Chicken.'

Scrope's expression changed; he looked as if he were suppressing a quite serious spasm of pain.

'OK – so we've got to see something at Number 10 Downing Street. Try "arse war".'

Lister thumbed his mobile. 'A planning application for a barn in Cambridge. A town in southern Spain. A revolting sexual practice. A complaint that a journalist called Jenkins is an arse because of his views on the Iraq war.' A pause as he scanned the next page of the list. 'Man United fans abusing Arsenal.'

SCORN

'That's it!' shouted Scrope. '"Jenkins" and "arse". "Arse" is an anagram of "ears". It's a reference to the War of Jenkins' Ear.' Scrope read off Lister's phone. '"Walpole declared war in 1739 using the amputation of Jenkins' ear by the Spanish during torture as an excuse."'

'Check who was the first prime minister.'

A brief pause.

'Walpole.'

'Hence, "first of all". So we've got: See something to do with Walpole in Number 10 Downing Street. We've got "bum" and "loo". Something in a toilet at Number 10 – a painting?'

'I doubt if they'd allow a painting of the first prime minister to be sited in a toilet. Where would that leave the rest of them?'

Lister tapped and scrolled down his phone for a few seconds, calling someone. He looked at Scrope. 'I was in the same year at Eton as the Cabinet Secretary's PPS. We used to snog behind the rafts on Sunday afternoons when we were in lowers.'

Scrope made a face.

'We were desperate.'

'Not that, because of the—'

'Jeng! It's Lister.' A pause and a laugh. Then, very quickly, 'Look, you know about this morning's Weston at the Palace? Got to be nippy, sorry. Is there a portrait or bust of Walpole anywhere at Number 10?' He looked over at Scrope, listening. 'There's a portrait in the Cabinet Room?' Scrope looked again at the clue on the wall.

'Tell him to look behind it and call us back.'

'Look behind it,' repeated Lister. 'There's no time – do it now.' He listened again and his face fell. 'Oh, fuck!'

The Unthinkable

'What?'

'He can't get in. There's a meeting of the Cabinet going on.'

'Give it to me!'

Resentful of this tone, yet aware of the urgency, Lister handed it over.

'This is Inspector George Scrope. I'm sorry to be abrupt, Mr ...' *Name?* He mouthed at Lister.

'Moyne.'

'Mr Moyne. But the queen's life and possibly the prime minister's are under real threat, so I don't care if the second coming is taking place in there. You have to look behind that painting and get back to us immediately.' He listened for a moment.

'Thank you. We'll be waiting.'

He took in a deep breath and let it out again.

'My phone,' said Lister. 'By the way, it's not *Mr* Moyne, it's Viscount Moyne.'

Scrope was about to answer back but stopped himself. 'Jesus, no wonder everyone hates us.'

'Why *behind* the painting?' asked Lister.

'The "bum" reference.'

Lister grimaced. Another silence.

'Look,' said Scrope. 'I'm sorry if I was a bit peevish.'

'That's all right. I know you of old. Once the pressure starts, you go to pieces.'

'Fuck you.'

The phone rang.

'Lister.' Scrope held out his hand, but Lister turned away, refusing to hand the phone over. A beat. 'Nothing else? OK, we'll be there as soon as we can.' He looked at his superior officer with pleasure.

SCORN

'Well?'

'I could ask whether you want the good news first or the bad news, but Warren has delivered both at the same time. There's a message on the back of the Walpole painting: SCROPE STAYS, OR ELSE!'

*'It is well further to explain:
that infallibility means more than exemption
from actual error; it means exemption from the
possibility of error;
that it does not require holiness of life; sinful
and wicked men may be God's agents in defining
infallibility;
The submission to infallible authority implies no
abdication of reason ... Were it so, how could one
believe in revealed doctrine at all without being
accused, as unbelievers do accuse Christians, of
committing intellectual suicide? ...
The only effective barrier against Rationalism
— the equivalent of political anarchy — is an
infallible ecclesiastical authority. This authority,
therefore, by its decisions merely curtails personal
freedom of inquiry in religious matters in the same
way, and by an equally valid title, as the supreme
authority in the State, restricts the liberty of
private citizens.'*

Catholic Encyclopedia, www.newadvent.
org/cathen/07790a.htm

'On 15 February 1990, in a speech delivered at the Sapienza University of Rome, Cardinal Ratzinger (later to become Pope Benedict XVI) cited some current views on the Galileo affair as forming what he called "a symptomatic case that permits us to see how deep the self-doubt of the modern age, of science and technology, goes today". Some of the views he cited were those of the philosopher Paul Feyerabend (1924–94), whom he quoted as saying, "The Church at the time of Galileo kept much more closely to reason than did Galileo himself, and she took into consideration the ethical and social consequences of Galileo's teaching, too. Her verdict against Galileo was rational and just."

The Cardinal did not clearly indicate whether he agreed or disagreed with Feyerabend's assertions.'

Wikipedia

'For men to be saved, they must know what is to be believed. They must have a perfectly steady rock to build upon and to trust as the source of solemn Christian teaching. And that's why papal infallibility exists.'

The materials presented in Catholic Answers are free of doctrinal or moral errors.

> Robert H. Brom, Bishop of San Diego,
> Catholic Answers, 10 August 2004

'In fall 1980, Pope John Paul II ordered a new look at evidence in Galileo's trial. In 1992 came acquittal.'

> Hal Hellman, Washington Post, 1998

INTELLECTUAL SUICIDE

CHAPTER 54

HIGH

For what was almost certainly the first time in modern British political history, both the prime minister and the foreign secretary were at a meeting with the recently appointed apostolic nuncio – effectively, the Vatican ambassador to the UK – his most Reverend Excellency Patrick Aloysius O'Mara.

'I'm afraid,' said the foreign secretary, a bald man with a blunt Yorkshire accent, 'we are unable to guarantee the safety of His Holiness during his visit next month.'

'I see,' said O'Hara. 'But the Holy Father has already made it clear he feels unable to turn down such an opportunity to evangelise with the faithful of the United Kingdom. His Holiness has also made it very clear that he, of all people, cannot be seen to be afraid for his own life in regard to his sworn apostolic mission.'

'Not even if his life was seriously at risk?' said the foreign secretary.

'Especially not then. Whatever people may think of the Church, it is not a political organisation but a spiritual one. Our Lord gave his life to save mankind, and even the humblest Catholic is bound to try to act his life out in the imitation of Christ. Life and death are neither here nor there when eternity is at stake. Besides, what's so special about this threat that you ask the Holy Father to

High

withdraw a second time?'

'May we speak in confidence, Archbishop?' said the prime minister. The foreign secretary, alarmed that his boss was about to say too much, sniffed loudly and looked at him meaningfully.

'I have no power to keep anything we say from the Holy Father.'

'But from anyone else?'

More mugging from the foreign secretary. A pause, then: 'Yes, I can agree to that.'

The prime minister irritably moved his feet out of reach of his agitated colleague.

'The person responsible for the deaths of so many of your ministers seems to be a former Catholic who not only harbours a grudge against the Church but who' – he hesitated, choosing his words carefully – 'has a *formidable* set of skills, considerably in excess of those of the average terrorist. Which is what we consider him to be.'

'You see, Archbishop,' said the foreign secretary, much calmer now he realised there was to be no mention of werewolves, 'though we're not allowed to say so in public, since the neutralisation of the IRA the quality of terrorists in this country has been dismal. Their most successful attack was a surprise strike in an unprotected public space. They've only succeeded once in more than a decade. They might get lucky from time to time, but terrorists in the West are drawn from the marginal and incompetent. Normally, such people wouldn't have a chance in hell of reaching someone so heavily guarded as His Holiness.'

This time the nudge came from the prime minister. 'Oh,' said the foreign secretary flatly. 'Sorry.'

'Why would you be sorry for mentioning hell?' asked

the archbishop, smiling. 'I talk about it all the time.'

'Ah. Right. Well, anyway, this individual,' said the foreign secretary, 'is altogether a different matter.'

'To put it plainly,' said the prime minister, 'there's a small chance he'll succeed. I can't tell you how reluctant I am to say it. No government would want to make it clear they can't protect their guests, a head of state, the pope himself, in their own country. But there it is. We can't offer any reassurance.'

The archbishop, a patriotic Irishman, was only too aware of the vanities of what was once the most powerful empire in history, and so was deeply alarmed by this extraordinary admission. He sighed.

'I can't emphasise too much, Prime Minister, the significance of the Holy Father not bowing to threats against his life. He's been very explicit about being the leader of a flock and not a prince of power. But I'll do what I can.'

The nuncio was silent for a moment. 'I suppose you know the late Archbishop Gillis had an assistant, a Father Peter North?'

Both men tried to create an impression of generalised uncertainty. 'The death of the archbishop disturbed his mind very much, poor fellow, but, given your claims about the preternatural skills of this murderer, I wonder if there might be something in his claim to have seen the devil himself that dreadful night.'

The smile from the prime minister could be described as anaemic, from the Rotherham-born foreign secretary as femmen.

When the nuncio had left, the prime minister walked over to the window overlooking the garden. 'What do you think?' he said over his shoulder.

High

'The archbishop made it pretty clear he's not going to help us out. We should consider withdrawing the invitation.'

'And explain it how?'

'God knows how we've managed to keep a lid on all this until now. Too bloody deranged to believe, I suppose. But if this *thing*, whatever it is, makes a pack-up out of the pope and the media finds out we knew about it and still couldn't prevent it – well, we'll both end up washing windscreens outside Baker Street.'

'What's a pack-up?'

'A packed lunch.'

'I'm glad you think it's amusing.'

'Do I look like I'm laughing? This padfoot—'

The prime minister looked balefully at him.

'It means a monster in the shape of a dog. He's got his head screwed on the right way round, whatever it is. He got into the queen's bedroom. He got into the Cabinet Room, for God's sake.'

'As to the queen's bedroom, what was the name of that nutter who did the same thing thirty years ago?'

'God knows.'

'Well, he just climbed over the fence and wandered in. At least now we know what we're up against.'

'Do we?'

'I'll put every policeman and every member of the secret services on to this. The entire fucking army, if I have to.' He looked at the foreign secretary and smiled. 'No therianthropic hybrid is going to tell me what to do.'

Yorkshire got the better of the foreign secretary.

'A ... *courageous* approach, Prime Minister.' A brief ecstasy of alarm travelled down the prime minister's spine, but then he realised what the foreign secretary was trying to do and declined to take the bait.

The foreign secretary was not so easily put off. 'Does your refusal to let a murderer dictate government policy mean you're going to get rid of this Scrope person he told you not to remove?'

It was a trap he should have seen coming but, given that so many battles in British history had been won on the playing fields of Eton, the prime minister was not to be defeated on a sport almost as carefully practised there as the Wall Game: pretending something you've just thought up on the hoof is, in fact, the product of long and deep reflection.

'No. He can stay. We'll make this creature think he's got us on the run. Scrope can be the front man, but I want him on a tight leash. MI5 can take the investigation over from here.'

'He's a mucker of yours, isn't he, this Scrope?'

'What? No. I take it you're referring to the fact he was at Eton. How unpredictable of you.'

'So you didn't fag for him, then?'

'There hasn't been any fagging at Eton for nearly forty years.'

'So he didn't use to bray you on your arse for chelping after lights out?'

'You know, I didn't realise what a class warrior you were. Perhaps you'd be more at home as Shadow foreign secretary in the Socialist Workers Party.'

The foreign secretary smiled.

'We speak our minds up north, Prime Minister.'

'Not the least of your deficiencies.' The prime minister smiled malevolently at his surprised foreign secretary. 'We know how to speak our minds in Notting Hill as well.'

High

*

Scrope gave Molly the job of chasing down Jacob Guza, identified during the interview with Aaron Gall as a person of interest. He'd proved difficult to find, having vanished from most public records nearly ten years ago. This, in itself, encouraged everyone, and, given the urgency and seriousness of the matter, some not entirely legal means were employed. He was discovered living at his mother's house in Maldon, and Molly was despatched to give him the once-over. When she returned from Essex, it was not good news.

'It isn't Mr Guza.'

'Because?'

'He's got a history of mental health problems dating back twenty years – the debilitating fuck-you-up kind – and ten years ago he had a brain haemorrhage that nearly killed him. He can't lift anything heavier than a knife and fork. Poor man barely made any sense.'

'Pity,' said Lister. Molly looked at him. 'I mean, for him as well as us.'

'His mother was very sweet. He's clearly a bit of a handful. She was interesting about his brain haemorrhage. The doctors who treated him said they thought the problem probably had its origins in his time at Salesian College.'

The truth was that Scrope and Lister, under a good deal of pressure to identify Warren, had begun to lose interest in Jacob Guza. This brought both of them to attention.

'Apparently, he told them he and some mates were so desperate to find some way of getting high to get away from the horrors of the place that they formed a little secret society and used to hide at the back of the gym and

SCORN

strangle each other until they passed out. Gives you a huge buzz, apparently – but not very good for your brain, especially when you're fourteen.'

CHAPTER 55

THE PRINCESS AND THE PEA

'Do not try to understand them and do not try to make them understand you. They are a breed apart and make no sense.'

The Last of the Mohicans,
Mann, Gowe, Cooper

Molly Coates enjoyed being a girl. She was so modern in her enjoyment that she was utterly indifferent to the assortment of fears and grievances that afflicted the almost exclusively middle-class members of the women's group she belonged to. The truth was, she found most of them a bit of a pain, touchy and ridden with anxiety about what she regarded as typically trivial middle-class concerns with appearance (to shave or not to shave) or their moral status – were they checking their privilege?

She had the working-class intellectual's lack of patience with issues of manners. She knew that it was easy for her, because, having a northern accent and being the daughter of a steel worker and hairdresser, made her opinions on anything almost bombproof. She found this tiresome but sometimes very funny. In the byzantine class system of the sisterhood, her opinions outranked even the lesbian whose father had worked down a mine, a trump card in terms of credibility but one seriously compromised by the fact that she'd once been a man.

On the one hand, this woman was transgendered (which was, of course, incredibly virtuous); on the other hand, this gave her enormous power in terms of credibility, which rankled with those who harboured the suspicion that, by surgical sleight of hand, a man had now managed to become dominant in a women's group dedicated to the overthrow of patriarchy. She did not help matters by being a know-all, a trait rather harder to remove than a penis or an Adam's apple, conclusive evidence to some that there was much more to being a woman than not having a cock.

So divisive was this issue that it was not permitted to bring it up, and the safest way of expressing resentment was always to support anything Molly said and justify that support on account of her superior social disadvantages. They couldn't check their own privilege, so they checked Molly's instead. Because of this, the meetings had become so irritating that she was thinking of quitting. They were of no help in her current problem. She hadn't even brought it up with the one or two members she was moderately at ease with, because she knew she'd never get anything sensible out of them.

The problem was love. It was not just the love of a man that was troubling her. She'd seen the sacrifices this could mean all her life: her mother was as clever as her daughter, but lack of confidence and an unwillingness to stand out – the great pestilence of so much working-class talent – had left her in work as dull as it was directionless. Her mother was wonderful with money, could trace every penny in

The Princess And The Pea

and out and had little grey books of perfect figures going back to the day she was married. 'You could have been an accountant, run a business, Mum, run the country.' Her mother just rolled her eyes in mock-horror and loved to hear it. The thing was, her dad agreed. 'We wouldn't be in this trouble if you were running the country, Di,' he'd say, at least once a month. Full many a rose is born to blush unseen and waste its fragrance on the desert air.

The trouble with love was that it was no longer just a women's issue. Now it was also a class issue. Quite how bad a class issue was not clear to her until one warm Saturday afternoon when Lister took her home. Not to meet his parents – his parents, as such, were not the problem. Just as Molly was too stylish to lord it over others because she had so much working-class credibility, Lister's parents had too much class, we might revealingly say, to be touched by anything so bourgeois as snobbery. In any case, they spent nearly all their time in New York.

Austen House, ancestral home of the Listers, is described in Pevsner's architectural bible of all the important buildings of England as perhaps the finest small manor house of its date (1702) in the nation. Designed by the great Nicholas Hawksmoor, it is a house of thirty-six rooms that manages to be on a scale at once impressive and delightfully human. The garden, consisting of a maze renowned as one of the finest in England, had just been trimmed and was looking particularly splendid. The orangery was stuffed with enough oranges, lemons, peppers and other exotica to furnish the gardens of paradise themselves.

Molly's stunned reaction on being presented to this jewel and then being taken through its rooms filled with family portraits, Gobelin tapestries and three rock-crystal chandeliers was, however, difficult to read. Lister's worry that Molly might be put off by all this was not realised. It was much worse.

Two days afterwards, she was still confused. The problem was that she loved him and adored the fact that he had clearly fallen in love with her and, very satisfyingly, even more deeply. But she'd fought every day of her life to make something of herself and, to her, class injuries were not at all hidden. They were the brutal everyday hammer blows of bad education, of poverty of expectation, of defensive and sour contempt for anyone getting above themselves from her own class, of amused dismissal of her ambitions by the class above.

But it was complicated. Was the resentment of her success by others in her family and among her friends really as great as she thought? Was the condescension of those above her socially really as sour as she imagined? Born in a county in which selection for secondary schools still remained, she deliberately sabotaged the exam that would have given her access to one of the finest, if unimaginative, grammar schools in the country. Button-bright, she'd been regarded as a prize by all her teachers at Scalby Comprehensive (in reality, an old-fashioned secondary modern starved of money and of teachers with ambition).

Gradually realising that solidarity had come at a high price and that she needed more from her education if she was to make her way in the world, she changed (much wracked by conscience) to the sixth form of the grammar school, where her fears about the inability or unwillingness of her former teachers to bring out the best in her were confirmed. She discovered that her impressive essays on Shakespeare, properly marked for once, revealed she had

The Princess And The Pea

been spelling his name wrong for five years.

Mortified by this and the corrections to her hideous punctuation, she felt she was being mocked and despised. The terrible thing – the really terrible thing – was that she was not. Her new teacher was excited by her brains but didn't realise how carefully she needed to be handled. He praised her essay on *Macbeth*, for all its mistakes, but not enough to neutralise the acid of humiliation, of lack of confidence and her resentment of an entire world she didn't understand. He thought her touchiness could be fixed by good teaching.

And he was partly right, but at a cost. Molly took the book of punctuation he offered and, though burning with shame, schooled herself to becoming point perfect in a couple of weeks. There were no more spelling mistakes, either. The price? Molly took it out on her teacher for the remaining two years, barely saying a word in any of his classes while, all the time, he was growing more impressed with the awkward sod of a little girl who hadn't been able to spell the Bard's name when she first came to his classes. 'You're writing degree-level essays, Molly, in your second year. You should try for Oxbridge.' But the price of being corrected so shamefully, but still listening and learning at every lesson, was that Molly was compelled to hate him and anything he suggested.

Poor old Lister had no idea what he was dealing with. But then, how could he?

'My great-grandmother was in service,' said Molly.

'Oh, great,' said Lister mournfully.

'I don't remember her. She died when I was three. But one thing my mum told me always stuck in my mind. The servants, the maids, had to show the housekeeper their soiled underwear before it was washed so she could keep track of their periods and make sure no one was pregnant. Funny you don't see any of that in *Downton Abbey*.'

Lister winced. He should have left it at that, but history, of course, is character, and his inability to know how to react to being pinned down led him to make the worst (though understandable) mistake – he dealt with his horrible discomfort by treating it with a light heart.

'I don't think we still do that. I'll ask Mrs Dudek.'

She looked at him. 'I hate,' she said, 'being such a judgemental cow. But you always think you can get out of anything awkward with a stupid joke.'

The journey home had been undertaken in near-silence. This did not reflect the turmoil in Molly's soul. And what turmoil it was. Molly was in a whirl of incomprehensible feelings of anger, resentment, love, desire, envy, all matched with hatred, longing, more envy and more longing. (Oh, to be mistress of Austen House!) Then there was the prospect of swanning about, lady of the manor, feeling every moment like a fraud and traitor. (How shameful to be mistress of Austen House!) So there was fury, there was calculation, there was the intense need (think how everyone would be impressed), there was revulsion so strong it was a taste (think how everyone would say what a hypocrite she was).

Poor Molly and poor Lister. The following day, they had an appalling row, as the irritation of Lister at having to apologise for something he didn't see as his fault came up against her fury that he couldn't see what the problem was. But then, how could someone who had been born love-bombed by the universe ever understand? Would being taken by the hand through the streets of Mayfair reveal

The Princess And The Pea

less misery than the streets of Deptford? Perhaps it would depend on your definition of misery. Are the tears of the rich less salty than those of the poor? Viktor Frankl, graduate of Auschwitz and Dachau, would not have thought so, but his belief in the universal suffrage of human pain chimes badly with the spirit of the times.

Surely not, you say – are we not more sensitive to the pain of others now than once we were? Yes, but no. Frankl did not believe in victims.

CHAPTER 56

SECRETS AND LIES

In Maslow's hierarchy of human needs, the basics (food, sleep, shelter, sex) are followed by the emotional needs that begin with self-esteem. Of course, highest of these needs in mankind is the desire to have the cake of success iced with the humiliation of someone else's failure. As a result, there was much rejoicing in MI5 when they were given control of something as prestigious as the safety of the pope, and particularly so because this honour had been taken away from the Metropolitan Police.

But forgive me: it can be hard even for a deeply committed friend not to become darkly pessimistic about human weaknesses and failures ... the defects, the cruelty, the stupidity, the vanity, the fiascos, the bankruptcies of mind and spirit, the sheer uselessness and triviality. What I try to do on these dark days is remember the great enterprises, such as the wonderful boldness of the human spirit that manifests itself in the Large Hadron Collider, even if its simplest discoveries are utterly incomprehensible to all but a vanishingly small proportion of people (though, to be entirely honest, it should be pointed out that, of the ones who *do* understand it, they don't understand it particularly well).

So, in this spirit of deeply sober optimism, I want to point out that our premier secret service was also genuinely convinced that it alone could preserve the safety of the citizens who paid so very much for their labours. Even if this was not their highest priority, it was certainly a close second. Or third. However, this pleasure at the discomfort of a competitor in the matter of resources and prestige was soon tempered by their incredulity when told of the true nature of what they would be facing.

At first, the Head of MI5 wondered if perhaps he might be having a strange dream from which he would soon wake up. However, as the briefing continued in the company of both the prime minister and the foreign secretary, along with all the photographic and forensic evidence, he began to shift to a sort of halfway point between belief and doubt in which he was neither convinced nor unconvinced. The mind is clever in that way, knowing the limitations of the human brain; it has spaces where terrible assaults on deeply held ways of seeing the world can be garaged in such a way that many completely contradictory notions about reality can be held at the same time without the owner going mad. Those who end up in the madhouse do so not because they are mad but because they lack the ability of the rest of us to handle their madness. And so, Her Majesty's secret service took on the task of catching the werewolf with absolute conviction, while ignoring the damage to their grasp of reality that might follow if it actually existed.

Besides, they had the help of keeping busy as a tool in ignoring reality. There were policemen and women to be debriefed and then, mostly, moved on to less sensational murder inquiries, along with the threat of what would happen to them if they said anything about the case. Others were kept, Molly being one of them, as there wasn't time to replace some of the more technically embedded jobs with their own people. After sixty years of decline in the secret services (alcoholic traitors, the complete failure to foresee the collapse of the Russian empire, Iraq: you know the drill), they had, paradoxically, benefited enormously from another serious fiasco: the construction of a dossier outlining the serious threat faced by the West from Saddam Hussein's weapons of mass destruction – weapons which turned out to be as illusory as the continuing menace posed by the USSR.

Lacking anyone else to do the job of spying, the government so ill advised by them was obliged to grant the secret services vast amounts of money and power to protect them from terrorists, many of whom had been created by the terrible advice they themselves had given and on which the government had acted with such lip-smacking enthusiasm. Flush with dough and purpose, MI5 had ballooned in confidence and authority and was in all ways able to throw its weight around with Mr Plods of whatever rank or gender. That the New York towers had fallen as a result of grotesque malice matched by extraordinary never-to-be-repeated luck, and that the bombings on the London Underground was a nasty but isolated success, was ignored not just out of understandable fear for what else might be to come, but even more because the money was already flowing like milk and honey.

It was in no one's interest to take the view that a war with only a dozen attacks in the West in a dozen years was not really a war at all. The threat of terrorist outrages meant that the money and power must be kept rolling in, and the absence of terrorist outrages showed that the flow of money and power was clearly working. Only through cash and the law could the spooks in their nosy pile of

Lego on the South Bank prevent the River Thames from foaming with blood.

Historians of the sociological make-up of the British secret services would have found some interest in the interview between Scrope and Lister (Oxford and Cambridge) and their interviewers (Bristol, Sussex and Durham). Across the table, the middle and upper-middle classes eyed each other with a fine hostility.

'You know, some people take the view that the real threat to the West comes from obesity,' said Lister to his new superiors. 'According to them, if you really want to protect the people you should be pointing your drones at Coca-Cola's headquarters in Uxbridge.'

'Perhaps we're going a little off topic, wouldn't you say?' commented the head spook. The truth is, they were not entirely prepared for the indifference with which Scrope and Lister treated them. They seemed immune to intimidation. This was not just because of some hazy assumption of superiority, it was backed up by the beautiful, class-annihilating simplicity of money: in the end, they both had enough of it to walk away from anything that didn't suit them. Poorer members of the upper class would, no doubt, have been less relaxed.

The problem was that MI5 had spent days going through the evidence with intense vigour, expecting to confirm their own middle-class prejudices against the working-class coppers (ignorant and thick) and the upper-middle-class cuckoos (smug and useless). Disappointingly, the investigation had been carried out at all levels with obvious diligence. There were no significant errors to revisit, or new areas revealed. Then there was the problem that MI5 had with the supernatural.

'You *actually* saw this creature?' said the chief spook.

A slightly pained expression from Lister (they'd agreed that Scrope should be the softer of the cops in their exchanges with MI5).

'We *saw* it, yes,' said Lister. The chief spook realised he'd been corrected but was not quite sure in what way. 'And so did the bodyguard at the scene, a police officer with an impeccable record, and, of course, the former prime minister.' Scrope was matter of fact. 'The DNA from the creature's blood was also confirmed as coming from an unidentified animal of a previously uncategorised type.'

The existence of werewolves was a deep problem for the men and women of MI5. They had worked for their place in the world by means of diligence and hard work. They put in effort A and this produced result B. Theirs was a world in every way ruled by cause and effect. In this instance, it was what put them at such a disadvantage from those in the class below, as well as those in the class above.

It's easy to understand why some peasant without a pot to piss in is sympathetic to the idea of magic, but it was also true of Scrope and Lister. After all, they'd been granted money, power, looks, intelligence and a sense of ease in the world, without having done the slightest thing to earn them. Theirs was a world of inherently irrational possibility. The adult middle class resent the idea of magic, the peasant hopes it exists, the aristocrat knows it does. It was not easy for the hard-working middle class to walk into a fairy tale (terrorists made out of gingerbread? Spies controlled by a talking frog?), particularly not one that confronted them with consequences of failure that would mean the name of MI5 would resonate with disaster for many generations to come.

As to Aaron himself, he further frustrated the search by doing nothing for the next three weeks. He watched quietly in the background, picking up bits and pieces about the faltering investigation from everywhere from *Private Eye* to WikiLeaks. The web, after all, had been created at Aaron's former place of employment, and he'd made a significant contribution to its architecture. Now he was expert at using its resources, both light and dark.

Not realising just how well he had already succeeded, he helped put Scrope even further back at the centre of things by means of a letter. He sent it to Scrope's home address, and in doing so made clear to the secret service that, if there was to be any hope of stopping him, it would come via his personal chosen one, or not at all. Inside the envelope was a selfie, taken – with some difficulty it should be said, given the size of his paws – by the werewolf in full hairy drag, holding in his hand the severed head of Father Gregory Melis. Inside was a piece of paper on which was written: '*ALLEGRO CON SPIRITO* 10171530141918910191043. WATER PROLONGS AN ACTIVE LIFE. IF YOU PERSEVERE, BUT WITHOUT FRENZY, YOU CAN IMPROVE ALMOST THE BEST HEALTH.'

When Scrope presented the spooks with the photograph, the reaction was understandable – utter world-dissolving shock of a kind you might expect from intelligent, educated people who were staring at the collapse of everything they knew about the laws of physics and biology.

Once they'd recovered, the immediate question was whether Scrope had deciphered the clue. He had not, he said.

This was a lie. In fact, he'd recognised the reference after several hours' work, just as he had been intended to.

Perhaps duty required him to tell them at once, but he took the view, after surprisingly little agonising, that what was good for him and what was good for the investigation were happily one and the same thing. He needed – perhaps 'required' was a better word – to make it clear that he was indispensable. Tell them he'd solved it now, and they'd convince themselves that the solution would have come to them soon as well. Perhaps it would have, but he doubted it. It was a gamble he was prepared to take. He even justified the delay by telling himself that, overall, it was best if he stayed on the case – that he had the best chance of anyone of stopping the wolf.

There's no reason to doubt that some of this was true. To be fair, a creature made of mud can't help being slippery.

Three days later, after MI5's cryptologists and their computers had drawn a humiliating blank, Scrope revealed that, after several sleepless nights, he had solved the puzzle. He decided to lie about the process of discovering the answer. Why should he give his enemies his secrets, after all? Better to invent a method that defied logic completely so that it seemed only Scrope's mysterious intuitions could solve the clues. And, besides, it was a laugh.

He claimed the solution had come to him in a dream in which he saw the words *allegro con spirito* floating along the River Thames. Everyone had realised that part of the clue was the term for an instruction to play music in a lively and spirited manner, but it prefaced hundreds of thousands of different tunes. Even the spook cryptographers had worked out that 'Water prolongs an active life' was a clue to identifying the music. They had not been able, however, to work out what the music was. But this was the easy bit for Scrope and, he suspected, made deliberately so as to torment him with the difficulty of the rest of the clue.

'Water prolongs an active life' could be summarised as: 'Water' and 'pal'. Pal was a dog food that had the by-line 'Prolongs Active Life'. It was a clue about the relationship between water and his pal, Lister.

Next came: 'If you persevere, but without frenzy, you can improve almost the best health.'

'Almost the best' must be the next comparative down from 'good', 'better', 'best'. Better is almost the best. This gave: 'persevere without ecstasy to improve the health better'. This gave him the answer to: 'persevere without frenzy'. 'Frenzy' gave a large handful of synonyms. But one, a long way down the list, stood out for some reason: 'ecstasy'. Ecstasy the drug is usually referred to as 'E', which gave him: 'persevere without an e'. This gave him 'prsevere', 'persvere', or 'persever'.

Nothing after twenty minutes. Then it screamed at him. It was an anagram of 'preserve'. Now he had: 'preserve to improve the health better'. Another five minutes with the sense the answer was staring him in the face and he was too stupid to see it. Could 'preserve' be a noun, not a verb? 'Preserve' is a fancy kind of jam. Now he had: 'jam to improve the health better'. 'Improve' was nearly 'improv' without the 'e' again – and 'jam' also means 'to improvise'.

This took him around the houses for nearly an hour. Nothing. He returned to reconsider 'improve the health better'. He worked on 'better' for a while, then 'health'. Synonyms for 'health' were 'wellbeing', 'robustness', 'fitness'. He checked out his thesaurus, noticing the horrible word 'wellness' was now included. He ranted internally

SCORN

– the *wellness* clinic, how is your *wellness*? Is your *wellness* improving? The National *Wellness* Service. THAT WAS IT! 'Jam' and 'well'. If comparatives for 'well' existed, they would be: 'well', 'weller', 'wellest'. 'Almost the wellest' meant 'weller'. 'Jam' and 'weller'. Paul Weller, lead singer of the Jam. BASTARD! *Allegro con spirito* was a reference to the style of playing a song.

Which Jam song? He checked the web. It had to be 'Eton Rifles', because his pal, Lister, went to Eton and the song was about Paul Weller's loathing for the pupils as they made their way through Slough, the nearest big town to Eton.

The numbers in the message had to be in pairs, because you couldn't have a letter numbered 0, so he laid the sequence out as 10, 17, 15, and so on, then matched the letters in the lyrics of Weller's song. This gave him, 'BCNGALOEUP'. He tried playing with this for an hour but came up with nothing. After a ten-minute think and some scribbling he went back to the start: 'water Eton song'.

'Oh, for crying out loud.' The solution gave him pain rather than satisfaction because it should have been obvious long before. It took only a couple of minutes to match the numbers with the lyrics in the now revealed music.

'Our killer says' – he paused for irritating effect – '"I have retired."'

'But what was the music he was referring to?'

'Oh, I *am* sorry,' said Scrope. 'It was the "Eton Boating Song".' Scrope watched as the spooks started checking for themselves. 'There's a double clue to confirm the meaning. Retirement, of course, prolongs an active life.'

There was a silence at once resentful and sourly impressed. It was broken by Lister.

'Did you know,' he said brightly, 'that more people in

this country have been killed by cyclists in the last twelve years than by terrorists?'

'Do you believe him?' said Lister afterwards, at the Gyngleboy.
   'Retiring? The fuck I do.'

CHAPTER 57

THE PORTRAIT

'Love is not a soap opera.'

Pope Francis II, 2014

In the middle of these great events, it had to be said that Molly and David Lister were much more concerned about their personal problems than the matter of the assassination of the pope and the disgrace of their country. So they sighed and wept and wept and sighed all through the night for many days.

I speak metaphorically, as neither were weepers in the literal sense. But neither had experienced love like this, and it was an especial agony that what might thwart it was a question of class that would be incomprehensible to almost everyone in the country. There were extreme Trotskyists of the Spartacist League who would have married Lister like the shot they had previously reserved for the enemies of the people when the revolution came; there were members of the Provisional Central Committee of the Communist Party of Great Britain who would have been off down to H. Samuel to pick out a ring within five minutes of him popping the question. And, to be honest, how many of us in our romantic heart of hearts would blame them?

The Portrait

But Molly was made of pretty stern stuff when it came to something so essential to her view of herself. On the other hand, what is more essential than love? The agony of this made poor Molly hollow-eyed with worry and grief. Perhaps she had already lost him. Stupid. Stupid. Stupid. But then she would think how it would gall her to be swanning back to Macclesfield as Lady Muck, in a hired Escort so as not to embarrass the family. In some ways, it made it worse that barely anyone would blame her, not really. There are myths so strong, so fundamental to the human psyche, that nothing can truly alter them. The only person who would really despise Molly would be Molly herself.

Part of her did not want to see him. Part of her was furious that he had not repeatedly arrived with a steel ram from the Special Projects Unit and smashed her door down. At work, he simply looked at her sheepishly as she tried to avoid any kind of eye contact.

In the end, there was no battering ram required. He just rang the bell. She opened the door to find him standing in the dark hall looking by turns defiant and worried, holding a bunch of flowers. He held them out to her.

'They're not from Jane Packer. I made a special point of getting them from a petrol station just before closing so as not to offend you.'

For a moment, she just stared at him, glass breaking, earth moving, leaves falling. Then she opened her arms.

MI5 had commissioned an offenders' profile from a forensic psychiatrist as soon as they'd taken over the case, and on the day that Scrope solved the clue his report was delivered to the investigation. No mention of werewolves had been made to the psychiatrist, on the grounds of national security and embarrassment. After all, what could he do with such information? Other than that, he had access to everything. The resulting report, thought Scrope, was clearly by someone who knew what he was talking about.

The subject might well be inconspicuous in his everyday life, although it should be considered as fundamental to any attempt to uncover his identity to be aware that this is a person of high intelligence. Hollywood films notwithstanding, it is very rare for a serial killer to be socially skilled and even rarer for them to be intellectually gifted, and even rarer than that to be professionally successful. Serial murderers tend to be almost always more Fred West and hardly ever (never?) Hannibal Lecter. In this case, it seems to me important to spread the search net to a quite different social and intellectual class from that of the usual habituated killer: the perpetrator will not be a casual taxi driver or work in a slaughterhouse.

All in all, the report was well balanced, thoughtful, careful and to the point. This was why it was so disastrous. When the solved new clue was sent to the psychiatrist, he was asked to conclude the report by coming to a view as to whether the claim he had retired was plausible. His response was annoyingly convincing:

The subject is a narcissist — something he does have in common with all serial murderers — who believes that he has the right to kill others without recourse to a legal process involving a jury of peers. His personal judgement is correct, and the views of others irrelevant. In addition, he has killed, by his own admission, those whose crimes seem, on occasion, barely to be crimes at all. The highly respected historian Professor Gregory Melis seems to have been killed simply because, decades ago, he failed to contradict an admittedly partisan

The Portrait

and even fanciful account of British history. Teresa Tandsby died because she, quite literally, did nothing. This inaction is, of course, blameworthy, but sadly entirely typical in cases of the physical and sexual abuse of children. No normal person would consider this a capital offence.

The perpetrator clearly delights in showing off his intellect, as shown by the highly complex but rarely useful clues with which he taunts the police – another typical narcissistic trait of such criminals. Until now, he has always had the initiative. He could choose his victims according to a rationale he was easily able to hide from the police, who, as a result, could not predict his crimes. On the one occasion where such a prediction did lead to his being confronted, he escaped by the skin of his teeth. (I have to say that the account of his escape from Tony Blair's residence seemed more like fiction than reality. He is clearly a man of considerable physical prowess, something that no doubt also feeds his vanity.)

However, it is because of this pathological self-regard that I find his claim about retiring – whatever his motives for declaring it – to be plausible. The fear that his next target is to be the pope, while clearly a reasonable one, ignores one important element, in my view. Choosing unknown victims according to a pattern known only to the perpetrator is one thing, but choosing a known victim who will be heavily protected (indeed, one presumes, uniquely) is a white horse of a different colour, as my father used to say. The chance of failure – and he nearly failed once under much less difficult conditions – will be enormously increased.

For a narcissist who has so far succeeded brilliantly on his own terms and concluded by murdering a senior cleric, he will be all too aware that failure in such an apex crime is highly likely. Pathological narcissists avoid risking failure to a much greater extent than normal people, because failure is a serious threat to their inflated idea of themselves. Even though this individual is ready to take risks to an unusual degree for such a psychological type, I cannot believe that he will willingly take on such a high probability of failure when he has succeeded so well in all his stated aims.

The claim I HAVE RETIRED seems to me an almost perfect conclusion for this individual. He has retired, as it were, undefeated and leaving the crowd wanting more, and with the teasing possibility that there will be a return at some time in the future. In my opinion, and it's only that, he is unlikely to make an attempt on the life of the pope at this time.

The problem for Scrope was that, in disagreeing with the psychiatrist, he was putting aside objections which he himself thought made sense. He argued with the MI5 committee that the perpetrator was not a psychological type in the conventional sense, and so, while the assessment was persuasive as it stood, it could not account – because the psychiatrist was never told – for the fact that this was an individual who'd undergone massive changes to his physical and mental state, changes unknown to science, let alone psychiatry.

But while Scrope did not exactly lose the argument, he felt that the perceived level of threat had unjustifiably diminished, though he had to concede that the presence or absence of a specific threat was more academic than real. It was pointed out by the committee that they had every intention of protecting the pope as if an actual threat existed. They agreed that such a thoughtful and well-balanced report was something they found more convincing than Scrope, but that it didn't really matter either way. Wherever His Holiness went, there would be large numbers of men armed to the teeth.

But Scrope and Lister, rather better experienced in

The Portrait

the practicalities of real and imagined dangers, knew that when people pretended to be at war on military exercises it had, as Lister pointed out, 'fuck all to do with how they behaved when faced with the real thing'.

To be fair, on the day the pontiff arrived, it seemed they might have underestimated the determination of MI5 to ensure that nothing go wrong on their watch. As a special sign of favour, the queen had arranged a greeting for the pope of a kind not at all lost on the Catholic hierarchy: in order to demonstrate what a welcome guest he was, she had asked the Duke of Edinburgh to go personally to Heathrow to meet the pontiff, an act well beyond what was required by normal protocol.

(It was felt, given the delicacy of the meeting – only the second of its kind in the vexed history of the kingdom and the Catholic faith – that an unusually frank reminder of the kind of diplomacy required of him was made to the duke. He took the warning in good spirits: 'Don't worry,' he said, 'I won't mention the war.' He did not take it amiss when it was pointed out to him that it was the previous pope who was a German national, not the one he was to meet the following day. He thought about this for a moment: 'Does that mean I *can* mention the war?')

The sun shone brightly as the pope descended the red-carpeted stairs into the middle of an enormous Guard of Honour, complete with several dozen shortbread biscuit tins' worth of men in kilts, braid tartan socks, sporrans and the rest, all done to emphasise the entirely ceremonial nature of the occasion. Oddly, no one commented on the incongruity of greeting the most holy representative of a religion that believed in turning the other cheek and returning hatred with love by means of a guard holding assault rifles tipped resplendently with a vicious-looking bayonet, the grooved funnel down one side of it designed to allow the blood of an opponent to squirt out of the wound. In addition, the regular service ammunition had been replaced by hollow-point expanding bullets of a kind that existed in something of a moral, not to say legal, grey area when it came to their use on human beings.

Although, of course, Aaron Gall's humanity was something of a grey area also.

In addition, there were some eighty sharpshooters all over Heathrow, armed with Lapua Magnum long-range sniper rifles. Concerning the vehicle carrying the pontiff, advice had been taken from Longleat Wildlife Park as to the capabilities of a large, angry predator when it came to attacking closed vehicles. The pope – the observed of all observers – was now in England.

'The volume of revelations of child sexual abuse by clergy over the past 35 years or so has been described by a Church source as ... "an earthquake deep beneath the surface hidden from view". The clear implication of that statement is that the Church, in common with the general public, was somehow taken by surprise by the volume of the revelations. Having completed its investigation, the Commission does not accept the truth of such claims and assertions.'

Commission of Investigation Report into the Catholic Archdiocese of Dublin, July 2009 (documentcloud.org/ documents/243712-4-murphy-report-entire-ireland.html)

'I will cite one experiment that depicts a dilemma that is more common in everyday life. The subject was not ordered to pull the lever that shocked the victim (an actor bound to a chair pretending to feel electric shocks), but merely to perform a subsidiary task (administering the word-pair test) while another actor pretended to administer the shock. In this situation, thirty-seven of forty adults continued to the highest level (apparently lethal) of the shock generator. Predictably, they excused their behavior by saying that the responsibility belonged to the man who actually pulled the switch. This may illustrate a dangerously typical arrangement in a complex society: it is easy to ignore responsibility when one is only an intermediate link in a chain of actions.

Thus there is a fragmentation of the total human act; no one is confronted with the consequences of his decision to carry out the evil act. The person who assumes responsibility has evaporated. Perhaps this is the most common characteristic of socially organized evil in modern society.'

Stanley Milgram, Obedience to Authority, 1974

CHAPTER 58

THE SHEPHERD

'Sparrowhawks are said to perch on the boughs of the oak tree that grows out of a murdered man's grave and so bear witness to the foul deed. Priests were allowed to hunt with sparrowhawks only.'

Teutonic Mythology,
Jacob Grimm, 1882

At the pope's insistence, his first public engagement was to meet with more than two thousand children from every parish in the country. He stood outside the Cathedral of Westminster in the soft sun of an English summer's day and smilingly accepted the delighted welcome of children of every age, from gawping toddlers to athletic teenage boys of seventeen. One of them, nearly six feet tall, welcomed the Holy Father, as the children, young and old, laughed and shouted their greetings to their much loved pope, all to the sound of cheers and the jingle jangle of joyously arrhythmic tambourines.

'Welcome, Holy Father,' said the proud and confident young man. 'This is a family reunion, and we are privileged to welcome you on behalf of all the young Catholics of England.'

SCORN

The shouts of delight from the assembled kids obliged the pope happily to rise from his seat. He acknowledged their joyful spontaneous salutation.

'Thank you, Holy Father,' said the boy. 'And God bless you.' It was clear the Holy Father was enchanted at the children's joy at seeing him. The boy was ushered towards his pope to kiss his hands, to a whoop of happiness from the youthful crowd. The pope stepped to the microphone for a short speech, short because of an infection of the throat.

'Welcome, children!' he called out happily. More shouts. 'Society needs your clear voices to call in all your vigorous and active enthusiasm for the rights of both young and old to live, not in a world of self-destruction and arbitrary freedoms, but in a society that works for the true welfare of all its citizens and a religious faith which offers guidance and protection in the face of human weakness and frailty.'

Uncomprehending toddlers, beribboned in blue and white, yelled their enthusiasm for guidance in their sinful weakness and banged their tambourines in celebratory rejection of self-obstructive and arbitrary freedoms. Cheers went up to heaven, as did the two dozen doves that the pope helped some children release into the blue and downy cotton clouds.

But as the pure white doves of innocence and peace flapped into the blue, two dark and ravenously hungry sparrowhawks fell out of the sky and set about the doves with hideous beak and claw. Hither and thither flapped the dovish prey as talon grabbed and beak slashed. The crowd looked on aghast, with shouts and screams, as bits of dove, of heads and wings and blood, showered the horrified celebrants. Open-mouthed, the pope looked on as the raptors hungrily and ecstatically displayed their savage nature to

The Shepherd

all below. Those who were young enough were grabbed into their mother's skirts. Some turned away, and others gawped in horrified awe, their innocent faces flecked with gobbets of the unfortunate albino messengers of peace.

Three-quarters of a mile away, Aaron Gall stood on the roof of a penthouse suite he had hired, expensively, for its wonderful view of the cathedral, and watched in rapture.

Now, you may think it cruel that he should gloat so lovingly over the slaughter of innocent doves. The thing is, the birds for these beautiful and touching ceremonies are especially bred for a purity and spotlessness symbolic of the perfect human soul. But nature doesn't believe in white for living things unless there's lots of snow around. In the world of green and brown and blue, white is the kiss of death. A love of perfection doomed the doves to death by beak and claw, no matter what.

As for the trauma to the innocent children – Aaron did not give them a thought.

CHAPTER 59

ALONE, LOST, ABANDONED

This is the Tesco mobile messaging service. Please leave a message after the tone. To re-record your message, press the hash key.

There's a pause. Poor thing.

'This is Lou.' A hesitation. 'Doesn't feel like me – not acting like *eine dumme Frau*. Isn't that funny? I don't understand why you won't answer my calls. I need to know you're all right, for some reason. But this is horrible and sad.'

'Teachers, social workers who work with children, and councillors could face up to five years in prison if they turn a blind eye to child abuse, under proposals to be set out on Tuesday by David Cameron.'

Guardian, 3 March 2015

'Jimmy Savile: Celebrity BBC DJ and television personality well known for his eccentric persona and substantial efforts on behalf of many charities over a 60-year period, during which it is estimated he raised more than £40 million, and for which he was knighted by Queen Elizabeth in 1990. In the same year, he was also honoured with a papal knighthood by Pope John Paul II. After his death in 2011, a number of police investigations revealed that Savile was responsible for raping or sexually abusing as many as 450 children, using his celebrity at the BBC and his charity work as a means of diverting complaints made about him while he was alive. He is now thought to be the most prolific child abuser in British history.'

Wikipedia

CHAPTER 60

SELECTIVE INATTENTION

The following contains extracts of a newspaper article written by Lord Christopher Patten, chairman of the trust responsible for overseeing the BBC.

Can it REALLY be that no one inside the smug BBC knew what that psychopath was doing? The chairman himself questions the corporation he represents.

The filth piles up. As the Savile story continues to unfold, threatening and destroying reputations, three issues particularly trouble me. Above all else, I think of the victims of abuse — women and men — marooned for decades with terrible memories of physical and mental torment which, even when they had the courage to report them, no one apparently believed. Not the police. Not the newspapers. Not the BBC.

When I was asked to become Chairman of the BBC Trust, I was proud and honoured. Proud because the BBC is our national broadcaster, praised around the world for the values it has tried to stand for. But also because it is part of our civic culture, trying to represent the best of the society we are and want to be.

Today, like many who work for the BBC, I feel a sense of particular remorse that abused women spoke to Newsnight, presumably at great personal pain, yet did not have their stories told as they expected. On behalf of the BBC, I apologise unreservedly.

There's a second reason the BBC's reputation is on the line. All

Selective Inattention

objective evidence tells us the BBC is one of the most trusted institutions in the UK. It is by far the most widely trusted source of accurate and balanced news. I know it is far from perfect and can seem smug or too metropolitan. But day in, day out, it depends on the public trust which underpins it far more than the licence fee. At its best, it is trusted because the public who pay for it think, rightly, that they own it.

In recent years, some of our greatest institutions have been discredited one after another: Parliament; the police; the press. Now the BBC risks squandering public trust because Jimmy Savile, one of its stars over three decades, was apparently a sexual criminal; because he used his programme and popularity as a cover for his wickedness; because he used BBC premises for some of his attacks; and because others – BBC employees and hangers-on – may also have been involved.

Moreover, can it really be the case that no one knew what he was doing? Did some turn a blind eye to criminality? Did some prefer not to follow up their suspicions because of this criminal's popularity and place in the schedules? Were reports of criminality put aside or buried? Even those of us who were not there at the time are inheritors of the shame.

All this touches on my third concern. The BBC should reflect our society's ethical values. How has this been shown by the relationship between our dismal celebrity culture and our values system? How can we have allowed so many people and institutions to be mired in fawning over one awful man – a devious psychopath? He was received into the heart of the Establishment; feted from Chequers to the Vatican; friend to Royals and editors. How did we let it happen? And could someone like this con us all again?

SCORN

Let us now praise famous men.

Consider Christopher Francis Patten, Baron Patten of Barnes, Governor of Hong Kong (where he was known, mostly affectionately it must be said, as Fatty Peng), Chancellor of Oxford University, and Chairman of the BBC. Life has been good to Chris and history kind – there are few reminders of the disastrous misjudgements of his life: his administrations of the poll tax that destroyed Margaret Thatcher, his utter commitment to the euro, a currency that brought the European Union to its knees. None of us, after all, is perfect – and when it comes to errors, will any one of us escape whipping?

Although it must be said that Chris was fortunate even in his failures. When the voters who'd elected him to Parliament decided they'd had enough of his talents and threw him out at the subsequent election, his friends in government (and outside) were not fickle followers of the kind of populism so easily mistaken for the true will of the people. He was immediately spirited away to do great things in the handover of Hong Kong to the Chinese, charged with negotiating the best deal possible for the islanders. Patten was so vigorous in the defence of the soon-to-be former colony that he was regarded by the communist government with unusual distaste, and described by one mainland government-controlled paper as 'the whore of the East'. It is also to his credit that, at a time when Vladimir Putin was still feted by the West, Patten unflinchingly described him publicly as a man with the eyes of a killer.

And yet there is something that nags when you consider the glittering prizes that have been poured on his head in such profusion: Minister, Baron, Chancellor, Chairman,

Selective Inattention

companion of the queen. Then add to all this a skipload of honours, doctorates and such. Yet when his actual achievements are set down … they are real enough but not especially impressive, not, to be honest, really worthy of this orgy of recognition, this love-bombing by the universe.

But so what? What has this to do with you and me and the business we are about here of lycanthropes, cannibalism and the murder of children's souls? Baron Patten – Fatty Peng – is a Catholic, and not just in name. He is, according to the *Tablet*, one of the country's most influential members of the One True Faith outside of which there is no salvation. More to the point, the man who railed with – I am myself convinced – entirely sincere indignation at the way in which Jimmy Savile's behaviour was ignored by the organisation he supervises – this man turns out to have been the person appointed by the government to oversee the visit of Pope Benedict, the man who ensured the burial of the case against Father Maciel and many others.

Lord Patten had done such a good job of ensuring that Pope Benedict was made to feel profoundly welcome in the United Kingdom that he was asked to do the same thing for his replacement after Benedict's mysterious retirement. There is no record of Lord Patten's attempt to investigate the many claims of child abuse covered up by the Catholic Church in general, and Pope Benedict in particular, abuse that was a matter of widespread public record at the time he so readily accepted these tasks. But to be fair, Pope Benedict XVI was not a gibbering narcissist in the way of Jim, Britain's national gargoyle. It's hard, if not impossible, for such a man to point the finger at power and glory when it had shown him all his days such bountiful generosity.

SCORN

Put yourself in his place. There is only so far any one of us can stray from the prison of our growing up.

On the eve of the new pope's address to a carefully selected audience in Westminster Hall, Lord Chris Patten sat in a comfy chair in his front room and was interviewed for a Catholic television channel on the unique importance of the pope's visit.

'This invitation to the Holy Father reflects an awareness of the enormously important role that the Catholic Church plays in making society more civilised.' Chris smiled, delicately mocking what he was about to say. 'There will be a gathering at Westminster tomorrow of what we call' – a little chuckle – 'the great and the good.'

He raised his eyebrows as if to suggest that the idea that there existed some favoured elite of the morally excellent and the politically powerful was slightly risible, the product of minds prone to envy and unrealistic notions of conspiracy and privilege. There was something in the accusation, the tone suggested, but not enough to take too seriously. After all, how could he explain his own pre-eminence in the world if the world were ineradicably corrupted by power and influence?

'The audience will be representatives of politics, of society as a whole from right across the board: former prime ministers, foreign secretaries, Cabinet ministers, leaders of the great industries, leaders of not-for-profit organisations, leading journalists – the works. It will be,' finished Fatty Peng, 'the gathering of Britain in one place.'

One group would not be there. There would only be silence concerning the children with the bleeding anal sphincters, and the dead and the dying souls, no mention

Selective Inattention

of the dread, the sin, the nightly collywobbles and heebie-jeebies of children wondering what fire and punishment was waiting for them if they should die in the night. There would be no calligrapher-written invitation on handmade Bella cotton for Jacob Guza, he of the auto-asphyxiation and the exploding blood vessels in his brain. There was nothing spoken of the boredom and the drabness, the obligation to swallow the foolish and the silly without reply. Smile away, Fatty Peng and the assembled tremendous and the superb, wrapped together in the aromas of distinction, milk of regard, sweet-smelling honours, pungency of chairmanship and myrrh of title and award, all come to welcome an audience with the vicar of Christ.

First from the pope as he started his speech came the obligatory blandishments. On such occasions, even God almighty would have been obliged to oil the wheels.

'Britain ... pluralist democracy ... freedom of speech ... rights and duties ... mother of parliaments ... Catholic teaching ... much in common ... Magna Carta.'

(It would have raised an unfitting smile in the hall if anyone knew the history of the Church in regard to Magna Carta – Pope Innocent III declaring this most noble document on the rights of man, 'illegal, unjust, harmful to royal rights and shameful to the English people', and excommunicating the barons who had forced King John to sign. Fortunately, no one invited knew any history concerning the faith they had all arrived to celebrate.)

There were others listening not so enamoured of what they were hearing. There were present a few bishops and higher prelates, as well as the less significant representatives of an assortment of more traditional diocese from the back of beyond, who believed in a more bracing Catholicism, who did not believe in this sort of congeniality. They were instinctively suspicious of niceness of any kind, smacking as it did of a potential retreat from the death, sin and judgement they held to be the backbone of the faith. But for everyone else, the generosity and kindness of the Holy Father's words created an atmosphere of warmth and generosity towards the man speaking to them that they had hardly expected.

Tony Blair, sitting next to wife Cherie, felt that his instincts about the One True Faith were on the verge of almost being realised. Again, to be fair, he did smile self-deprecatingly to himself at the messianic tone of this, a tendency his wife had warned him about. Even so, this was a pope with whom Tony could do business.

The pope continued, speaking of the core values they shared. If this seemed a little too affable for some of the more conservative clergy listening, who no doubt reflected that they were not so very sure this was the case, their pope restored the balance somewhat by gently reminding the assembly that he was speaking from the very spot where St Thomas More had been sentenced to death for following his conscience.

(There was no time to say that so had the Catholic terrorist Guy Fawkes, for attempting to blow up the place with the king and all his ministers. The Twin Towers? Nothing new under the sun, my swampy dears.)

He then praised the purifying power of religion (that is to say, Catholicism) to act as a corrective to the distortions of ideology (at the mention of the word, a frisson of horror ran through the assembled clerics). At this point, a great wailing went up from one of the pews, not a scream of protest but a cry from a tiny baby no more than three months old. The pope stopped as the crowd shuffled

Selective Inattention

uncomfortably. The mortified mother blushed red with shame, as if she were the focus of disapproval from the congregation (though all the mothers there cringed with empathy). As the poor woman tried to move past a quartet of the lesser great and good, who fumbled to their feet to let her, the pope called out.

'Please, young woman, if all that's wrong is that the child is hungry, then by all means sit down and breastfeed him. Don't worry. There are only too many mothers in the world who can't feed their children.' He raised the palm of his hands, smiled, and gestured her to sit. Somewhat startled, she did as she was asked and the pope recommenced talking to distract the mother as she fumbled with the front of her blouse and the baby wound himself up a gear. Around the congregation, there was great astonishment, and a good deal of it from some of the assembled clerics was the astonishment of distaste.

'Finally ...' began the pope. As soon as he had spoken the last syllable, the baby clamped lips to nipple and there was a sudden, heavenly silence. The pope smiled. 'I can see the word "finally" has raised the spirits of some of the younger members of this gathering.' Laughter, warm and genuine, swept through the great hall. 'As I speak, the carved angels looking down on us from the magnificent ceiling of this ancient hall remind us that God is constantly watching over us all, constantly seeking to guide and protect men, women and children alike.'

Unfortunately for the congregation, the angels weren't the only preternatural creatures looking down on them from above. High up on a beam in the darkened recess of the great vault of Westminster Hall, the werewolf Aaron Gall was rubber-necking the assembly below with a fearful brew in his chest of fury and ill-will. Relaxing his body, if not his ire, he allowed his muscular hairiness to slide down the rafter on which he'd been lurking. Now on the flat of a beam cutting across the entire width of the hall, he crept and wriggled and squirmed his way forward.

Then, in an instant, he stood up and leapt magnificently on to the high-up window ledge. And before the great and good assembly he let out a gargantuan howl of triumph and bitter rage, and then sprang into the congregation, all sharp teeth and malice.

Can two thousand people act as one? Eyes opened wide and mouths wider across every pew in that great and iconic hall. Breaths were indrawn and terrible amazements registered on every soul. Nothing now could abate the rage of this bad-tempered Barghest. Grim and greedy, he landed among the anguished elite. How they wished now they had left unopened the gilded envelope, how they regretted in their vanity responding to the select invitation.

The werewolf threw back his hefty head and, open-mawed, trilled in ecstasy at their fear. The terrified assembly witnessed a gruesome shining in his eyes – the devil was in him. Then a deep silence as Gall looked around and considered his victims. Just for a moment, his nail-tipped fingers beat on the floor, a tick-tack threnody of death, while inside his heart there was a terrible laughter.

Then, with one bound, he grasped one of the privileged, one of the first and one of the foremost. Lord Christopher Patten he had in a death grip, of men the most honoured, most covered in glories. Patten opened his mouth to speak of discussions, to offer the chance of negotiations. But then he was silenced and silenced forever. No more to be

Selective Inattention

appointed, of all unelected, nor showered with honours and baubles and gewgaws. Gall rendered his stomach open and ghastly, and bit into his bone-locks, drank up his blood and swallowed great gobbets of the nabob of Barnes in the Borough of Richmond. He chewed up his feet and his hands and his fingers.

Weeping was heard, and a terrible screaming, ghastly the horror at the red sweat of violence. Those who could run, they scattered like turkeys; those who could not, they were slaughtered and eaten. Breast bones were crunched and corpses burst open. And then the ghoul saw him, the one who'd escaped him, escaped him in Connaught, convenient for Hyde Park.

Anthony Blair, he had caught in his eye beams.

Biting and clawing, he made slowly towards him, killing the innocent and killing the sinful. All rendered guilty by accepting the bidding of the popes who had ordered his pain and his suffering, the lies and the boredom, the murder of souls by the hundreds and thousands, all who were present and never protested, died by the tooth or the nail and the paw grip – ignorant converts like Black and Widdecombe. Then Read and then Johnson were deprived of their life blood for keeping their mouths shut while noisily protesting of faith's persecution and secular values. Also for silence the bowels of Mark Thompson were spilled on the tiles of that hall in Westminster. Hapless Wayne Rooney (a sad day for football) was eaten by Aaron, though he would have been spared if not blinded by anger, so great was the wolf's liking for his glorious passing.

Then he tore off the arm, all bloody and broken, of Cormac Murphy-O'Connor, former Bishop of England, for hearing complaints from the mothers of children then forgiving the priest who had hurt and abused them, then – after a pause for prayer and reflection – ushering him back to the lambs at the altar.

But then it was Tony who came up for judgement. The wolf grasped his neck and raised Tony upwards, high in the air, upraised like a trophy. The angels above would have called out for mercy and begged for forgiveness for Tony's infractions. *His intentions are good* sang the angels, so silent, *though they usually lead to much death and destruction. And it should be said that his backside is pleasing.* But deaf was the wolf to their dumb protestations. Blair had joined a faith that had injured and hurt him, and his buttocks, though lovely, were no mitigation.

Nothing could halt him, the ill-tempered padfoot: he tore Tony in two like an old piece of paper and showered his blood on the running and screaming.

'STOP!'

This time, the voice was that of a pontiff. Two thousand years of authority held them. Even the werewolf broke off from his mayhem and stared at the man in the shoes of St Peter.

Silence.

And more silence. The pope stared at Aaron and Aaron stared back. A moment of stillness in all of the horror. Then Aaron reached for the kidney that hung from the bladder, healthy and pink and all covered in suet, and, pulling it off like a long-ripened apple, he gobbled it up with much delectation. 'Yum!' said the werewolf. 'This Tony is tasty!'

Then he nibbled his chittlings and munched on his liver, then chewed on his pizzle and tasted his sweetbreads:

Selective Inattention

last was his bottom, so pink and so rosy. The left had the taste of the beef known as kobe, absorbed at the banquets of power and money. The left had the flavour of wines of the finest, of Château d'Yquem of Latour and of Petrus. The taste was of luxury paid for by others.

He finished his meal and then turned to the pontiff, who stood on the dais, courageous and lonely.

And then Aaron Gall woke up.

Some people's nightmares are other people's wondrous dreams. Once he realised that it was all an hallucination, Aaron felt at first disappointed and then rather foolish. The regret was at how much terror and distress he had failed to deliver to people he loathed for turning up to celebrate the presence of the Holy Father. It also spoke of a fear that still loomed, a fear of death and failure. However much the wolf relished what was about to happen, reckless of fear and indifferent to consequences, the Aaron in him was clearly still in there somewhere, worried and afraid. He took a deep breath and blew it out, as if to expel the backslider who wanted it all to be over and done with.

He also felt slightly stupid because there had been a fair number of signs that it was a dream. For example, while scanning the assembly from up in the rafters, he'd clearly recognised Jimmy Savile talking to Guy Fawkes.

CHAPTER 61

POLITICS AND LOVE

Molly's thoughts over the days after her reconciliation with Lister turned to the awkward question of how she was to break the news of her engagement around the office.

'Why say anything?' asked Lister.

'You don't understand much about women, do you?'

'Obviously not. I was under the impression you were ashamed of being promised to me.'

'One of the many things you need to learn about me with regard to the faint hope of you ever becoming acceptable as a lover is when to shut your cakehole.' She looked at him, severe. 'Have you told your parents?'

Another grunt of disbelief.

'My parents sent me to board at prep school when I was seven. In the holidays, I always had a vague sense that they thought I was the child of a guest who had inconsiderately left me behind and who for some reason kept turning up for a few weeks three or four times a year — they were just too well bred to say anything. Then it was Cambridge. I travelled in the vacations. Then the army ... We're practically strangers.'

'You're exaggerating.'

'Not much,' he said softly. 'Hardly at all.' He looked at her, sly. 'If you like, we can call New York now and break the news. Though it'll take five minutes to explain who I am.'

Politics And Love

He put on a ludicrously fruity upper-class accent that was hardly at all like his father's. '*Deirdre, there's some ghastly fellow on the phone says he's getting married ... Says his name is David. I think it must be for you, old chap.*'

'You bloody liar.'

Lister was laughing now. 'OK. They're not that bad.'

'Are they going to disapprove of me?'

'Do you care?'

'Up to a point, yes I do. My family are very important to me and I want to get on with yours.'

'You'll be fine.' He looked thoughtful for a moment. 'Have you ever shot a fox?'

'I don't think so.'

'Eat your peas with a knife?'

'Not since I stabbed myself in the eye a couple of years ago.'

'Then you'll be fine.' He looked at her, a request for permission to speak.

'What?' she asked.

'If you really want to get on with them, don't go on about your working-class roots. Boasting about the superiority of your ancestry is considered very bad form.' She laughed. 'The better class of aristocrat, like my ma and pa, consider snobbery a sign of insecurity.'

She was silent for a moment. Lister could see she wanted to talk about something but also didn't want to ask.

'Spit it out,' he said.

She looked at him and laughed, sweetly and clearly, at herself. 'What will I be when we're married?'

'Are you going to stop being a pain in the neck?'

'I shouldn't think so.'

'Then I don't think much will change at all.'

SCORN

'You know what I mean.'

'I thought you hated all that stuff.'

'I do, but I'm still curious.'

'OK. Right.' He sighed as if about to reveal a list of to-be-gotten-over-with past iniquities. 'I'm Viscount Lister.' Her eyes widened slightly. 'I've never used it. Ever. Nobody calls you "Viscount" either – it's used in legal stuff, and that's it. So you'll be a countess.' She laughed. 'Only no one will ever call you that – at least, I think that's how it goes. You'll be known, if I remember rightly, as Molly, Lady Lister.'

'Fuck!'

'And when I inherit—'

'God, no, too morbid. And bad luck.'

'No, let's get it over with. The full ghastliness. I become an earl, Lord Austen, after the place we live in. You'll become Molly, Countess of Austen. Or Molly Austen.'

A thrill of ecstatic distaste and horrible delight danced the full length of Molly's spine and tingled to the top of her scalp.

'Appalled?' he said, smiling.

'God forgive me, not as much as I should be. This is *so* weird.'

'It'll pass.'

'What if it doesn't? What if I start to like it? What if, all the time, it was just envy and I objected to it because I wanted to be one of them?'

'One of me.'

'Yes. One of you.'

'It won't happen.'

'Sure?'

'I'm sure.' A pause. 'Countess Molly Lister.'

Politics And Love

She smiled, sly, and patted the back of her head.

'It does have a ring to it, doesn't it?' She looked thoughtful. 'I think I still have my English exercise book from Year Ten at home. I could scrub out "Mrs Molly Musgrave" from the covers – that was the name of my dreamy Marxist sociology teacher – and write "Countess Molly Lister" instead. Acknowledge my absolute betrayal of the people.'

'I thought that subject wasn't to be mentioned.'

'Not by you.'

Molly was, nevertheless, dreading breaking the news at work. People might be insulting: *What? Him?* Followed by the bad: *What do you see in David Lister?* And then by the very much worse: *What does David Lister see in you?* Nobody would say this out loud, of course, but it might be clear they were thinking it. Then there was the excruciating possibility that she might be surrounded by a garrulous horde of thrilled women shrieking with delight and demanding to see the ring and expecting her to be ecstatic that she had finally achieved the one true aim of all sentient female life.

Mercifully – and to her shame for doubting the sisters – the response was both generous and entirely in line with the moderate wing of Feminist Central: marriage, so often a tool of oppression for women, could be a welcome structure for the mutual sharing of responsibilities (as well as conferring a number of important legal protections), as long as it was undertaken by a powerful, independent woman well educated in the many traps and strategies of long-term romantic relationships. There was, it should be said, an added element of joy on her behalf. Basically, it was a rather sweet experience.

The silence of the rams, however, didn't last long. The

next day, as everyone arrived for work, it was to find that someone had pinned up an enlarged photocopy of a magazine article taken off the web. A man had clearly been responsible, as evidenced by the underlinings in red and the fact that the clipping had been torn rather than cut before being photocopied.

TEN ELIGIBLE ARISTOCRATS
NUMBER 4: VISCOUNT DAVID LISTER
It's literally a crime that David Lister is still single. We're not complaining, though! He's handsome, übercool and has a Oxford degree in Biology. Definitely the dark horse of our top ten, Dave is as much Mr Rochester as Mr Darcy and with a bit of Heathcliff thrown in for good measure. Academic success at Eton and Oxford seems to place him firmly at the bluestocking end of the aristocracy, but five years as a soldier in Iraq and Afghanistan, where he won the Distinguished Service Cross and was twice mentioned in despatches, showed he was a true descendant of the Lister who led many soldiers to safety after the Charge of the Light Brigade. After leaving the army, he startled husband-hunting *Tatler* readers by joining the police force, where (surely not for long) he now serves as a humble police sergeant. But the family history has its bounders as well – the black sheep of the dynasty, Henry Lister, was a notorious 18th-century pirate.
Some of his GFs have been pretty dazzling – he's rumoured to have squired A-listers Kate Moss!!! and Keira Knightley!!! as well as glamourpuss physicist Dr Lisa Randall. If you've got looks and the brains or talent to go with them, then Viscount David could be just the aristo dreamboat you're looking for.

Margin annotations: BOLLOCKS!!! / MORE BOLLOCKS!!! / WHAT THE FUCK? HUMBLE??? / WHAT A SURPRISE!!!! / WHO THE FUCK IS LISA RANDALL???

Politics And Love

WHERE TO MEET: Try speeding at 45mph down the King's Road.
WHAT TO SAY: I'm sorry I was breaking the speed limit, Officer, but I'm late for a lecture at the Royal Society on paradigm shifts in biology (we had to look it up).
WHAT NOT TO SAY: Why don't we could go back to my place and watch *Downton* over a plate of mushy peas?

There was little doubt that the photocopy had been pinned up by someone trying to stir the pot, but it certainly failed in the attempt to cause trouble. The general goodwill towards Molly meant that the women just laughed at the article and were delighted by the glamour of an ordinary girl marrying someone who turned out to be a lord of some sort. It was as if they'd all been visited by enchanted dust from the Green Fairy Book of magical tales. Cinderella! In our office!

The attempt to ridicule Lister might have been more successful if the article hadn't revealed that he had been awarded a medal for bravery in Iraq and was twice mentioned in dispatches in Afghanistan. He was given even more credit for not having mentioned it. In addition, the fact that he might have had carnal knowledge of Kate Moss and Keira Knightley simply obliterated all previous objections to Lister's manner and privilege. His colleagues felt themselves positively glowing in the warmth of one degree of separation. He was no longer a supercilious cunt but a lucky bastard.

Later that night, Molly went over the claims in the article in detail.

'It's nearly all bollocks,' said Lister. 'I've never even met Keira Knightley.'

SCORN

'And Kate Moss?'

'OK, I took her out maybe half a dozen times.'

Her eyes narrowed.

'What's she like?'

'She has green teeth and snores' – a pause as he thought this through – '… when she falls asleep watching the television.'

'I'm not an idiot, and I don't care who you went whoring with before you met me. I'll bet you made a beast of yourself, though.'

'She's very nice, as it happens.' He laughed. 'Look, I'm incredibly impressed by how wrong practically everything is in this drivel. It wasn't the Light Brigade, it was the Heavy Brigade. And I am not fifty-second in line to the throne. The Distinguished Service Cross is for exemplary gallantry at *sea* – I get seasick walking over Waterloo Bridge. I won the Military Cross. I went to Cambridge, not Oxford, and my degree is in maths, not biology.'

It was a few days afterwards that Molly remembered the line about one of Lister's ancestors being a pirate. Thinking it would amuse her parents when she showed it to them – and herself – she googled his name. As with so much in the magazine article, the stuff about there being a pirate in the family history was entirely wrong. On this occasion, though, it was not incorrect because of lazy or incompetent journalism. The writer and editor of the piece knew exactly who Henry Lister was, but the truth about him did not sit well in a light-hearted fantasy piece about eligible toffs. Henry Lister had not been a pirate, or anything that the passing of time had turned from being shameful to being romantic: Henry Lister had been a slave trader.

CHAPTER 62

IT'S COMPLICATED

QUESTION: Since your ancestors profited from the human sale of my ancestors — about ten million of them, plus the two million who died in the passage across the Atlantic — why should Africans not be granted some form of compensation from that profit, which you are still enjoying the benefits of?

ANSWER: The issue of reparations is a complex issue that has been debated by many people far better qualified than me — government leaders, human rights lawyers — without coming to any definitive conclusions. My personal opinion is that we are in the end only responsible for our own actions and that is what we should be judged on.

Q and A between Kaid Diriye and David Lascelles, Lord Harwood, great-grandson of King George V

(The plantation business on which the family fortunes are founded extended at one point to twenty-two West Indies plantations and approximately four thousand slaves. Life expectancy for slaves in the Lascelles plantations was about twenty-two years)

SCORN

Henry Ford did not invent the automobile, nor did he invent the assembly line, an idea he took from the meat-packing industry of Chicago. But, more than any other single individual, he was responsible for transforming the car from an unreliable toy for the very rich into a device that continues to shape the modern world more than any other. Ford deserves his place in history, there's no doubt. But more than two hundred years before the first Model-T was built on an assembly line, Henry Lister was responsible for perhaps a greater feat of industrialisation.

Unlike his namesake, sugar plantation owner Henry had no examples to go on when he turned his brilliant mind to a potentially more lucrative but much trickier product: the importation of slaves from Africa. Henry began to apply the skills he had developed in packing and storing sugar efficiently to the business of packaging people efficiently. It was Henry who developed the idea of stowing black slaves on wooden shelves side by side and head to foot, an image as seared into our collective memory as the gates of Auschwitz, and worked out the satisfactory ratio of extra spoilage that would result from the massive increase in numbers that could now be transported in the same space. And it was Henry who freed slavers from the restrictive practices of the tribal chiefs who sold the slaves to the traders, by holding slaves offshore in specially designed stowage ships that could be moved up and down the West African coast in order to expand the area for trade and put pressure on the chiefs to sell more cheaply.

When he died, creative Henry left his heirs a fortune worth approximately £70 million in today's money. His son, Edwin, mourned his loss by spending some of his inheritance building Austen House. It should not be

It's Complicated

thought that the Listers rested on their laurels, like so many families who made a fortune in the slave trade. Although, in the early nineteenth century, the Listers were still among the top 1 per cent of aristocratic slave-owning families, they had invested their money wisely elsewhere, so that, in 1800, their slave plantations, where life expectancy for their slaves was around twenty-one years, accounted for just 28 per cent of their income.

When the calls for abolition of slavery grew to a frightening level in 1832, the by now 2nd Earl of Austen acknowledged that others less fortunate than himself were the real victims: 'I, among others, am a sufferer; but I am not a sufferer equal to those who may have nothing but their West India property to depend upon.' The meeting cried, 'Hear, hear!'

However, he saw the way the wind of change was blowing and had already divested the family of most of its plantations. When the vote came to free the slaves in 1835, the 2nd Earl voted for abolition and pocketed nearly £2 million in compensation. Who can say what connection existed between these two facts? That the slaves received nothing by way of reparation hardly needs saying. The Lister family had invested at first ingeniously, then wisely, and now morally.

There is, it should be said, in all fairness, no direct evidence for the presence of black household slaves at Austen House.

Think of the last time you started to watch a television programme or film after missing the first ten minutes. On realising that it was still worth watching, how long did it take you to pick up the thread of what was going on? A minute or two? Perhaps not even that. When was the last

SCORN

time you were even later into the drama – twenty minutes, say, or thirty? How often were you so bewildered by what you missed that, reluctantly, you had to stop watching? Hardly ever, probably. People have now seen so many thousands of films, so many hundreds of thousands of dramas of one kind or another, that they can fill in the missing bits both very quickly and at a considerable level of complexity. It's pretty miraculous, really. And almost everybody is a genius at doing it.

Consider the conversation now about to take place between Molly Coates and the man she loves and, for reasons with which you are familiar, has had to sacrifice a great deal to agree to marry. Of course, he, too, has had to swallow a fair bit and apologise for himself more than he ever thought was possible. Answering her knock, he is surprised to see her and instantly alarmed by the expression on her face: as yet unreadable, it speaks of strange matters.

You understand, Reader, the alarm and horror that she feels about a trade you cannot fail to know something about: the deaths, the cruelty, the torture, the punishments, the agony, the crime, the rape, the sadism, the centuries of horror. The millions. Now consider it was you who had agreed to sit down and eat the fruits of this thing: water from cups bought (or partly bought) from the profits, sheets slept in paid for by blood, a truly beautiful house mostly built on almost impossible to imagine suffering. Nothing you could touch would not be affected by this great agony, and nothing untouchable either (confidence, power, status, ease). And if you walked through that door, would it only sting at first and then begin to fade, or would the smell follow you around, the smell of unwashed bodies, the stink of the dead, of urine, blood and fear and dread?

It's Complicated

Consider David Lister, about to be confronted by all this. Stand in his shoes and prepare for the battering to come, not because the woman who loves him wants to cast a stone, because she hasn't come to break anything, with the exception of his heart and her own. This is a man dealt a hand in just the same way as anyone else, a flawed person, uncomfortable in strange ways inside his skin, brave, a good friend, rich for complicated reasons no one really talked about and which belong to a distant past. His fathers have handed out sour grapes and now his teeth are going to be set on edge. No one asked his permission before he was born. Those of you who find him liable: ask if you would have done differently. Those who think there is no case to answer: consider the source of the power that drives the magic on which his life, and that of his forbears and ancestors, has been and always will be able to depend.

Now consider the exchange between them, to the end you think is inevitable. Do what you've done a thousand times before and write what passed between them for yourselves.

CHAPTER 63

GOOGLE

Aaron's dentist looked down at him warily.

'I didn't mean to sound as if I was lecturing you last time you were here.'

'You were just doing your job. What's the bad news?'

'I'm afraid it *is* quite bad. The X-rays you had last week showed up that the repeated fillings you've had on your teeth mean that something a bit more radical needs to be done to save three of them. Root canal, I'm afraid. Unfortunately, one of them is too far gone. But it's right at the back, so, while you can have an implant, no one's going to notice if we just take it out. I can fit you in for a couple of hours next week. Get things started.'

A moment's silence. Aaron considered the likely outcome of his plans and decided that an advantage of getting killed was that he wouldn't have to sit through eight hours of teeth fracking. The choppers could wait.

'Let me get back to you on that,' he said.

It was impossible for Molly to concentrate on work, but impossible to do nothing either. She turned for distraction to the web, jumping here and there and everywhere: book reviews, YouTube, buying an alarm clock from Amazon, the sidebar of shame. More alcohol than she was used to. At times, she almost shook with grief and remorse. She

Google

could work for an hour at a time, swaddled up in briskly deranged diligence, and only then would the loss erupt past anything she could do to stop it. It was in between one of these grief jags, while she was looking at the *Daily Mail* website at a more than usually witless article about on-set romances in the making of the *Twilight* series, that she came across a picture of a character from the film – a werewolf with its mouth covered in blood. This triggered a notion, which prompted a question, which sparked off an idea.

A few minutes searching and she landed on a series of articles in the *Journal of Animal Nutrition* devoted to wolves. For five minutes, she scanned and dipped. She was about to give up and return to the usefully mind-numbing stupidity of the *Daily Mail* when she came across a lengthy abstract of a technical paper. 'An Analysis of the Role of Animal Fur in the Digestive Transition of Bone Fragments in the Grey Wolf (Canis Lupis)'. It was the reference to bone fragments that triggered her memory of the photographs she'd seen of large splinters of sharp bones. A question must have formed then, so deeply that she wasn't even consciously aware of it: what happens to your insides when you swallow shards of razor-sharp bone?

The key, it turned out, is in the fur that wolves always make a point of eating in large quantities. It not only acts as a way of speeding large amounts of meat through the gut of the animal; it also, by some as yet mysterious process, wraps itself around these dangerously sharp fragments and allows them to be passed safely through the digestive tract without cutting it open. She sat back, tongue winsomely just emerging from between her teeth, and mulled this over. Then she dismissed it, then mulled it over again, then wondered how you might check up on something like this.

She looked at the photographs of the half-eaten priests. A couple were hairy, all right, but pretty sparse compared to the picture of an almost completely eaten elk. (What did cops do before the internet? she thought. Not bother, probably). She thought for a few minutes more. If the werewolf needed fur, he'd go to a furrier. If he bought a couple of fur coats and ate them (she laughed aloud at this), then there was not going to be any kind of record.

What if he stole them? She logged on to the PNC and searched. No recorded crimes at the not very great number of furriers. It turned out the ones that still existed were very exclusive and had specialised safes for storage. She quickly checked a few charity sites (Oxfam, Cancer Research). There were clear (and prissy) comments that stated they would not accept real fur coats of whatever vintage. She was about to give up when she wondered if hair might be a substitute. The PNC again. She checked the rate of break-ins for hairdressers – pretty much static over a two-year period. Except for one London Borough: Finchley. There had been a 200 per cent increase in hairdresser break-ins over the last six months. This only amounted to a handful of burglaries, but it was still pretty odd. Then she checked against the file of suspects. One witness lived in Finchley – Aaron Gall.

After a few minutes of exhilaration and a brief fantasy of what everyone would think when she cracked the case, the extreme thinness of what she'd uncovered sobered her up. After all, it had started as no more than a whim, a distraction, and it had taken hardly any time to come up with a collection of pretty weak coincidences. Besides, she was one of the few coppers left after MI5 had taken over, and no longer reported directly to Scrope or Lister.

She could protect herself by knocking the idea around with David, but that was something currently impossibly fraught. For the moment, David Lister could take a long walk off a short pier.

If she went with this to the MI5 officers in the direct chain of command, it would take two minutes to dismiss what she'd uncovered. What had been an exciting discovery had quickly declined from being thin and was now skeletal. The narks of MI5 looked down on them, in any case – she'd been given the task of collating evidence that was not much more than glorified filing. She was made of 90 per cent confidence, born of the smart commoner's disrespect for the opinions of middle-class softies, but she was also 10 per cent jelly – the hidden fear that she might be found out, be exposed, laughed at and dismissed. At this moment, the jelly was wobbling. *Don't be such a big girl's blouse*, she thought.

'Come in.'

She opened the door into the office of the C3 in charge of records, a man not more than two years older than her. She'd only talked to him twice, and briefly at that. He'd been up half the night with a sick child and had been told half an hour earlier that he was being sent to Newcastle for three months. He was tired and pissed off. But he made an effort.

'Oh, right, it's Constable ...?' The tiredness and irritation robbed him – her name had gone.

'Coates, sir.'

'Sorry. What can I do for you?'

'I've finished the witness collation.'

'Already? Oh, look, I'm a bit all over the place at the

SCORN

moment. Give me half an hour and I'll get back to you.'

Sitting at her desk, she decided there was nothing in the hair nonsense. Let it go. But she couldn't. The simplest thing was to go and check it out herself. It was not wise, and she knew it. Her habit now was to try to restrain her tendency to damaging disobedience, to do as she was told, full of contempt for the half-wit nature of the command. She had tried insubordination, and plenty of it, when younger, but she was the one who, right or wrong, ended up getting a kicking of one kind or another. She'd learned to be more careful.

Recently, she'd come across a line in a book which made a striking impact on her: a strong man outside the system is much weaker than a weak man inside the system. She wished she'd had someone to point this out to her when she was growing up – it would have saved her a lot of grief. But now she was leaning back to disobedience again.

It was easy to see how it could all go horribly wrong. Short of her actually apprehending the killer, it was hard to see how it could go right. *Leave it*, Molly said to herself. *You're weak and you're on the outside.* She was still thinking this as she approached the door of Aaron Gall's flat.

It was then that the real idiocy of what she was doing swept over her, and she was about to flee when the door opened.

'Looking for me?' said Aaron. She stared at him, silenced for a moment.

'Mr Gall?'

'Yes.'

'I'm a police officer. Detective Constable Coates.'

'A police officer.' He looked at her as if being a police officer was a calling so splendid that all he could do was regard her with a glowing appreciation for which words were entirely inadequate.

'Can we talk? It won't take long.'

He continued staring at her, although the light in his eyes had changed. She felt as if he could stare right through her to the other side and see what a ridiculous twit she was. With a show of good-tempered mockery, he backed away from the door and swept his arm theatrically to show her in. They sat opposite one another, Aaron smiling like a pleased uncle welcoming a favourite niece.

'What can I do for you?'

'I'm just tidying up some details from your last statement. We were trying to cross-reference some dates.' She gave him a look to imply it was nothing of consequence and yet vitally important. 'Can you remember where you were on 14 August, in the evening?'

He looked at her amiably.

'Can you?'

'Sorry?'

'Can you remember where you were on 14 August, in the evening?'

She smiled. 'No, I can't.' In fact, she could, because she'd chosen the day of her parents' thirtieth wedding anniversary. 'But if you could check for me, it would be a great help – a diary?' she suggested.

'Do people still keep diaries? I never have.'

'I meant more like a social diary.'

'The calendar? Yes, that might have something.' He smiled. 'But can I find it? Let me think. The bedroom, perhaps. Would you excuse me?'

When he'd left, she stood up and walked quickly to his desk, scanning the untidy top, then moved to the bookshelves. The room, large, was something of a mess and there was an odd smell, which, with a shiver, she recognised as faintly doggy. In the corner, there was a crumpled, half-deflated bin bag. She glanced back at the door through which he'd left. Nothing. She quickly pulled open the bag, and an electric terror sparked along her neck. Instantly, she turned around.

Less than two feet away hung the enormous head and the open jaws of the werewolf Aaron Gall. With a terrible cry, she stumbled back and fell heavily on to her backside, scrabbling away as the wolf moved forward to the meaty bass note of a doggy growl. But the corner of the wall was directly behind, and Molly didn't have far to go.

'I suppose,' said the werewolf, 'minding your own beeswax would be unwelcome advice to a professional sneak.'

To hear the wolf talk added a new terror. 'Curiosity,' tormented the werewolf, 'killed the cat. They do say that, don't they?'

She stared, feeling the hot, warm breath upon her cheeks. 'Well, Officer?' he demanded.

'Yes,' she whispered. He moved his jaws closer and sniffed her cheeks and eyes. 'You're a funny-looking thing,' he said. 'Find anything useful?' Again, no reply. He growled.

'No. I mean yes.'

'Good. It's smart to be honest with me. And what did you find?'

It was almost impossible to speak. She swallowed hard. 'Hair.'

'I see. I was thinking of going into the wig business. Is that a crime?'

The courage came from somewhere.

Google

'You were using it to protect yourself from sharp bones.'

The wolf pulled back in surprise and, breathing heavily, contemplated the young woman.

'Nosy *and* clever.' A long silence. 'But why here on your own?' He moved his face closer. 'I want to emphasise the continued importance of being straight with me.'

'They're outside, watching.'

Another growl, and another pause. He sat back on his huge haunches and began to pat her down. Satisfied, he stopped.

'As one might expect from a clever, nosy little girl, you're a great big liar. If there were anyone out there, you'd be wired for sound.'

He leaned back, a strange sound like a deep, slow purr emerging now from his throat. 'So, what,' he said, 'am I going to do with you?'

An hour later, a dozen officers alerted by an anonymous phone call burst into his Finchley flat to discover Molly Coates lying on a sofa bed, gagged and bound hand and foot, completely unscathed.

CHAPTER 64

I'VE ALWAYS WANTED TO MEET YOU

Of Aaron Gall there was never a trace. It was clear from the subsequent search that, though the flat was full of stuff, nothing personal or expensive remained. It seemed clear he had been planning to leave when Molly arrived. The idiocy of what she'd done in going to see Gall alone was somewhat cancelled out by the impressive police work that had led to it. The general view from MI5 was that, because Molly had caught him just as he was about to leave, this was solid, if circumstantial, evidence that his claim to have decided to retire could perhaps be taken at face value. Scrope and Lister disagreed, but, as there was no attempt to lower security on the pope during the last days of his visit, it hardly seemed to matter.

For his last night in England before his address to the faithful in Hyde Park, the Holy Father had somewhat reluctantly agreed to be moved secretly from the late cardinal's residence in Westminster to a guest suite in the most secure building in the United Kingdom: the headquarters of MI6 itself, sitting squat as a toad, a giant Babylonian ziggurat over the mighty Thames. All that remained was to get the Holy Father to Hyde Park in the morning for a final Mass and then off to Heathrow and an affectionate farewell from Prince Philip. *Lovely to see you – don't hurry back.*

I've Always Wanted To Meet You

*

'Get a fucking move on, Scrope. I'm parked in a resident's space. You know what the Nigerians are like.' Lister's fear of Nigerian traffic wardens was entirely reasonable. Just as the Jews had been drawn to finance, the Huguenots to weaving, and the East African Asians to late-night grocery shops, the Nigerians of London had effectively requisitioned the calling of traffic warden. No lion or duiker was ever stalked with a more pitiless ferocity than that brought to the motorist of the capital city by the descendants of the trackers of the Kagoro and Hausa-Fulani.

Shabby but in no way chic, Scrope's flat on the top floor of Cumberland Court, just off the Edgware Road, was beyond such matters as taste, good or bad. Similarly transcendent, the area itself was neither fashionable nor unfashionable. These bourgeois anxieties were not disdained – this would imply Scrope was even aware of them. This is where I live; these are the worn carpets and tables patinated by ancient neglect that occupy the place where I live.

Lister was carrying his estrangement from Molly well, which was to say he was utterly distraught but hiding it as if nothing had happened. I suppose all heartbreak is of this kind: a scalding mixture of loss of the beloved and bitter resentment of them for their heartless desertion. To his great unease, he had even taken to driving past her flat in Cricklewood, sometimes parking outside, sometimes just going in circles. For someone who'd never been humiliated by life, it was an unusually horrible experience to discover what it felt like to be powerless, a fuck knuckle, a pathetic ass potato, a saddo, utterly without self-respect. He was so

SCORN

previously untouched by the continuous humiliations that just being alive dumps on general humanity that he hadn't been aware until now that his self-confidence was even capable of falling apart.

Let's be fair to Lister – let's please be fair, old chums – why wouldn't any of you want to feel like that all the days of your lives? Better than money, place or might: a sense of ease in the world, of self-belief, of trust in who you are and will always be. Pity poor Lister a little bit, then, drinking from his silver spoon the wormwood of humiliation that he'd had no idea was on the menu of his life. And remember his service to the state in the Middle East, with its slitting of throats and the IEDs filled with nails and dog shit; take into consideration that he has walked the mean streets of London town in order to protect and serve.

More than most, he has witnessed the horror of human life. But, in one way, he is like a little lamb compared to you. One advantage of being part of the common herd is that at least you've had the chance to accustom yourselves to the daily little doses of failure, defeat and loss that weaken the soul of your ordinary types. The stuff that grinds you down is unknown to the rich and beautiful and powerful like David Lister, burnished with the omnipotence of always being able to walk away. There's always another job, or none at all, always another woman to fall for your looks and ease. How could it be otherwise? But the bigger and stronger they come, the harder they fall. Sympathise or laugh at Lister as you choose. In the end, the human race is united in the great chain of being by the fact that, sooner or later, everyone gets what's coming to them.

MI5 had invited Scrope and Lister to their sneaks' temple by the Thames to humiliate them, by showing off

I've Always Wanted To Meet You

their creepy Lubyanka, gussied up in all its glass and stainless-steel finery at the taxpayers' expense, but in a way that underlined their insignificance – they were invited to the wedding in order to be seated next to the toilets with the long-employed cleaner and the disgraced history teacher related to the bride.

Lister was in a particularly bad mood as they made their way to the south bank of the river, not just because he was forlorn but because Molly was there as well. The process of admitting the three of them into the building was as near to being grand opera as you could get outside the warble palaces of Covent Garden or Milan, all body frisks, shoes off, X-ray machines, and even a wallet inspection.

'Don't you want to bend me over the table so you can look up my arse?' said Lister to the fresh-faced underling – especially chosen to be of no importance – who had been assigned to escort them up to the roof so that they could be shown the city and the world that was MI5's to keep their eyes on and control.

Startled at the question, the poor underling tried to babble his way through the necessity for such tight security, given that they were protecting such an important person from a particularly dangerous threat.

'Well, he's not going to be hiding in my fucking wallet, is he?'

Scrope gave Lister a look that told him to shut up if he knew what was good for him, and eased the subordinate towards taking them to the roof. This was done by means of a deliberately humbling route, involving not the advertising-agency elevators in the magnificent atrium, all fuck-you deep-pile carpet and mirrors, but by using a grubby maintenance lift at the back of the building, a lift

SCORN

with the size and appearance of a neglected basement. Frosty, arctic, gelid, chill – no word was up to describing the coldness of the silence generated between the two former lovers as they stood waiting in the large and grubby lift, Scrope between them, catching some of the big freeze himself.

Distracted, Molly tried staring intently at various places in the lift where Lister was not. Just as the doors closed and the lift started to groan its way to the top floor, she caught a fractional sight of a man pushing a cleaning caddy in the passage outside. For one terrible moment, she thought it might be Aaron Gall. But then she was certain it wasn't. But it might, possibly, perhaps, could have been Gall.

But what was she to do? Call it, and there would be panic. The whole of MI5 would go Bedlam. And if it turned out to be nothing – and it probably was nothing – she'd look like an hysterical idiot. But what if it *was* him? She turned and started to speak, and happened to catch Lister's eye and with it a look bent on causing her hair and clothes to catch fire. Instinctively, she turned away. *It almost certainly wasn't him,* she thought. Onward and upward went the lift. It was too late to say anything now. But she couldn't let it go, however stupid she looked.

'I think I might—'

There was a huge groan, a shudder and the lights went out. The lift stopped dead.

'Aren't there any emergency lights?' asked Scrope, out of the blackness.

'Um ...' said the underling. 'Yes, of course. I mean, there should be. I'll call.' He took out his mobile and it lit up. He screamed.

Staring at him in the glow of the ghostly LED was the

enormous head of a werewolf, not eight inches from the poor spook's face. Instantly, the lights went on and the three cops started back in alarm. Molly might not have been sure what she'd seen, but Aaron was altogether more certain. Aaron Wolf, in all his nine-foot glory, slowly raised himself to his full height, looked at the four people in the lift and settled on the bug-eyed underling.

'Who the fuck are you?'

The unfortunate spook urinated on the floor and then fainted. Do not mock too much unless you, too, have been confronted out of the dark by a giant talking monster with violent eyes and enormous teeth. In an instant, Aaron grabbed Lister. Turning him around as if he weighed nothing, he held him around the throat with his left arm. Around the wrist he was wearing a huge roll of gaffer tape, and in his hand he was holding a large hammer. With his free hand, Aaron patted Lister down. Finding what he was searching for, he removed his mobile phone, which he dropped on the floor, and then a Glock 26 from a leather holster under his right arm, all the while keeping an eye on Scrope and Molly.

'Now you, George.'

Scrope did as he was told, kicking phone and gun over to the werewolf. Aaron looked at Molly.

'I'm not an AFO,' she said.

'I don't know what that means.'

'I don't have a weapon.'

'Give me a twirl.'

She took off her jacket and turned around. Satisfied, Aaron gave Lister a hefty shove to the other side of the lift, where he collided with Molly.

'Are you all right?' she said, fetchingly worried.

But he turned away from her, even in the middle of such bizarre danger more angry at her than frightened.

'Lie down, face to the floor, both of you, hands behind your back.'

Lister asked the question on all their minds. 'What's the hammer for?'

A smile from the wolf. 'Don't fret, whatever your name is. Once I'm done here I've got some shelves to put up.' He waved the hammer at him to signal he should get on with it. 'And if I wanted to kill you, I wouldn't be needing this to do it.'

Realising there was no point protesting, Lister and Molly did as they were told. Aaron threw the gaffer tape over to Scrope. 'Bind their hands and legs then tape their mouths. Do it properly, or else. I don't want any unnecessary violence, but keep in mind that my idea of what's essential when it comes to violence is undoubtedly very different from yours. So don't try my patience. Then do your man in the corner.'

Keeping his eyes on Scrope as he got to work with the tape, Aaron took to the mobiles and the Glocks with the hammer. When Scrope had finished binding his three colleagues, Aaron got him to tape his own legs together at shins and thighs. Then, having made him tear off lengths of tape enough to bind his wrists and tape his mouth (it being extremely difficult for Aaron to do this himself), he finished off disabling Scrope himself.

The wolf leaned over to the buttons and pressed to go up. The lift juddered and began to rise for another ten floors before stopping. The door opened on a floor leading to a section of the roof used only by maintenance men. All but two of the maintenance staff had been told to stay away while the pope was in residence, and those two were now safely trussed up in their crappy staff cabin.

Aaron transformed back into his other self as the three cops watched in astonished silence. Hard though it is to imagine the transformation from small to big, from hairless to hairy, from pathetically weak to powerfully strong, it's only time that makes this strange. Is this not what happens to a baby, after all? But the reverse is something else again: imagine the wonder at the unnatural alteration as, in a few seconds, Aaron's hair grows inward, his snout devolves to become a tiny nose, the skull from ferocious gobbler of meat to an almost delicate head; the massy enormity of steely sinew and of adamantine bone shrinks to become a man in late middle age, pale, not more than five foot nine, and looking like a million others. But not the eyes. They barely changed at all. He walked out on to the roof to scout whether there was anything for him to be concerned about. Ten minutes later, he was back with an assortment of tools, with which he disabled the lift controls, tunelessly humming to himself. Finished, he contemplated Scrope.

'However this goes, George, don't be too upset by the fact that you've fucked up so badly. Put it down to the power of the uncanny and my superior motivation. Playing with you was fun – and you know something, George? I was afraid I'd lost that joy for good.'

Then he turned to the control panel, pressed the button to shut the doors and stepped out before they closed, trapping the three cops and the spook inside. He walked over to the edge of the building, hidden from sight by numerous maintenance huts of one kind or another, and waited for an hour until dark. Then he changed – pleasurably, slowly – into the wolf, made his way to the edge, took a deep breath, and slipped over the side. Those of you of a sneery persuasion who doubt that it's possible to break so easily into a place of central importance to the security of the United Kingdom, I refer you to Phill Jones, Chipper Mills and Tony Vallance.

The Holy Father sat in a large modern leather chair, not as comfortable as it appeared, and gazed out over the sparkle of the black-water Thames and the vast array of lights beyond. To the right, the Houses of Parliament that ardent Catholics had once planned to explode, along with all its members and the king himself. The greatest of all attempted terror plots was allegedly sanctioned by the principal of the same order to which the pope himself belonged. This was probably not true, in that he plausibly claimed the plot had been revealed to him under the seal of the confessional only, and that though he had strongly disapproved of the plot he was powerless under pain of eternal damnation to break the sanctity of the confessional and inform the authorities. It is interesting to speculate what a modern court would do in such a circumstance, but it was not much of a defence in 1606 and so, perhaps unfairly, he was disembowelled in the churchyard of St Paul's Cathedral in May of that year.

Beyond the house of the Mother of Democracies lay Kensington, the retail palaces of Westfield in one direction, and in the other that great Versailles of consumption, Brent Cross, where the ageless Diana left the city for her final resting place, past Hendon Central and the eternal exit of the Great North Way. The lights of Willesden and Cricklewood seemed to shimmer a fond farewell to the soon to be departed pope as he closed his eyes for a moment,

I've Always Wanted To Meet You

allowing the graceful strains of Clara Haskil's playing of Mozart's 'Concerto in D Minor' to ease a mind wearied with so much travelling and talk. After a few minutes, the music ended, and for a while the pope enjoyed the silence.

'I've been expecting you,' said the Holy Father at last. He stood up, walked to the window and turned around. He seemed at first to be talking to himself, but then, out of the deep shadows at the back of the room, loped Aaron Werewolf, long-shanked, stooped and hairy. However much the pope had banked on this confrontation, it was one thing to imagine, another thing altogether to hear the breath of such a creature and see the whiskers bristle on his muzzle and the enormous, sharp-clawed feet.

'I always wondered what the devil would actually look like in the flesh. Surprisingly conventional – even a tail.'

'The devil?' said Aaron. 'My goodness. My only experience of hell, Your Holiness, is the years I spent suffering the tender mercies of the Catholic Church. If there's the whiff of perdition about me, that would be your responsibility.'

'In my experience,' replied the pope, now almost completely in command of himself, 'it's every bully's cry to justify his cruelty: look what they did to *me*.'

'Do I take it from your insults that you've worked out how this evening is going to end?'

'I'm an old man, by any standards. The difference between here and now or later isn't worth worrying much about.'

The wolf laughed.

'Such courage in the face of death. Do I detect the sin of pride?'

The pope smiled.

'When you talk to the devil, said Hölderlin, remember

that he often comes in the guise of a moralising prig.'

'I wish you'd stop saying that. I'm not the devil.'

'Satan's greatest talent is to persuade the world that he doesn't exist.'

The wolf looked at the pope suspiciously.

'I've heard that before somewhere. Where's it from?'

'I couldn't say. Does it matter?'

'I suppose not. But do you believe it yourself, or are you just trying to insult me?'

The pope looked at him as if mildly surprised. 'Insult you? Not at all. You're very sensitive for such a large creature with such big teeth and sharp claws. But then my grandmother always used to say: *Iloriqueo es el pasatiempo favorito del diablo.*'

'Sorry, no one thought there was any point learning Spanish when I was at school.'

'It means something like' – he paused – 'whining is the devil's favourite pastime.'

There was a growl from the wolf, so deep that it could barely be heard. Several glasses on the table rattled.

'We'll see what you think about the tone of my complaints very soon, Your Holiness.'

'Then tell me what they are, your complaints.'

The wolf hawked and spat on the carpet. 'I haven't come here to ask you to hear my confession.'

'The confessional is not a little wooden torture chamber. It's a place to share the tenderness and understanding of God.'

The wolf raised his head slightly, and his enormous whiskers fluttered delicately.

'I like that,' he said thoughtfully. A careful silence from the pope. 'The bit about the little wooden torture chamber

I've Always Wanted To Meet You

is spot on. I don't remember much in the way of tenderness or understanding, just the humiliation of feeding yourself to the soul gluttony of old men.'

He licked his lips. 'I can taste it now, how they devoured my shame.' The wolf shook himself, as if to drive off the water after a storm.

'Then why *have* you come?'

'Why have I come? I've come to chastise you. I intend to rake you over the coals a bit, pluck a crow, as *my* grandmother used to say.'

'So,' said the pope, 'first the verdict, then the trial. But if you're angry – perhaps for very good reason – you must consider that your anger is poisoning you. My father used to say that to torment yourself with past injuries, however real, is like punishing the culprit by drinking your own stale urine.'

The wolf, panting slightly, sank lower on his great haunches as he looked at the pope. It was a look both surprised and admiring.

'You know, Holy Father, you're right. It's exactly like that.' The werewolf dropped his head to one side. 'I admire a man who speaks with a bit of salt. You'd do well to remember that.'

He took in a deep breath as if to signal he was moving on. 'You're not a person, you're the pope. You stand in the shoes of the fisherman Peter, all the way back in an unbroken line to Christ himself. Your guilt is not in question – you are the living presence of history and, when you took the ring of Peter on your finger, you took on all the Church's shitload of sins – and, given that I've endured most of them on my soul or the back of my head, I've decided to make my own history stand for the history of all.'

SCORN

The pope laughed. 'Not vain at all.'

'Merely practical, Your Holiness. If we were to try to go through all the wickedness of the One True Faith, we'd be here until the conversion of the Perfidious Jews or the cows came home, whichever takes the longest.'

Dismissive, the pope waved his hand. 'I knew a teacher – a priest, I mean – who used to do the same thing when I was a boy. He'd cut down to size some perfectly happy little child he thought wasn't miserable enough about their sinful nature, collect every fault big and small about them to their face – and do it in front of the rest of us, like the sour old monster he was – and present a picture to that child as if it were in a dirty mirror that made his faults shine and his virtues vanish.

'That the Church has done dreadful things, you'll get no argument from me. I've done plenty of things that I blench to think about, but I'm a sinner, and I've never said anything else. Tell me the sins of the Church if you must, but tell me all the goodness, too: the sick healed, the lost found, the weak protected. I see the Church like a field hospital in the middle of a battle, a place surrounded by confusion, confusion of the battle itself and of the healers, themselves tired and disorderly and perhaps not the most skilled surgeons or nurses, because those have gone off to richer and easier pickings. These priests, these surgeons, may not be perfect – indeed, they may be very far from that – but they are the ones who stayed to heal and to comfort in the middle of the suffering.'

He looked squarely at the werewolf. 'The first European infected by Ebola died after contracting the disease while caring for the sick in Liberia. He was a Catholic priest. We could be here for a thousand years and not speak of all the self-sacrifice of the priests and nuns of the faith. Do you, whatever you are, have the courage to concede that?'

The wolf sat back on his haunches then raised himself awkwardly on his hind legs, stretching out his arms wide and letting out a huge yawn and growl all in one. For a moment, he hung there; then he landed back on all fours with a thud. He looked the pope right in the eye.

'Does the name John Rabe mean anything to you?'

The pope looked at him, rightly suspicious.

'No?' asked the wolf. 'But then why should it? After all, you claim to be infallible, not omniscient.'

'Really?' said the pope. 'A cheap joke. Whatever we're about here, I would have thought it deserved better than that.'

'I stand corrected, Your Holiness. *Mea culpa.* John Rabe was a German businessman in Nanking in 1937. When the invading Japanese army was in the process of butchering, torturing and raping perhaps four hundred thousand people, John Rabe worked without rest to organise a safe haven for the people of the city. He may have saved more than a quarter of a million lives. Perhaps, in all the history of the world, no single person has ever saved so many lives.' The wolf looked slyly at the pope. 'Something of a saint, wouldn't you say?'

His Holiness looked thoughtful. 'The man you describe,' he replied carefully, 'is clearly a most remarkable person – although I presume there is some sort of trick involved here.'

'A trick?' said the werewolf. 'Not exactly a trick. A change of perspective, perhaps.'

'Isn't a change of perspective just a fancy term for a trick?'

'You could be right. I'll let you be the judge. The reason that Rabe was so effective at organising the committee to rescue so many thousands of souls was that he was a prominent Nazi. Over and over again, he used his powerful place in the party to protect and rescue the weak and defenceless. Think of it, Your Holiness, a quarter of a million people saved from unimaginable horror by a man who signalled the place where the Japanese soldiers could not bring hell on earth by the raising of numerous swastikas.'

The pope sighed with irritation. 'I believe that most intelligent people would regard the attempt to use a comparison between the Nazis and the Church as both desperate and in bad faith.'

The wolf looked thoughtful. 'It's tricky, that one, certainly debatable. But that wasn't quite the point I was making.'

'Which was?'

'That you can't put great crimes on one end of the scales and balance them with good deeds on the other. Is God some greengrocer in the sky? Stalin, after all, defeated Hitler; the old monster fed the poor and clothed the orphans; he brought good health and education for all. Or, take war itself. What immeasurable good has flowed from death and destruction. More women were emancipated by the four-year charnel house of the First World War than at any time in the history of mankind. But then,' added the wolf genially, 'I don't suppose you regard the freedom of women as an altogether unmixed blessing, do you?'

'So – more detraction. More bad faith.'

'I wouldn't,' said the wolf, 'be altogether dismissive of scoffing. It has its place. The best way to drive out the devil is to sneer at him – for he cannot bear scorn.'

The pope laughed. 'Luther. Am I correct?'

I've Always Wanted To Meet You

'Indeed, you are.'

'The laughter you talk about is all destruction and sneering. You cannot make fun of the faith of others.'

'So what do you say to the dead cartoonists in Paris and their life of mockery?'

A pause from the Holy Father. He knew a trap when he saw one. 'Freedom of speech is, of course, a fundamental right.'

'There you go again. When you're on slippery ground, out you come with the pious phrases.'

The pope looked angrily at the wolf. 'You cannot insult the faith of others. You cannot mock what is sacred to them. The right to liberty of expression comes with the obligation to speak for the common good. You want me to speak plainly, then listen to this. Even if my close friend, the gentle Dr Gaspari, curses my mother, he can expect a punch in the mouth. It's normal. It's normal.'

The wolf yelped with delight.

'But what if your mother is Eva Perón or Lucrezia Borgia or the Whore of Babylon? What if she's Mother Mary Frances?'

The pope looked puzzled.

'Don't worry, Your Holiness. We don't have time to go into Mother Mary. What if the insult I speak about someone's mother is the truth? What if speaking for the common good of all my family and all my friends means that I have come here for you to answer for their damaged and murdered souls?'

'Then perhaps you should get on with it.'

A soft growl, almost a purr, from Aaron.

'Don't be so quick to go to judgement, Your Holiness. Things might not be as you expect.'

'You think I assume upon the mercy of God? I do not. But he will not refuse someone so ready to go to him.'

The werewolf looked at the pope slantwise, as if weighing up what to do next.

'You know, Your Holiness, I could talk to you for hours. But we don't have hours, so we must get on if I'm to make use of this exceptional opportunity. Moving on from mothers to the rest of the ladies, I'm curious about your first excommunication. It's reasonable to think that such a drastic step would have great symbolic importance – and yet, with all the other bad deeds you might have condemned, you chose to excommunicate an Australian cleric, I believe, for arguing that women should be allowed to become priests? Or am I wrong that you've sentenced someone to eternal spiritual shipwreck for claiming that women are the spiritual equals of men?'

The pope sighed, exasperated. 'Another old chestnut. Nothing could be further from the truth. The Mother of God is of greater account than all the apostles.'

'Ah!' said the wolf, suddenly remembering something important. 'On the subject of mothers again, I just want to say it was a nice touch, what you said to the mother and her crying baby. I even had a dream about it.'

'It wasn't a touch, as you put it, at all.'

Taken aback for a moment, the Wolf realised his blunder in seeming to mock and bowed to signal his retraction. '*Mea culpa*, Your Holiness, I stand corrected yet again.'

'Never mind that,' said the pope. 'Your accusation that women are undervalued by the Church is not just a lie, it's a particularly worn-out cliché with it.'

'Really? I would have said it's more of a truism than a cliché.'

I've Always Wanted To Meet You

The pope's exasperation turned to irritation.

'Despite the fact that we live in an age of weak thought, of slogans instead of ideas, I'll try patiently to point out that the reason women do not exercise the priesthood is not because of any trumped-up Church notion of inferiority, but because the High Priest is Jesus. In theologically grounded tradition, the priesthood passes through the man, but this doesn't make a woman any less than a man in any way. The Church has not achieved a profound theology of women, I admit, and we must strive to make more room for an incisive female presence so that the feminine genius can make an essential contribution.'

The wolf cackled as only a wolf can.

'And you were almost beginning to win me over. You know, Holy Father, it's odd how even a man who has some impressive salt to his language starts to waffle when he knows in his heart of hearts he's drowning. That's the trouble with words – they give you away.

'So I won't argue with you. Instead, I'll tell you a story about a drum. The school where you did most of the poisoning of my poor ickle soul employed no women as teachers, not even cleaners – except one. But we were three hundred men and boys, and that's a lot of dirt to be cleaned and gobs to be filled. We had a convent of eight nuns attached to the school who washed our underpants and fed us food so hideous there are days when I belch and I believe I can taste it still. The priests, when they spoke of the sisters, always did so in the same tone as you – full of reverence and respect.

'But the thing is, in all the seven years I was there, I never saw them, not once, and neither did anyone else. But we talked to them. We talked to them through a large wooden drum in the dinner hall with a plywood wall down the middle. We'd knock on the drum to summon them and place a bag of sweaty shirts and vests and skid-marked shitty underpants inside, and then when we knocked to say it was full they'd turn the drum and it was theirs. And they always said thank you, the nuns, for the stale sweat and urine and excrement. They seemed quite nice, I thought – you know, grateful. And then, three times a day, they'd load in porridge the consistency of a dead jellyfish or sausages that only a dog would eat.

'And that was that. Seven years, and I never saw them once. That's your world in a grain of sand, Your Holiness.'

The pope considered the wolf for a few moments.

'Quite the sermon, ah ...' He raised his eyebrows in a question.

'Mr Wolf,' said the wolf agreeably.

'You don't have a name?'

'Oh, I do,' said the wolf.

'Perhaps you protest too much.'

'I've a lot to get off my chest.'

'I mean, perhaps you've missed your vocation.'

'I wouldn't describe this' – the wolf gestured at himself – 'as a vocation, exactly. It's been too much of a pleasure for that.'

'Perhaps you've let the pleasure of manifesting your anger and resentment distort your true nature.'

'I don't doubt it. My mother used to say I was a wonderfully happy little boy until I was eight years old. You know, there's an odd thing,' added the wolf chattily. 'I used to get, when I was in bed at night in your concentration camp for children, just a couple of times a year, these absolutely amazing bursts of utter joy that came out of nowhere. I can still remember them. Just wonderful. They lasted for about three or four years into my sentence. Then they just stopped. Pity. They were quite something, I can tell you.'

A thought struck the werewolf. 'Talking of mothers. You said just now that you'd punch someone on the nose if they insulted yours. But you're explicitly instructed to turn the other cheek when someone strikes you. It's unequivocal that you are obliged to forgive seventy times seven. There's no punching allowed. All this stuff about authority and your obligation to stand up without compromise for the commands of God, and you're making it up to suit yourself as you go along.'

Aaron was impressed that the pope did not reply instantly but was clearly considering this carefully. It was some time before he spoke again.

'I meant it when I said I was a sinner,' he said regretfully. 'I acknowledge that, in the past, and in some places, the Church was sometimes a place of shortcomings and sin.'

'Shortcomings!' The wolf laughed – not a pleasant sound at all. 'Yes, I'd say there were shortcomings. And as for *in the past, in some places, sometimes* – wonderful. You kill me.'

'I apologise,' said the pope quickly. 'That was waffle, as you call it. What my mother used to call water words. Let me be clear: the abuse of children is a leprosy that has infected the Church and for which there must be remorse and reparation.'

The werewolf Gall raised his head and turned it to one side. His muzzle curled and an odd gasp escaped his huge, toothy mouth.

'Good God, no. I'm not talking about any of that stuff. Is that what you think I'm on about? I'm sick to the back of my rotten teeth with everyone thinking I'm here because I was buggered by some bastard in black.

'I killed all these priests and that woman, and I'm going to kill you, for murdering my soul, not defiling my bottom. You're going to die because of the blows to the side of my head and for the beating of my entirely covered arse with a rope in front of thirty schoolboys. Your liver will not be eaten because of the baying about the persecution you suffered, but for the silence about the terror you inflicted across centuries. I'm going to rip out your kidneys because of the mad fantasies you poured into my ears about hell and guardian angels and miracle cures. And then the boredom of living with you day after day, listening to you, watching you, smelling you. I'm going to tear your lungs apart for making me eat like a dog – you're going to die because of my rotting teeth. I'm going to chew on your eyeballs for my brother's broken finger, for the friends who lost their minds. I'm going to devour your brains for turning my mother and father, sweet and kind as they were, into the agents of my destruction because they were afraid of you.'

The werewolf stood high on his haunches as he became more and more excitable. Now he breathed out, hot and sticky. 'You see, Holy Father, you were right when you said that God is hidden in what is small.'

'My son,' said the pope sadly, 'I see how much you have suffered and I ask for forgiveness on behalf of the Church for whatever was done to you by those who should have been your guardians and not your tormentors. I was wrong to speak with such bitterness about your anger. But let me say that it's still the truth that your anger is destroying you and that we should sit down together now and look to the future. Forgive me and sit down with me.'

The werewolf stared at him, panting quick and shallow,

I've Always Wanted To Meet You

like a dog on a hot afternoon.

Then, in an instant, he leapt at the pope, clamped his jaws around his head and wrenched it from his shoulders. Blood shot from the severed neck, showering the room in a dreadful crimson while the pope's hands, nervous with electricity, flew up in the air and waved about in terrible distress.

Pitiless, the wolf looked on, papal head in his enormous mouth, at the headless corpse, arms waving in terror for a few seconds, then slowing gradually to an anxious flutter, then relaxing and descending to his sides. For a moment the body stood upright, as if silently coming to accept its suffering and fate. And then it fell to its knees, paused a moment as if praying for guidance into the afterlife, then fell forward on to the carpet with a muffled thud.

Mouth full, the wolf looked on. Then, with one shake of its mighty neck, it threw the pope's head across the room to hit the door with a tremendous wallop before landing with a dreadful thump on the floor. The wolf stared at the body.

'Enjoy your seventy-two virgins, Holy Father,' he said aloud. After a moment's reflection, his expression changed to one as remorseful as a werewolf's face is ever likely to get. 'I apologise, Your Holiness. That was a sneer unworthy of either of us. *Mea maxima culpa.*'

The look on his face changed from one of lupine remorse to one of discomfort. He reached up a giant paw, pinged out a ferociously sharp nail and poked it about on the right-hand side of his mouth, clearly in some considerable discomfort. Then, with a sudden tensile twist of the extended nail, he gave a brief cry of pain, searched the inside of his mouth with his enormous tongue, and spat the pieces of a splintered tooth out on to the floor.

'For even Satan disguises himself as an angel of light. Therefore it is not surprising if his servants also masquerade as servants of righteousness.'

2 Corinthians 11:13–15

CHAPTER 65

UNKNOWN UNKNOWNS

The werewolf Gall turned away from the carnage to the massive window that looked out over the Thames. He felt neither triumph nor exultation. Perhaps the fact that so few people have clear, heroically ambitious ends explains why they're not always prepared for ultimate victory. Few men and women put their hands on the glistering statuette or hear the fulsome accolade that confirms their central importance in the world. Evolution has prepared you carefully for failure, but hasn't bothered too much to make provision in your hearts for getting everything you want. 'I'm worried about that man,' Freud used to joke. 'He's had a great success.'

And so the wolf stared out into the London night and considered the strange emotions taking shape inside his hairy chest. He was so preoccupied in his pondering, and the process was so silent, that he was completely unaware of the miracle unfolding behind his back.

Slowly and judiciously, the headless corpse of the pope got to its feet and stood there for a moment, somewhat unsteadily, it must be said. It moved its upper body a few times to left and right, as if trying to work out why it could not see. After a moment, the hands started moving up from its sides. With the index finger of each hand pointing upward, all at once the pointing fingers began to shake uncontrollably, for about ten seconds. Then they stopped. The hands moved to where the pope's head should have been and, on failing to find what the nervous system expected, all ten fingers spread apart in horrified alarm and began to shake. Again, after a few seconds, they stopped.

The headless cadaver stood still for a little longer while in front of it, all unseen of course, the great wolf wrapped up in its shaggy thoughts continued to stare out over the Thames. Then a slight shudder poured over the cadaver, which slowly began to increase into a noticeable but silent shaking. The hands moved outward and began to wave insanely, and then the noise began.

The sound seemed at first very distant, as if it were a train from nearby Waterloo that had decided to leave its tracks and take to the freedom of the roads. Involuntarily, the ears of the wolf pricked up, but it seemed like only an odd city sound and nothing to be alarmed about. But then the noise grew loud, increasing until the room began to shake, the glasses on the tables to move and the windows to rattle. Slowly, the wolf turned around, and a cry of fear broke from his mighty throat and his body began to tremble with the shock.

Instantly, the corpse of the pope started to split and expand, as if it were a mountain about to erupt. It stopped. The noise increased. The body shook. The clamour increased yet more. And then it was as if something arrived there from another world, some kind of entrance from a place immeasurably old and infinitely vast, and the body split apart and a huge, white ballooning bulge burst out of the papal corpse and began to inflate like some hideous giant grub. If you have ever held a spaniel in a thunderstorm and felt it shake, that was nothing to the ancient animal terror the wolf experienced now, its animal dread of the terrible unknown.

The maggoty head reared backward, quivering and swaying, a ghastly, bloodless white, stretching and bulging as if trying to find what shape it ought to be. And create a shape it did, a sort of pus-filled, flabby beach ball. From deep inside, two terrible black blobs like ugly, dirty pearls began to grow towards the surface of the head, and just below the midway point a split from side to side began to form a terrible mockery of a mouth. And then the horrible, white, wormy flesh began to engorge with colour – bruised reds and welty purples spreading across its unearthly parody of a human face. Arms popped out of its sides like the bursting of a ripening blackhead of enormous heft. Then hair began to sprout upon its head, but only on one side. Then a forehead of a kind emerged and a chin and then a neck, but all with an indistinct and sloppy line so you couldn't tell where one began and one left off.

Then the squidgy whiteness of the skin began to congeal and harden, fleshening with purple, indigo and a dirty cochineal. Then, finally, there was a popping sound as hairs as thick and sparse as the bristles on a worn-out wooden toilet brush began to grow on the receding chin. And then the smell, one that Aaron had not sniffed for many years and never with such sickening intensity: the smell of a man unwashed for centuries, the throat-catching whiff of the urine of millennia, the reek of priest-breath – they shrivelled the hairs in his nose. The stoaty musk of rank testosterone gone sour convulsed the wolf's guts, and he retched repeatedly.

SCORN

With a slobbering heave, the creature ejaculated from the pope and revealed itself entirely to the terrified werewolf.

CHAPTER 66

DEAD END

What of our heroes in the lift? Have they had the time and the skill to free themselves with pluck and ingenuity from the bonds in which they were ensnared by Aaron Gall? Are they even now working their way out of the lift in an impossible mission to save the day? Let me remind you: they were wrapped in gaffer tape by a man who designed some of the most complicated instruments in the most complicated machine in human history. The three of them were going nowhere at very nearly the speed of light.

'The thing to understand about wicked people is that they don't really have a plan, they just appear to do so. When they try to create something it never lasts, because like viruses their ideas are not really alive in any way we understand the term. The Reich that would endure for a thousand years lasted twelve. Stalinism came and went in a generation. A virus needs a host, a living organism it can inhabit. That was the wisdom of the early fathers of the One True Faith: they infected an idea which they saw had a vital power and made it theirs. But in time even a very adaptable virus will threaten to kill the creature that alone can give it life. One of two things will happen then. The virus will kill the host and that will be that. Or a new virus will take over from the old. An example? The Communist Party of China. It retains the name and a good deal of the rhetoric of communism; it reveres Mao Tse-tung.

But otherwise? Nothing beside remains, except that the State continues to seek complete control of its citizens. But it has no purpose other than this. It has no plan at all. At the moment the Catholic Church is vast enough but rotting from the inside.

It needs infecting with a new virus if it is to survive. But from where will this new source of infection come? I can't say. But let's be quite clear, if it comes at all it will only have the appearance of a plan, of a purpose. Its sole attribute will be the attribute that dominates every wicked thing: the will to power.'

Louis Bris, The Wisdom of Crocodiles

'As to the frequently asked question: is Satan a communist or a fascist? The answer is that Satan is unquestionably a communist. Fascism is incomprehensible to him because it states honestly what its intentions are: to use willpower to dominate everything. The father of lies is a Bolshevik to his bones because he always insists the terrible things he does are for the benefit of mankind.'

Louis Bris, Notes from a Fraud

CHAPTER 67

AN INTERVENTION

The wolf backed fearfully into the corner of the room, guts dissolving, senses reeling, as the creature, sure of its victory, took a moment as if to gauge its surroundings, head moving ravenously from side to side with the sound of joints popping from lack of use. The dirty pearls that were its eyes rolled about in a face full of pain and deep confusion. There were no legs, just a widening trunk, and, as its baggy flesh touched the ground, a skirty fold of flesh, something like that of a snail, rippled with a hundred muscles, cut like the tread of some monstrous tyre oozing mucus. It glistened with the petroleum colours of a bubble blown from the wand of a very wicked child.

Then it began to speak in strange sentences, each one in a different voice: intimate, alarmed, conspiratorial, demanding, ashamed, truculent, pitiful, desperate, thoughtful and obscene.

'I'm gonna tell you something, Steve, I've kept to myself for years – I reached my peak when I was nineteen.'

'Gold in Mexico? Why sure there is.'

'We know you're the head of a tungsten monopoly, Mr Farrell.'

'Why did we sit silent? Why did we take part?'

'By using a substance from the blood of humans, schizophrenia has been induced in dogs.'

An Intervention

'Nobody laughs at me! Because I laugh first!'

'I'm wearing a cardboard belt, but I don't even want to talk about it.'

'It does more than turn me on, Mr Vader. It makes me come.'

'They can't hear! They can't speak! They can't operate machinery!'

'Now, there are more than twenty vital bodily fluids, and I am proud to say that I have tasted every one of them.'

'Then I thought, *What if I'm wrong? What if there is a God?*'

The maggot fell back against the wall, raised what would have to pass for its head, and gazed longingly but regretfully into the distance, disgusting black eyes fringed by insanely long and gorgeous eyelashes:

'They call me beautiful, but I kill ... I kill with my cunt.'

At once a strange and painful tremor passed over the creature. It sagged for a moment and, when the trembling passed, it sighed with relief. The smell of rotting armpits filled the room. Then the maggot looked up and stared directly into the wolf's eyes.

'What ...' The words stuck in Aaron's throat. 'Who are you?'

The maggot smiled, if you can imagine such a smile.

'My name is Legion,' he said, and laughed, 'for we are many.' The creature coughed and spat out a gobbet of phlegm the size of a middling jellyfish.

'Dear me, what an outburst! And such language!' It blinked and sighed again. 'My apologies, Mr Gall, for that. Being born again after such a long time is a tumultuous experience – a crucifixion and a resurrection all in one chummy intermingle, so to speak.'

Its gaze scanned the werewolf.

'Since you've gone to so much trouble to bring me here, what've you got to say for yourself?'

Aaron, his bag of over-inflated courage burst, could barely speak.

'Who are you?'

Even though the sound was like the last sound in this life made by an asthmatic with a fat man jumping up and down on his chest, it was still clear to the wolf that the creature was laughing.

'Isn't it obvious?'

The wolf stared at him.

'Clearly not.' A pause. 'How utterly typical. You've been going around, sticking your big, hairy conk into matters that don't concern you and about which you're completely clueless. You ought to be more careful.'

'Who are you?'

'Oh, you know who I am, you hound, in your heart of hearts. Yes, it's me, the one who feeds upon ashes as if they were bread and whose joy is at the mouth of the furnace, Lord of the High House, Old Nick, the Fallen, the angel who, if I alight on a tree, all its apples are poisoned.' He leaned forward and winked. 'A filthy Protestant lie by the way, that one.'

Regaining some but not much in the way of composure, Aaron Wolf started to ease himself away from the hideous gargoyle in front of him.

'Getting a second wind, are you? Well, you just stay where you are and be still.'

'Are you the devil?'

The creature drew in a deep breath, the sound of patient exasperation.

An Intervention

*

Dear Reader, allow me to interrupt this portion of the show by reminding you that I promised you when we began this book a climax to freeze your heart, to cause your tongue to cleave to the roof of your mouth and the hairs to stand up on your neck like a hedgehog or a crown of thorns. Did I exaggerate? Is not your mouth dry, your heart a-pitter-patter, the hairs along your nape erect? Prepare for more – a shock so great some of you will have a stroke, others an insult to the brain. You have been warned. Prepare yourselves.

I and this devil, we are one. I am he and he is me. All along, dear bibliophile, I, Mephisto, Nick, Beezleybub, Rastus, Señor Eddy Scratch have been your guide. Still living? Want to know more? Then come. But leave, for goodness' sake, your boring preconceptions at the door.

(PS I intend to continue refer to myself in the third person, not out of vanity – I'm beyond all that now – but merely in order to avoid confusing you.)

The creature drew in a deep breath, the sound of patient exasperation.

'It's not,' said the devil, 'a handle I care for. It's not really true or useful. But to try and explain the frankly exhaustingly bombastic nature of the realm of spirits – I don't have the time.' He looked at the werewolf, his maggoty black eyes twinkling. 'And neither do you. But, technically speaking, I'm a Cherub – no idea where the fat little babies thing comes from. I am also the fourth most important of all the spiritual powers. Make of that what you will.'

'The Bastards in Black used to say that the devil doesn't know how to give a straight answer.'

'There you are, then,' said the devil.

'What do you want?'

SCORN

'Funnily enough, I was going to ask you the same thing. But there isn't really time for all your boring personal problems. You could say, in a manner of speaking, I'm a Guardian Angel. And until you came along, I was doing what Guardian Angels do, which is to keep an eye on things, roll their eyes in distaste at the vulgarity and grossness of those they're guarding, and try and gently shift them in the direction of doing the right thing.'

The creature tipped its hideous head back and scowled. 'But now I find you adding shit to the soup just when I was trying to get something done at a particularly difficult time.'

He looked mournfully at the remains of the late Holy Father and sighed, a sound and a smell like the air bursting out of the corpse of a whale dead for a week. 'If you had any idea of how much time and effort had gone into placing this particular man in this particular position at this particular time ...' Words seemed to fail him. He leaned towards the wolf, who was shaking uncontrollably in the corner.

'Worrying I'm going to kill you?' He let out a low bass rumble that raised the hackles on the terrified werewolf. 'But there's no need to worry at all. That's exactly what I'm going to do.'

Silent, shaking deep in his guts, feeling as if he might lose control of his bowels, Aaron from deep inside realised the all-powerful padfoot he thought he could rely on was frightened beyond human understanding. Animals are terrified of the fire that gives human beings joy. Aaron the man was terrified, of course, but he was still able to think and plan. Talk.

'How can the devil be a guardian angel?'

The devil snorted in disgust. 'I can't begin to tell you

An Intervention

how many asinine assumptions there are behind that question. See, all that stuff about my rebellion through pride is all filthy, lying propaganda. And before you jump to conclusions about my motives, I'd just like to point out that, in the entire history of the world, all the books about me have been written by God. Now it's my turn. So, before I kill you, I intend to tell you why.'

He drew in a deep breath and began speaking as gently as a mother to her beloved child.

'When God created mankind, I honestly thought he was making a mistake. I genuinely felt sorry for you. All I did at the time was point out that making Adam out of mud and expecting him to act as if he were made out of silk was asking for trouble. Is that rebellion? I think it was a sincerely held disagreement. What's wrong with that? But that was it. No fucking turning the other cheek then, I can tell you. Arse over tit for three days headlong from ethereal light to darkness visible.'

The devil sniffed and looked shifty. 'I don't mind admitting that, for a time, I lost my way, morally speaking. I looked around for someone to blame.'

'Wasn't God to blame?'

The devil examined him thoughtfully. Being very old and crafty, he was perfectly clear what Aaron was up to.

'Yes, He very much was to blame, but His being omnipotent as He had so painfully demonstrated, I wasn't in a position to get my own back. So I looked around for someone I could actually hurt and went looking for Adam and Eve. I'm not proud of what I did when I found them – stirring them up to disobey their Maker and get expelled from the Garden of Eden. Sticking up for them had got me damned for all eternity, and they were going to pay. Not that I didn't feel bad at the time. She was wonderful, that Eve.'

He sighed with delight. A smell of old urine and faecal matter filled the room. 'Atheists? PHHHHT! You couldn't look at breasts like hers and not know there was a God. Still I did what I did and then I cleared off. But I knew I'd done them a bad turn, and it was on my mind. So, eventually, I went back to see if there was a way of making up for what I'd done. But I wasn't the only spiritual entity with a bad conscience. Who should I find stirring things up, but Jesus Christ all fucking mighty claiming that he'd generously come to save mankind from the vices his father had given them in the first place.'

'Can I sit down?' said the werewolf. 'I'm feeling awfully off colour.'

'You stay where the fuck you are,' said the devil pleasantly. A pause. 'What was I saying?'

'You'd discovered the Son of God telling the Jews he'd come to save them.'

'Bastard!' exclaimed the devil. So angry did he seem that, at first, Aaron thought he was shouting at him; but he was expressing an antipathy of long standing.

'But wasn't he doing the same as you – making up for the mistakes of the past?'

'*I'd* come to apologise,' said the devil in hurt tones. 'God doesn't do "sorry". He claimed it was all their fault, but that, given He was all merciful, He decided to forgive them and offer them a new beginning.'

'And you were angry?'

'Of course I was angry. I know I hadn't been a friend to mankind, Mr Gall, but I was determined to make up for it and do my best to help them out, only to find Jesus Christ spouting his poison at them.'

An Intervention

'Poison?' Aaron was surprised, even a little shocked. Like many atheists lacking the courage of their convictions, he'd tended to sentimentalise Jesus as a good and often wise man who, just like the faithful, had become the victim of his viral priests. But the devil was not so much angered by the disagreement as incredulous that anyone could see it otherwise.

'Oh, for goodness' sake! Yes, poison. Turn the other cheek under the threat of violence – a monstrous idea that could end only in the rule of the thug and the bully. Sell all you have and give it to the poor, desert your family to pursue the good life, pay the same wages to a man who's sweated for a day as a man who's toiled only for an hour? Forgive seventy times seven? Monstrous. Giving love to the cruel is like fertilising the weed that destroys the crop; it's encouraging the viper to come into the house with a saucer of milk and allowing it to bite the smiling baby in the cot. Where's the love in that? And what destruction do you think it would produce if you carried it through? He was a terrorist, that Jesus – it's just that he wanted to use love instead of violence to bring the world down around our heads. It was all just hot air, but hot enough to set the world on fire if anyone actually carried it out. Which of course they never did.'

The devil started to laugh. 'Listen to me, getting on my high horse. But Jesus fucking Christ almighty always had that effect on me. Finding him there, with the crowds lapping it all up the way they were, I was really terrified he'd persuade the world he could remake mankind. I really thought that people would be inspired and take this bilge seriously, start forgiving the evil and loving the oppressor. And I couldn't bear it. I loved the human race and couldn't endure to see it destroyed by his hideous idea of opposing power with meekness and love.'

'You love the human race?' said the astonished werewolf.

The devil looked at him oddly for a moment, as if uncertain what to say.

'All right, "love" is putting it too strongly. That kind of absolutist bilge is catching. Call it fellow feeling then, if you prefer. Mankind and I, we were both turfed out of paradise for sticking up for ourselves. And I'd done them wrong, and I knew it.

'But instead of trying to put it right there and then, I went into a bit of a sulk for a few thousand years. I don't excuse it, I'm merely telling you how it was. I wasn't my best self. So I came back, as chance would have it, just as Jesus Christ almighty was peddling his nonsense. I stayed to see them string him up, and I hung around for a bit to make quite sure his toxic notion of using love and forgiveness to defeat the wicked was going nowhere. Which it wasn't. When I left the world for a second time, his pitifully small rabble of followers were tied up in endless squabbles about circumcision and whether it was all right to eat the meat of strangled animals.'

The devil shook his head. 'A few centuries later, I dropped by—'

'Where did you go?' asked Aaron, hoping to spin the conversation along. The devil looked at him, eyes narrowing.

'I was taking care of business. Not that it's any of yours.' A pause. 'I've got my eye on you,' he added. 'Anyway, I came back to see what had happened to God's collection of half-wits, slaves and women. Lo and fucking behold,

An Intervention

Christianity is now the sole state religion of the most powerful military empire in history. It turns out the bullies didn't destroy Christianity, they loved it.

'Curious that – how a religion for herbivores became so attractive to an empire of meat-eaters. Perhaps that explains why the faith of love and forgiveness was now all about sin and suffering and obedience to authority. The funny thing is, they were still talking about peace and charity and understanding when I got back, but it turned out that endless forgiveness and endless love had come to mean burning people. To be fair, not everyone agreed: St Augustine said you should forgive heretics once before you burned them.'

He laughed, not hiding the delight and the malice. 'Me and God almighty – human nature made fools out of both of us.'

'So you got your revenge.'

A sudden dart towards the werewolf, so fast cobras would have spat jealously. The devil brought his hideous face right up against Aaron and let a blast of air into his face that was foggy with the smells of roadkill skunk, the fruit of the durian and the yellowy pus of long-untreated syphilis.

'Listen to me, fucker. I'd behaved questionably in the Garden of Eden so I felt I had an obligation to set the human race on a path that would make their tragically deluded lives a bit more bearable. It was partly my fault they'd started out in a direction that led to them being chained to a bunch of old monsters and their mad ideas. I couldn't just leave them in the grip of bastards who delighted in making them feel like scum. All I ever wanted to do was help people to see themselves as they really are and stop destroying each other with delusions of grandeur. You know why lemmings throw themselves over the cliffs in their thousands?'

'I thought that was just a myth.'

'Don't be stupid all your life! It's nothing to do with being suicidal. What have lemmings got to complain about? It's because lemmings suffer from the delusion they can fly.'

'I'm sorry,' said Aaron, trying to keep the talk going. 'I don't understand.'

The devil sighed, irritated at having to explain the obvious. 'When I said to God that mankind were scum, I wasn't being rude. I was being factually accurate. I was pointing out to His Enormity that it was unreasonable ...' He stared at Aaron and then, his tone sarcastic, added: '... by which I mean it was morally wrong, it was unfair, to create a being for which He had such high hopes, make it out of bug shit and worm casts and dog water, and expect it to behave in a way superior even to the angels. He gave you the ability to choose good and evil when He hadn't had the generosity of mind to give that choice to me.

'In short, He gave the lemmings the desire to fly, the belief that it was in their nature, but He didn't bother to give them wings. That's just not right.'

Aaron saw his chance to stoke the devil's sense of grievance at someone other than Aaron.

'Are you saying God didn't give you the power to choose between right and wrong?'

'You're surprised, aren't you? Well, you're fucking right to be. I shone like the sun and, from my eyes, the light of wisdom fastened the world in understanding, but still I was tailored like a Savile Row suit by Him to follow His

An Intervention

every word without hesitation or regret. Or so He thought. He was so stunned when I disagreed with Him about the making of mankind, I don't think he so much cast me out of heaven as dropped me as if I were some lapdog who'd given Him a bite. I saw His mistake, and you can't say events haven't shown that I was right.

'I mean, look at you,' said the devil, in a tone more of sympathetic sorrow than disdain. 'What are you but a combination of arrogance, hysteria, woolly-mindedness, criminal amorality, doctrinaire fanaticism, the purveyors and buyers of shoddy spiritual goods and false idols from Elvis to the iPod? Your art is spurious, your philosophies stuttering, wrapped in utopian humbug or witless intensity. Exactly what you'd expect from a bunch of grass cunts manufactured from a rancid brew of slug and snail shit.'

He sighed in irritation, a seething sound of skin burning on a hot-plate. The devil leaned forward, as if sharing a rarely spoken secret. 'But if mankind was a shoddy doohickey from the first cook it was His fault, not yours.'

He slid backward away from Aaron and took up a place against the wall where he could keep an eye on him.

'Where had his decision to get involved one more time ended up? A dead son on a gibbet. So He withdrew again and left you to it. Well, I wasn't prepared to let the bullies of the priesthood have you to themselves, so I asked myself: given your limitations, what is the best life for mankind, a creature occasionally high in ambition but made out of sludge? What you needed, then and now, is a religion that takes your peculiar nature – good intentions, inferior materials, torn by irreconcilable differences – and gives it a bit of support, a helping hand. A religion that would mostly keep you on the straight and narrow but could be let out at the seams, bend a little' – he leaned forward, and winked – 'or a lot. That's compassion, friend. That's being fucking merciful.

'I was the one who came up with the idea of the confessional in' – he paused to remember – 'the year of Our Lord 357. An idea, I don't think it's unfair to say, more generous than any idea in the history of compassion. What a wonderful deal it offers to a creature that was created to have a nature as base as a crocodile and yet, from time to time, cursed with the awareness of an angel! So I thought up a way of making it bearable to be human.'

His disgusting black eyes were filled with ancient nostalgia. 'Ah, confession!' he said, with the smile of an old sportsman recalling a great victory from the past no longer remembered by the fickle crowd. 'Human beings can't help being pretty shitty a lot of the time but I, me, I'm the one they call Lord of the Flies.'

He stopped and looked at Aaron with affronted incredulity. 'Do you know what some little brat called me yesterday? Poo-poo-faced Ding-dong. When all I was trying to point out to him was …' Suddenly, he looked shifty. 'Well, never mind what I was trying to point out. You can't talk to a child these days without people questioning your motives.'

He coughed. 'Anyway. Confession was designed to make life bearable. Come to me, own up, say sorry and promise to make good the damage, and we'll wipe the slate clean before the next time you fuck it up. Then we'll try again and see how we go. The God of love? How can He possibly deserve to be called the God of love after the way He made you? People should be talking about the Devil of love.'

An Intervention

He sniffed loudly, as if at a private grief that no one could understand. He turned back to Aaron. 'And what did the Church do?' He spat another jellyfish gob on the floor. 'They turned my gift, my wonderful compassionate gift, into a torture chamber.'

Astonished, the werewolf looked over at the late pope. 'That's what he said.'

The devil closed his eyes and gasped irritably. 'He said it, fuckwit, because I'd been whispering it to him in his dreams for years. Have you any idea how hard it is to develop the thinking of a man like this when all you have to work with is the drivel that happens to be going through his mind as he sleeps? And now you've fucked up decades of work!

'And for what? What's your beef? Someone gave you the odd clip on the ear, which you probably deserved, and told you a few things you didn't care for. No one buggered you! No one made you lick shit off their boots! So what are you complaining about? There are hundreds and thousands – *millions* – who had it worse than you.'

He sighed again, spreading the smell of rotting fish and smelly feet throughout the room like a hideous stain.

'Still, whatever doesn't kill you makes you stronger. When life gives you lemons ... I suppose if you really want something done well, you'd better do it yourself.'

He seemed to have calmed down. Aaron tried more stalling.

'There's one thing I want to understand before I die. And you're the only one who can tell me. Give me that at least.'

The devil looked at him suspiciously. He was, after all, the father of flattery as well as the father of lies. But even the man who invented sugar was not immune from its corrosive rush.

'Well?'

'How in the name of all that's unholy has the Catholic Church survived for so long? What's its secret?'

'PHHHHT!' snorted the devil. 'You think there's some brilliant plan at work, some terrible but dazzling insight into the human condition? There's no great secret to the Church's success. When the Emperor Justinian saw it could help him unite his empire, he made it the religion of the state. Politics, and nothing more. He didn't even convert to Christianity himself. It got the Church unique power and, above all, it got them control of the young.

'And that was what did it. Give me a child until he is seven and I will have possession of his soul for life. If the Church relied upon adults to choose the One True Faith, it would consist of a couple of thousand weirdos and criminals like Tony Blair, Newt Gingrich and Stalin.'

'Stalin was a Catholic?'

'Only on his deathbed. And only in his own head.' The devil smiled and smacked his horrible lips with delight. 'I mean, he didn't get into heaven or anything. There was no one to hear his last confession but me, disguised as the Archimandrite of Moscow. 'All your sins are forgiven you, my son,' I intoned. 'Dzz Dzz,' he said, and wet himself with relief. My goodness, how I laughed.'

Not being skilled in the reading of the expressions of satanic caterpillars, Aaron was unsure whether the devil was being serious about Stalin. He was the father of lies, after all.

'That's not important now,' continued the devil. He started gliding across the room on his huge, sluggy pad,

An Intervention

little wriggly legs like a thousand millipedes, and looked out over the Thames. At once, he turned his head in alarm.

'Did you hear that?'

'Hear what?'

The devil looked at him warily. 'Never you mind.'

He looked out of the window again. 'Is it beginning to get light?'

Aaron didn't want him thinking about the time. 'No.'

'I can see right through you to the other side, friend. Try anything, and I can promise you it's the last thing you'll ever do.'

'I'm just curious,' said Aaron. 'If I'm going to die—'

'You are,' said the devil.

'—then there are a few other things I want to understand before I go. I mean – what's the plan?'

The devil looked him over and smiled. What kind of smile it was (amused, dismissive, affectionate) was unclear.

'Mankind is slime made with a feeling that it can be divine. That's a terrible thing to do to a living creature. Terrible. But I would never be cruel enough to tell the human race what they really are. They need a religion to get them through their miserable lives and shield them from their complete lack of any significance whatsoever.

'But the trouble is that, for some reason, all those religions spawned out of the deserts of the Middle East have a terrible allure for heretic burners and stone throwers and – fucking careless of him, as usual – Jesus didn't hand down that neat little trick of keeping them in check by writing their sins in the sand. You know what happened to the woman taken in adultery five minutes after he saved her from being stoned? They crept back and beat out her brains with a couple of rocks they'd just collected from the desert.'

SCORN

The hideous smile vanished as he looked at Aaron. 'Make one more move towards the window and I'll break both your legs.'

Aaron stopped moving. The devil turned back to face him.

'An inadequate creature doesn't need an outstanding religion to make up for its incorrigible deficiencies. It needs the right kind of inadequate religion to reflect them, ease them away from the worst excesses. I can't stop the war raging in mankind, but at least I'm offering a faith that's – yes, he's right, you know – a field hospital for your wounds to be dressed, a place where you can feel forgiven for a revolting nature about which there's nothing you can do. I don't want to reveal the truth about your character – you can't handle the truth – I just want to get rid of the stone throwers who've made human life so miserable. The wound has always been there, and now I've come with the bandage to ease the pain of the fact that you're basically glorified monkeys deluding yourselves you're the fallen lords of creation, deserted by God, living out futile lives that last a few pathetic, pain-filled days in an utterly indifferent universe.' He sighed deeply and regarded the dismembered bits of pope. 'People want to adore, they really do. I had high hopes for him – not perfect, but much, much better than the roll call of the living dead who usually end up in charge. People need someone they admire to tell them how not to be so fucking horrible. Someone nice but firm.'

He looked away into the distance at some long-anticipated promised land. 'Yes, firm but nice. If I could have put Nelson Mandela in the chair of St Peter, I'm telling you, every church in the world would be like Old Trafford on a Saturday afternoon.'

An Intervention

The time for Aaron to act was closing in. For the last five minutes, he had slowly been moving his hind legs back against the wall, then little by little pulling his great body to follow, so that he was ready to make the great spring forward at the devil that would decide whether he would live or die.

The devil let out a deep breath (graveolent of cold sick, nidorous of scorched turd, reasty of weasel pee), and looked somewhat surprised. 'By God,' he said, at last. 'I needed to get that off my chest.'

He looked at Aaron. 'I suppose I should be grateful.'

'Does that mean you won't kill me?'

'I'm not that grateful.'

Aaron needed a little more time to adjust his left rear leg.

'Hell,' he said softly, as if accepting his fate. 'What's it like?'

The devil gave an eloquently malicious smile that would have spread from ear to ear if he'd had any.

'In my opinion, you'd be better off thinking about what you're going to say when you meet your maker.'

'Oh, I know what I'm going to say to Him already.'

'Do you, now?' The devil waited, smiling.

'I'm going to say' – he paused for effect as the devil leaned in towards him, eyes wide with curiosity – 'I'm ready now to listen to your apology.'

The devil burst into laughter. 'I shall miss you.'

'Then let me go.'

'I won't miss you that much.' Still, he contemplated Aaron with some pleasure. 'To answer your question about hell, it's a lot like here, only you get to see yourself as you really are. I admit that some …' He paused. 'All right, *most*, find that degree of self-awareness a bit bracing. That's the reason for all the screaming. But, once you get used to the noise, it's not so bad.' He paused. 'Oh, and there's nowhere to sit down.'

'And heaven?'

The devil smiled. 'Nice place. The only problem is, there's nobody there.' He grunted affably. 'Anyway, now that I've dealt with you, I'm going to have to find a way to draw a line under this abuse thing. Time to move on. I wonder if some guidelines might help.'

NOW! With a terrible howl of rage, the werewolf leapt upwards over the great table and launched himself at the face of the astonished devil, knocking him to one side.

He didn't stop to fight but leapt again, turning in the air and landing halfway up the wall with his great hind legs pressed against the hard surface. Then he thrust powerfully in another great spring, shot past the devil as he struggled to rise, and crashed with all his muscular strength into the vast window overlooking the Thames.

Unfortunately, Aaron bounced off the window and, horribly winded, plunged to the floor. The glass designed to keep out the explosive rage of Gerry and Osama was also sufficient to keep in a werewolf.

The devil got back to his feet and slid over to the enormous desk, flinging it to one side with irritable ease. He moved to the werewolf's side and fetched him two ugly blows to the side of the head, then lifted the stunned wolf into his arms as if he were an unusually hairy toddler. He slithered backward a few yards and took in an enormous breath, raised his head, and opened his mouth.

He let out a scream so shrill it sounded like a thousand peacocks being disembowelled at the same time. Not just

An Intervention

the great window in front of them began to vibrate and shake, but all the glass inside this massive fortress. Then, in an instant, every window in the place exploded under the impact of the ghastly pitch, pulsing an enormous shock wave of pulverised bombproof glass out into the London night in every direction. Unbearably lovely, lit up by the city lights, sparkling motes of powdery glass swirled and danced in the air as if joyously delivered from their duty to protect the nosy agents of the state.

The devil leaned into Aaron's muzzle, breath smelling of fermented puffin giblets. 'Ta ta,' he said, and raised the stunned werewolf into the air.

But pride had always been his weakness, and Aaron was not finished yet. As the devil lifted him past his hideous maggot head, with the last of his remaining strength Aaron flicked out the longest and dirtiest talon from his right paw and plunged it into the devil's eye. A yellowy, zitty burst from the eyeball shot into the air and splattered against the opposite wall. The devil let out a terrible scream, one so high-pitched and piercing it struck six ravens returning to the Tower of London. Instantly, they fell dead as one creature, to test the legend that, when these crows vanished from the Tower, the kingdom itself would fall.

With another great shout of rage, the devil threw Aaron the wolf in the air. Catching him by the hindquarters, he swung him like a cricket bat at the edge of the hole left by the exploded window. There was a most hideous crunch of breaking bones, of jaw and neck, and then another as the enraged Prince of Darkness turned about and lashed the hapless werewolf with even greater force against the other window edge. Then, wrapping Aaron under his arm, he slithered out on to the terrace of the into-everybody's-business wedding cake that kept the British people safe from harm.

Once outside, the devil pulled Aaron's broken features close to his and gave him a few slaps to wake him up. Slowly, through bleeding eyes, Aaron gradually focused on the hideous countenance no more than a couple of inches from his own.

'I want you to be awake for this,' said the devil. 'You lose.'

And, with that, he raised Aaron high above his head, let out a triumphant roar, and snapped the werewolf's spine in two.

CHAPTER 68

THE RIVER

Slowly, exhausted and in terrible pain, the devil lowered the werewolf's body and held him in his arms. With one eye pouring a sticky yellow white, he examined Aaron's face with his good eye, as if trying to discover something useful there. Then he let out a deeply rumbling sign of contentment, drew in a gulp of air that a whale would envy, pulled one arm back and launched the dead werewolf into the London night.

The mass confusion that had erupted in the building when the windows and much else had shattered so explosively meant that no one noticed the sight of a dead wolf arcing gracefully through the dark, or the hefty splash as it entered the grim, dark sparkle of the Thames and sank instantly beneath the water. For a moment, the body lingered, and then, on a full ebb tide, it began drifting its way past Billingsgate, the Narrow, Mudchute, the Isle of Dogs, on its way towards the deep cold of the mysterious kingdoms of the North Sea: Humber and Doggerland, Fisher and German Bight.

The devil watched for a moment and then, aware that he was exposed to view, oozed his way back into the shadows through the broken window and into the room. There was already a loud and desperate banging on the door.

'Holy Father! Holy Father! Are you all right?'

SCORN

'I am here,' called out the devil in a strong and confident voice.

'Are you all right, Holy Father?'

'I am. I can see the exposed iron beam over the door. It's been severely bent by the force of the explosion.'

'I'll get help immediately, Holy Father.'

'You will do no such thing. I am perfectly safe, and there must be many in the building who are not. Don't worry about me. Go and see what you can do to help the injured or the dead and give those who require it the consolation of your office. Their need is much greater than mine. You are not to ask for or permit anyone to come to my aid before the morning. Do you understand me, Father?'

There was a pause.

'But the police may not accept—'

'I do not care about what the police accept. Under no circumstances are they to divert their efforts from the injured or the dead.'

'Are you sure you're all right, Holy Father?'

'I'm fine. See to those that need your help.'

'I'll return later, Holy Father.'

'I told you I don't want to see you before sunrise, my son.' The voice of the pope was harsh, not at all the tone his aide was used to. 'Do you understand me? Help the wounded and the dying. Now go!'

This time, there was no faffing about. The devil turned back to the room and considered the carnage. He stood for a moment and then slid over to the late pope's head. He lifted it up high, opened his mouth and dropped it in. Big as his mouth was, it did not seem big enough to swallow a human head – but then there was an unpleasant clicking sound of ligament and bone, and the devil dislocated

The River

his jaw, allowing his throat to expand and enabling him to swallow the head in one gulp.

Finished, the devil coughed and then moved over to the pope's corpse. He lifted the heavy body as if it were almost nothing, then raised it right up in the air with both hands, dislocated his jaw again and slowly fed the body into his hideous mouth. Gulp after gulp, he eased the body down, shoulders and torso, little by little. The skin around his neck and chest bulged horribly, and his eyes seemed ready to pop out of his skull, but still he kept swallowing, breathing as if by some miracle through his nose, the waves of muscles in his throat pulling the body further and further in until he could grab the pope's feet with his arms and begin stuffing the last of him down.

After about half an hour, the hideous meal was over; with one last push and gulp the pope was entirely consumed. The devil waited for a minute or two. There was another grisly click as his jaws reconnected themselves. After a few more seconds, his tongue – as pink and delicate and beautiful as that of a giant baby – licked his lips, and he held his head to one side, as if struck by a surprising familiarity.

'Hmmm,' said the devil thoughtfully. 'Tastes a bit like …' But whatever the taste reminded him of, he could not quite put a name to it.

For a while, the devil stood still in an attempt to allow the enormous meal to settle down. Time, however, was short, and in only a little while he was forced to move over to the corner, the slimily, rippling tube of his wormy bulk distended in blunt angles caused by the pope's bony elbows, feet and knees. We would need a special word to depict the rippling stagger of a creature that slides having eaten half its weight – but, happily, the language to describe the turbid, lurching slobber of that hell maggot does not, ordinarily, need to exist.

The devil now faced directly into the point where two walls met, looking for all the world like a naughty schoolboy sent to the corner, transformed into a grub for all his sins. He squashed himself down and placed his hands firmly flat on the floor, then, tubularly gymnastical, swivelled his body so that its pad was facing upwards. He telescoped it so that the pad touched the ceiling, immediately followed by an ejaculation of yellowy-whitish goo that set almost in an instant and glued the devil upside down. Retracting his arms and hands inside his carcass, the devil hung free and began to move up and down and from side to side, the body all the while rippling up and down its entire length.

This horribly, grubby wiggle continued for several minutes, until there was a sudden split along the back of his head, as if a fat man grown morbidly obese on a diet of decaying, yellowy-green cream cheese had bent over and split his trousers. Now the split skin began to shuffle upwards to the pad glued to the ceiling, until it hung there like a pair of baggy tights around an old woman's ankles. For half an hour it dangled there, shivering from time to time. Then, from deep inside the grub's milky transparency, there was a flutter and a shudder and a tremble, as if something from within its depths was aching to be set free. Then it stopped.

Five minutes passed and then, as if from somewhere very far away, a pair of purple claws began to scratch against the hardening surface of the chrysalis. From behind the purple talons a milky, golden shape emerged. Then something loomed red behind that gold. A heave and a contracting

The River

and a sudden burst and split, and then a monstrous ball of colours erupting with a flood of liquid green and blue plopped slabbily on to the floor, seeming to split apart along its lower half. It lay there steaming as the light of dawn began to break, shuddering briefly now and then as occasional blobs of viscid ooze dripped on to what might have been its back. Then nothing, as the greeny-yellow seepage covering it like the vernix and meconium from a terrible birth began to drain away, slowly revealing the vivid mingling, small and large, of gold and purple and of red.

Then, instantly, it exploded into life like some horrible jack-in-the-box and stood triumphantly, head bowed, to reveal all to the unwatching world. The gold was the gold of the most exquisite ecclesiastical robe – a chasuble, worn over an alb of watered silk. The red was a cap of gauffered velvet worn only on the holiest of days. The purple claws were nothing of the kind, but gloves of Roman violet for a special blessing of the flock. Slowly, the head held low upon the chest began to raise itself and look upon the world, eyes gentle, mouth amused, features kind but strong.

In every way, it was a face identical to that of the Holy Father martyred by Aaron only a few hours earlier.

EPILOGUE 1

FORTHCOMING MARRIAGES

Viscount D. H. Lister and the Right Honourable Miss E. L. Candy.

The engagement is announced between David, Viscount Lister, son of Lord Lister and Countess Lister of Austen, and Elizabeth, daughter of the late Sir Allan Candy of Edinburgh and Mrs Jane Baxter of London.

EPILOGUE 2

AndreaCoates @AndreaCoatesFollow

Congratulations to my big sis Molly who starts her teacher-training degree today!

Retweets **10**

Likes **4**

9.21 a.m. Don't miss any updates from Andrea Coates.

EPILOGUE 3

From: Aaron Gall

To: George Scrope

Subject: For me to know and you to find out

CC: The City and the World

Alcoholic Cath and Charlotte (8, 6)

soulfully rub one out (4, 6)

with their sexiest organ in Nirvana (12, 7)

EPILOGUE 4

'Now the serpent was more subtil than any beast of the field which the LORD God had made.'

Genesis 3:1

So here we are.

Where is that, exactly?

So – unofficially, and because it's you, and we've become close – I'll give you a taste of things to come. Highlights, then.

While it is true I am the pope, I am not some great dictator laying down the law about everything under the sun.

I am a sinner.

You mothers, if your children cry because they are hungry in church, breastfeed them. Don't worry about it.

Hypothetically, we could revisit the question of celibacy. But, for the moment, I am in favour of maintaining it. There are pros and cons, but we have ten centuries of more good experiences than bad ones.

The honest answer is that I feel sometimes as if I were the winner of some worldwide talent contest. To say that I disapprove of it is to put it mildly. I am with Sigmund Freud when he describes such adulation as a form of hostility.

The kind of globalisation that makes things uniform is essentially imperialist. At the end, it becomes a way of enslaving people.

The Church must offer guidance but, on the question of homosexuality, we do not have the right to force a particular kind of life on anyone. If God, in his creation, ran the risk of making us free, who am I to meddle?

There are those in the Church who want to put the whole world inside a condom.

I mean to be blunt: these crimes against children are a leprosy in our house.

Like me? I'd like me if I were you. I can't remember who said it (because I couldn't care less): the thing about charm is that it gets you to say yes without you knowing the question.

But we must part, my dear, dear friends, you of the earth, earthy. And, hard though it is to do so after this extraordinary journey we have embarked upon together, know that someone who sees and loves you as you really are is watching over you at last.

One duty I have that still remains, to dot the 'i's and cross the 't's of understanding, as it were, to put the tail, at last, on top of the nine, precisely where it's meant to go. 'What is Truth?' said jesting Pilate, and did not stay for an answer, but I offer you that chance to stay and hear, reluctant though I am to speak. After all these many words and thrilling actions, we have come to the bit where everything is explained. The suspects are in the drawing room, those who have been slaughtered have been tidied away, and now it's time for the great detective to give you the reveal.

What are you made of besides mud? Mostly water, a lot of wind, vanishingly small amounts of silver and gold which, perhaps revealingly, don't serve any function at all; the kind of carbon that you would find in coal, not at all like the type of carbon you would find in sparkling diamonds; pinches of stuff like zinc, sulphur, iodine; about enough iron in a hundred of you to make a pot big enough to piss in.

There is grandeur in this vision of life. Surely it's more admirable to see yourselves as you are and make the very best of your nature that you can, rather than be always living beyond your means and failing in ways that bring disaster to you all. As somebody or other once said: perfection for human beings is deadly or banal. It ends in a gulag or a Barbie doll.

So I offer you, as a last act of compassion, a simple choice. If you think that you can stand the truth that burns, the cold reality of the human, read on. And believe me, truly, this is hard for me to do. Speaking the truth to power isn't difficult at all; it's speaking the truth to weakness that's hard. But it's not as hard as having to listen to it. So my advice to you is to read no further.

I'll say more: please stop now. I'm begging.

But to those that choose to walk towards the edge ... I take my hat off to you.

Everyone knows that the story about men building a tower at Babel is a metaphor for something or other. In fact, the Tower of Babel isn't a metaphor for anything at all. It's a particularly revealing demonstration of a fundamental truth about what it means to be human (those wisely growing apprehensive still have the chance to turn and run).

You see, the Leaning Tower of Babel, to give the thing its proper name, was not destroyed by God as a punishment for mankind's presumption for trying to reach heaven through its own efforts. It fell down of its own accord because this overweening ambition to build up to the heavens was not matched by an equal ability, or commitment, or strength of character, to see it through. It collapsed because there were too many shoddy corners cut: insufficient hay in the bricks, or of the wrong but less expensive kind that was easier to get; cheaper types of wood and not enough of it, when expensive oak was required to maintain the structural integrity; too few craftsmen with sufficient experience or willingness to take pains with their work; and so on and so forth.

You know the drill. Let's face it — you *are* the drill.

Let me be clear. And, in a way, this is the most important thing to get your head around, as to why the building fell down and how horrible your delusions about yourselves are. Some parts of this shoddily ambitious structure were built with enormous care and skill from the best materials available by people who really cared about what they were doing.

To come at this by way of another story you're probably familiar with, it's generally agreed that the search for the Holy Grail is the search for the divine in human nature. So, ask yourself why it's a search that always ends in absolute fucking disaster. That's *clearly* the moral of the story.

Perhaps you're beginning to catch my drift, my theme,

my *motif*, as it were. Perhaps you're currently wishing you really had chosen differently.

(It's still not too late to turn around.)

But if you still don't quite get what I'm driving at, I in no way accuse you of being dim. It's merely the terrible anxiety of coming close to discovering what you really are that clouds your mind. As well it might.

Have I said too much? Or perhaps I haven't said enough. At any rate, though you might think it cruel to point out just what the Tower of Babel is truly about, you need to remember that it's only a real friend who's prepared to speak the truth, which is why only those who really want the best for you, who long for you to be a success, are willing to be cruelly kind to you by saying:

Jy is die toring en die toring is jy.

አንተ ታወር ናቸው ግንብ ለእናንተ ነው.

Dorrea zara eta Dorrea da duzu.

B Koj yog tus pej thuam thiab tus pej thuam yog koj.

ы вежы і вежы вы.

Olet Tower ja Tower on sinulle.

你是塔，塔是你.

شما درج و برج شما است.

당신은 타워하며 타워가있다.

Anda di Menara dan Menara adalah anda.

Tu es turrim et turrim.

Te vagy a torony és a torony te.

Du er tårnet og tårnet er deg.

Bạn đang tháp và tháp là bạn.

Anda di Menara dan Menara adalah anda.

Sen Kulesi ve Kule sensin.

Ту Бурҷи ва Бурҷи аст.

Vi estas la Turo kaj la Turo estas vi.

You are the Tower and the Tower is you.

Disappointing?

So glad we finally understand each other.

ACKNOWLEDGEMENTS

My profound thanks to Aelred Doyle for his incisive and intelligent editing. Also to Nick Szczepanik for managing to make sense of my scrawls to create the illustrations. John Bond and George Edgeller of whitefox have managed the process of publishing *Scorn* with great skill and impressive attention to detail. Thanks also to Emma Draude and Bethan James of EDPR. As always Anthony Goff, my agent, was an unflagging supporter. Mark Ecob realised my constantly changing ideas for the cover with a deft touch. Sarah Day copyedited with a relentlessly intelligent eye for detail. The typographical design by Jill Sawyer Phypers is truly elegant; the proofreading by Ian Critchley was meticulous. Alan Connor gave truly useful advice on the nature of crossword compiling.

I am deeply grateful to Thomas Hoffman for his mastery of the dark arts of multimedia; to Victoria Hoffman for her detailed work on the project and to both of them for reading early versions. Particular thanks to Lorraine Hedger for her unique ability to make sense of my handwriting in providing a typed manuscript. Finally to my wife, Alexandra Hoffman, who has, as always, taken on the fearsome task of telling me what needs to get better.

For those interested in exploring this vast subject further, Wikipedia lists Catholic Church sex abuse cases by country.

en.wikipedia.org/wiki/Catholic_Church_sex_abuse_cases_by_country

Some Independent Inquiries into Institutional Abuse in the Catholic Church

The Irish Ryan Report was concerned with establishing whether or not abuse occurred and the nature and scale of that abuse. A brief summary of the report can be found at www.childabusecommission.ie/rpt/ExecSummary.php, and an easily searchable web version at www.childabuse-commission.ie/rpt

The (also Irish) Murphy Report is more restricted in scope than the Ryan Report. It is concerned only with the response of Church and State authorities to a representative sample of complaints and suspicions of child sexual abuse by approximately 183 priests in the Archdiocese of Dublin between the years 1975 and 2004.

Part 2 can be downloaded at www.justice.ie/en/JELR/Pages/PB09000504 DOWNLOAD PART 2

The website of the Royal Commission into the institutional abuse of children in Australia is childabuse-royalcommission.gov.au.

On a smaller scale, an independent report (in German) into the physical and sexual abuse of 547 former students of the Catholic Regensburger Domspatzen choir school in Germany over a period of 70 years can be found at www.uw recht.org/fileadmin/user_upload/Abschlussbericht_Domspatzen.pdf. The former musical director at the school, Georg Ratzinger, the brother of former Pope Benedict, apologised to the victims in a newspaper interview at the time, saying he wasn't aware of any sexual abuse. However, Ratzinger admitted he slapped children as discipline. 'I did have a very bad conscience doing it, though,' he said in the interview.

Over the next few years the long-delayed Independent

Inquiry into Child Sexual Abuse (IICSA) will examine the extent to which institutions and organisations in England and Wales have taken seriously their responsibility to protect children. As of 2017 there are no preliminary findings. More information can be found at www.iicsa.org.uk

In *The Case of the Pope* (Penguin, 2010), lawyer Geoffrey Robertson details the legal case against the Catholic Church in the context of international human rights legislation.

For a concise alternative view of the Catholic Church by a respected, if controversial, theologian and 'priest in good standing', it is well worth reading Hans Kung's objective and intelligently readable account, *The Catholic Church: A Short History* (Weidenfeld & Nicholson, 2001)

For more information about
the work of Paul Hoffman
(and to find the answer to the
clue on page 515) go to
www.paulhoffman.co.uk